CHRISTIAN CAIN

Fracture Zone

The Echo of Broken Time

First published by CainCyberLabs, LLC 2025

First edition

ISBN: 979-8-9941470-1-6

Contents

Preface

In the world of cybersecurity, there is a fundamental truth that every analyst learns early: you can build the perfect firewall, write the most elegant encryption, and design an unbreachable network, but eventually, it will fail. It won't fail because of the math. It will fail because of the human.

Someone clicks a link they shouldn't. Someone writes a password on a sticky note. Someone hesitates.

I spent years studying systems—both in the military and in the private sector. I learned that order is not a natural state; it is an act of will imposed upon a universe that prefers chaos. *Fracture Zone* was born from that realization. I wanted to explore what happens when that imposition of order goes too far, and what happens when the universe decides to push back.

Ravn Vidar's journey is not just a trek across a broken wasteland; it is a confrontation with the terrifying reality that we cannot code our way out of our own humanity. The "flaw" in the system is not a bug to be fixed; it is the feature that makes us worth saving.

Thank you for picking up this book. I hope you enjoy the glitch.

Christian Cain, 2025

1

A Flaw in the Design

T he calipers were cold against the woody scales of the pinecone, a sharp, metallic truth in the quiet of the cabin.

Ravn Vidar held his breath, a habit he'd developed to still the tremor in his hands—a faint but persistent legacy of the day the world had broken.

His eye, pressed to the jeweler's loupe, saw a world magnified into perfect, geometric clarity. He turned the specimen slowly, reverently, in the clean, white circle of light cast by his battery-powered lamp.

Outside, the late afternoon sun bled through the dense canopy of the Cascade wilderness, a chaotic tangle of green and brown that clawed at the edges of his small window. The world outside was a storm of illogical, untamed variables: wind shear, barometric pressure, the chaotic branching of ferns, the unpredictable scatter of seeds.

But in here, there was only order.

His single-room cabin was a laboratory of exile, every object within it a testament to a desperate, self-imposed control. The cot in the corner was made with military precision, the single wool blanket pulled taut enough to bounce a coin. The small wood stove was cold, its cast-iron surface wiped clean of ash, the firewood next to it stacked in a perfect, interlocking grid.

The shelves that lined one wall held no novels, no poetry, no distractions from the hard, empirical truth of things. They were packed with the tools of his penance: worn textbooks like Feynman's Lectures on Physics and Gray's Anatomy, a treatise on geometric morphometrics, and stacks of his own leather-bound journals.

Five years of meticulous, joyless observations, a data-thick wall built against the howling void of his memory.

On the corner of his desk, separate from his main workspace, sat a small, silver-framed photograph, turned permanently face down on a square of black velvet. He never touched it. He never moved it. But he was always aware of it, a small, cold mass in his peripheral vision, the ghost at the feast of his logic.

This small circle of light on a rough-hewn pine desk was his altar. For five years, the ritual had been the same. It began at dawn with the checking of his snare lines—a joyless task that produced little. Then came the filtering of water, the cataloging of supplies, the endless, monotonous maintenance of a life reduced to its barest components.

The rest of the day was for work. He would venture out, collect a specimen, and bring it back to be cross-examined. A fern frond unspooling in a perfect spiral of Crozier. A snail shell's elegant logarithmic curve. Each was an affirmation, proof that the laws of nature were constant and unbreakable.

This meticulous process, more akin to a religious rite than science, was the only thing that kept the memory contained: the catastrophic failure of his quantum experiment at the Aethelburg research facility.

That was the true anomaly—the one that had cost him everything.

Today's subject was phyllotaxis. The divine mathematics of botany. A soft science, Lena would have called it, her lips quirking into a wry smile. She and Aris had often teased him for his obsession with the "macro" world, for finding comfort in the predictable elegance of biology while they wrestled with the chaotic, paradoxical nature of the quantum realm.

It was that wrestling that had torn a hole in the universe. Now, this soft science was all he had left.

As he prepared his instruments, a ghost of a memory surfaced, unwelcome and sharp. He was in the clean, white-walled Aethelburg lab, the air humming with processing power and the faint scent of coffee and static.

Aris, younger and buzzing with an energy that seemed to bend light around him, was excitedly scrawling the Fibonacci sequence across a whiteboard, the marker squeaking in his haste.

"It's not just a pattern, Ravn," Aris had said, his eyes alight with discovery, gesturing wildly with the marker. "It's the universe's source code. A recursive algorithm that builds everything from the arms of a galaxy to... this!"

He'd tossed a pinecone from his own desk into Ravn's hands.

"God is a mathematician, and he left his notes everywhere."

Ravn squeezed his eyes shut, pushing the memory down with a familiar, practiced motion. The memory was a variable he could not control. He had to focus on the data.

That was the man he was now—not the passionate collaborator, but the joyless custodian of his brother's last, beautiful idea. He was searching for proof that Aris had been right, that God was a mathematician and not, as Ravn secretly feared, a careless child who had abandoned his experiment.

With a soft click, he locked the calipers on the distance between two scales on a single winding track. 1.618 millimeters. The golden ratio, perfect and serene. He recorded the number, his graphite whispering across the page.

He began to trace the spirals, counting with a quiet, desperate intensity. The ones winding to the left... one, two, three... all the way to eight.

He paused, letting out a slow breath. A perfect, reassuring integer. A number of the sequence. He felt a familiar, fleeting sense of peace. The system was stable. The math still held.

He shifted the pinecone slightly under the light and began to count the spirals winding to the right. One... five... eight... twelve... thirteen.

It was always thirteen. The reassuring counterpart to eight.

He picked up his pencil, ready to capture this small victory, this fresh proof that the universe still made sense, that the chaos was confined to his own past.

He froze.

The pencil hovered over the paper. A cold dread, sharp and sudden as a needle in the heart, seized him. His hand, steady moments before, now felt alien, a clumsy appendage of meat and bone he couldn't quite control.

The pencil dropped from his fingers, rolling silently across the floor into the shadows. He ignored it.

He snatched the loupe, his heart beginning a frantic, irregular rhythm against his ribs, a panicked bird trapped in a cage of bone.

It was a mistake. It had to be. His own error.

He brought the pinecone back into focus, the magnified scales filling his vision. He forced himself to breathe, a slow, methodical intake of air, just as he had been trained to do when an experiment threatened to run away from him. He would re-verify the data. That's what a scientist did. He would isolate the anomalous variable, and that variable would be himself.

He counted the right-winding spirals again, his lips moving without sound. One. Two. Three... a frantic scramble through the familiar sequence... eight... thirteen...

Fourteen.

The number was a physical blow. Impossible. He set the pinecone down and rubbed his eyes with the heels of his hands, seeing flashes of light against the darkness.

It was eye strain. It had to be. He'd been working for hours under the focused glare of the lamp.

He took a clean, soft cloth and meticulously polished the lens of the loupe, then held it to the light, checking for imperfections. There were none. He picked up the brass calipers, running a thumb over their cool, smooth surface, checking their calibration against the edge of a steel ruler he kept for just that purpose.

Perfect.

The flaw was not in his tools. It was in him.

He stood up, pacing the small cabin. He was tired. His nutrition was poor. The psychological strain of five years of isolation was finally taking its toll. He was hallucinating. That was the only logical explanation.

To confirm it, he needed a control subject. From a carefully cataloged box on his shelf, he retrieved another specimen, Specimen 734, a Ponderosa Pine cone he had analyzed two years prior. Its perfection had been a comfort to him for a week.

He placed it under the lamp and began the ritual again, his movements now sharp with urgency. Left-winding spirals: five. Right-winding spirals: eight. He measured the angles, the distances. Everything was perfect. The universe, according to Specimen 734, was still sane.

He slid the control specimen aside and pulled the anomaly back into the light. His hands were slick with a sudden sweat. He was the flaw. He had miscounted.

He began again, tracing each spiral with the tip of a pick, his voice a dry, rasping whisper in the silent cabin.

"...twelve... thirteen..." He paused at the final, impossible ridge, his throat closing. "...fourteen."

It was not his error. The flaw was in the design.

The realization arrived as a slow, grinding collapse of the foundations of his sanity. For five years, he had built a fortress of logic, its walls mortared with the elegant certainty of mathematics. And a single, insignificant pinecone had just smashed a hole in the cornerstone.

If this one simple law could be broken, then all laws were provisional. All order was a temporary illusion. And the chaos of Aethelburg wasn't an anomaly. It was the rule.

The number was a shard of glass in the clean machine of his world. And the lie was a key. It turned a lock deep in his mind, and the cage flew open.

The smell hit him first—acrid static and the sterile, biting cold of super-cooled helium that burned his sinuses. It wasn't a memory; it was a sensory assault, present and suffocating. The scent of cedar and pine in the cabin vanished, overwritten by the smell of a tomb of his own making.

Then the sound. Not just the alarm, but voices, tinny and strained over an intercom.

"Ravn, the K-field is fluctuating beyond predicted parameters! We're seeing decoherence across the entire array!"

It was Lena's voice, tight with a professional urgency that bordered on panic.

Then the sight: the air in the cabin shimmered, it blazed with Cherenkov radiation. A brilliant, lethal blue washed over the log walls and his simple wooden furniture, making the solid objects seem translucent, unreal. The light cast no shadows.

Through the impossible glare, he was at his console again, the data a waterfall of impossible numbers. He saw Lena's hand, her fingers outstretched, reaching for Aris's across the control room.

And Aris's voice, not over the intercom, but live, breathless with a terrifying ecstasy.

"It's working! It's not just tunneling, it's resonating with something! Do you see the data, Ravn? It's beautiful!"

His own memory surfaced, the core of his guilt. He saw the critical warning alarms flashing on his screen, the ones he should have acted on. But for a fatal half-second, he had been mesmerized, paralyzed by the sublime, impossible elegance of the data Aris was seeing.

He hesitated.

The high-frequency shriek of the final containment alarm screamed in the present tense, a physical pressure against his eardrums. And beneath it, his brother's last, desperate shout, distorted by the storm of energy.

It was a shout of pure, unadulterated, scientific awe. The sound of a man witnessing God and the Devil in the same, terrible instant, a sound of sublime, ultimate discovery that had ripped the world apart.

The psychic whiplash threw him back in his chair. He gasped, a wave of nausea washing over him. The cabin returned, but its sanctity was gone, violated. The flaw in the pinecone was no longer a botanical curiosity. It was a multiversal wound, and it was bleeding into his reality.

He scrambled from his desk, the legs of his chair screeching against the floorboards as he shoved it back. A cold sweat plastered his shirt to his back, and the acrid phantom-smell of ozone still burned in his sinuses.

The cabin was just a cabin again—wood and glass and the scent of pine— but the psychic residue of the vision, the lingering afterimage of lethal blue light, had tainted it forever.

He stumbled to the window, his breath fogging the cool glass, desperate for an external, verifiable truth to refute the evidence of his own fracturing mind.

He looked past the humming anemometer, the small device that had, for five years, been his connection to a rational, measurable world. But the world it was measuring was no longer rational.

The sun was too low in the sky, a sick, jaundiced yellow, casting shadows of the firs that were impossibly long and sharp, stretching like black daggers across the clearing. His watch read 15:32. The sun should have been high overhead. The shadows were wrong. The light was wrong.

It was a simple, brutal violation of orbital mechanics.

His gaze lifted to the sky, and the cold dread in his gut turned to ice.

It was a deep, star-frowned twilight, a bruised purple that bled into an inky blackness at its zenith. And in that blackness, the stars themselves were screaming that the universe had gone mad.

He searched for Polaris, the celestial anchor, the constant that had guided humanity for millennia. It wasn't there.

In its place, a trio of impossibly bright blue suns burned with a cold, fierce light, a baleful, alien trinity.

He frantically scanned for Orion, for the familiar belt, the sword, the shield, the comforting shape from a thousand childhood nights. He found a ragged, swirling nebula of violent violet, a cosmic bruise that seemed to be actively choking the life from the ancient constellation, its stars flickering like dying embers.

The laws of physics, the grand, elegant equations of relativity and celestial mechanics, were not just unraveling; they were being rewritten by a mad god.

This was it. The cascade failure. The final, horrifying conclusion to a theoretical paper he and Aris had co-authored, a paper that had been dismissed by the review board as "brilliant but needlessly alarmist."

He wasn't panicked. Panic was an inefficient variable, a chaotic emotion that corrupted data. He was a scientist. And this was the final, ultimate observation.

It was a compulsion, a need that overrode fear. He had to measure it. He had to record it.

He moved with a sudden, sharp purpose, grabbing his leather journal and a handheld spectroscope from a shelf. If the world were ending, he would take notes.

He unlatched the cabin door and stepped outside into the strange twilight.

The air was thin, carrying a static charge that made the hairs on his arms stand on end and tasted faintly of copper, just like the memory. A low, sub-audible hum vibrated through the soles of his boots, a sound that was felt more than heard.

The world was... de-rendering.

He perceived it as the quantum information theorist he was. His senses, honed by a lifetime of seeing the universe as a complex system of data, could now see the system crashing in real time.

He saw the shimmering, unstable quantum foam that underpinned all matter, the very source code of existence, bubbling up through the surface of things like digital artifacts on a corrupted screen.

He raised the spectroscope to his eye, pointing it at a nearby fir tree. The readout was impossible—a chaotic smear of emission lines that defied the laws of chemistry.

He lowered the instrument and stared. The tree was no longer a solid object; it flickered between states, its bark resolving for a nanosecond into cascading lines of emerald green code.

He recognized the syntax, a variation on a self-replicating algorithm he and Aris had designed for modeling organic growth. And within the code, he saw a specific, elegant subroutine for calculating needle distribution that Lena had written, a piece of her beautiful mind, now highlighted in a stark, alien red, flagged for deletion.

The mountain on the horizon was a wireframe model against the impossible sky, its majestic solidity stripped away to reveal the raw, polygonal geometry beneath. It flickered, its level of detail shifting, as if a cosmic processor was struggling to render the image, shedding polygons to save on memory.

He remembered a long, sleepless night with Aris, arguing about the theoretical computational power required to simulate a single, stable universe. Aris had called it the "God Algorithm." Now, Ravn was watching that algorithm fail.

He looked at his own hand, holding it up in the fractured light.

He saw the layers peel back in his perception. Skin gave way to the intricate network of capillaries, a map of pulsing red. That dissolved into the white lattice of bone, and then... then the final substrate.

He saw not flesh and bone, calluses and scars, but the raw, flowing data stream of his own existence, a beautiful and terrifying river of pure, conscious information.

It was the most beautiful thing he had ever seen. It was the most horrifying. It was the ultimate confirmation of their life's work, realized as an apocalypse.

He was the sole witness to a truth no one else could understand, a solitary mind cataloging the death of his own reality.

This moment of absolute, terrible understanding was the last thing his consciousness could process. He was a scientist standing before a god of pure data, a being of mathematics and light, and the sheer scale of the revelation was an insurmountable weight.

He was witnessing the universe's source code unfurling, a sight no human mind was ever meant to comprehend.

The pearlescent wave of new information, the leading edge of a new reality, washed over him.

It struck as an informational force. His mind, his very quantum signature, was flooded. It was like trying to pour an ocean into a thimble.

Trillions of zetabytes of raw, universal data—the history of every star, the biological code of every alien microbe, the geometric laws of a thousand other dimensions—crashed against the fragile architecture of his human consciousness.

He felt his own memories, his identity, his love for his brother, his grief, his failures, his name, all of it becoming just one more line of code in an infinite program, about to be debugged.

His mind, a processor pushed far beyond its limits, simply shorted out.

The world, both the one he knew and the one he was now witnessing, went silent.

He awoke to the taste of ash.

It was a dry, chemical bitterness that coated his tongue and the back of his throat, the flavor of a world incinerated and remade.

For a long moment, it was his only reality. He coughed, a dry, racking sound that was swallowed by a profound, alien silence.

He slowly became aware of other sensations. The feeling of the ground beneath his cheek. He ran his fingers over it; it was a slick, spongy moss that felt unnervingly warm to the touch, like the skin of a living thing.

A deep, cellular weariness radiated from his bones, an ache born not of injury, but of fundamental violation, as if he'd been disassembled and hastily put back together again.

He pushed himself onto his elbows, the world swimming in and out of focus. The air was next. It was thick and heavy, and when he drew a breath, it filled his lungs with the scent of damp, fertile soil and something cloyingly sweet, like rotting honey.

It was a smell devoid of the clean, sharp notes of pine and fir he had known his whole life. This was the smell of a different biology, a different kind of decay.

The silence pressed in. There were no birds. No squirrels chittering in the branches. No distant hum of a passing airplane. The rich, layered soundscape of his old world was gone, replaced by a dead, flat quiet.

The only sound was the rasp of his own breathing and the soft squelch of the moss beneath him.

Finally, he opened his eyes and took in the sight of his new reality.

The sky above was a bruised purple he had no name for, choked with alien constellations.

He was in a forest, but it was a perversion of one. The trees were nightmares of botany, their bark a slick, oily black that reflected the faint, sickly green bio-luminescence pulsing from their leaves. Strange, fungal growths clung to their trunks, glowing with a soft, blue light that did little to push back the oppressive gloom.

He performed a slow, methodical self-assessment, a scientist trying to impose order on his own shock. No broken bones. No immediate wounds. Just the profound, soul-deep exhaustion.

He scrambled to his feet, a wave of vertigo threatening to send him back to the ground.

He turned in a slow, desperate circle, searching for his cabin, for the small point of order he had carved out of the wilderness.

It was gone. Not burned down, not destroyed. Erased. There was no clearing, no foundation, no flattened grass, no sign that it—or he—had ever been there.

He was a castaway on the shores of a new and broken world, a ghost in a reality that had already forgotten him.

A voice spoke, not to his ears, but directly into the core of his mind. It was cold, analytical, and terrifyingly familiar, like a diagnostic report from a cosmic machine.

System corrupt. Variable anchored. Equation unsolved. Survive. Understand. Find the Heart.

2

The Taste of Ash

The voice faded, but the words were etched into his mind like a burn. *System corrupt. Variable anchored. Equation unsolved. Survive. Understand. Find the Heart.*

They were a command structure, a mission objective. The only piece of logic in a world gone mad.

He clung to it as his own reality swam back into focus, a drowning man clutching a piece of jagged, unforgiving driftwood.

The first sensation was the taste. A dry, chemical bitterness coated his tongue and the back of his throat, the flavor of a world incinerated and remade.

Ash.

He pushed himself up, a groan escaping his lips as his muscles screamed in protest. Every joint ached with a deep, cellular weariness, as if he'd been disassembled and hastily put back together again by a blind and careless god.

He was lying in a patch of the rust-colored moss he had cataloged before the fall. It was slick, slightly oily, and felt unnervingly warm to the touch.

He took a moment, forcing down the rising panic, and did what he was trained to do: observe, gather data.

The sky was the same bruised twilight he had witnessed in the final moments of the cabin, lit by the three alien blue suns. The trees remained

12

nightmares of botany—slick, black bark and pulsing, sickly green leaves.

His cabin, his journal, his entire life's work—gone. Erased.

Survive. The first directive. A problem to be solved.

Ravn stumbled to his feet, his body feeling clumsy and weak, a foreign piece of machinery he no longer knew how to operate.

Basic needs first. He ran a systems diagnostic on himself. Vitals: elevated heart rate, signs of dehydration. Primary objective: Water.

His old knowledge, the comforting logic of a world that no longer existed, told him to look for low-lying ground, for the tell-tale green of water-loving vegetation, for the faintest sound of a gurgling stream. But here, everything was low-lying, and everything was a sickly, glowing green. The ground itself seemed to breathe, the moss rising and falling in a slow, rhythmic pulse. The very concept of geology felt provisional.

He pushed through foliage that left a greasy, phosphorescent residue on his skin and clothes, his ears straining for the sound of running water.

He found it after an hour of stumbling, a stream cutting a dark, silent line through the glowing flora. But the water itself was a violation. It wasn't clear; it was faintly milky, and an oily, iridescent sheen, like a slick of gasoline, swirled on its surface.

It flowed not with a gurgle, but with a low, viscous hum, as if it were thick with suspended particles.

His scientific mind screamed danger. His internal monologue was a frantic triage of hypotheses: heavy mineral suspension? Biological contamination from a new kingdom of microorganisms? Complex, oil-like hydrocarbons? Every possibility was a death sentence.

But the thirst was a roaring fire in his throat, a physical torment that overrode all his logic. His tongue was a dry rasp of sandpaper in his mouth, and a dull, pounding headache had begun behind his eyes.

He knelt, his reflection in the oily water a distorted, monstrous caricature. He cupped the strange, lukewarm liquid in his hands. It felt thick, heavier than water had any right to be.

He hesitated for a final, agonizing second, then drank.

It was almost syrupy and tasted of minerals and burnt copper. It quenched the immediate fire in his throat but settled heavy and cold in his stomach, a foreign, leaden weight.

He had drunk the poison. He had survived the first test, for now.

Next, shelter. Then, orientation. He looked up at the three blue suns, trying to triangulate a position, to find a celestial anchor. But their positions seemed to shift in relation to one another, their light diffuse and unhelpful. He tried to apply the principles of parallax, but the numbers were nonsensical.

It was cosmic vertigo, the profound, gut-wrenching dislocation of a man with no north, no south, no frame of reference. He was a variable in an equation with no constants.

He gave up on the sky and focused on the ground. He tried to build a simple lean-to, a basic structure against whatever predators this new world held.

He found a fallen tree, its oily bark flaking away. He broke off a branch. It didn't snap with the satisfying crack of pine or oak; it splintered in his hands, flaking away in razor-sharp, glassy shards that cut his palms.

He dropped it with a curse, looking at the thin, red lines welling up on his skin.

He tried another tree, one with a more fibrous-looking bark. The wood was bizarrely pliant, rubbery, and useless, bending under his weight without offering any resistance.

He attempted to lash branches together with vines, but they were either as brittle as glass or slick with a slime that prevented him from tying a knot.

Every attempt was a failure. Every piece of knowledge he possessed, every law of physics and material science he had trusted, was now a defunct data set.

The first forty-eight hours were a blur of tainted water, gnawing fear, and utter failure. He was exposed, exhausted, and haunted by the chilling realization that in this new world, his intellect, the very core of his identity, was not an asset. It was a liability.

The initial shock, the intellectual horror of his displacement, began to fade, worn down by the sheer, grinding attrition of survival. It was replaced

14

by a new, more urgent imperative.

Hunger.

It began as a hollow, aching void in his gut, but by the third day, it had become a physical beast, clawing at him from the inside. It was a constant, gnawing pain that frayed the edges of his reason.

His thoughts, usually so clear and linear, became sluggish and circular, always returning to the singular, obsessive need for sustenance. The world grew slightly unreal, a dizzying landscape seen through a haze of light-headedness.

His scientific mind, the part of him that cataloged and analyzed, was being silenced by the screaming, biological demand for calories.

His first logical approach was botany. He had spent years studying the elegant systems of terrestrial plant life. He began to forage, his eyes scanning the alien foliage for familiar patterns—the tri-lobed leaf of a potential berry, the tell-tale shape of a root system.

But this world was a mockery of his knowledge. A plant with soft, inviting-looking leaves would be covered in microscopic, glassy thorns that embedded themselves in his skin. A brilliantly colored fruit, shaped like a pear, would burst when touched, releasing a puff of narcotic spores that made his head swim for an hour.

Desperation was his only guide, a frantic, illogical impulse driving him through the world's insidious chaos. He tested everything with trembling fingers and a keen, terrified eye, tasting small slivers and waiting for the burn or the numbness that signaled death.

Bitter. Burning. Numbing.

After hours of searching, he finally found a patch of gnarled, pale roots that smelled faintly of starch rather than poison. He dug them up with his bare hands, his fingers raw and bleeding, and took a bite.

The texture was woody and fibrous, and the taste was like bitter chalk. He forced himself to chew and swallow, the act feeling more like consuming medicine than food. It did nothing to quell the fire in his stomach.

Food would have to be hunted. He saw small creatures skittering in the undergrowth—things with too many legs, with carapaces that shimmered in the gloom, with soft, multi-faceted eyes that watched him with unnerving intelligence.

He recalled the design of a simple trigger-and-loop snare from a manual he'd once read. The logic was simple, the physics sound. He spent half a day trying to build one.

The glassy wood he found was too brittle for the trigger mechanism, shattering in his hands. The rubbery wood was too pliant to hold the necessary tension. The vines he tried to use for a noose were either slimy and slick, refusing to hold a knot, or so dry they crumbled to dust in his fingers.

His hands, so adept at calibrating micro-fittings and manipulating quantum arrays, were clumsy and useless at these simple, primitive tasks. Every failed knot, every splintered branch, was another piece of evidence of his own inadequacy.

He abandoned traps and tried direct force. He saw one of the six-legged creatures, the size of a rabbit, nibbling on a glowing fungus. He picked up a heavy, flat stone, judged the distance, and threw it.

In his old world, he could have calculated the trajectory, the arc, the force needed. Here, the creature simply moved. It skittered sideways with a burst of impossible, frictionless speed, vanishing into the undergrowth before the stone even hit the ground.

Failure after failure mounted, each one chipping away at the scientist and feeding the desperate animal inside. The gnawing in his gut was no longer just a physical sensation; it was a state of being. It was a predator, and it was consuming him from within, devouring his reason, his patience, and the last vestiges of the man he had once been.

He was no longer thinking. He was just hungry. And the hunger demanded to be fed.

The hunger had won. The careful, logical man, the scientist who observed and recorded, was gone—starved out of existence. In his place was an animal, gaunt and hollow-eyed, moving with a predator's single-minded purpose.

He was no longer thinking about snares or trajectories; he was simply hunting, his senses raw and unnaturally sharp. Every rustle of a leaf, every skittering sound in the undergrowth, was a potential meal.

He found one cornered in a small, rocky alcove, a natural dead end.

It was the size of a rabbit, its body low to the ground, supported by six spindly legs that ended in delicate, multi-jointed claws. Its back was covered in a shell of iridescent chitin that shimmered with oily rainbows in the faint, green light of the pulsating flora.

It trembled, its two large, liquid-black eyes fixed on him. It made no sound, its terror a silent, palpable thing in the still air.

Ravn stopped at the mouth of the alcove, his own gaunt frame blocking the only escape.

He saw his reflection in those huge, dark eyes, and for a horrifying second, he didn't recognize the man staring back at him: a filthy, wild-eyed creature with matted hair and the hollowed-out look of a wolf.

The scientist, the last remnant of his old self, recoiled in horror. This was a life-form, a unique product of this new world's evolution. It deserved to be studied, cataloged, and understood.

But the beast in his gut roared, a physical pain that convulsed his stomach and clouded his vision. It didn't care about understanding. It only cared about eating.

His weapon was a stone he'd been carrying for the last hour, its weight familiar in his palm, one edge flaked away to a crude but effective sharpness.

He didn't think about the act. He couldn't afford to. He simply moved, a lurching, clumsy predator.

The first blow was a disaster. He swung the rock with all his strength, but his weak, trembling muscles betrayed him. Instead of a clean strike to the head, the stone glanced off the creature's iridescent carapace with a sickening, wet crack.

The chitin splintered, but didn't break. The creature shrieked, a high, whistling sound that lanced through the air, a sound of pure, unadulterated pain. It tried to scramble away on its spindly legs, two of them dragging uselessly behind it, shattered by the clumsy impact.

The sound paralyzed him for a moment, the sheer agony of it a physical blow. The scientist in him recoiled, cataloging the brutality, the inefficiency, the sheer, horrifying cruelty of the act. He had taken a living thing and had only broken it.

But the animal in him, awakened and enraged by the scent of its own potential meal, struck again.

The world narrowed to the feeling of stone against shell, a wet, percussive impact that vibrated up his arm.

And again. He was no longer in control. He was a passenger in his own body, a ghost watching a savage perform a butcher's work. The whistling shrieks devolved into wet, gurgling sounds, and then, finally, a last, shuddering sigh.

Silence.

It descended like a shroud, thick and absolute. The only sound was his own ragged breathing, his chest heaving.

He stood over the broken thing, the rock slick and heavy in his hand. It was coated in a deep, viscous indigo fluid, its thick droplets pattering onto the rust-colored moss below.

He had done it. He had survived. He had killed.

He let the rock fall from his numb fingers. The cost of his meal was written in the shattered iridescence of the creature's shell and the silent, black pools of its unseeing eyes.

The beast in his stomach was quiet now, but a new, colder hollowness had taken its place, a void in his very soul.

He stared at the broken creature, the indigo blood stark against the rust-colored moss. The silence of the alcove was absolute, a ringing vacuum where the creature's pained shrieks had been moments before.

He knew what came next. The logical, procedural next step. He had to process the kill.

He retrieved his small, utilitarian knife from his pack. The blade felt unnervingly clean in his stained hands. He knelt, forcing himself into a state of clinical detachment.

This was no different from a dissection in a biology lab. It was a specimen. A problem of mass and energy. He made the first cut, the knife struggling to pierce the strange, semi-pliable chitin.

The work was slow and gruesome. The creature's anatomy was a puzzle of alien biology, its organs unfamiliar shapes and colors. He was working by guesswork, his mind a distant, horrified observer cataloging the butcher's work of his hands.

He managed to harvest a few strips of pale, fibrous muscle tissue, wrapping them in a large, waxy leaf.

He looked at the remains, the discarded shell and viscera, and felt a wave of nausea. He had not just taken a life; he had desecrated it, reducing a unique and complex organism to a set of components for his own fuel.

He quickly buried the rest of the carcass under a pile of loose rocks, a crude and hurried burial for a creature whose only crime was to be edible.

Making a fire was its own special kind of hell. The glassy wood he had found earlier refused to catch, its surface too smooth for friction. The rubbery wood simply smoldered, producing a thick, acrid smoke but no flame. It took him another hour of desperate searching before he found a dead, brittle husk of a tree whose fibrous interior could hold a spark.

He worked with a grim, mechanical determination, his knuckles raw, until a tiny, flickering flame finally sputtered to life. As he fed it slivers of the strange wood, the fire burned with a foul, chemical stink, its light a sickly orange that did little to warm the oppressive gloom.

He skewered a piece of the creature's meat on a stick and held it over the struggling flame. It sizzled and spat, releasing an alien, coppery aroma that was nothing like the familiar scent of roasting meat. It was the smell of survival, and it made him want to vomit.

When the meat was charred on the outside, he pulled it from the fire.

He sat on the cold ground, the piece of alien flesh in his hands, and forced himself to eat.

The texture was wrong, stringy and tough, with a strange, gritty quality he couldn't identify. The flavor was worse—a sharp, acrid taste, metallic and bitter.

And beneath it all was the faint, pervasive taste of ash, a flavor that seemed to come not from the fire, but from the meat itself, as if he were consuming the very essence of this dead, broken world.

He ate until the gnawing in his stomach subsided, his jaw aching from the effort of chewing. His body, desperate for calories, accepted the fuel. His mind, his soul, rejected every single bite.

He dropped the half-eaten stick and looked at his hands.

They were stained with dirt, cuts, and the deep, indelible indigo of the creature's blood. They were not the hands of a physicist, hands that had once danced across holographic interfaces and calibrated quantum sensors. They were the hands of a butcher. A savage.

A wave of profound self-loathing washed over him, so powerful it made him gag. He hadn't just killed a creature. He had violated a fundamental law of his own being.

The man who had lived by the clean, elegant logic of the cosmos, who had found a sacred beauty in the predictable mathematics of life, was now a monster who bludgeoned that life to death with a rock to feed his own gut.

He had solved the first part of the Axiom's equation. He had survived.

But as he sat there in the alien twilight, shivering with a cold that came from within, he felt the terrible cost of the answer.

He was psychically soiled, a man remade in the image of this horrifying new reality.

He had eaten the ash, and now it was a part of him.

3

The Aperture

The self-loathing was a heavier burden than the hunger had been. In the days that followed his first kill, the sharp, violent horror of the act had faded, but it was replaced by something worse: a dull, grinding numbness, a spiritual gangrene that was slowly consuming what was left of his soul.

He had killed again. And again. The second time was no easier, but it was faster. The third time, he felt almost nothing at all, his mind retreating to a cold, clinical distance as his hands performed the butcher's work.

He had learned to identify the creatures by their chitin patterns, to predict their skittering movements, to find the weak point just behind their multifaceted eyes. He had become an efficient predator. The thought brought him no pride, only a profound, hollowing shame.

Ravn moved through the alien forest like a ghost, haunted by the memory of indigo blood on his hands.

The Axiom's words, once a lifeline of logic in a sea of madness, now felt like a curse. *Survive.* It was a mandate to perform acts that violated his very being, to become the savage he had seen reflected in that first creature's eyes. *Understand.* How could he understand a universe whose fundamental laws were a lie, a world built on a foundation of chaos and violence? And *Find the Heart…* it was a meaningless abstraction, a fool's errand in a world that clearly had no heart at all.

He was adrift in a chaotic sea, and the mission he clung to was a sinking raft.

His body was failing as surely as his spirit. The viscous, chemically-tainted water kept him from dying of thirst, but it offered no true relief. It sat heavy in his gut, a constant, low-grade poison that left him with a perpetual feeling of nausea and dull cramps that radiated from his core. The alien meat, the stringy, ash-flavored protein he now consumed with mechanical regularity, gave him calories but no strength.

He felt a deep, cellular weariness, as if his body was struggling to process fuel it was never designed to burn. He was weak, dehydrated again, and utterly lost. The three blue suns offered no guidance, their positions in the bruised purple sky shifting with an unpredictable, maddening rhythm.

He had abandoned any attempt at orientation. He was simply moving, driven by a low-level, animal instinct to avoid staying in one place for too long.

The world around him was a blur of hostile beauty. The pulsating, bio-luminescent flora, the crystalline growths that sprouted from the slick, black bark of the trees, the shimmering, heat-haze distortions in the air—he saw it all, but he no longer had the will to catalog or analyze it. It was just the landscape of his own personal hell.

He was leaning against the oily trunk of a pulsating tree, the rhythmic thrum of its internal processes vibrating through his exhausted body. His legs gave out, and he slid down into the rust-colored moss, the warmth of the alien ground seeping into his back.

He had no more strength to hunt, no more will to force down the tainted water. He could simply stop. He could close his eyes and let the world reclaim him, let the equation of his miserable existence finally resolve to zero.

It would be a relief.

He closed his eyes, the oppressive silence of the forest pressing in on him. This was it. The end of the variable. He was ready to be pruned, this time for good.

It was then that he heard it.

At first, he dismissed it as a symptom of his own collapse, an auditory hallucination born of starvation and despair. It was a low, resonant hum, so faint it seemed to exist at the very edge of his perception.

He pressed the heels of his hands into his eyes, waiting for it to fade with the other phantoms. But it didn't. It remained a constant and unwavering presence in the dead silence.

He lifted his head, turning it slowly, trying to triangulate the source. The sound felt deeper, resonating in the bones of his skull and the fillings in his teeth. He placed a hand on the warm, mossy ground, and he could feel it there, too—a faint, rhythmic thrumming, like a colossal, sleeping heart beating miles below him.

His scientific mind, battered and starved but not yet dead, began to analyze.

The sound was a perfect, pure sine wave. There was no wavering of pitch, no complex overtones. Nature, in all its chaotic glory, did not produce pure sine waves. Wind, water, the cries of animals—they were all a complex, noisy hash of frequencies.

A pure tone like this was almost always a sign of one thing: technology. It was artificial.

And that terrified him more than anything he had yet encountered.

Every rational instinct, every lesson from a thousand half-forgotten survival manuals, screamed at him to run. An artificial signal in a hostile, alien world was not an invitation; it was a threat. It was the lure of an angler fish, the territorial call of a predator he couldn't comprehend.

The logical, survival-oriented choice was to put as much distance between himself and the source as possible. To be a variable is to survive, and survival meant avoiding the unknown.

He even tried to stand, to force his aching limbs to carry him away. But he couldn't. Because he was already dying. His logic had led him here, to this point of collapse, starving and alone at the base of a pulsating tree. His caution had earned him nothing but a slower death. What, really, did he have left to lose?

And the hum… it was more than a potential threat. It was a clue.

It was a single, impossibly elegant piece of order in a universe that had abandoned it. It was a constant in a world of terrifying variables.

For a man who had dedicated his life to finding the signal in the noise, this was a siren song he could not resist. His curiosity, the core of the man he had been, flared to life, a single, defiant spark in the ashes of his despair.

It was a mystery. And a mystery demanded to be solved.

The debate in his mind was short and one-sided. Cautious logic offered only a continuation of this miserable, failing existence. Desperate curiosity offered a different outcome, even if that outcome was a swifter end. He chose the latter.

He pushed himself away from the tree, his muscles protesting with a dull, burning ache. He took a single, shuffling step in the direction the hum felt strongest, then another.

The sound, or the feeling of it, grew marginally stronger, a physical presence in the air that seemed to make the iridescent particles of dust dance. He pushed aside a curtain of thick, fleshy leaves that felt like cold skin and stumbled forward into the gloom, a moth drawn to a flame he knew would almost certainly consume him.

He stumbled into a small, sunken clearing. The hum was overwhelming here, a physical presence in the air that seemed to vibrate the world into a low, resonant thrum. Not only in his bones anymore; it was a pressure against his eardrums, a deep, pure tone that drowned out all other sensation.

And in the center of the clearing, he saw it.

Partially embedded in the rust-colored moss was an object. It was a dodecahedron, no larger than his fist, and it was the most impossible thing he had ever seen.

His scientific mind, starved for stimulus, flared to life with a ferocious intensity that burned through the fog of his exhaustion. He approached it slowly, cautiously, his heart hammering against his ribs.

The object was crafted from a material that seemed to drink the faint, green-blue light of the clearing. It wasn't metal or crystal, but something in between, its surface a seamless, matte black that was so absolute it seemed to possess no texture at all. It looked less like a physical object and more

24

like a hole carved in reality, a piece of pure, three-dimensional emptiness.

He knelt, his eyes scanning every facet. There were no seams, no scratches, no signs of wear or manufacturing. It was perfect.

A perfect Platonic solid, one of the five fundamental shapes of sacred geometry, resting in the mud of an alien world as if it had simply willed itself into existence. It was a profound and beautiful violation of entropy.

The hum emanated from its core, a sound of immense, sleeping power. It was a contradiction on every conceivable level.

The world he was in was a testament to decay, to the violent, chaotic breakdown of systems. The flora was twisted and asymmetrical. The fauna was a hodgepodge of mismatched limbs and carapaces. The very laws of physics felt provisional, frayed at the edges.

But this object... this object was a statement of perfect, unshakable, intelligent order.

His mind raced through hypotheses, each one more ludicrous than the last. A geological formation? Impossible. No natural crystalline process could create a seamless dodecahedron of this complexity and perfection. A piece of technology, then? Left behind by a pre-Fracture survey team? Unlikely. The material was unlike any alloy he had ever encountered, and there was no visible power source, no interface, no markings of any kind.

It was alien. But not alien in the way the pulsating trees and the six-legged creatures were. They were products of a chaotic, runaway biology. This was the product of a cold, precise, and impossibly advanced intelligence.

It was a clue.

The flawed pinecone had been the first clue, a sign that the old rules were broken. This was the second. It was a sign that new rules had been written.

He stared at it for a long time, the scientist warring with the survivor. The survivor screamed at him to back away, to leave this impossible thing alone, to recognize it as a threat far greater than any simple predator.

But the scientist, the man he had been, the man who had followed his curiosity into the heart of the Aethelburg Anomaly, was utterly captivated. It was the most profound puzzle he had ever encountered, and the need to understand it, to gather data, was a more powerful drive than fear.

He reached out a trembling hand, his fingers caked with dirt. He could feel the low-frequency vibration of the hum intensifying as he drew closer, the air growing thick and heavy.

This was a choice. A leap of faith into an abyss of pure, terrifying, beautiful mystery.

His fingers brushed the matte black surface. It was neither warm nor cold, and for an infinitesimal fraction of a second, he felt nothing at all.

Then the world vanished.

A total, instantaneous cessation of all sensory input, a perfect vacuum.

The clearing, the trees, the ground beneath his knees, the very air in his lungs—all of it was gone. He was a disembodied consciousness floating in an endless, featureless void.

The hum became a roar that filled that void, a sound that was also a feeling and a color and a concept. An avalanche of pure information crashed through the firewalls of his mind.

It arrived as raw, direct, experiential data.

He felt the slow, crushing pressure of a thousand millennia of geological strata forming beneath him, the heat and weight of a planet's history compressed into a single, agonizing moment. He felt the intricate, silent latticework of the mycelial network, a planetary intelligence of root and spore, and for a timeless second, he was part of its slow, patient consciousness, feeling the flow of nutrients through the soil and the collective hum of a billion living things.

His perception then fractured, shifting from the organic to the analytical. He saw the local topography not as a landscape, but as a three-dimensional wireframe of shimmering light, a perfect map unfolding in his mind's eye. On that map, every living thing within a five-kilometer radius glowed with a distinct heat signature, from the smallest insects to the largest predators, each a pulsing, living flame.

Then the data turned inward. Schematics for the object in his hand—an energy cell of impossible efficiency, a bio-scanner capable of reading a creature's DNA from a distance, a data-conduit that interfaced directly with the quantum foam—unfurled behind his eyelids like blueprints made of light.

It was too much. His consciousness, his very sense of self, began to fray under the colossal weight of the data stream. His own memories—of Aris, of Lena, of the pinecone, of his own name—became small, insignificant files in a torrent of cosmic information.

He was a single kilobyte of data in a universe-sized archive, on the verge of being overwritten, his identity dissolving into the overwhelming whole. He was experiencing the death of the self, a blissful and terrifying dissolution.

Just as the last anchor of his identity was about to slip away, the device itself resonated with a single, overriding informational tag, which the Axiom—his mind's stabilizing anchor—instantly processed and named:

The Aperture. A tool to measure the equation.

The flood of information did not recede. It was organized. The roaring avalanche was channeled and categorized, settling from a chaotic, overwhelming deluge into a quiet, intuitive layer of his perception.

He felt the solid ground beneath his knees again. He smelled the cloying, sweet air. The clearing returned.

He could still feel the world around him, but it was now overlaid with a calm, clean heads-up display of data that moved with his gaze.

A compass materialized in the upper right of his vision, its needle not pointing to a magnetic north, but to a powerful energy source deep in the distance, labeled simply: *THE HEART*.

The pulsating flora around him was now tagged with its biological properties: *TOXIC, NARCOTIC, EDIBLE [MINIMAL NUTRITIONAL VALUE]*. A small, six-legged creature scurrying nearby was highlighted with a simple, pragmatic tag: *PROTEIN SOURCE*.

He looked at the object in his hand. The Aperture.

Among its functions, now intuitively understood, he noticed a locked, encrypted interface in the corner of his vision, a file he could not open, labeled simply: *[ROOT]*.

A wave of something he hadn't felt since before Aethelburg washed over him: hope.

It was a fragile, terrifying, and exquisitely precious thing.

The mission, once an abstraction, was now a tangible objective.

Survive. Understand. Find the Heart.

He finally had a tool for the first two. And now, a compass to point the way to the third.

He was no longer a ghost being hunted. He was an explorer. He had a map to the heart of the scar.

4

The Weight of a Choice

Hope was a dangerous variable, a notoriously unstable element in any closed system. Ravn knew this. For five years, he had ruthlessly purged it from his own life, replacing it with the cold, hard certainty of mathematics.

Yet, as the days passed since his discovery of the Aperture, he could feel the treacherous, unfamiliar emotion taking root in the barren soil of his soul.

The device was a constant, cool weight on his wrist, a silent, logical partner in the hostile wilderness. The overwhelming flood of information he'd experienced upon first touching it—the feeling of drowning in the planet's data—had subsided. It had settled into a calm, persistent overlay of augmented reality that moved with his gaze, tagging the chaotic world with comforting, predictable labels.

It had transformed the Fracture Zone from an incomprehensible nightmare into a complex but solvable equation.

He was no longer just a ghost being hunted; he was a field researcher again, gathering data in the most hostile environment imaginable. His new routine was grim, but it was a routine. And in a world of madness, routine was a form of prayer.

His priority each twilight cycle was water. In the desperate days before the Aperture, he had been forced to drink from the viscous, iridescent streams, his body wracked with cramps and nausea as his liver fought against unknown isotopes. Now, the Aperture guided him. Following its topographical analysis of the landscape, it led him away from the poisoned lowlands and toward the base of colossal, mushroom-like flora that grew on the ridgelines.

He watched the data scroll across his vision as he approached a towering fungal stalk.

TARGET: MYCO-CISTERN. CONTENTS: H20. TRACE MINERALS: ACCEPTABLE. BIOLOGICAL CONTAMINANTS: 0.02%.

He learned to use his knife to pierce the plant's tough, leathery skin at the precise angle indicated by the Aperture's schematic. Cool, clear water dripped from the wound, tasting slightly metallic but blissfully clean. He filled his canteen, the sound of the trickling water the sweetest music he had ever heard.

It was a small, daily miracle of applied data.

Food was no longer a matter of brutal, desperate violence against creatures he didn't understand. The Aperture's bio-scanner was a ruthless editor of the landscape. It painted the forest in a binary of life and death.

It tagged the vast majority of the luscious, inviting fruit with flashing crimson warnings: *TOXIC, NEUROTOXIC, PARALYTIC AGENT.* But occasionally, amidst the poison, it would highlight a patch of gnarled, pale roots or a cluster of deep blue berries with a reassuring green tag: *EDIBLE. HIGH IN CARBOHYDRATES.*

The food was alien, often flavorless or possessing a texture like wet chalk, but it was fuel. The gnawing, maddening hunger that had driven him to savagery in the first days was gone, replaced by the simple, manageable ache of a body running on a caloric deficit.

He was no longer starving. He was sustaining.

And he had shelter. The Aperture's constant geological scanning had revealed a network of dry, defensible caves in a nearby rock formation. He had chosen one with a narrow entrance and a deep inner chamber, a place where he could finally escape the perpetual, bruising twilight and the unblinking gaze of the three blue suns.

For the first time since the Convergence, he slept for more than an hour at a time. He had wedged a heavy stone across the mouth of the cave, a silent, unfeeling sentinel against the dark.

He was in control.

It was a fragile, provisional control, a thin layer of logic stretched taut over an abyss of chaos, but it was real. In the quiet of his cave, illuminated by the soft blue light of the Aperture's screen, he would study the device. He traced the perfect lines of the matte black dodecahedron, marveling at the impossible science it represented.

The Axiom's words no longer felt like a curse, but like a solvable problem set.

Survive. He was doing that. *Understand.* He was beginning to catalog the physics of this broken world one scan at a time. *Find the Heart.* The compass in his vision pointed ever onward, a constant, unwavering guide toward a distant energy source.

He left the cave after a few hours of fitful, dreamless sleep. The fragile sense of control was a fuel, burning clean and bright, pushing him onward.

For two days, he traveled, following the steady, silent pull of the Aperture's compass. He moved with a newfound confidence, his steps measured, his eyes constantly scanning the data overlay that was now as natural to him as his own vision.

The world was still a place of profound danger, but it was no longer a place of profound mystery. It was a system, and he was finally beginning to understand its rules.

It was this flicker of control, this nascent, dangerous hope, that made the encounter so devastating.

He was navigating a shallow, rocky valley where the air was thick with the sweet, cloying scent he'd come to associate with biological decay when the Aperture flashed a new icon in his vision.

An amber triangle flashed, a signifier he hadn't seen before.

BIOLOGICAL SIGNATURE DETECTED: HOMO SAPIENS. VITALS: CRITICAL.

Ravn froze, dropping into a low crouch behind a slick, black boulder. A

31

human. Another survivor.

In all his weeks in the Fracture Zone, he hadn't seen another soul. He had begun to believe he was the only one left.

He crept to the edge of the boulder and peered into the clearing below.

He found the man huddled by a stream whose water shimmered with a toxic, iridescent film. He was old, his skin drawn tight over his bones, possessing a strange, grayish pallor that spoke of a deep sickness. He was shivering violently, despite the unnatural warmth radiating from the mossy ground, and his lips were cracked and tinged with blue.

He was in the advanced stages of dehydration and what looked like systemic poisoning, clutching a small, dented canteen with white-knuckled hands. He was muttering to himself, his words a delirious, nonsensical slur.

Ravn felt a pang of something he hadn't felt in years: a clinical, detached pity.

The man was a failing system, his biological processes on the verge of total collapse. He had clearly been drinking the tainted water, a fatal error in judgment.

Ravn's first, cold instinct was to back away, to leave the dying variable to its inevitable conclusion. He was not a factor in Ravn's own equation for survival.

But as he began to retreat, the man, Caleb, looked up.

His eyes, cloudy with delirium, scanned the clearing without focus until they landed on Ravn. Or, more specifically, on the simple, tube-like water purifier hanging from Ravn's pack.

Recognition flared in the man's eyes, a spark of lucid intelligence in the fog of his sickness. He was not just seeing a tool; he understood its function. A lifetime of knowledge, of engineering or science, was still flickering in his dying brain.

He didn't beg for water from Ravn's canteen; he made a more desperate, technical plea, appealing to their shared understanding of this new world's dangers.

He pushed himself up, his arms trembling with the effort.

"The filter..." he croaked, his voice a dry, agonizing rasp, each word a struggle.

He held up his own empty canteen, a gesture of desperate hope. "Please... just one canteen's worth through the filter. I know the stream is poison..."

The request slammed into Ravn, bypassing pity and triggering a cold, frantic panic in his scientific mind.

This wasn't a simple plea for a drink. It was a complex problem, a new, unwanted variable that threatened to destabilize his entire, fragile system of survival.

For a fleeting moment, he felt a pang of empathy, a visceral memory of his own sandpaper tongue and the pounding headache of dehydration. He saw not a stranger, but a fellow man, another scientist perhaps, trapped in the same nightmare. The impulse to help was there, a brief, warm flicker in the cold void of his fear.

He immediately suppressed it.

Empathy was a dangerous variable. It was an emotion that had no place in this new world's brutal calculus. It was a bug in the system, a path to inefficiency and, ultimately, death. He had learned that lesson in the ashes of Aethelburg. He had hesitated then, mesmerized by the beautiful data, and the cost had been everything.

He would not make that mistake again. He walled off the feeling, compartmentalizing it, and allowed the cold, detached analyst to take control. He didn't see a dying man; he saw an equation with an unacceptable outcome.

A high-speed, cost-benefit analysis scrolled through his thoughts, crisp and logical, a process that took only seconds but felt like an eternity.

Initial State: Subject Ravn possesses a single, functional water purifier. A filter cartridge is a polymer membrane with a finite lifespan. Current estimated capacity: ~400 liters. This is the primary survival asset. It is the clock.

Input Variable: Subject Caleb, dehydration critical. Request: one liter of purified water. A single, immediate cost of 0.25% of the total asset lifespan.

Projected Outcome, Scenario A: Refusal. Ravn conserves the resource. Subject Caleb's survival probability remains unchanged, trending toward zero. Ravn's survival probability remains at baseline.

Projected Outcome, Scenario B: Assent. Ravn expends one liter. Subject Caleb's immediate survival probability increases. However, the act creates a dependent variable and establishes a precedent.

Sub-Analysis, Scenario B: Caleb, now with a reason to hope, will observe a functioning resource. He is weak, but mobile. He will follow. Probability: >95%. This creates a two-variable system. Resource expenditure will increase. The daily water requirement for two subjects doubles. The operational window of the filter cartridge is reduced by 50%. Ravn's mobility will be compromised by Caleb's weakened state, reducing daily travel distance and increasing exposure to potential threats.

The long-term probability of the system (Ravn + Caleb) reaching a stable, sustainable resource zone before asset depletion decreases significantly. The probability of at least one variable (Ravn) reaching that zone alone is substantially higher.

His mind, almost against his will, performed the final, chilling calculation. The introduction of the new variable, with all its attendant risks and resource drains, decreased his personal long-term survival probability by a horrifyingly precise 47.3%.

Conclusion: The logical, optimal path to ensure the survival of at least one node in the system is to conserve the resource. To decline the request. It was math. It was the cold, hard, unforgiving truth of their new reality.

The horrifying logic settled in his chest, a block of ice.

While this frantic, silent simulation ran its course, he had stood perfectly still, his face an unreadable mask. To Caleb, it looked like he was considering the plea with solemn gravity. In reality, he had already run the numbers and made his choice.

The calculation was complete. The conclusion was absolute. Now came the execution.

Ravn's body felt stiff and heavy, each movement a conscious effort against a current of profound, internal resistance. He forced his hand to move, to unclip the purifier from his pack. The simple plastic tube felt impossibly heavy.

It was a cruel gesture, he knew, to show the dying man the very instrument of salvation he was about to deny him. But it was part of the lie, a necessary component of the performance.

He held it up, his gaze fixed on the small, color-coded indicator on the side of the cartridge, a meaningless piece of data he was about to weaponize. He refused to meet Caleb's pleading, delirious eyes.

"It's almost depleted," Ravn said. His voice was a monotone, flat, and devoid of the emotion that was churning in his gut. It was the voice of a scientist delivering a disappointing but unavoidable result. "I don't think it has another liter in it. I'm sorry."

The lie tasted like ash in his mouth. He could feel the weight of the water in his own canteen, a sloshing, life-giving accusation against his ribs.

He watched as the last, flickering spark of lucid hope in Caleb's eyes died, replaced by a vacant, hollow despair. The old man's shoulders slumped, his entire body seeming to collapse inward on itself. He didn't argue. He didn't plead further. He had no energy left for it.

He simply sank back to the ground, a system shutting down.

Ravn turned and walked away. He did not run. He forced himself into a steady, measured pace, maintaining the façade of a man who had made a difficult but necessary choice. Every step was a hammer blow against his conscience. The crunch of his boots on the rocky ground was the only sound, a rhythm marking his retreat from the scene of his own quiet, profound moral crime.

He didn't get far. He had just moved out of sight behind a ridge of glistening black rock, the silence of the valley wrapping around him, when the sound reached him.

Ragged, despairing sobs echoed of a man completely and utterly broken. It was the sound of a soul surrendering, a raw, ragged noise that was horribly, inefficiently human.

The sound bypassed all of his logical defenses and struck him like a physical blow. He froze in his tracks, his back pressed against the cold rock.

The equation, which had seemed so clear and absolute moments before, now felt like a monstrous lie. The 47.3% was a meaningless number in the face of this absolute, present-tense suffering. He should go back. He had to go back.

A deep, silent paralysis seized him. He squeezed his eyes shut, wishing the sound away, wishing the whole equation away, but the ragged, miserable sobs continued, a profound, unfixable error in his calculus. He stood frozen, unable to move forward to save the man, and unable to run away from the sound of his own moral decay. He realized with terrifying clarity that the logic hadn't protected him; it had only provided a sophisticated language for his cowardice. He wasn't calculating survival; he was calculating the price of his own humanity, and he had found it cheap.

Before he could decide, before he could act on the resurgence of his own buried humanity, the sobs were cut short by a piercing, predatory shriek that echoed off the valley walls.

Ravn dropped into a crouch, his heart pounding against his ribs, adrenaline a hot, metallic flood in his veins. The beast attack wasn't his fault, not directly. But he knew, with a certainty that defied all calculation, that the man's cries of despair, a direct result of his refusal, had been a beacon in the twilight.

He heard a brief, terrible struggle from the other side of the ridge—tearing sounds, the wet snap of bone, a single, choked-off scream that was abruptly silenced.

He stayed hidden. He listened, his breath held, every muscle in his body screaming at him to run.

But he remained, paralyzed. He made another choice. He did not intervene. He stayed silent, passively using the dying man as a distraction, as a sacrifice to ensure his own escape.

The sounds faded, replaced by the wet, rhythmic noise of a predator feeding.

Ravn remained pressed against the cold rock, every muscle locked, his breath a shallow, controlled tremor in his chest. He was waiting. Waiting for the creature to move on, to leave him alone in the quiet tomb of his own making.

He listened, his hearing strained to an almost painful degree, trying to parse the direction of the beast from the faint, alien sounds of the valley. He heard a low, guttural snort from the other side of the ridge. Then, the sound of sniffing, a series of deep, powerful inhalations.

It had scented two prey items, but had only claimed one. It was still hunting.

The predator, a sleek, four-limbed creature with skin like oiled leather, emerged from the direction of the stream, its head low to the ground. It moved with a liquid, unnerving grace, its muscles coiling and uncoiling. It raised its head, its featureless face turning slowly, sniffing the air.

Ravn's blood ran cold.

The creature's head stopped, its entire body freezing, oriented directly at his hiding place. It had found him.

Terror, absolute and primordial, seized him. The weight of his guilt for Caleb, the memory of his own recent death, and the immediacy of this new, impending one all crashed together in his mind.

It was a feedback loop, a recursive error that his consciousness could not resolve.

His perception of reality, already fragile, finally shattered. For a split second, his mind fractured.

The world dissolved. The rocks, the trees, the very air around him de-rendered into a dizzying cascade of shimmering green code.

He was no longer in a valley; he was inside a crashing simulation. The predator was no longer flesh and blood but a complex, hostile algorithm, a knot of aggressive subroutines. And in the waterfall of data, a single, critical line of its immediate behavior script was highlighted in stark, terrifying crimson:

[LUNGE: TARGET_ACQUIRED. VECTOR: 34.8. PROBABILITY: 98.9%.]

He didn't have time to think, only to process the data. His body moved without his conscious command, reacting to the raw information as if it were a physical law.

He didn't dive or scramble; he simply pressed himself flat against the rough surface of the rock, making his profile as small as mathematically possible an instant before the creature launched itself through the air.

He felt the wind of its passage, a hot, musky gust against his cheek. He heard the shriek of its claws scraping sparks from the stone inches from where his head had been. The sheer, kinetic force of its lunge shook the very ground he was lying on.

Just as quickly, the world snapped back into focus. The green code solidified back into rock and moss and pulsing leaves.

The predator, having overshot its target, landed with a low growl of frustration. It cast one last, confused look back at the empty rock face, then turned, dragging Caleb's limp body into the glowing woods until it was swallowed by the gloom.

Silence descended. Ravn pushed himself to his feet, his body trembling uncontrollably.

The adrenaline of survival faded, and the cold, crushing weight of his choices rushed in to fill the void.

He had survived. But the cost was unbearable.

His mind fractured again. This time, there was no code, no data, no tactical advantage.

Just a single, silent, vivid image burned into his consciousness: his brother Aris, standing in the clean, white light of the Aethelburg lab, looking at him not with awe or terror, but with a gaze of profound, quiet disappointment.

It was a look that said, *I believed in you.*

The vision vanished. He was alone in the valley, the silence broken only by the sound of his own ragged, broken sobs.

He was alive because he had lied. He was alive because he had listened to a man die. He was alive because his own mind was coming apart at the seams, haunted now by the ghost of a man he had condemned and the ghost of a man he had failed.

5

A Debt in Time

The vision of his brother's disappointed face was a brand on his mind, more terrifying than any physical threat.

Ravn scrambled to his feet and fled the valley, not with the calculated caution of a survivor, but with the blind panic of a soul trying to outrun its own damnation.

He crashed through thickets of glowing flora, the greasy residue of the leaves smearing on his skin, tearing his clothes, and leaving stinging welts on his arms. He ignored the tactical data scrolling across his vision from the Aperture. The optimal paths, the threat assessments, the hydration warnings—all of it was rendered meaningless by the storm in his own head.

The memory of Caleb's sobbing, the wet sound of the predator feeding, and the quiet judgment in Aris's eyes formed a cacophony he was desperate to escape. He was a walking wound, bleeding guilt and terror into the alien atmosphere.

And in the strange, interconnected ecosystem of the Fracture Zone, such a powerful broadcast of distress did not go unnoticed. He was no longer a quiet variable moving cautiously through the system. He was a beacon of pure, chaotic panic.

He was halfway up a loose scree slope, his lungs burning and his legs shaking with exhaustion, when the Aperture finally cut through his mental static.

A shrill, internal alarm tone shattered the calm, a sound he had never heard before, pulsed in his ears, and the entire field of his vision was washed with a crimson alert.

[!!WARNING: THREAT DETECTED. CLASS 7 BIOLOGICAL!!]
[DESIGNATION: REAPER]
[VELOCITY: 90 KPH. DISTANCE: 400 METERS & CLOSING]
[ANALYSIS: APEX PREDATOR. EVASION PROBABILITY: < 0.1%]

The numbers were so absolute, so final, that they momentarily silenced the ghosts in his head. A Class 7? The creature that had killed Caleb had been a Class 3. Evasion probability is less than one-tenth of one percent. It read like an obituary.

Then he heard it. A sound like a distant landslide, a deep, grinding roar that seemed to vibrate up through the soles of his boots and rattle the marrow of his bones.

He glanced back over his shoulder, down into the valley he had just fled. The tops of the oily black trees at the far end of the valley were shaking violently, thrashing as if caught in a gale, then snapping like twigs. Something massive was coming.

It burst from the tree line, and his blood ran cold.

It was a hulking predator built of serrated black chitin and raw, exposed muscle, its body low to the ground like some nightmarish crocodile the size of a transport truck. It moved with an impossible, earth-shaking speed, six powerful, insectoid legs churning up the mossy ground, each stride covering a dozen meters. Multiple, unblinking red eyes, set deep in its armored head, scanned the landscape with a cold, biological certainty.

This was an unstoppable force of nature, a living engine of destruction. It had found his trail. The chase had begun.

There was no time for analysis, no time for a plan. There was only the thunder of its six legs eating up the ground behind him and the primal, all-consuming need to run.

He scrambled up the rest of the scree slope, loose rock sliding away beneath his boots, robbing him of momentum. The Aperture's data overlay was a frantic, useless scramble of red warning icons and proximity alerts.

His intellect was a dead weight. This was a problem that could not be solved with math.

His first instinct was to use the terrain. He reached the top of the slope and found himself at the base of a sheer rock face, a vertical wall of glistening black stone. It was a suicidal climb, but the alternative was worse. He found handholds in the rough, alien rock and began to pull himself upward, his muscles screaming in protest.

A normal predator, no matter how large, would be slowed by such an obstacle.

He glanced down and saw the Reaper reach the base of the cliff. Instead of slowing or searching for a different path. It simply coiled its powerful legs and leaped.

It was a terrifying, impossible sight—a creature the size of a truck launching itself thirty meters into the air. It slammed into the cliff face just below him with the force of a wrecking ball, its obsidian-hard claws digging into the stone to arrest its momentum. It didn't climb; it bounded, a vertical avalanche of controlled destruction, shattering rock with each impact.

Panic gave way to a cold, strategic terror. He couldn't out-climb it. He needed a chokepoint.

He hauled himself over the lip of the cliff and consulted the Aperture's topographical map, his mind racing. He saw it—a hundred meters ahead, a narrow fissure in the rock, a slot canyon barely a meter wide. A perfect trap.

He sprinted across the rocky plateau, the Reaper gaining on him with every earth-shaking stride. He reached the fissure and threw himself into the narrow opening, the rough walls scraping against his clothes.

He was through. He pressed himself against the stone, his chest heaving, listening to the approaching thunder.

The Reaper arrived at the entrance. He heard it snort, a sound like grinding stone. Then came a sound of immense pressure, of groaning, fracturing rock. The creature was making the opening bigger.

With a deafening crack, a huge section of the canyon wall beside him exploded inward. The Reaper smashed its way through the stone, widening the fissure with sheer brute force, its red eyes glowing in the dust and gloom.

He scrambled away, deeper into the canyon. His intellect screamed for a solution.

His eyes darted to the canyon walls. They were composed of sedimentary layers of unstable, silicate shale.

Structural integrity: Compromised, his mind registered, the old habits of a physicist overriding the panic of the prey.

He grabbed a heavy, iron-dense stone from the ground. He didn't throw it at the beast. He spun and hurled it high, aiming for a specific, protruding shelf of rock thirty feet above the narrowest point of the path—a keystone holding back tons of loose scree.

The stone struck the shelf with a sharp clack. The vibration traveled through the unstable shale. Then, gravity did the work his muscles couldn't. The shelf sheared. A landslide of razor-sharp shale thundered down, burying the path behind him in a cloud of choking dust.

It wouldn't stop the Reaper—he knew that—but he had bought himself seconds using physics, not luck.

He broke through the far side of the dust cloud, and his heart sank.

It was a dead-end canyon, a perfect, natural trap. Sheer, unclimbable walls of glistening black rock rose on three sides, converging to a point a few hundred meters ahead. There was nowhere to run. Nowhere to hide. The chase was over.

He was exhausted, his lungs burning with an acid fire, his legs trembling so violently they could barely hold his weight. He stumbled to a halt in the center of the rocky basin, a profound and final sense of futility washing over him. He could keep running, scramble for purchase on the sheer walls, and be plucked from the rock like an insect. Or he could face it.

He chose to face it. He would not die fleeing.

He turned, the useless pulse rifle held loosely in his hands, and waited. The Reaper entered the canyon.

It was no longer charging at its earth-shaking, impossible speed. It knew he was trapped. It moved with a slow, deliberate, almost reptilian grace that was somehow more terrifying than its full-on assault.

The thunder of its charge was replaced by the sharp, rhythmic click-clack of its six, multi-jointed legs on the stone floor, a sound that echoed off the high canyon walls like a monstrous, ticking clock.

As it drew closer, Ravn got his first clear, up-close look at the creature.

It was a masterpiece of biological horror. Its body was a series of overlapping, serrated plates of black chitin that looked like volcanic rock, glistening with some kind of oily secretion. Pale, exposed muscle tissue, thick as steel cables, pulsed in the gaps between the armor. Steam vented in soft hisses from articulated joints near its powerful legs.

Its head was a solid, armored wedge, and set deep within it were not two, but six unblinking, crimson eyes that glowed with a faint, internal light. They stared with a complete and unnerving lack of any discernible emotion.

His scientific mind, even in the face of absolute terror, was still working, a ghost in the machine of his own fear. It was cataloging, analyzing. Arthropodal-reptilian hybrid. Exoskeleton appears to be a carbon-silicate matrix. *No visible respiratory system... likely a diffusive process through the musculature...* It was a final, futile act of understanding, an attempt to impose logic on the agent of his own extinction.

The Reaper stopped ten meters from him. It lowered its head, and a complex mandible structure, a terrifying array of smaller, needle-like appendages, unfurled from beneath its jaw with a soft, wet clicking sound.

It tilted its head, its six red eyes regarding him with a cold, biological certainty. In that moment, Ravn understood. There was no malice here. No cruelty. He was not an enemy to be defeated. He was a resource. A caloric anomaly to be processed. He was simply the next logical step in the creature's survival algorithm.

It coiled, its massive legs bunching under its body, the ground vibrating with the tension of its stored kinetic energy. It lunged.

Pain was the first reality to de-render.

It was an absolute, all-consuming, white-hot supernova of agony as the Reaper's chitinous claws sheared through flesh, muscle, and bone. It was the universe reduced to a single, screaming data point of pure, physical trauma.

And then, just as suddenly as it had arrived, it was gone. Not faded, not dulled, but simply... switched off. The sensation became an abstract tag in his fading perception, a logical flag labeled *[FATAL_ERROR]*, detached from any actual feeling.

Sight dissolved next. The image of the creature's open maw, its six crimson eyes burning with cold, biological fire, shattered into a screaming static of red and black pixels. His vision collapsed inward from the periphery, the world dissolving into a noisy, corrupting artifact until there was only a single, pinprick of light, which then winked out into absolute, featureless black. The visual data stream had been terminated.

Sound went last. The roar of the beast, the wet crunch of his own body, the frantic pounding of his heart—all of it collapsed into a single, attenuated sine wave, a pure, high-frequency tone that spiraled down, down, down into a silence more profound and empty than any he had ever known.

His consciousness, now untethered from its physical anchor, was pulled violently away.

He experienced his own life as a corrupted data file being force-deleted by a cosmic administrator. Time ran backward in a violent, chaotic rush.

He was in the canyon, turning to face the beast. He was in the glassy forest, blasting the trees into shards. He was squeezing through the fissure in the rock. He was hiding behind the boulder, listening to Caleb's final, choked-off scream. He was walking away from the stream, the lie a cold stone in his gut. He was watching the hope die in Caleb's eyes.

He was seeing the world as green, cascading code. He felt the phantom weight of a creature's head resting on his shoulder in what looked like a grotto. He saw a brass machine projecting a map of a broken sky. He was laughing with a madman in a moving fortress of rust and smoke, sharing a joke at the end of the world. He was watching a man with swirling eyes trade his humanity for the song of the hive. He was hearing Aris's voice on a data log he hadn't found yet. He was staring into the cold, blue eyes of a General who wore Lena's face like a mask of ice.

He was vomiting on the moss, the memory of his own death and his brother's fused to his soul. He was killing for the first time, the rock slick with indigo blood. He was drinking the tainted water, tasting ash and ozone. He was staring at the flawed pinecone, the fourteen spirals an indictment of a broken universe.

He was in the Aethelburg control room. The Cherenkov blue light blazed. Lena's hand reached for Aris's. His brother's face was a mask of sublime, terrible awe. He saw the warning on his own console. He hesitated.

The memories were not just images; they were being stripped away, their emotional weight and informational content ripped from his being. His consciousness, his very "I," was being unwritten. He was a paradox in the system, a failed timeline, an error in the equation.

He was being pruned.

He awoke with a gasp, a violent, involuntary spasm that arched his back off a cold, stone floor.

Air flooded his lungs, raw and thin. He was on his back, staring up at the familiar, rough-hewn roof of the small, dry cave he had slept in two nights ago.

For a disoriented moment, he thought it had all been a nightmare—the chase, the canyon, the Reaper.

He sat up, his heart hammering, and frantically ran his hands over his body. He checked his chest, his arms, his legs, expecting to find the horrific, shearing wounds from the creature's claws, the wetness of his own blood.

There was nothing. No wounds. No blood. His clothes weren't even torn. He was whole.

He was alive.

The relief was a brief, sunlit flash that was immediately consumed by a profound and chilling wrongness.

The memory of his own death was not a dream. It was a searing, high-fidelity recording etched into his consciousness. He could still feel the phantom sensation of the claws, still see the static of his collapsing vision, still hear the silence as his world ended.

The paradox between his memory and his physical reality was a chasm of impossibility that his logical mind could not bridge.

He scrambled to the mouth of the cave, desperate for an external data point, for something to make sense. He looked out, and the true horror of his situation crashed down on him.

The world was... leached.

The vibrant, sickly greens and rust-reds of the landscape were gone, replaced by a dead, monochromatic palette of muted, washed-out shades of gray. The gentle, bioluminescent pulse of the alien flora was now a harsh, stuttering flicker, like a dying fluorescent bulb. The light from the three blue suns was a flat, sterile white that cast sharp, grating shadows with no color or warmth.

It was a dead photograph of a world that had once been terrifyingly alive.

The sounds were worse. The air, once thick with alien smells and a low, organic hum, was now thin, sterile, and unnaturally silent. Every small noise was amplified and distorted, sharp and painful against his eardrums. A hollow, aching void resided in his chest. It was a physical sensation, a literal lack of substance in the space where his core being should be.

He felt... thinner. Less real. He was a phantom, a translucent echo of himself, and he was viewing the world through a dirty, gray pane of glass. His own spirit felt cracked and fragmented, like a shattered mirror that could no longer form a coherent reflection.

He had survived death. He was not resurrected; he was displaced. He had left a piece of himself behind in that dead timeline, a debt in time that he could feel with every gray, shallow breath.

He was an echo anchored in a failed reality.

His eyes narrowed as the analytical part of his mind, cold and detached even now, performed a rapid assessment. If he was here, where was the Reaper?

Ahead, through the gray haze of the valley, he saw a shape. It was the massive, chitinous carcass of the predator that had killed him. It lay where it had fallen, but in this Desynchronized State, its form was indistinct and gray.

The beast's quantum signature must have been catastrophically corrupted by the same informational backlash that triggered his own Echoic Resonance. His death was a reality-breaking event; the Reaper's demise was the necessary, localized consequence of that paradox.

Killing him broke the timeline around them both.

6

The Ghost in the Machine

The gray world was a razor's edge against his senses.

He remained at the mouth of the cave, his knuckles white where he gripped the rock, trying to reconcile the vivid, high-fidelity memory of his own annihilation with the impossible fact of his continued existence. The paradox was a grinding gear in his mind, threatening to tear his sanity apart.

The wrongness permeated every single photon, every single vibration of the world around him.

He focused on sight first, the scientist in him trying to catalog the data. The world was not merely leached of color; it was as if the very concept of the visible spectrum had been corrupted. The landscape was a study in harsh, overexposed whites and deep, information-less blacks, with a thousand shades of grating gray in between.

The gentle, bioluminescent pulse of the alien flora was gone, replaced by a harsh, stuttering flicker, a frantic, sickly strobing that made his eyes ache and his head swim. It was a dying monitor, the refresh rate failing, struggling to render a last, corrupted image of reality.

Then he analyzed the sound, or the lack of it. The rich, ambient hum of the living world was gone. In its place was a dead, flat silence, a zero-frequency that felt like a physical pressure against his eardrums.

Every sound that broke it was an act of violence. The drip from a rock hit with the sharp crack of striking glass. The distant skittering of an unseen insect sounded of metal scraping against stone, a grating, digital artifact in a corrupted audio file.

The air itself felt wrong. It was thin and sterile, devoid of the thick, organic smells of soil and decay. It tasted of nothing, of a vacuum. And it was cold, a profound, penetrating cold that had nothing to do with the temperature. It was the cold of absence, the cold of a system from which all warmth, all energy, all life had been bled away.

But the most horrifying sensation was the one inside him.

The hollow, aching void in his chest was a constant, physical presence. It was a literal lack of substance, a negative pressure in the space where his core being should be. It felt like a wound, and it was pulling inward, a tiny black hole demanding to be filled.

He felt thin. Less real. A phantom, a translucent echo of himself, his own spirit cracked and fragmented.

He knew, with a certainty that was as physical as the ache in his chest, that he had to get back. Back to the canyon. Back to the site of his death.

The void was a vacuum demanding to be filled, a negative pressure pulling him toward the source of the wound.

He raised the Aperture. The device still functioned, but its data was distorted, the clean lines of its interface flickering like a dying monitor. The compass, however, was steady. It no longer pointed toward the distant, abstract "Heart." It pointed back the way he had come. Toward his own ghost.

He took a shuffling step out of the cave, into the gray, stuttering light.

And he saw that he was not alone.

Flickering at the edges of his vision were shimmering distortions in the air, phantom-like creatures that drifted through the dead landscape with a silent, unnerving purpose.

He named them Glimmers. They were glitches left over from other failed timelines, and he learned their nature through terrifying trial and error. They were not a single type of entity, but a whole ecosystem of psychic predators.

The first kind he encountered were the Chaos-Glimmers. They appeared as small, swarming clouds of static gnats, buzzing with a visual noise that hurt to look at. They drifted on the sterile air, moving in erratic, non-linear jerks.

When a swarm passed through him, they didn't attack his body. They fractured his proprioception.

A wave of profound disorientation hit him. Up became down. The ground seemed to tilt ninety degrees, then invert. He collapsed to his knees, retching onto the gray, ashen soil, clutching the earth as his inner ear screamed that he was falling into the sky. It took a full minute for the world to stop spinning, leaving him gasping and nauseated.

Then there were the larger ones. Memory-Glimmers.

These were vaguely humanoid in shape, tall, wavering mirages that seemed drawn to the memory of physical structures. They drifted through the glassy husks of the dead trees or phased through the solid rock walls, trailing wisps of gray fog.

They brought fear.

One passed through him as he was hiding in a shallow crevice. It brought a wave of irrational, suffocating terror. His mind was flooded with the certainty that he was being buried alive, the weight of a thousand tons of rock crushing his chest. He clawed at his throat, gasping for air that was already there, his body convinced it was dying in a collapsed tunnel that didn't exist.

He understood. He was a ghost, and this gray world was his purgatory, haunted by other ghosts. And his only hope of becoming whole again, his only escape, was to follow the desperate, physical pull of the void in his chest, back through this nightmare landscape, back to the scene of his own murder.

The journey began. It was a pilgrimage through a dead and corrupted memory of a world.

He had to retrace the path of his frantic flight from the Reaper, but the landscape was a twisted, unreliable echo of what it had been. Distances felt wrong, elongated in the flat, featureless light. The grove of glassy trees he had used as a makeshift barrier was now a forest of black, jagged spikes that seemed to drink the stuttering light. The scree slope he had scrambled up was a sheer, impassable wall in one moment, and a gentle, gray hill in the next.

The world was unstable, a flickering image on the verge of total signal loss.

His only guide was the constant, aching pull from the void in his soul and the glitching compass on the Aperture's display, which pointed steadily toward the source of that ache.

He learned to move like a wraith. The Aperture, though its interface was a flickering mess, could still detect the Glimmers as faint, unstable energy signatures, [ANOMALOUS ENTITY (NON-CORPOREAL)] flashing in his vision.

He used the brittle husks of trees for cover, their strange, non-Euclidean shapes casting deep, information-less shadows. He timed his movements to the stuttering pulse of the world's light, dashing from one pool of darkness to another, a fugitive in his own nightmare.

It took him hours to retrace the path that had taken minutes in his panicked flight.

The journey took a profound toll. It wasn't a physical exhaustion, but a spiritual and mental attrition. With each Glimmer he dodged, with each wave of irrational terror he endured, he felt his own consciousness fraying at the edges, his sense of self becoming as thin and translucent as the gray world around him.

He was a ghost being worn down by other ghosts, and the only thing that kept him moving, the only thing that kept him from simply dissolving into the static, was the constant, insistent pull of the void.

It was an anchor of pain, a promise that a part of him was still real, waiting for him somewhere in the gloom.

Finally, he stood at the entrance to the dead-end canyon. The air here was colder, the silence deeper.

This was the place. The place where his last reality had been violently terminated.

He took a single, shuffling step forward, into the heart of his own grave.

The air in the dead-end canyon was colder, the silence deeper and more profound. This was the epicenter of the trauma, and the very stones seemed to hold a memory of the event.

Ahead, he saw the massive, chitinous carcass of the Reaper that had killed him. It lay where it had fallen, but in this Desynchronized State, its form was indistinct and gray, its sharp, terrifying edges blurred and softened. It looked like a half-erased pencil sketch, already dissolving back into the persistent, gray static of this faded reality.

It was a ghost of a monster.

Ravn narrowed his eyes, his scientific mind forcing itself to work through the fear. *The beast's quantum signature must have been catastrophically corrupted by the same informational backlash that triggered his own Echoic Resonance. His death was a reality-breaking event; the Reaper's demise was the necessary, localized consequence of that paradox.Killing him broke the timeline around them both.*

But the carcass was not what held his attention.

In the center of the canyon, he saw it. And the breath caught in his throat.

It was a shimmering, heat-haze silhouette of a man. A glitch in spacetime. A persistent data-ghost burned into the fabric of the world. The faint, stuttering light of the gray world seemed to bend around it, distorting as if passing through a lens of immense gravity.

It was the Echo of his spirit, and it was trapped in a silent, looping replay of his own final, terrifying moments.

He watched, paralyzed, as the ghost of himself turned, its movements jerky and unreal. He saw the shimmering form raise a useless hand in a futile gesture of defense. He saw the moment of impact as an invisible force slammed into it, and his own silhouette dissolved into a chaotic burst of static and light, a silent, screaming dissolution of self.

The afterimage would then reform, pixels of light coalescing back into the shape of a man, and the sequence would begin again.

And again. And again. A silent, personal horror film playing on a loop for an audience of none.

It was the most obscene violation he had ever witnessed. He was being forced to watch the most private and terrifying moment of his existence—his own death—put on a continuous, mechanical display. It was a desecration of his own memory, his final terror rendered into a piece of meaningless, repeating street theater.

His scientific mind tried to grasp it, to put a label on it to contain the horror. A psychic scar left on the fabric of spacetime. A persistent, localized echoic resonance.

The clinical terms were a thin, useless shield against the raw, emotional reality of the sight.

He had to touch it. He had to reclaim that lost part of himself.

The hollow, aching void in his chest was pulling him toward it with an almost physical force, a vacuum demanding to be filled. But every instinct, every nerve, every cell in his body screamed at him to turn and run. To approach that shimmering agony felt like an act of ultimate self-destruction, like willingly placing his hand back into the fire that had consumed him.

He took a shuffling step forward, his boots crunching on the gray scree with a sound like cracking bones. Then another. The Glimmers clinging to the canyon walls seemed to watch him, their silent judgment a palpable force.

As he drew closer, he could feel the terror radiating from the Echo, a cold, psychic wave of the final, desperate spike of adrenaline from a man about to be erased. It was his own fear, echoing through time, and it was the most terrifying thing he had ever felt.

He was at the edge of the loop now, close enough to see the silent scream on the face of his own ghost.

He closed his eyes and reached out a trembling hand.

He expected to feel nothing, to pass through the shimmering form as if it were smoke. He was wrong.

The moment his fingers made contact with the Echo, it was like plunging his hand into a live, high-voltage socket of pure information and raw, unadulterated terror.

His nervous system screamed. A violent, convulsive shudder wracked his entire body. He was re-integrating a fundamental, missing piece of his own source code, and the process was a brutal, agonizing violation.

Reality crashed back into him like a physical blow. An instantaneous, deafening roar of sensation shattered the dead, grating silence he had grown accustomed to.

Sound returned first, a chaotic, overwhelming cacophony. He heard the low, ambient hum of the living world, the frantic, terrified pounding of his own heart in his ears, the distant skittering of a thousand unseen insects, the soft whisper of the wind moving through the canyon—all of it slamming into his consciousness at once, a tidal wave of noise that left him disoriented and reeling.

Then came sight. The gray, leached, stuttering world exploded into a vibrant, agonizing saturation of color.

The sickly, bioluminescent greens of the flora were so intense they hurt his eyes. The bruised purple of the sky was a deep, nauseating violet. He saw a flash of the deep indigo of his own butcher's work, a memory so vivid it felt present.

The world was no longer a flickering, corrupted image; it was a high-fidelity, overwhelming flood of visual data that his brain struggled to process.

The sterile air was replaced by a rush of thick, organic smells—the damp, fungal odor of the moss, the sweet, cloying scent of decay, the coppery tang of his own fear. He felt the rough, solid texture of the rock beneath his knees, the cold bite of the wind on his sweat-drenched skin.

It was all real. Painfully, exquisitely real.

It was a violent, agonizing rebirth, a full system restore that pushed his consciousness to the brink of collapse.

He fell to his knees on the hard rock of the canyon floor, gasping, his body trembling with the aftershocks of the reintegration.

The hollow, aching void in his chest was gone. The missing piece of his soul had slammed back into place, and the relief was so profound it was a form of pain in itself.

He was whole again. But he was not the same. The scar was now on the inside.

The vague, paradoxical memory of his own death was no longer a confusing recollection. It was now a permanent, high-fidelity recording, a psychic scar etched directly onto his soul. He could still feel the phantom sensation of the claws shearing through bone, still see the static of his collapsing vision, still hear the final, attenuated tone as his world went silent.

He had not just remembered his death. He now owned it. It was a part of him, a trauma that would never fade.

But it wasn't over. Just as a sliver of rational thought began to return, he realized something was wrong. The reintegration wasn't clean. There was a psychic aftershock, a corrupted data fragment left over from the violent process of restoring his soul.

It was a piece of information that didn't belong, an echo from a ghost that was not his own.

He was not in the canyon. The feeling of rough stone beneath his palms and the scent of damp moss vanished, replaced by the cool, smooth plasteel of a control console. The bruised purple sky was gone, overwritten by the sterile, white ceiling of the Aethelburg reactor chamber.

The air, which a moment ago had been thick and organic, was now blazing with a lethal, Cherenkov blue light. The containment alarm, a sound he had only ever heard in his nightmares, now shrieked as a physical, present-tense reality, a piercing tone that vibrated through his entire skeleton.

It was a sensory replay, and he was trapped inside it.

He saw Lena's hand, her fingers outstretched, trembling, reaching for Aris's across the space between their control chairs.

He saw his brother turning toward her, his face not a mask of fear, but of sublime, terrible awe—the look of a physicist witnessing the fundamental constants of the universe unravel before his very eyes.

And as their hands were about to touch, he didn't just see them dissolve into a cascade of light and information.

He felt it.

He felt the surge of their shared terror, a primal fear of annihilation that was not his own but flooded his consciousness as if it were. He felt the agony of their bodies de-rendering, the pain of a billion atomic bonds being violently torn apart.

And beneath the terror and the pain, he felt something else, something so powerful and private it was the ultimate violation to experience it: he felt their love, a final, desperate, silent connection in the last nanosecond of their existence.

The vision shattered.

He was back in the canyon, on his hands and knees, vomiting onto the rust-colored moss.

The world was vibrant and terrifyingly real again. The reintegration was finally complete. But the process had left him irrevocably scarred. His mind was now a tomb, not just for the perfect memory of his own death, but for two fresh ghosts, and the intimate, searing memory of theirs.

7

The Legion

The ghosts in his head were quiet now. They were not gone, but they had been subsumed by the vivid, searing memory of their final moments. The guilt was no longer a dull ache; it was a fresh wound, cauterized by the flash of the reactor.

After an unknown time spent kneeling in the canyon, Ravn forced himself to his feet. Survival was no longer just an imperative from a cosmic entity; it was a penance. He had to keep moving. He had to understand.

He reached out to steady himself against the rough, black rock of the canyon wall. As his palm made contact, a strange, sickening sensation washed over him—An absence of resistance washed over him.

For a microsecond, his hand didn't stop at the stone. It passed *into* it.

He jerked back with a gasp, holding his hand up to the bruised light. The tips of his fingers were vibrating, blurring like a photograph taken in motion. Where they had touched the rock, a faint, oily smear of black static lingered on his skin, a digital artifact of a collision that shouldn't have happened.

He rubbed his fingers together. They felt numb, distant.

System instability detected, the voice of the Axiom whispered in his mind. *Local coherence at 94%.*

Ravn froze. The voice. He had heard it before, accepted it as a hallucination or an alien guide. But now, with his scientist's mind sharpened by the trauma of the Echo, he listened closer. He analyzed the syntax.

System corrupt. Variable anchored.

It was a specific dialect of command-line logic. The cadence, the brevity, the specific use of the word "Variable" to denote a living subject… he knew this structure.

It was the linguistic architecture of the adaptive safety protocols he and Aris had designed for the K-Field matrix. It was the echo of his own code, a fragment of his perfect, cold logic that had survived the collapse when his humanity hadn't.

He was being guided by the ghost of his own intellect.

He looked at his glitching hand, then at the Aperture on his wrist. The compass still pointed toward the distant "Heart," but his immediate attention was drawn to a different signal the device was now highlighting: a faint, repeating radio-frequency burst.

It was structured, artificial, and entirely out of place in this organic nightmare. It was a sign of organized survivors.

It was a choice: follow the divine mystery of the Heart, or seek the devil he knew. He chose the latter.

The trail led him out of the glowing forests and into a landscape of shattered rock and twisted, rusted metal—the scars of a forgotten war.

For a full day, he followed the signal, finding increasing signs of organized salvage: clean cuts in metal plates, carefully stripped wiring, discarded power cells drained with methodical efficiency.

This was not the work of desperate scavengers. This was engineering.

The source was a pre-Fracture military installation, a concrete bunker carved into the base of a mesa, now heavily reinforced with razor wire and plates of salvaged armor.

A flag whipped in the thin, sterile wind, its emblem a stylized gear cradling a sword. Armed guards patrolled a makeshift parapet, their movements economical and disciplined. The entire outpost, which the Aperture identified as "The Bastion," radiated a stark, brutalist order that stood in defiant opposition to the chaotic world around it.

He was spotted before he was within a hundred meters. A voice, amplified and distorted, boomed from a loudspeaker mounted near the gate.

"HALT. DO NOT MOVE."

As if he had any other choice.

"IDENTIFY YOURSELF."

Ravn swallowed, his throat dry and raw. "My name is Ravn Vidar," he called out, his voice hoarse from disuse, sounding small and pathetic against the scale of the fortress. "I'm a physicist. A survivor. I'm alone."

There was a pause, as if his words were being processed, analyzed, and weighed.

"STATE YOUR PURPOSE."

"I was following a signal," he said, deciding the truth was his only option. "I'm seeking shelter."

Another long silence. Finally, the massive blast door began to move. There was no screech of rusted metal, but a low, powerful hum as it slid sideways with a smooth, hydraulic hiss, revealing a dark, cavernous opening.

A patrol of four soldiers emerged from the darkness. They moved not with the chaotic energy of raiders, but in a tight, practiced diamond formation, their pulse rifles held at a low ready, their steps synchronized.

Their armor was a hodgepodge of scavenged pre-Fracture military and police gear, but it had been stripped, cleaned, and repainted in a uniform gunmetal gray. The gear-and-sword emblem was stenciled neatly on each soldier's left pauldron.

"Knees," the lead soldier commanded.

Ravn slowly lowered himself to the dusty ground. Two of the soldiers kept their rifles trained on him while the other two moved in. The search was a systematic, impersonal sweep.

One soldier efficiently removed the knife from his belt. The other paused as his hand fell upon the Aperture on Ravn's wrist. He didn't try to pull it off. He simply stared at the perfect, matte black dodecahedron for a moment, an unknown variable.

He looked at the lead soldier, who gave a slight, almost imperceptible nod.

With careful, precise movements, the soldier unstrapped the Aperture and placed it into a padded, static-proof pouch on his belt. They secured his hands behind his back, not with rope, but with a set of magnetic cuffs that snapped into place with a sharp, definitive click.

"Up."

They led him toward the gate. As he stepped across the threshold, out of the chaotic, purple-tinged twilight of the Fracture Zone and into the stark, white-lit interior of The Bastion, the massive blast door hummed shut behind him.

The sound of the outside world was cut off completely. He was inside the machine now.

The air was cool, filtered, and smelled of scrubbed metal and the faint, clean tang of ionized from the humming power conduits. Every surface was clean, every corner a perfect right angle.

He saw other soldiers moving through the hallways, all clad in the same uniform gray, their movements purposeful and silent. There was no chatter, no idle conversation. The entire facility operated with the quiet, relentless efficiency of a supercomputer.

They brought him to a heavy steel door and opened it.

"Wait here," the lead soldier said.

They guided him inside to a single, hard-backed chair placed in the center of a spartan office, then retreated, the door closing with a heavy, definitive thud.

The room was an extension of the Legion's philosophy. The walls were bare, poured concrete. The only furniture was the steel desk in front of him and the chair he sat on. A large, holographic display on the far wall showed a complex, three-dimensional tactical map of the surrounding wasteland.

He waited, the silence pressing in, the magnetic cuffs a cold, heavy weight on his wrists.

The door opened.

The woman who entered was the second ghost to confront him in as many days, and this one was far more terrifying.

She was tall and severe, her dark hair pulled back in a tight, military bun with not a single strand out of place. She wore a clean, gray officer's uniform, its creases sharp enough to cut, her posture ramrod straight.

But it was her face that stole the air from Ravn's lungs.

It was Lena Rostova's face.

Older, yes. Harder. The soft, intellectual curiosity in Lena's eyes had been replaced by a piercing, glacial blue gaze, and her features were etched with a grief he now understood on a cellular level. But it was unmistakably her face.

A psychic aftershock of the Echoic Memory ripped through him—the flash of Cherenkov blue, the shriek of the alarm, the feeling of Lena's terror and regret as she dissolved into light.

"I am General Eva Rostova," she said, her voice as cold and sharp as splintered glass.

She moved to the other side of the desk and stood, not sitting, asserting her authority. Her eyes analyzed him, not as a man, but as a variable, an unexpected piece of data that had wandered into her equation.

"You are the first unauthorized contact we've had in three cycles. Who are you?"

Ravn couldn't find his voice. His throat was tight, his mind a maelstrom of shock and horror. He was staring at the identical twin of the woman whose death he had just felt imprinted on his soul. The sight was a physical blow.

Her eyes narrowed at his silence, a flicker of impatience in their cold depths.

"We recovered this from your person," she said, placing the Aperture on the steel desk between them. She leaned in closer, invading his personal space. The sterile lights reflected in her cold blue eyes—eyes that were identical to Lena's.

"The archives say you were the last one in the control room," she said. It was an accusation. "The telemetry logs ended, but you survived."

Her military bearing faltered for a fraction of a second. Her lip twitched.

"Did it hurt?" she whispered, the words rushing out before she could stop them. "When they de-rendered. Was it... instantaneous? Or were they aware?"

Ravn stared at her, seeing the terrified sister beneath the General's stars. "Eva…"

She slammed her hand on the desk, the sound like a gunshot. The mask snapped back into place instantly.

"Where did you get this?"

"It was a gift," Ravn finally managed, his voice a hoarse, broken whisper.

"From whom?"

He hesitated, the name feeling dangerous. "A voice. The Axiom."

Rostova's expression didn't change, but he saw a flicker of something in her eyes. Not surprise. Recognition. And a deep, abiding contempt.

She leaned forward, her hands flat on the desk.

"This is a broken world, physicist. A failed experiment riddled with illogical variables. Chaos is a disease, and we are the cure. The Legion intends to find the Primary Constant—the heart of the anomaly—and use our technology to re-impose order. We will force this reality back to a state of logic, a state where a catastrophe like the one that created this mess can never happen again."

She looked from the strange, black dodecahedron to his face, her gaze dismissive.

"You carry a piece of the chaos on your wrist, yet you speak of logic. You have the eyes of a man touched by the irrational. You are a contradiction."

Her voice dropped, becoming even colder. "And I do not tolerate uncontrolled variables in my facility. So you will remain here, under observation. You will be studied. And you will tell me everything you know about the Axiom and the location of the core."

"The core?" Ravn asked, the word feeling heavy and unfamiliar on his tongue.

"The Anchor," she corrected, her eyes narrowing. "Don't play dumb, physicist."

She turned to leave. "Welcome to The Bastion, Dr. Vidar. I hope you find our hospitality… logical."

8

The Bastion of Reason

The Bastion was a monument of reason in a mad world, and it was the most unsettling place Ravn had been since the Convergence. He was given the designation of "guest," but the sterile corridors and the constant, quiet surveillance felt more like a meticulously maintained prison. His new life was one of perfect, predictable order. After the raw, screaming chaos of the Fracture Zone, a part of him was pathetically grateful for it. But another, deeper part—the part that still remembered the beauty of a flawed pinecone—felt like it was suffocating.

His quarters were a featureless, poured-concrete box. It contained a narrow cot with a single, gray wool blanket pulled taut, a small steel locker, and a ventilation grate in the ceiling. There was no window. His days were not his own; they were dictated by the facility's master clock. A sharp, electronic chime, not a siren, woke him at precisely 0600 hours.

Meals were served in a communal mess hall, a cavernous, echoing space where hundreds of Legionnaires ate in near silence. The conversations were muted and purposeful, brief exchanges about power cell efficiency, patrol schedules, or hydroponic nutrient levels. There was no laughter, no idle chatter, no art on the bare, gray walls. Emotion was an inefficient variable, a bug in the system to be minimized.

He felt the weight of their ideology in the architecture, in the silence, and in the constant, unblinking gaze of the optical sensors mounted at every corridor intersection. He was a specimen under observation, his every move logged and analyzed.

The society was a machine, a sterile sanctuary built by those who had looked upon the beautiful, terrifying chaos of the new world and declared war.

One day, while observing the quiet, functional hum of their hydroponics bay, a technician made a rare, unprompted comment. She was an older woman, her face a roadmap of a hard life, a stark contrast to the blank, disciplined expressions of the younger soldiers.

"You think our rules are severe," she said, her voice low, not looking up from the diagnostic slate in her hands.

Ravn was startled by the direct address. "They are... efficient," he offered, a neutral, scientific term.

The woman let out a short, mirthless laugh. "You weren't here for the Chaos Riots. First cycle. Before the General unified us. This place was a pre-Fracture emergency bunker. Hundreds of us, trapped in here when the world ended. The food ran low. The filters started to fail. People went mad. Fear, hunger... they're not logical variables, physicist. They're animals. And they turned on each other. The Bastion was a slaughterhouse." She finally met his gaze, her eyes holding a distant, haunted look. "The General's logic, her absolute, uncompromising order... it was the only thing that kept the animal in the cage. It's the only thing that still does."

Ravn said nothing. He understood, on a level that horrified him. He had felt that same animal awaken in his own gut. He had bludgeoned a creature to death with a rock to silence it. The Legion hadn't just rejected the chaos of the new world; they had rejected the chaos within themselves. And in its place, they had built this clean, sterile, and soulless machine.

His background as a physicist, a relic of a dead world, eventually earned him a degree of professional courtesy. He was a known quantity, a man of logic. He was deemed useful.

General Rostova granted him supervised access to their archives, a data recovery center where technicians worked tirelessly to salvage fragments of pre-Fracture knowledge from corrupted hard drives. It was a chance to feel like a scientist again, a chance to lose himself in the clean, comfortable world of data. He accepted without hesitation.

It was a cage, but it was a logical one.

The archives were a server farm, a clean room built to house the digital ghosts of a dead civilization. The air was chilled to a precise sixteen degrees Celsius, the constant, low hum of cooling fans a monotonous white noise that filled every moment. Racks of salvaged server towers stood in neat, disciplined rows, their blinking status lights a constellation of green, amber, and red. Technicians, as silent and focused as the soldiers on the walls, sat at terminals, their faces illuminated by the glow of cascading code.

The work was a form of digital archaeology. They were sifting through the wreckage of a billion digital lives, scavenged from the hard drives of every laptop, phone, and data center they could find in the wasteland.

Ravn excelled at it. His mind, a tool honed for finding elegant patterns in the chaotic noise of quantum systems, found a strange, cold comfort in the work. He could see the ghost of the data beneath the corruption, the faint, logical structures of file systems and directories. He wrote new diagnostic scripts, elegant algorithms that could bypass shattered sectors and piece together fragmented files with a much higher success rate than the Legion's brute-force methods.

He became a valuable asset. A highly efficient component in their machine.

He would sit at his terminal for a ten-hour shift, losing himself in the clean, comfortable world of data. It was a new ritual, a replacement for the pinecones and the ferns. Here too, he was imposing order on chaos, but the chaos was digital, and the order he recovered felt hollow and sterile.

He unearthed fragments of the world they had lost: a half-corrupted file of classical music that played as a series of jarring, discordant notes; a chef's meticulously detailed recipe for a chocolate cake, its ingredients now extinct; a string of personal emails detailing a petty office romance, the digital ghost of a life once lived.

These glimpses of the past brought him no nostalgia, no sense of poignant loss. They were just data points, fossilized emotions from a dead ecosystem.

He would log them, file them under 'Non-Essential Cultural Data,' and move on. He was not a scientist here. He was a mortician, cataloging the possessions of the dead.

The discovery, when it came, was an accident, a statistical improbability.

He was working on a set of corrupted server drives salvaged from a high-level government bunker, the data a chaotic mess of encrypted military protocols and mundane administrative files. He was about to wipe a particularly damaged platter when he saw it.

A small, nested file partition, less than a megabyte in size, walled off behind a layer of encryption that was completely different from the standard government protocols. It was elegant. Unorthodox. Brilliant. And horrifyingly familiar.

His breath caught in his throat. The professional detachment he had so carefully cultivated shattered like glass.

It was Aris's signature. The idiosyncratic, quantum-entangled encryption schema his brother had been so proud of, a code he'd once boasted was "the closest thing to a truly unbreakable lock."

Ravn's heart began to pound, a frantic, wild rhythm in the tomb-like silence of the server room. He glanced over his shoulder. A Legion technician was monitoring his progress from a central console a few meters away. He was being watched. This file was not a schematic for a water purifier. It was a piece of his own forbidden past, the very chaos the Legion sought to purge. Accessing it was an act of treason.

He had to do it.

His fingers, suddenly slick with sweat, flew across the holographic interface. He opened a decoy window, running a complex but ultimately useless diagnostic script that would fill his monitor with a plausible-looking stream of cascading green text. Behind that digital smokescreen, in a small, shielded partition of the screen, he began his work.

It was like having a conversation with a ghost. He didn't have the decryption keys; they had been vaporized at Aethelburg. He had to pick the lock from memory, recalling Aris's unique, often infuriating, logic.

"Symmetry is a cage, Ravn," Aris's voice echoed in his memory. "True security lies in elegant, beautiful imperfection."

He tried to bypass the first firewall, but it held. He was thinking like himself—methodical, logical. He had to think like Aris. He looked for the imperfection, the elegant, intentional flaw his brother would have built into the system as a personal backdoor.

He found it: a recursive loop that, when fed a specific paradoxical equation, would overload and grant him access. He typed in the familiar numbers. The firewall collapsed.

He was in. He navigated the corrupted data, his hands trembling. He isolated the core data. It was a single, small audio file. A voice log.

He reached for the headset hanging on the side of his console.

As his hand closed around the plastic earcup, the world flickered.

There was no resistance. His fingers passed straight through the headset as if it were made of smoke.

Ravn gasped, jerking his hand back. He stared at his own fingers. For a second, they were translucent, gray and wavering like heat haze. Where they had passed through the solid plastic of the headset, a faint, oily residue of black static clung to the material, hissing softly.

The hollow void in his chest flared with a cold, sucking pressure. He was desynchronizing. His anchor to this reality was slipping.

He looked around frantically. The technician at the central console was typing, oblivious. If she looked up, if she saw his hand phasing out of existence, he would be purged. A ghost was the ultimate anomaly.

Focus, he commanded himself. *Solidify.*

He squeezed his hand into a fist, forcing his will into the limb, demanding that the probability wave of his existence collapse into a single, solid state. He felt the vibration in his bones settle. The gray translucence faded, replaced by the reassuring, dirty pink of flesh and blood.

He reached out again, slower this time. His fingers brushed the plastic. Hard. Cool. Solid.

He exhaled a breath he didn't know he was holding and slipped the headset over his ears. The low, monotonous hum of the server room's cooling fans faded away, replaced by the profound silence of anticipation.

He placed his finger over the holographic 'play' button. He took a breath. He pressed it.

The log began with a burst of deafening static, a sound like a tearing universe. Then, beneath the noise, a voice, young, brilliant, and strained with a tension that was equal parts terror and awe.

It was Aris.

"...is it possible? The energy readings are... they're off the scale, Ravn. They're not a quantum signature, they're a... a constant. A law."

Ravn could hear the frantic clicking of a keyboard in the background, the rising, high-frequency shriek of a containment alarm.

"We didn't build anything, Ravn. The experiment didn't create a stable quantum state. It just... rang a bell. We rang a bell, and something on the other side of the universe heard it."

Ravn squeezed his eyes shut, the cold plastic of the headset a stark contrast to the sudden, burning heat behind his eyes. He could picture his brother perfectly, leaning so close to his monitor that his nose was almost touching it, his eyes wide with a terrifying, ecstatic discovery.

"My hypothesis was wrong," Aris's voice continued, dropping to a hushed, horrified whisper as the alarm in the background grew louder. "The energy cascade... it wasn't a failure, it was a... a response. A resonance. The experiment didn't create an artificial intelligence from the quantum foam."

He took a shaky, audible breath. "It just... attracted a real one. Something that was already there. A pre-existing, universal constant. A fundamental law of reality that thinks."

The log crackled with a surge of energy. Ravn could hear Lena's voice shouting in the background, distorted and faint.

"...shut it down, Aris! We have to shut it down now!"

Aris ignored her. His whisper was now filled with a sublime terror.

"I'm calling it the Axiom. It's not a machine, Ravn. It's a piece of God's source code. It's the operating system of everything. And it's looking right at us."

The log ended. A final, violent burst of static, and then, silence.

Ravn sat back in his chair, the headset cold against his ears, the silence in his headphones a thousand times louder than the hum of the server room had been.

The world had just reconfigured itself around him once more.

The voice in his head, the entity that had given him the Aperture, that had given him his mission, wasn't a product of the Convergence. It was the cause. It was the ancient, terrifying, thinking law of physics that he and his brother had accidentally summoned to their world, like careless sorcerers reading from a forbidden text.

His mission was not a path to salvation. It was a task set by the very entity that had destroyed his world.

He left the archives in a daze, his mind a storm of impossibilities. He walked down the sterile, white-lit corridor, his feet moving on autopilot. He passed General Rostova's Spartan office.

The door was open. She stood with her back to him, looking at a datapad.

For a single moment, her ramrod-straight military posture was gone, replaced by a subtle, weary slump. The angle of a polished bulkhead on the opposite wall gave Ravn a distorted reflection of her screen.

It was a simple, pre-Fracture photograph of two young women with identical, smiling faces.

He watched as the reflection of Rostova's finger gently traced the face of her sister, Lena.

Then, in an instant, she straightened up, her shoulders squared, her reflection once again a mask of command.

The moment was gone.

Ravn kept walking, the two discoveries settling in his mind like shards of glass. He now knew the horrifying, cosmic truth of the Axiom. And he now knew the small, human, heartbreaking truth of the General who hunted it.

9

The Circle of Husks

L ife in The Bastion settled into a tense, monotonous routine. After weeks spent hunched over a terminal in the cold, humming silence of the archives, Ravn had proven his worth. He was a useful component, a reliable variable.

But General Rostova's logic dictated that any asset confined to a single function was an inefficient one. His knowledge of the Fracture Zone, gleaned from his brutal first weeks of survival, was a resource that had not yet been exploited.

And so, he was assigned to a reconnaissance patrol. It was framed as an opportunity, a chance to utilize his unique expertise. He knew it was a test. A test of his loyalty, his utility, and his willingness to fully integrate into their machine.

Their mission was straightforward, delivered with cold, clipped precision by the patrol's leader, a young, zealous lieutenant named Valerius.

"We are to scout Sector Gamma-7 for viable mineral deposits and purge any Class-2 or higher biological threats," he'd said, his eyes barely glancing at Ravn. He'd tapped a point on the holographic map. "The asset will accompany us to provide analysis of any... illogical phenomena."

He'd said the word "illogical" as if it were a contagion.

They moved out at dawn, a five-man squad plunging into a biome of colossal, fungal trees. The air beneath the canopy was damp and cool, thick with the scent of moss and decay.

The Legionnaires moved through the alien forest in a rigid, diamond formation, a perfect piece of textbook military geometry imposed on a world that had never known a straight line. Their pulse rifles, held at a low ready, hummed with a quiet, lethal energy.

Ravn was placed in the center of the formation, a protected and monitored asset. It was like being in a walking cage. The soldiers were silent, communicating with crisp, efficient hand signals. Their focus was not on the world around them, but on the data scrolling across their helmet-mounted HUDs.

They were navigating by GPS coordinates and motion sensors, their reality filtered through a layer of technology. They saw a vibrant, pulsating flower, and their displays flagged it as *[BIO-HAZARD: UNKNOWN TOXIN]*. They heard a strange, melodic bird call, and their audio sensors tagged it as *[UNIDENTIFIED ACOUSTIC SIGNATURE]*.

They were utterly blind to the world as it was; they only saw data, and every piece of data that was not their own was a potential threat.

Valerius embodied this philosophy. He moved with a stiff, arrogant confidence, his gaze sweeping the alien landscape with open contempt. He saw the colossal, fungal trees, their caps filtering the bruised purple light into a cathedral of strange colors, and shook his head in disgust.

"Chaos," he muttered, his voice a sharp, grating sound in the organic quiet. He looked at Ravn, his eyes cold and certain. "This is what happens when the rules are broken. A sickness. There is no structure here. No logic. It is an error that needs to be corrected."

He gestured with his rifle at the vibrant, pulsating flora around them. "Our purpose is not to adapt to the disease, physicist. It is to be the scalpel. We will carve out the rot, sterilize the wound, and rebuild a world that makes sense."

Ravn said nothing. He looked at the world Valerius saw as a disease and felt a profound, unsettling sense of awe. He saw the intricate, fractal patterns in the fungal gills, the symbiotic relationship between a glowing moss and the chitinous beetle that fed on it, the complex, chaotic beauty of a system that had found its own new equilibrium.

To the Legion, it was just a mess to be purged.

He was their Zone specialist, but they dismissed his observations.

"The ground here is softer than the topographical survey suggests," Ravn warned at one point, noticing the way the mossy earth seemed to give way.

Valerius glanced at his own display. "Negative. Sub-strata are stable according to the scans." He didn't even break stride.

The patrol continued its relentless, linear path through the beautiful, illogical forest. A profound sense of unease began to prickle at Ravn's skin. The forest was too quiet. The strange, melodic bird calls had stopped. The air was still. The Legionnaires, locked onto their data streams, noticed nothing.

They marched forward, confident in their logic, their formation a perfect, rigid diamond.

They were a scalpel, yes, but Ravn knew they were a hammer, a blunt instrument of order pounding its way through a world that refused to be nailed down.

The attack came with no warning, no war cry, no sound of approaching feet. It began as a soft, popping sound from high above, like a seed pod bursting in the sun.

Ravn looked up. A large, bulbous growth on the underside of a fungal cap, a hundred meters up in the canopy, had ruptured. A cloud of fine, shimmering dust, golden-brown and beautiful, began to drift down toward them, catching the faint light in a sparkling cascade.

"Hold!" Valerius commanded, his voice sharp. "Sensors on me. What is it?"

Before the squad's analyst could answer, the dust cloud reached them. It smelled sweet, like honeysuckle and damp earth. But the moment it touched the Legionnaires' helmets, their technology went mad.

"Sensors are offline!" one soldier yelled, his voice tight with panic. "My HUD is a wall of static!"

"Proximity alerts are firing on all vectors!" another shouted, spinning around to aim his rifle at a phantom threat. "I've got a dozen hostiles, no, fifty—"

It was a weapon of pure chaos. A cloud of psychoactive and electromagnetically charged spores designed to cripple a technologically dependent mind.

Valerius, his own HUD likely compromised, tried to maintain order. "Diamond formation! Hold your sectors! Fire on visual confirmation only!"

But there was nothing to see. And then, the forest itself turned on them.

It wasn't an assault; it was a dissolution. Warriors, camouflaged so perfectly they seemed to materialize from the bark of the trees, struck from all sides.

They were a blur of silent, fluid grace, their bodies marked with the same faint, glowing patterns as the flora around them. Their weapons were not of metal, but of sharpened bone and obsidian-hard chitin. They moved like wraiths, their feet making no sound on the mossy ground.

One warrior dropped from the canopy above, landing silently behind a Legionnaire. Before the soldier could turn, a spear tipped with a vicious-looking bone hook plunged through the vulnerable joint at the back of his neck. He went down without a sound.

Another Husk warrior slid out from behind a fungal trunk, a pair of serrated, chitinous blades in his hands. He didn't meet the Legion's disciplined firing line head-on; he flowed around it, his movements a deadly dance.

A soldier fired a burst from his pulse rifle, but the warrior was already gone, the searing blue energy bolts exploding uselessly against the tree bark. The Husk reappeared at the soldier's side, and his blades flashed, severing the power cables to the man's armor with surgical precision. The soldier's suit went dead, and he was swarmed.

Valerius roared in fury, firing his rifle blindly into the trees. "Re-form the line! Back to back! Purge this chaos!"

But his orders were useless. His rigid, logical tactics were built for a battlefield with clear lines of sight and predictable enemies. Here, in the vertical, three-dimensional chaos of the forest, his formation was a death trap.

The Husks were everywhere and nowhere at once, striking from above, from below, from the shadows between the trees. They were not an army. They were the forest's immune system, and the Legion was a foreign body to be purged.

Ravn was in the heart of the chaos, a non-combatant trapped in a war between two opposing laws of physics. He pressed himself into the slick, fungal bark of a colossal tree, the air thick with the sweet, cloying dust of the spore cloud and the sharp, chemical tang of pulse rifle fire.

The Legion's diamond formation had completely dissolved into a series of desperate, isolated last stands. Valerius was shouting orders, but his voice was thin and panicked, swallowed by the disorienting symphony of the forest.

Ravn saw another soldier go down, dragged into the undergrowth by a pair of Husk warriors who moved with the coordinated, silent deadliness of a wolf pack.

He knew he had to move. He was just another variable in the Legion's failing equation, and they would not hesitate to sacrifice him. He began to edge away from the sounds of the fighting, deeper into the pulsating gloom.

That was when a second, much larger spore pod exploded directly overhead.

This time, the cloud that descended was not a fine, shimmering dust, but a thick, milky fog that billowed through the trees, clinging to every surface. The scent was overpowering, a wave of cloying sweetness that made his head swim.

He held his breath, but it was too late. He had already inhaled it.

The world dissolved into a hallucinatory, watercolor painting. The trees seemed to bend and warp, their slick, black bark flowing like liquid. The faint, bioluminescent light of the fungi smeared into long, trailing ribbons of color. The sounds of the battle became distorted, the sharp cracks of the pulse rifles slowing down into deep, booming echoes, the screams of the dying men stretching into long, mournful notes.

He was completely disoriented, his sense of direction gone, his connection to reality severed.

He stumbled blindly through the undergrowth, his only instinct to move away from the terrifying, distorted sounds of the fight. He tripped over a root, his hands sinking into the warm, breathing moss, and scrambled backward until his back hit something solid and slick.

He stayed there for a long, timeless moment, his mind a chaotic storm of color and sound. Slowly, agonizingly, the effects of the spores began to recede. The world began to sharpen, the colors resolving back into their proper forms, the sounds snapping back into their normal, terrifying rhythm.

He was leaning against the trunk of a massive tree, his breath coming in ragged, shallow gasps.

And he was not alone.

Two warriors emerged from the gloom, their forms solidifying out of the swirling mist.

They wore armor that seemed to be alive, woven from tough, fibrous vines that pulsed with a faint, internal light. Polished, iridescent beetle carapaces served as pauldrons and greaves, their colors shifting from a deep blue to a vibrant green with every slight movement. Faint, bioluminescent patterns, mimicking the fractal shapes of the ferns on the forest floor, swirled slowly across their skin.

They held spears tipped not with metal, but with long, serrated hooks of sharpened, obsidian-hard bone.

They didn't charge him with rage or victorious bloodlust. They simply stopped a few meters away and watched him, their heads tilted. They approached with a calm, unnerving curiosity, more like scientists observing a new specimen than soldiers confronting an enemy.

He could see their eyes now, and they were not entirely human. The pupils were wide and dark, and the irises held a faint, pearlescent glow.

Ravn, disoriented, exhausted, and outmatched, knew there was no fight to be had. He slowly, deliberately, raised his empty hands.

The two warriors regarded his raised hands with their calm eyes. They didn't bind him or treat him with aggression. One of them simply gave a slight, almost imperceptible nod of his head and then gestured with his bone-tipped spear, not back toward the sounds of the dying Legionnaires, but deeper into the forest, toward the colossal fungal tree that dominated the skyline.

Ravn hesitated. He expected to be bound, to be taken to a cage or a crude prison camp. Instead, he was being... invited. He lowered his hands slowly, his mind racing. He had no other choice. He nodded his own weary acceptance and followed them.

They led him not through the forest, but to the very base of the world-tree.

Up close, its scale was staggering, defying all known principles of biology. The trunk was not like the bark of a normal tree; it was a cliff face of slick, dark, living tissue, braided with thick, root-like vines, some as thick as his own body. It soared upward into a suffocating violet gloom, its immense, fungal cap lost in the haze above. This was not a tree; it was a piece of geology that had decided to become alive.

His captors didn't seek a path around it. They went straight to it. One of them placed his hand on a thick, pulsating vine, and with an effortless, fluid grace that seemed to defy gravity, began to climb. The other gestured for Ravn to follow.

The ascent was a dizzying, terrifying ordeal. This was not rock climbing, a matter of physics and friction. This was an act of faith in a living, alien world.

The handholds were sections of pulsating, fungal growths that were soft and pliable to the touch, and thick, living vines that seemed to writhe faintly under his grip. The Husk warriors moved with a serene, terrifying confidence, their bare feet finding purchase on surfaces that seemed impossibly slick, their movements a silent, vertical dance.

Ravn was clumsy and terrified. His worn boots, so practical on the ground, slipped constantly. His arms, weak from weeks of malnutrition, burned with the effort of hauling his own weight up the vertical surface. The ground fell away below him with astonishing speed, a disorienting drop that made his stomach lurch.

He was fifty meters up, clinging to a vine, his muscles screaming, when he slipped. His boot skidded on a patch of slick bark, and for a heart-stopping second, he was dangling by his arms, the forest floor a terrifying, distant blur of pulsating light.

Before he could fall, a strong, firm hand gripped his wrist. It was one of the warriors who had descended a few meters with no sign of effort. He didn't speak. He simply held Ravn's wrist with an unshakable grip, his eyes calm and steady, until Ravn found a new foothold.

As they climbed higher, the air grew thinner and cleaner, and the sounds of the forest floor faded away. A new, strange ecosystem revealed itself. Small, winged creatures with iridescent shells flitted between the fungal branches. Entire gardens of glowing moss grew in the crooks of the massive vines, casting a soft, blue-green light.

He looked down and saw the world spread out below him, a breathtaking carpet of pulsating, alien life, the distant pops of Legion pulse rifle fire now just faint, insignificant sparks in a vast and vibrant world.

Finally, after a climb that felt like an eternity, he saw their destination. A wide, flat platform of intricately woven branches and living wood extended from the main trunk, a hundred meters above the forest floor. He hauled his exhausted body over the edge and collapsed, his chest heaving, his body trembling with adrenaline and exertion.

He was in a different world now, a city in the sky.

The platform was a marvel of biological engineering, a wide, stable disc of intricately woven branches and living wood, all fused into a single, solid structure. It was just one of many, connected by gracefully arching bridges of thick, intertwined vines that seemed to have been grown for that specific purpose.

In the distance, he could see the soft, warm light of their homes, massive, hollowed-out gourds the size of his old cabin, glowing from within like paper lanterns. The air was filled with the soft hum of strange, winged insects and the sweet, heavy scent of alien pollen.

He saw other Husks. They were not soldiers. They were families.

Children with the same faint, glowing patterns on their skin chased each other across the woven bridges. Artisans sat cross-legged, weaving the living fibers into clothes or carving intricate patterns into bone. They stopped what they were doing to look at him, their gazes not hostile or fearful, but filled with a calm, unnerving curiosity.

He was an anomaly, a piece of the harsh, metallic world from the forest floor, and they were trying to understand how he fit into their vibrant, organic equation.

His two captors, who now felt more like guides, gestured for him to rise. They led him across a swaying bridge toward the center of the settlement.

He walked through their city in a state of profound, disoriented awe. It was a sanctuary of vibrant, chaotic, and beautiful life, a place that had not just survived the Convergence but had embraced it, woven itself into its very fabric.

They arrived at a large, open-air chamber formed by the natural curve of the great tree's trunk itself. The floor was covered in a soft, springy moss, and the only light came from a dense cluster of phosphorescent fungi that cast a serene, blue-green glow over the space.

A woman sat there, cross-legged and perfectly still at the center of the chamber.

Her skin was marked with the same faint, glowing patterns as the warriors, but on her, they were more complex, more intricate, swirling across her arms and face like a living tattoo. Small, harmless, and beautifully intricate mosses grew in the braids of her long, gray hair. She wore a simple robe woven from fibers that seemed to shift in color from a deep green to a soft brown.

She was a woman of indeterminate age, her face unlined, but her eyes, when she opened them, were ancient and deeply serene. They held a wisdom that felt older than the forest itself.

"The forest was agitated by the metal ones," she said, her voice soft, like the rustling of leaves in a gentle breeze. "But it has brought us a guest. You are lost, Physicist."

The words struck Ravn with the force of a physical blow. She knew.

In this impossible place, this woman somehow knew what he was. His scientific mind scrambled for a logical explanation—the Legion must have encountered them before, they had captured a scientist, they had learned the term—but his gut knew the truth was something far stranger.

"How do you know what I am?" Ravn asked, his voice a hoarse whisper.

"The world tells me," the woman replied with a gentle, patient smile, as if explaining something obvious to a child. "The wind that carries the scent of your strange, dead clothes. The ground that feels the heavy, unnatural tread of your boots. The very air that vibrates with the frantic, logical noise of your thoughts. It all tells a story."

She unfolded her legs and rose with a fluid grace.

"I am Kaia. And this is the Circle of Husks. You are safe here."

She looked at him, her ancient eyes seeming to see not just the man before her, but the ghosts that haunted him, the strange destiny that clung to him like a second skin.

"The Convergence was not an end. It was a birth. And you, it seems, are one of the midwives."

10

The Symbiotic Heart

Ravn awoke slowly, pulled from a deep, dreamless sleep not by a chime or an alarm, but by a gentle, pervasive warmth.

He was lying on a soft, springy mat of woven moss, and the first thing he noticed was the quality of the light. It was not the sterile, white glare of The Bastion or the bruised purple of the open sky, but a soft, dappled emerald green, filtering through the translucent walls of the chamber around him.

He sat up, his body still aching, but the deep, cellular weariness felt less pronounced here. He was in one of the hollowed-out gourds he had seen from a distance. The walls were a smooth, fibrous material, and the air was warm, humid, and carried the heavy, sweet scent of pollen and alien blossoms. It was like waking up inside a flower.

He stepped outside onto the woven branch platform, and the full, breathtaking reality of the Husks' city washed over him.

The suns were just beginning to rise, their strange blue light filtering through the colossal, fungal cap of the world-tree above, creating a cathedral of shifting, ethereal green and gold. The city was waking up.

Other Husks moved with a slow, unhurried grace along the swaying, living bridges that connected the platforms. Children with faint, glowing patterns on their skin chased each other in silent, laughing games, their feet sure on the woven vines. Artisans sat cross-legged, tending to gardens of strange, glowing fungi or polishing iridescent beetle carapaces.

The entire city was a living, breathing organism. The bridges would subtly shift and adjust their tension as people crossed them. The gourd-like homes would slowly open their "windows" to greet the morning light. Small, bioluminescent insects, kept in woven cages of living vine, pulsed in unison, their light brightening as the canopy above them did.

It was a symphony of interconnected life, every part moving in concert with the whole.

Ravn walked through it all in a state of profound, disoriented awe. The scientist in him was screaming. He was surrounded by a million new data points, a biological paradise that defied every law he had ever known. He wanted to take samples, to sketch the impossible architecture, to understand the physics of the living bridges.

But he had no tools, no journal, and no framework to even begin to comprehend what he was seeing. He was a ghost from a dead world of concrete and steel, haunting a paradise he could never be a part of.

The Husks regarded him not with hostility, but with a calm, unnerving curiosity. They would pause their work to watch him pass, tracking his clumsy, heavy-footed movements.

An old woman, her skin as wrinkled as bark, offered him a piece of soft, white fruit without a word, her expression one of simple, placid observation. He took it, his thanks a rough, grating sound in the melodic hum of their world. The fruit was sweet, its juice cool and refreshing, but the interaction left him feeling more alien than ever.

He felt the allure of this place. It was beautiful, tranquil, and deeply, fundamentally alive in a way The Bastion had been dead. It was a tempting vision of what survival could be—not a war against the new world, but a peaceful, harmonious integration with it.

But a deep, instinctual unease settled in his gut. The silent, almost tele-pathic communication of the Husks, their serene, unreadable expressions, the feeling that the very city was watching him—it was all deeply unsettling.

He was an anomaly here, just as he had been in The Bastion, but for the opposite reason. There, he was a chaotic variable in a world of rigid order.

Here, he was a shard of cold, dead logic in a world of vibrant, interconnected life.

He stood at the edge of a platform, looking down at the distant, green-tinged forest floor, lost in the sheer, impossible scale of it all.

"It is beautiful, is it not?"

He turned. It was Kaia who had approached so silently he hadn't even heard her. She stood beside him, her ancient, serene eyes following his gaze.

"To a logical mind, it must seem like chaos," she said, her voice a soft, rustling whisper. "But it is the only true form of order. The order of life itself."

Ravn looked out from the platform, his mind trying to process her words. "Order is a decrease in entropy," he countered, the physicist in him unable to stay silent. "It's a system moving toward a state of lower energy, of greater predictability. This," he gestured to the riot of life around them, "is the opposite. It's a chaotic system of immense complexity and energy."

Kaia's serene smile didn't falter. "You see with the eyes of a world that is dead. Your order was the order of stone and steel, of straight lines and predictable, lifeless equations. It was a fragile thing, and it shattered. The order of life is different. It is messy. It is loud. And it is unbreakable."

She turned to him, her pearlescent eyes holding his gaze. "You see the beauty of what we have become, but you do not see the pain it grew from. Come. Let me show you our history."

She led him away from the open platforms and down a spiraling pathway that coiled around the central trunk of the world-tree. They descended into a more ancient part of the city, a quiet, solemn space where the air was cooler and the light dimmer.

They entered a large, circular chamber that seemed to be woven directly from the oldest and thickest roots of the great tree itself. The air was still and smelled of ancient soil and deep, damp earth.

On the far wall, covering the entire curved surface, hung a massive tapestry.

It was unlike any work of art Ravn had ever seen. It was not woven from dead wool or cotton, but from a mosaic of different colored mosses, lichens, and living fibers, all painstakingly intertwined and kept alive by a trickle of nutrients from the roots they were attached to. The entire tapestry seemed to breathe, the colors shifting subtly, the textures a living, breathing thing.

It depicted a history of pain.

The first panel, on the far left, was a chaotic, abstract swirl of gray and black moss, a depiction of a world dissolving. Ravn could almost recognize the fractured, de-rendering shapes of buildings and the screaming, static-filled sky of the Convergence. Tiny figures, woven from pale, white fibers, were shown being torn apart by the chaos.

"The end of your world," Kaia said softly. "But perhaps a necessary end."

She touched the panel depicting the gray, lonely survivors. "Look at them, Ravn. Starving. Afraid. Why? Because they were separate. An individual is a closed system. Entropy eats them alive. They run out of energy. They die."

She turned to him, her eyes glowing with a terrifying benevolence. "To be alone is to be terminal. The only way to survive the infinite is to become infinite. We do not just live in the forest, Physicist. We are the forest. When the time comes, we do not die. We simply… disperse."

Ravn felt a chill. "And the cost? What happens to the 'I'?"

Kaia smiled, and it was the smile of a predator that eats souls. "The 'I' is the wound, Ravn. We cure it."

The figures of the survivors were gaunt, skeletal things, huddled together for warmth that did not exist. Their mouths, woven from a stark black fiber, were open in silent screams of hunger and despair.

In the corner, figures were shown turning on each other, their forms a tangle of violence.

"The first children of the Convergence," Kaia explained, her voice heavy with the memory. "We were starving, lost, and mad with fear. We were the last children of a logical world, and our logic was useless here. We were dying."

The third panel was the largest, the central focus of the entire work. The world was still gray and dead, but the central figure, a shamanistic woman with long, flowing hair, was on her knees, her arms outstretched to the sky. And from the top of the tapestry, a single, glowing thread of golden, phosphorescent moss descended, touching her outstretched hands.

It was a single point of light in an ocean of despair.

"And then, the world spoke to us," Kaia whispered, a note of awe in her voice. "It did not offer harmony. It offered a choice. Adapt, or perish. We chose to listen."

The final panel was a riot of vibrant life. The gray landscape was gone, replaced by a forest of deep green mosses and pulsating, fungal reds. The golden thread from the previous panel had spread, its fibers woven into the very fabric of the world, and into the people themselves.

The figures of the survivors were no longer screaming. They were walking calmly into the embrace of the new, living world, and on their skin, the first, faint, glowing patterns were beginning to appear.

Ravn stared at the living history, a scientist looking at a religious text. He tried to find a logical explanation—the golden thread was a targeted mutagen, a terraforming agent, a symbiotic organism that offered sustenance in exchange for a host—but the sheer, unshakeable faith that radiated from Kaia and from the tapestry itself was a force beyond his comprehension.

"Now you understand the price of our peace," Kaia said, turning to him. "Now you are ready to witness the affirmation of our choice."

"So the spore..." he began, his scientific mind grasping for a logical foothold, "it was a catalyst? A mutagen? It rewrote your biology to be compatible with the new ecosystem."

Kaia turned from the tapestry, her ancient eyes holding a look of gentle pity.

"You still try to place the world into your small, hard boxes of logic, Physicist. You seek to understand the river by measuring a single drop of its water. That is not understanding. It is merely description."

She gestured back at the final panel, at the serene figures walking into the vibrant forest. "To understand, you cannot stand apart from the current. You must feel it. You must join it."

She placed a gentle hand on his arm, her touch surprisingly warm. "Our history is not a thing of the past. It is a choice we reaffirm with every new generation. A choice we will reaffirm today."

A new, deeper sense of unease began to coil in Ravn's stomach. "What do you mean?"

"You have seen the memory of our first choice," Kaia said, her voice dropping to a low, reverent hum. "Now you must witness its living heart. Today, a young warrior, Kael, will undergo the Coming of the Heart. It is a great honor, the most joyful union a person can know. It is the moment one of us ceases to be a lonely, separate whisper and joins the great song of the world. It is the moment a Husk truly comes home."

Her words were beautiful, spiritual, and utterly terrifying.

"Union?" Ravn asked, the word feeling cold and heavy on his tongue.

"A perfect symbiosis," she answered, her smile serene. "An affirmation of the pact. He will give of himself, and the Zone will give of itself in return. He will become more."

Ravn's mind raced, his scientific training screaming that there was no such thing as a "perfect" symbiosis. There was always a cost, always a dominant partner. He pictured the strange, mindless grace of the Ascended warriors, their eyes holding a light that was no longer human.

He will become more. The words echoed with a chilling ambiguity. *More what?*

He wanted to refuse. Every instinct for self-preservation, every tenet of his logical, rational worldview, told him to turn away, to thank her for her hospitality and retreat to the edges of their society.

But the Axiom's directive, *Understand*, was a splinter in his mind. He was a scientist. His purpose was to gather data, to observe phenomena, no matter how unsettling. To refuse to witness their most sacred ritual would be to willingly blind himself, to abandon the very mission that was keeping him alive.

It would also be a profound insult, a rejection of the trust Kaia was showing him. He was trapped between his fear and his purpose.

"I..." he began, his voice hesitant. "I would be honored to witness it."

The words felt like a lie, but they were also a deeper truth. He had to know.

Kaia's smile widened, not with triumph, but with a deep, maternal understanding. "Good," she whispered. "Come. The song is already beginning."

She led him out of the quiet, solemn chamber of the roots and back up the spiraling pathway toward the central platforms of the city.

As they emerged, he could feel a change in the air. The gentle, ambient hum of the city had been replaced by a low, rhythmic chant that seemed to emanate from all the Husks at once. A palpable sense of sacred anticipation was building, a living energy that vibrated through the woven branches beneath his feet.

He was being carried by the current now, and he was deeply, profoundly afraid of where it was taking him.

She led him to the central and highest platform of the city, an open-air amphitheater woven from the thickest and oldest branches of the world-tree.

The entire community had gathered, their forms a silent, swaying sea in the dappled green light. The air was thick with the sweet, heavy scent of pollen and a low, rhythmic chant that vibrated up from the floor, through the soles of Ravn's boots, and into his very bones.

It was a hypnotic, resonant frequency that seemed to lull the logical, analytical part of his mind to sleep, and he had to actively fight to stay focused, to remain an observer.

In the center of the platform sat a young warrior, Kael, his face a mask of calm, ecstatic focus. He was stripped to the waist, his skin marked with intricate, temporary patterns of golden pollen. He did not look afraid. He looked like a man about to meet his god.

Before him, two attendants, their movements slow and reverent, held a glistening, chrysalis-like pod. It was a living thing, pulsing with a soft, internal light, and its surface was slick with a translucent, amber-colored mucus.

Ravn watched, his scientific curiosity at war with a rising sense of profound dread.

As the chanting reached its peak, a deep, resonant hum that was the sum of every voice, the pod began to split open. It unfurled like a time-lapse flower, its fleshy petals peeling back to reveal what lay within.

Inside was a creature of obscene beauty. It was something like a centipede, nearly a meter long, its body crafted from segments of what looked like iridescent, milky-white pearl. It unfurled from its coiled position, its many delicate, hair-like legs moving in a mesmerizing, hypnotic wave.

It had no discernible head or eyes, only a single, needle-sharp point of polished black chitin at one end. It was an organism of perfect, alien symmetry.

The young warrior, Kael, took a deep, shuddering breath, a sound of pure, blissful anticipation. He opened his arms in a gesture of absolute welcome.

The attendants, with the utmost care, lifted the creature from its pod and laid it on the warrior's bare chest.

Ravn felt a wave of nausea, his own skin crawling as he imagined the feeling of those hundreds of tiny, chitinous legs skittering across his own flesh.

The creature arched its back, raising its sharpened, black head. For a moment, it was poised, a living dagger held over the warrior's heart.

Then, it struck.

It did not bite or sting. It plunged its head directly into the warrior's sternum with a soft, wet, sickening sound.

Kael's back went rigid, arching off the ground in a violent, convulsive spasm. A silent scream contorted his face, his jaw clenched so tight Ravn could hear his teeth grinding, but no sound escaped his lips. His eyes rolled back in his head until only the whites were visible.

Ravn watched in pure, frozen horror, but the Husks around him watched in awe, their chant deepening, their faces filled with a look of shared, vicarious ecstasy.

Dark, indigo veins, the color of a deep bruise, spread from the entry point like lightning across Kael's skin, pulsing in time with the community's chant.

He began to convulse, his limbs thrashing against the woven floor, a low, guttural, inhuman growl rumbling in his chest. The pearlescent creature on his chest seemed to fuse with him, burrowing deeper until its tail vanished beneath his skin, its own internal light pulsing in sync with the spreading veins.

After a moment that stretched for an eternity, the warrior's convulsions subsided. He lay still, his body limp.

Then, slowly, he stood, not as a man in pain, but as something more.

He opened his eyes, and they were no longer human. The pupils and irises were gone, replaced by a swirling, nacreous nebula that seemed to contain the light of distant galaxies. A faint, chitinous sheen, like a thin layer of mother-of-pearl, now covered his skin, catching the light.

He turned his head, with a blur that defied the shutter-speed of the human eye, his new eyes tracking a tiny, winged insect a hundred meters away that Ravn couldn't even see.

The man that was Kael was gone. In his place stood an Ascended.

The Husks surrounding the platform let out a collective, sighing exhalation, a sound of shared, cathartic release. Some had tears of joy streaming down their faces. Others approached the newly transformed warrior with a deep, religious reverence, reaching out to gently touch the new, chitinous sheen on his skin.

Kael—or the thing that was Kael—turned its head, its swirling, pearlescent eyes seeing a world of details and energies that Ravn could not even begin to imagine.

"He is Ascended," Kaia whispered, her voice filled with a profound, beatific joy. She turned to Ravn, a serene smile on her face, clearly expecting him to share in her awe. "He has accepted the Heart of the Zone into his own. He can hear the song of the world-tree now, feel the flow of life in the soil beneath us. He is no longer a separate, lonely note. He is one with the great song of the world."

Her words were beautiful, poetic, and to Ravn, they were the most horrifying thing he had ever heard. He felt a cold dread wash over him, so powerful it almost brought him to his knees.

He looked from the transformed warrior to the joyous faces of the other Husks, and then back to Kaia's serene, smiling face, and he finally, truly, understood.

His scientific mind, a tool he could not turn off, was analyzing what he had just witnessed. It was a biological hijacking. A hostile, parasitic infection where the host was a willing, ecstatic participant.

He pictured the creature's nervous system burrowing into Kael's spinal cord, its tendrils wrapping around his brain stem, overwriting his personality, his memories, his very consciousness with its own alien imperatives.

The man had not "become more." He had been hollowed out and replaced.

But the philosophical horror was far worse. This was the price of their beautiful, harmonious world. It was the complete and utter surrender of the self. It was the erasure of the individual—with all of its messy, illogical, chaotic, and beautiful thoughts and feelings—in exchange for a peaceful, mindless place in the whole.

Their harmony was that of an ant colony, of a single, hive-minded organism. They hadn't adapted to the Fracture Zone; they had been consumed by it.

He looked around at the other Husks, at their calm, pearlescent eyes, and a new, chilling question took root in his mind.

How many of them were Ascended? Was Kaia? Were the children who played on the bridges still children, or were they just waiting for their own "Coming of the Heart"? Was there a single, truly independent human mind left in this entire city, or was he the last one? He felt a profound, suffocating sense of alienation. He was an individual standing in the heart of a collective, a dissonant chord of logic and selfhood in their great, harmonious song.

He now understood the price of the Husks' beautiful world. To achieve their balance, one had to stop being human. This place was not a sanctuary. It was a different kind of tomb—not a sterile, concrete one like The Bastion, but a vibrant, green, and living one, a place where the soul was willingly sacrificed for the sake of the body's survival.

And he knew, with an absolute certainty, that he had to get out.

11

The Iron Blight

L ife with the Husks was a study in contradictions. In the weeks that followed the horrifying ritual of the Ascended, Ravn found a strange, unsettling peace.

He was safe. The constant, grinding threat of starvation and predation was gone, replaced by a life of communal harmony. He learned the rhythms of the canopy city, the soft, melodic hum that signaled a shared meal, the way the glowing pods would dim as the three blue suns reached their zenith. He was a guest in their paradise, a silent observer of their tranquil existence.

And he was slowly going mad.

His mind, the restless, analytical engine that had defined his entire life, was starving. The Husks lived in a world of faith and feeling, of instinct and deep, silent connection to the Zone. Their knowledge was intuitive, biological. They knew which fungi held water and which held poison not by analysis, but by a deep, cellular empathy with the world around them.

When Ravn tried to speak to them of his own world, the world of data and diagnosis, he was met with gentle, uncomprehending smiles.

He once tried to explain the principles of orbital mechanics to a young Husk artisan, attempting to sketch the solar system in the dirt of a planter box. The artisan listened patiently, then picked up a fallen leaf, pointing to the elegant, fractal patterns of its veins.

"The world does not need to be measured to be understood," she had said, her voice soft. "It only needs to be felt." To them, his logic was a strange, dead language, the relic of a failed world. He felt his greatest asset, his intellect, beginning to atrophy in the warm, humid, and intellectually sterile air of their utopia.

He was a guest, but he was also a curiosity, a strange, sad creature who was deaf to the great song of the world, a man who still tried to count the waves instead of simply letting himself be carried by the tide.

This conflict, this deep, internal friction between his gratitude and his suffocation, led him to a secret heresy.

In the bottom of his pack, wrapped in a piece of oilcloth, he still carried the small, damaged data-slate he'd salvaged from a Legion corpse during the ambush. It was a shard of the old world, a piece of forbidden logic.

It was a blasphemy in this organic paradise. In the deepest part of the twilight cycle, when the city was asleep, and the only light came from the soft, pulsing glow of the fungi, he would slip away.

He found a secluded grotto, hidden behind a curtain of thick, hanging moss, a small, damp cave where the ever-present, communal hum of the Husks was faint and distant. This small, dark space became his secret laboratory, his confessional.

By the faint blue-green light of his Stalker, who would watch him with its silent, intelligent eyes, he would work.

He didn't know why, precisely. It was a compulsion. A need to feel the spark of his old self, to prove that the scientist within him had not yet been completely consumed by the survivor.

The data-slate was a wreck. Its casing was cracked, its screen a spiderweb of fractures, its power cell long dead. Repairing it with the tools at hand was a near-impossible task.

He used the sharpened edge of an obsidian flake to carefully pry open the casing. He used the tensile fibers of a particular vine, which he'd analyzed with the Aperture, to painstakingly re-route the microscopic, broken circuits on the main board. It was a maddening, delicate process, a surgeon performing microsurgery with a woodsman's tools.

For power, he had only one option. He would carefully unstrap the

Aperture from his wrist and, with a pair of makeshift copper contacts he'd stripped from the slate's own charging port, he would attempt to channel a tiny fraction of the Aperture's impossible energy into the dead device.

It was a dangerous, foolish act. But the challenge, the pure, logical problem of it, was the only thing that made him feel alive.

He was solving an equation again. And that, he realized, was a need as fundamental to his being as food or water.

After weeks of painstaking, secret work, the moment had come. The circuits were bridged, the power conduits rerouted. Ravn sat back on his heels in the gloom of the hidden grotto, the repaired data-slate resting on a flat stone before him.

The Stalker lay nearby, its head on its paws, its luminous eyes watching him with a quiet, animal intelligence. Everything came down to this. A single, desperate connection.

With surprisingly steady hands, he took the two makeshift copper contacts and pressed them to the terminals he had rigged on the slate's power port. He held his breath and touched the other ends to the exposed energy cell of the Aperture.

For a heart-stopping second, nothing happened. He felt a surge of bitter disappointment. It had all been for nothing.

Then, the cracked screen of the data-slate flickered once, twice, and sputtered to life, bathing the grotto in a cold, blue-white light that was utterly alien to the warm, organic glow of the Husks' world.

A wave of pure, triumphant joy, an emotion he had thought long dead, surged through him. He had done it. Against all odds, he had resurrected this small piece of a dead world.

The screen was a chaotic mess of fractured pixels and corrupted data, but in the center, a single line of text was miraculously, beautifully legible: *LEGION OS v.7.3 – RUNNING DIAGNOSTIC....*

The clean, sharp angles of the text were a balm to his logic-starved soul. It was the language of his people, the language of reason.

For a single, perfect moment, he was not a savage, not a survivor, not a guest in a paradise that was slowly suffocating him. He was a scientist again.

He did not know, in his moment of triumph, that the slate's emergency protocols, upon receiving power for the first time in years, were doing exactly what they were designed to do.

They sent out a powerful, encrypted, wide-spectrum diagnostic burst—a single, sharp pulse of pure, structured information, searching for a network that no longer existed.

To the Husks, it was a blasphemy. Miles away, in her chamber at the heart of the world-tree, Kaia gasped, her meditation shattered. She felt it as a spike of pure, physical pain in the world's consciousness, a dissonant chord of cold iron struck in the heart of their sacred, organic harmony.

It was a frequency of logic and death, a poison she had not felt in years. Her serene expression dissolved, replaced by a look of profound, sorrowful betrayal. She knew, instantly, where it had come from.

To the Legion, miles away in the opposite direction, it was a miracle.

The sensor technician on a long-range patrol, his eyes glazed over with the monotony of sweeping the forest for anomalies, sat bolt upright. An alert was screaming on his console, a signature so clean, so logical, it couldn't be real.

Not the chaotic energy of the Zone. It was a Legion diagnostic signature, a friendly IFF beacon in a sea of hostiles.

"Contact!" he yelled, his voice cracking with excitement. "Sector Delta-9! I have a positive Legion signature!"

The two forces, one of sorrow and one of steel, began to converge on the source of the signal. On Ravn.

He was still staring, mesmerized, at the screen when a shadow fell over him. He looked up.

Kaia stood at the mouth of the grotto, her face a mask of deep, heartbreaking sorrow.

"You have brought the Iron Blight into our heart, Ravn." Before he could explain, before he could even begin to process her words, the first sounds of the assault ripped through the tranquil air of the canopy city. It was the high-pitched, terrifying shriek of pulse rifle fire, echoing from the forest floor far below.

The Legion had found them. And it was his fault.

The shriek of pulse rifle fire from the forest floor below was a definitive, damning sentence. Kaia's accusation echoed in the sudden, violent noise. Ravn stood frozen in the grotto, the cold blue light of the data-slate painting his face in the colors of his crime.

He looked from the device—the shard of forbidden logic—to Kaia's face. He had expected anger, fury, a righteous condemnation. What he saw was worse. Her ancient, serene eyes were filled with a deep and profound sorrow, the look of a mother watching her child make a terrible, irreversible mistake. It was not anger. It was pity. And it was unbearable.

The battle below escalated. The clean, high-pitched hum of Legion pulse rifles was answered by the guttural, defiant war cries of the Husk warriors. He could hear the crackle of energy shields, the wet, percussive thud of bone blades finding their mark.

It was the same clash of ideologies he had fled from before, the war between the cold, hard line and the wild, living curve. But this time, he was the cause.

A crushing weight of guilt, heavier than any physical burden he had ever carried, settled on his soul. He was a walking sickness. A catalyst of chaos. His very nature, his obsessive need to analyze and understand, his inability to let go of the dead world's logic, was a poison.

He had brought a plague of cold iron into this living, breathing paradise, and now it was bleeding. He was a traitor to the only people who had shown him grace.

He looked at Kaia, who was now staring down through the woven branches, her face a mask of pained concentration as she listened to the sounds of her people fighting and dying.

He knew he could not stay and face her judgment. What would their justice even look like? Some form of serene, biological punishment as horrifying as their rituals?

And he could not be recaptured by Rostova. He was a compromised asset, a variable that had been contaminated by the "illogical" enemy. She would not see him as a returning prodigal; she would see him as a failed experiment to be dissected and discarded.

His position was untenable. He was trapped between two worlds, and welcome in neither.

His only option was the one he had grown so accustomed to. He had to run.

He used the chaos he had created as his cover. While Kaia's attention was fixed on the battle below, while the warriors of the canopy city descended to defend their home, Ravn took his chance.

He grabbed the data-slate, an instinct he couldn't explain, and shoved it into his pack. He gave the Stalker, who was watching him with confused, worried eyes, a soft, apologetic touch on its head.

Then he slipped out of the grotto and into the chaos of the city.

The air was filled with shouts and the scent of cordite. He found a forgotten service vine, thick and rough, that snaked down the far side of the colossal trunk, away from the main fighting.

Without a second thought, he began his desperate descent. He was an outcast once more, a fugitive from the faith he had betrayed and the logic he could not return to.

He reached the forest floor, his body scraped and bruised from the desperate descent. The sounds of the battle above—the clean shriek of pulse rifles and the guttural cries of the Husk warriors—faded behind him, swallowed by the immense, alien quiet of the wilderness.

He did not look back. He ran, the Stalker a silent, glowing shadow at his heels, the two of them plunging deeper into the unknown.

For hours, he moved, driven by a raw, primal surge of adrenaline and a crushing wave of guilt. He was a traitor. An outcast. A man with no allies and no home. He had fled the cold, sterile logic of the Legion only to betray the chaotic, vibrant life of the Husks.

He was a man caught between two worlds, and welcome in neither.

The landscape began to change as he put distance between himself and the Husks' world-tree. The colossal, fungal trees became smaller, then stunted and withered.

The rich, breathing moss that carpeted the ground grew thin, revealing patches of cracked, rust-colored earth beneath. The air, once thick and humid with the scent of pollen and decay, became thin, dry, and sharp in his lungs.

He was leaving the world of life and entering a world of death.

By the next cycle, the last of the twisted, fungal trees had vanished. He stood at the edge of a new biome, a desolate wasteland that stretched to the horizon in every direction.

The ground was a vast, empty expanse of rust-colored sand and jagged, wind-carved rock. The "rust" was not just a color; it was literal.

The air tasted of oxidized metal, and a fine, red-brown dust, the powdered remains of a billion tons of pre-Fracture steel, coated his tongue and stung his eyes.

The sky was a vast, empty canvas of **oppressive violet**, the three blue suns casting harsh, unforgiving shadows that seemed to carve the landscape into sharp, geometric shapes. This was a world without softness, a world of hard angles and sharp edges.

The only features were the skeletal remains of his own dead civilization: the twisted girders of a collapsed bridge reaching like desperate fingers from a dry riverbed; the silent, hollow shells of factories, their roofs long since caved in; and in the distance, a mountain range of scrap metal, a jagged, unnatural horizon of compressed cars and rusted-out machinery.

The vibrant, living symphony of the forest was gone, replaced by a profound, oppressive silence, broken only by the lonely, abrasive howl of the wind. It was a dead world, a monument to the failure of the very logic and industry he had once belonged to.

He trudged through the desolation, the Stalker padding silently at his side, its bioluminescent patterns a strange, lonely beacon of life in the overwhelming emptiness. The creature was uneasy here, its head low, its dark eyes constantly scanning the empty horizon.

Ravn, however, felt a strange, grim sense of homecoming. He had fled a world of overwhelming, interconnected life, a world that had threatened to consume his individuality. This place was the opposite. It was a world of profound, aggressive, and absolute emptiness.

It was a physical manifestation of his own exile, a perfect reflection of the barren, scoured landscape of his own soul. He was a broken man from a broken world, and he was finally home.

He had walked for a full day, the adrenaline of his escape long since burned away, leaving only a grim, weary determination. The silence of the wasteland was a profound, oppressive thing, broken only by the abrasive howl of the wind as it scoured the rust-colored dunes.

He was alone, a man with no allies and no home, a ghost in a graveyard of his own making.

It was the Stalker that sensed them first. The creature stopped, its body going rigid, a low, guttural growl rumbling deep in its chest. Its bioluminescent patterns flickered with agitation.

Ravn froze, straining his ears, but he heard nothing over the wind. Then, he felt it—a low, deep vibration in the soles of his boots, a rhythmic thrumming that was growing steadily stronger. It was a sound he hadn't heard since before the Convergence.

The roar of engines.

He scrambled to the top of a dune and looked out.

A convoy of vehicles was cresting the horizon, a nightmare of welded scrap metal and roaring exhaust pipes, kicking up a massive plume of rust-colored dust. There were stripped-down buggies with skulls welded to their grilles, hulking flatbed trucks with harpoon guns mounted on the back, and agile, three-wheeled bikes adorned with bones and strips of torn leather.

They saw him, a lone figure silhouetted against the purple sky, and a chorus of whooping, joyous war cries echoed across the waste. They turned and headed straight for him.

The hunt was short and brutal. He was a man on foot against a pack of baying, mechanical hounds. They didn't charge him directly. They toyed with him, herding him, their bikes cutting him off every time he tried to break for the cover of the rocky outcroppings.

A buggy with a grinning, masked warrior hanging off the side swerved close, the man lashing at him with a long, hooked chain. They were laughing. To them, this was sport.

Finally, they had him surrounded, their engines revving in a deafening, chaotic chorus. He was a captive audience in a theater of rust and gasoline. They were loud, clad in patchwork leather and scavenged armor, their faces hidden behind goggles and grimacing masks. They radiated a palpable, joyful menace.

He was bound and thrown onto the back of a flatbed truck, the convoy's prize.

They drove for hours, deeper into the desert, until he saw their home. It was a moving city, a colossal pre-Fracture mining vehicle that crawled across the wasteland on immense tracks, a fortress of rust and fire belching black smoke into the sky.

It was the Grinder.

The interior was a chaotic, multi-leveled maze of catwalks, roaring engines, and makeshift workshops where welders sent showers of sparks into the gloom. The air was thick with the smell of diesel, hot metal, and unwashed bodies.

It was a sensory assault, a stark and violent contrast to the sterile halls of The Bastion and the living beauty of the Husks' canopy city.

He was dragged from the truck and brought to the heart of the machine, a throne room built around a massive, still-thumping V-12 engine. The heat was immense, the noise a deafening, rhythmic roar.

On a throne of welded tailpipes and engine blocks sat their leader. He was a physically imposing man, covered in scars and makeshift tattoos, with a booming laugh that seemed to compete with the engine's roar.

He held a mug of some foul-smelling liquid in one hand and a cruel-looking, double-bitted axe in the other. Next to his throne, a sharpened spike of rebar held a single, grotesque trophy: a massive, dented helmet from a suit of pre-Fracture riot armor, its faceplate shattered.

"Well, look what the little hounds dragged in," the man bellowed, his smile both charming and predatory. "A stray. You run fast, stray. I like that."

He took a long drink. "I'm Jax. This here is the Grinder. And we are the Rust Lords." He gestured around at his roaring, chaotic war band. He then pointed a thumb at the spiked helmet. "That belonged to a man who thought he could make rules for us in the first days. He learned." Jax leaned forward, his eyes glinting with a dangerous intelligence. "So what's a soft-looking thing like you doing all alone in our scrapyard?" Ravn, exhausted and battered, met his gaze. "Surviving."

Jax let out another booming laugh. "Surviving! I like him!" He slammed his mug down on a metal drum, the sound a sharp clang against the engine's roar.

"Well, you survived us. That makes you interesting. You can have a place here, stray. We don't have fancy logic or tree-hugging prayers. We have this," he said, gesturing to the glorious, dangerous chaos around them.

"And this." He hefted his axe. "Here, there are no rules. Only what you can take and what you can hold. Welcome to the chaos."

12

The Orrery Puzzle

In the chaotic, roaring hierarchy of the Rust Lords, Ravn quickly learned that survival was a matter of utility.

He was not strong, he was not a warrior, and he was a terrible mechanic. But he could think.

In a world of brute force and instinct, his logical, analytical mind was a strange and valuable commodity.

Jax, recognizing this, had dubbed him the tribe's official "brainiac," a title that was both a privilege and a leash. It meant he was given a workshop of his own—a small, relatively quiet alcove carved out behind a massive bank of dead ventilation fans—and a larger share of the filtered water.

But it also meant he was at the warlord's beck and call, a pet intellectual to be trotted out whenever a problem arose that couldn't be solved with an axe or an explosive. The other Rust Lords, warriors who measured a man's worth in scars and salvaged engine parts, treated him with a mixture of contempt and superstitious suspicion.

He was Jax's creature, and that was the only reason he was still breathing.

One cycle, as the Grinder was plowing its way through a vast, glassed-over desert, two of Jax's lieutenants appeared at his workshop.

"Jax wants you," one of them grunted, and Ravn knew from his tone it wasn't a request.

He found the warlord in his throne room. The massive engine was idling, its rhythmic thumping a deep, resonant heartbeat for the entire moving city. Jax was perched on his throne of welded tailpipes, using a long, wicked-looking knife to pick his teeth. His axe rested against his knee.

"Echo!" he boomed, his voice echoing in the cavernous space. "Got a job for you. A legend. A prize." He kicked a dusty, metal crate toward Ravn. "Heard this from a Scrapper I picked up last cycle. Little rat was dying of rust-lung, but he paid for his water with a story." Jax leaned forward, his eyes glinting with a greedy fire.

"The story told of the 'Old World Sky-Watchers,' brainiacs like you, who lived on a high mountain before the big crack-up. This rat said they could read the secrets of the stars, and that before the world broke, they hid a map—a 'sky map'—that led to the greatest prize of the old world. A place he called the 'Anchor.'" Ravn's blood ran cold. The Anchor. The Heart. The Legion, the Husks, and now the Rust Lords—they were all hunting the same thing, even if they didn't know what it was.

"The little rat died before he could say what the prize was," Jax continued, tossing his knife from one hand to the other. "But what else could it be? Weapons. An armory of these Legion pea-shooters." He gestured dismissively. "Tech. Maybe a whole bunker full of the good stuff. Or fuel. A depot that'll keep the Grinder running for a hundred cycles." He grinned, a predatory, joyful expression. "Doesn't matter. Whatever it is, I want it. The legend says the map is in their old nest. A place called the 'Observatory.'" He pointed a greasy thumb at a crude map scrawled on a piece of flayed hide pinned to the wall. "You're a scientist. One of them. You can read their chicken scratch and make their junk work. You're gonna go up there, get my map, and bring it back." It was a command. "Spike and Grit will take you," he said, nodding to the two hulking warriors who had escorted Ravn. "Try anything stupid, and they'll bring me back your head in a box. Understand?" Ravn looked from Jax's hungry, ambitious face to the cold, dead eyes of his two guards. He was a tool. A key to be used to open a lock. And when the lock was open, keys were often discarded.

But he had no choice.

"I understand," he said, his voice flat. He had to get to the Anchor. If going as Jax's unwilling key was the only way, then that was the path he would take.

The journey to the observatory was a treacherous, rattling affair.

Ravn was given a small, three-wheeled scout vehicle, a skeletal contraption of rusted pipes and mismatched tires that belched a constant stream of black, oily smoke. His two guards, Spike and Grit, rode alongside on loud, heavily armed motorbikes, their expressions a permanent sneer of boredom and contempt. They were his keepers, there to ensure Jax's "brainiac" didn't get any ideas about running.

They drove for a full day, leaving the relative flatness of the rust-colored desert and climbing into the jagged, wind-carved peaks of a mountain range. The path was a barely-there goat track, a crumbling ribbon of ancient asphalt clinging to the side of the cliffs.

At one point, they came to a collapsed bridge spanning a deep chasm. Spike and Grit, with a series of guttural shouts and practiced efficiency, produced a set of heavy grappling hooks and winches. They secured the lines to an outcropping on the far side and, with a terrifying lack of ceremony, winched Ravn's flimsy vehicle across the abyss, the trike swaying sickeningly in the high, thin wind.

As they climbed higher, the air grew cold, and the wind howled with a lonely, mournful sound.

Finally, they reached the peak. The observatory was a rusted, white dome against the indigo vault, a forgotten pearl in a setting of jagged rock. A faded, pre-Fracture logo for some forgotten space agency was still barely visible on its side, cracked and peeling. The wind shrieked through its broken windows and the rents in its metal skin, the only voice left in this high, lonely place.

"We wait here," Grit grunted, dismounting his bike and pulling out a flask. "Don't take all day, brainiac. This place gives me the creeps." Ravn left them to their vigil and approached the main entrance.

The great doors had been torn from their hinges years ago, likely by the initial shockwave of the Convergence. He stepped inside, and the howling of the wind was instantly replaced by a profound, sad silence. The air was cold, still, and thick with the smell of dust, decaying paper, and the faint, metallic tang of old, dead electronics.

He walked through the derelict control rooms, his boots crunching on shattered glass and brittle, yellowed papers covered in faded equations. He saw overturned desks, banks of smashed monitors, and vast, astronomical charts peeling from the walls like old wallpaper, the familiar constellations now a mockery of a lost truth.

This place was a tomb for a dead science.

He saw the skeletal remains of the scientists who had been at their posts when the world ended. One was slumped in a chair, its bony fingers resting on a keyboard, a silent testament to a duty kept until the very last second.

Near another, lying on the floor amidst a scatter of broken instruments, he found a small, personal datapad. The screen was cracked, but when he tilted it to the light from the doorway, he could just make out the ghost of an image: a smiling man, a woman, and two small children, frozen in a moment of happiness from a world that no longer existed.

He felt a sharp, unexpected pang of kinship, a deep and profound sorrow for these nameless colleagues who had died in the heart of their own temple.

This was his world. These were his people.

He felt a surge of grim resolve. Jax wanted a weapon, a prize. But Ravn was here for something else. He was here to salvage a piece of his own lost world, to prove that the curiosity and wonder that had built this place had not died in vain.

He continued deeper into the facility, his footsteps echoing in the silence. He passed a massive, inert mass spectrometer and, through a shattered bay window, saw the colossal, skeletal frame of a radio telescope dish, pointed at the alien sky like a begging hand.

Finally, he entered the central chamber, directly beneath the massive, retractable dome.

He stopped, his breath catching in his throat. It was a breathtaking sight: a massive, mechanical orrery, a beautiful, intricate brass model of a solar system that no longer existed. Intricate, interlocking rings and gears, all crafted with the loving precision of a master watchmaker, were designed to spin in a complex, celestial ballet. But now, it stood silent and frozen, its brass surface tarnished and dull, a beautiful, broken clock in a universe where time itself had lost its meaning.

He spent the next few hours in a state of focused, almost reverent silence, his grief for the dead scientists channeled into a deep respect for their final, beautiful creation.

He walked the circumference of the orrery, his fingers lightly tracing the cool, tarnished brass. It was a masterpiece of mechanical engineering. Each gear was hand-tooled, each planetary model exquisitely detailed. He saw a tiny, silver Earth, its continents rendered in a faint, blue-green enamel. He saw the magnificent rings of a bronze Saturn, each one a perfect, concentric circle.

It was a perfect model of a perfect, logical system. A system that was now a ghost.

His first task was to find a power source. Following a thick, armored conduit from the orrery's base, he found the auxiliary power unit in a sub-level chamber. It was a massive, pre-Fracture generator, its systems long dead. But the core components, shielded behind layers of lead and steel, looked intact.

It was a puzzle, a problem of applied physics, and his mind, starved for such a challenge, latched onto it with a ferocious intensity.

He spent hours jury-rigging a solution. He used the Aperture's diagnostic tools to identify a functional ignition circuit. He bypassed the corroded primary conductors with heavy copper wiring he stripped from a wall panel.

For the final, critical step, he once again unhooked the energy cell from his Aperture, its strange, matte black surface a stark contrast to the rusted, old-world technology. He fashioned a makeshift connection and channeled a single, controlled pulse of its impossible energy into the generator's ignition.

For a moment, nothing happened. Then, with a deep, shuddering groan that echoed through the entire observatory, the ancient generator sputtered to life. Lights flickered on in the main chamber, and the great orrery began to hum with a low, ghostly energy.

Back in the main chamber, he watched as the machine tried to orient itself. The brass rings shifted, the planetary arms whirred, their internal sensors searching the sky through the dome's main aperture for alignment points that were no longer there. The orrery was trying to find Polaris. It was trying to find the familiar, comforting light of Sol.

It was a machine built for a universe that was gone.

With a final, grinding screech of protesting gears, the system faulted, its lights blinking a steady, diagnostic red. The malfunction was not mechanical; it was conceptual.

The only way forward was an act of scientific heresy.

He accessed the primary calibration interface, a complex holographic display that flickered to life at the base of the orrery. He found the root directory, its files labeled with the familiar, comforting names of his past: Sol, Terra, Jupiter, Saturnus.

He had to delete them. He had to manually, deliberately, erase the last digital ghost of his own home.

He paused, his finger hovering over the DELETE command for the file labeled Terra. It felt like a desecration, like pulling the plug on a life support machine. With a heavy, shuddering breath, he did it. One by one, he erased the solar system he had grown up in.

Now came the hard part. He had to build a new universe from scratch.

He ascended the gantry to the observatory's main telescope. With a groan of rusted metal, he opened the dome's massive iris, exposing the chamber to the bruised purple twilight and the three, baleful blue suns. He aimed the massive telescope, its optics miraculously intact, and began his work.

For the rest of the cycle, he was a scientist again, a cartographer of a broken cosmos. He mapped the positions of the three suns, calculating their strange, non-Keplerian orbits. He measured the spectral signature of the violet nebula that had consumed Orion.

He used the Aperture's data to cross-reference his own optical calculations, a strange and wonderful fusion of old-world optics and new-world physics. He was a man standing with one foot in a dead universe and the other in a new, impossible one, using the tools of both to draw a new map of reality.

He fed the new, "wrong" data into the orrery's navigation system. Then came the physical work. He had to climb into the heart of the machine itself, his body aching as he used a heavy wrench to manually loosen and realign the massive, planetary gear sets, the brass teeth thick with the dust of a dead world. He adjusted the heavy, optical lenses of the central projector, focusing them on the new coordinates he had just created.

Finally, it was done. He descended from the machine, his body covered in grime and grease, and initiated the alignment sequence again.

This time, there was no grinding protest. The great brass rings slid into their new positions with a quiet, satisfying hum. The planets of bronze and silver moved to their new, impossible orbits, a perfect, clockwork model of a broken sky. The system was stable. But the final sequence, the one labeled *MAP_PROJECTION*, refused to activate.

A single, final component was missing.

He stood back, a deep sense of satisfaction warring with his exhaustion. The great machine hummed with a new, stable energy, its model of the impossible sky perfectly aligned. The three blue suns, cast in bronze, now held their proper, alien positions. The violet nebula was a beautiful, intricate etching on a polished brass ring. He had done it.

He had imposed a new, logical order on the chaos.

He returned to the holographic interface and initiated the final command: *EXECUTE: MAP_PROJECTION*.

The command blinked, and a single, frustrating line of text appeared below it: ERROR: CALIBRATION KEY NOT DETECTED. SEQUENCE ABORTED. A wave of cold, bitter frustration washed over him. He had done everything right. The power was stable. The coordinates were perfect. The physical gears were aligned.

He spent the next hour in a state of meticulous, mounting frustration, running every diagnostic the system had to offer. He re-checked his own calculations, searching for a misplaced decimal, a single flawed variable. He even climbed back into the machine's guts, re-examining the gear placements. Everything was perfect.

The machine was not broken. It was locked.

He began a minute, physical inspection of the orrery's core mechanism, the central housing from which the main projector was meant to emerge. And that's when he found the break. Tucked away behind the primary gearset, the main drive shaft was sheared.

The brass coupling had snapped, creating a jagged, spiraling gap between the motor and the projector. It was a catastrophic mechanical failure. The smooth gears of the old world couldn't bridge the gap. He needed something with friction. Something with a complex, gripping geometry to catch the teeth of the shattered shaft.

He slumped down at the control console, utterly defeated. The quest was over. He had come so close, only to be thwarted by a single, missing piece.

He leaned back in the dusty chair, the silence of the observatory pressing in on him, a monument to his own failure. Idly, his hand went into his pocket, his fingers searching for a familiar, grounding object. He found it.

The flawed pinecone. He pulled it out, its fourteen wrong spirals a familiar, painful sight.

For weeks, he had seen it as a symbol of the broken universe, the first sign that the laws of nature had been corrupted. It was an artifact of chaos.

He rolled it in his palm, feeling the rough texture of the woody scales. He looked at its base, where the scales converged in the impossible, asymmetrical spiral pattern that had so horrified him.

He looked up at the orrery's central mechanism, at the empty, spiraling socket.

A spark of an idea, so ludicrous, so profoundly illogical that he almost dismissed it, ignited in his mind.

The pattern... His heart began to pound, a slow, heavy rhythm. He stood and walked back to the great machine, a sense of disbelief and a wild, terrifying wonder warring with his scientific skepticism. This was not logic. This was not science. This was a leap of faith into the heart of a cosmic irony so perfect it felt like a mad god's private joke.

With a hand that trembled, he held the pinecone up to the sheared coupling. The fourteen-spiral mutation gave the cone a density and roughness that nature never intended. He didn't gently fit it; he jammed it into the gap. He used the mutated pinecone as a biological wedge, forcing its woody scales to mesh with the broken brass teeth.

It crunched, biting into the metal with a grip that a smooth machine part could never achieve.

The first anomaly of his new world had just solved the final puzzle of the old one.

For a moment, nothing happened. The orrery remained silent, a beautiful, completed machine waiting for its final command. He stood back from the orrery, a profound sense of disbelief warring with the undeniable truth before him.

The key had been in his pocket the entire time. The first symptom of his world's disease was the cure for its greatest puzzle.

He walked back to the control console, his heart pounding with a mixture of terror and a wild, exhilarating surge of scientific curiosity. His hands were trembling slightly as he reached for the holographic interface, not from fear, but from anticipation.

He re-entered the command, his fingers tracing the glowing blue letters. *EXECUTE: MAP_PROJECTION* He hit enter.

For a moment, nothing happened. Then, a deep, resonant chord, like the sound of a struck bell, echoed through the chamber. It was not the groan of rusted, ancient gears, but a smooth, powerful hum, as if the pinecone had not just completed a circuit, but had healed the very soul of the machine.

The great machine shuddered to life. The massive, interlocking brass rings began to turn, gliding silently on their tracks with a whisper of displaced air. The planets of bronze and silver slid along their new, impossible orbits, a perfect, clockwork model of a broken sky. The three blue suns at the center of the model began to glow with a soft, internal light.

It was a beautiful, terrifying, and elegant ballet of impossible physics.

A cylindrical housing rose from the core of the machine, its polished brass surface gleaming. A series of complex lenses telescoped out, clicking into focus with microscopic precision. A beam of faint blue light shot from the central projector, hitting the apex of the rusted dome above.

The light spread, and a shimmering, three-dimensional map resolved into existence in the dusty air of the chamber.

Ravn stared, his breath caught in his throat. It was a perfect, dynamic holographic projection of the entire Fracture Zone. He could see the colossal, fungal canopy of the Husks' world-tree, a vibrant green cluster of data in the east. He could see the stark, concrete walls of The Bastion, a cold, gray geometric shape to the west. He could even see the jagged peaks of the mountain range he was currently in, the observatory a tiny, blinking point of light.

It was a living, breathing map, with faint, shimmering lines indicating atmospheric currents and pockets of temporal instability.

And on that map, three specific locations, scattered across the vast and dangerous landscape, pulsed with a steady, insistent, golden light.

Each was marked with a strange, interlocking symbol he didn't recognize. They weren't random artifacts. The map identified them as *[SYS_RE-STORE_NODES]*—fragments of the Axiom's own code that had physicalized to stabilize the local reality.

One was in the heart of a region the map labeled a "Reality Tear." Another was in the submerged ruins of a pre-Fracture city.

The third was in a petrified forest known as the "Husk Graveyard." The Aperture on his wrist chirped, its scanner automatically interfacing with the holographic data.

COORDINATES LOGGED. ANOMALOUS SIGNATURES DETECTED:

SOURCE_ORGANIC [High Theta Variance].

SOURCE_KINETIC [Entropy Cascade].

SOURCE_STATIC [Null Data].

ANALYSIS: COMPATIBLE STABILIZATION AGENTS. He had found the path. This wasn't a map to a simple treasure of weapons or fuel. This was something more. This was a map to the very heart of his world's mystery.

The thing the Axiom had called "The Heart." The thing the Legion had called "The Anchor." He now knew that to reach it, he first had to find these three keys.

His journey was no longer a desperate, aimless trek of survival. It was a quest.

He stood there for a long time, bathed in the soft, blue light of the holographic map, the first true explorer of a new and broken world.

13

A Line in the Sand

The map to the keys was a death sentence. Ravn knew it the moment he returned to the Grinder, his body aching from the treacherous journey, his mind alight with the impossible discovery.

The holographic projection, which had filled him with a sense of scientific awe, was, to the Rust Lords, nothing more than a treasure map.

Jax had convened a war council in his throne room, a loud, chaotic gathering of his most trusted lieutenants and allied tribe leaders around a massive table made from the salvaged wing of a pre-Fracture cargo plane. The air was thick with the smell of oil, sweat, and roasting meat, and the constant, deafening roar of the Grinder's engine was a physical presence that vibrated through the metal floor.

Ravn stood before them, a small, quiet figure in their world of violent giants, the unwilling architect of their next conquest. He used the Aperture to project the 3D map above the table, the cool, silent, logical blue light a stark and unwelcome contrast to the flickering, fire-lit chaos of the throne room.

"There," Jax boomed, slamming a greasy hand down on the table with a force that made the mugs jump. He pointed a thick, grimy finger at the first pulsing, golden light on the map. "The brainiac says that's the first prize. The 'Husk Graveyard.'"

A scarred warrior named Grit, the same one who had escorted Ravn to the observatory, spat a stream of brown juice onto the floor. "Place is bad luck, Jax. Full of their tree-hugging ghosts. Nothing there but stone trees and bad wind."

Jax let out a booming laugh that was louder than the engine. "Ghosts can't stop a bullet, Grit! And their 'sacred shrine' is about to get a Rust Lord blessing!" He turned his wild, joyful gaze on the assembled warlords, his charisma a palpable force in the room. "Heard the stories, haven't ya? The Husks hoard the old world's magic. They talk to the trees, they sing to the dirt. They're soft. They're prey."

He picked up his axe, its polished edge gleaming in the firelight.

"This map leads to a weapon, a prize the Sky-Watchers hid. These Husks are sittin' on it, guarding it, keeping it locked away. They pray to their dirt while we bleed for every drop of fuel, for every scrap of metal that keeps us free!" His voice rose to a roar. "I say we pay them a visit! I say we take what's ours! We'll hit them so hard and so fast, they'll be too busy humming to their flowers to fight back. We'll take their prize, smash their little shrine to dust, and be gone before their tree-god even wakes up!"

A chorus of roared approvals, the stamping of heavy boots, and the clanging of metal mugs against the table filled the chamber. It was a symphony of bloodlust.

Ravn stood in silence, a cold knot of dread tightening in his stomach. He saw the map he had so carefully uncovered, a key to understanding the new world, being used as a blueprint for sacrilege and slaughter. His scientific discovery had become a weapon, and he was the one who had handed it to them.

He had to play his part. To show hesitation now would be suicide.

Jax turned his grin on him. "Well, brainiac? You're the one who can think in straight lines. How do we crack this nut?"

Ravn felt the eyes of every warlord in the room on him. He forced himself to adopt a clinical, detached tone, the voice of the Legion's technicians. He felt a cold, professional part of his brain take over, a part he hated, the part that had calculated Caleb's chances of survival.

"The map indicates the shrine is in a clearing on the forest floor," he began, his voice flat. "Their primary settlement, as I've observed, is in the high canopy. An assault on the shrine will be seen immediately. You'll be facing their full force."

"Let 'em come!" a one-eyed woman roared, slamming her fist on the table. "More skulls for the pit!"

"A direct, loud assault will draw their warriors down," Ravn continued, ignoring her, his mind a cold machine calculating the variables of a battle he found repulsive. "But it will be a concentrated defense at a single point, a bottleneck. A diversionary force, a smaller, faster group attacking the base of the world-tree from the north, could split their numbers. It would divide their attention between defending their home and defending their shrine. Their response will be fractured."

Jax's grin widened. "Fractured! I like that!" He clapped Ravn on the back with enough force to make him stumble. "See! The brainiac is good for something other than reading! He thinks like a hunter! He thinks like one of us!"

Ravn felt a wave of self-loathing so profound it was dizzying. He hadn't just handed them the map. He had just made their desecration more efficient, weaponizing his own intellect in the service of their barbarism.

Jax turned back to his warlords, his voice booming with absolute authority.

"You heard him! Grit, you take the fast-biters, you're the diversion! Hit 'em hard and pull 'em deep into the woods! The rest of us will hit the shrine and take the prize! We ride at dawn! And we will give their ghosts a new reason to cry!"

The journey began at dawn. The Grinder came to a halt with a deep, shuddering groan, its massive treads silencing for the first time in days, and the war party assembled in the pre-dawn gloom.

It was a chaotic muster of two dozen vehicles and nearly a hundred warriors, a mechanical beast preparing to uncoil. The air, usually just thick with the Grinder's exhaust, was now a cacophony of roaring engines, shouting men and women, and the distorted, pounding beat of scavenged music blasting from war-rig speakers. It was a rolling party of destruction, and Ravn was its guest of honor.

He was shoved into the cramped, rattling cab of a heavy transport truck driven by Grit. The hulking, scarred warrior shot him a look of pure contempt and spat a stream of brown juice that sizzled on the hot engine block. Spike, his other guard, climbed into the turret mounted on the roof, letting out a wild whoop as he racked the slide on a heavy-caliber machine gun.

The Stalker, sensing Ravn's terror, was a tense, glowing coil at his feet, a low, continuous growl rumbling in its chest.

The convoy roared out into the wasteland, leaving a wide, ugly scar on the rust-colored dunes. The noise was a physical assault. The heat from the exposed engines, the smell of unrefined ethanol and hot metal, the constant, bone-jarring rattle of the truck—it was a sensory overload designed to celebrate the glory of chaos.

Ravn stared out the reinforced window, watching the jagged landscape blur by, and felt like a prisoner being transported to his own execution.

"So, brainiac," Grit's voice boomed over the engine's roar, making Ravn jump. "What's a soft thing like you know about a fight?"

"I'm a scientist, not a soldier," Ravn said, his voice flat.

Grit laughed, a harsh, grating sound. "Heard that. So you think. But out here, everyone's a soldier. Or they're food." He gestured with his chin out the window. "See that ridge? Last cycle, we cornered a pack of Dust-Diggers there. Another tribe. Thought they could claim one of our wells." He grinned, revealing a row of stained, broken teeth. "They were wrong. Fought 'em for a day. Took their water, their fuel, and their scrap. That's the only law out here, scientist. The one who's left standing is the one who's right."

As if to prove his point, an outrider on a sleek, three-wheeled bike let out a whoop and swerved violently. Ahead of them, a small, six-legged Zone creature, its shell a beautiful pattern of iridescent blue, was skittering across the sand. It was harmless, a simple herbivore. The rider didn't slow. He accelerated, aiming directly for it.

Ravn watched in horror as the bike crushed the creature under its wheels, leaving a smear of indigo and shattered shell on the red dust. The rider laughed, raising a triumphant fist to the cheers of his fellow warriors.

This was the freedom Jax championed. A freedom from empathy, from restraint, from any law but the will to dominate.

Ravn fell into a state of cold, detached horror, his mind retreating to the sterile, logical cage he had built in The Bastion, the only place he could find refuge from the gleeful brutality around him. He contrasted this casual cruelty with the Husks' deep, spiritual reverence for all life, even the monstrous. He thought of the Legion's cold, non-malicious efficiency. They would have classified the creature, logged its position, and moved on. The Rust Lords killed it for fun. He felt utterly, profoundly alien, a man out of time and out of place.

They drove for a full day, a procession of noise and violence. As they neared the petrified forest, the landscape began to change. The red desert gave way to a cracked, gray plain, and the air grew still and cold.

The convoy slowed, the cacophony of engines and music dying down one by one, until an unnatural silence fell, a silence that felt heavier and more threatening than the noise had been.

Jax gave a sharp, cutting motion with his hand, and the convoy's engines died one by one, the sudden, profound silence a physical blow after the hours of engine roar. The Rust Lords, unaccustomed to quiet, grumbled as they dismounted, the clanking of their scrap-metal armor unnaturally loud in the still air.

"No horns," Jax's voice was a low, predatory growl that carried easily in the silence. "No engines. We go in quiet. We'll give the ghosts a proper surprise."

He moved through their ranks, his presence an immediate, intimidating force. He backhanded a warrior who had failed to muffle the clanking of a loose armor plate, the sound a sharp crack in the silence.

"Quiet," he hissed, his voice a low, predatory growl. "Or I'll give your throat to the ghosts myself."

The tribe fell into a tense, resentful silence, their chaotic energy now coiled and compressed, waiting to be unleashed. They were a pack of wolves, and Jax was their alpha, forcing them into a hunter's stalk.

Ravn and the Stalker followed them on foot into the Husk Graveyard.

It was a place of ancient, profound silence. Colossal, fossilized trees, their wood turned to pale, gray stone over centuries, stood like the bones of ancient, slumbering gods. Some were as tall as the skyscrapers of the Drowned City, their petrified branches reaching like skeletal fingers for a sky they no longer knew.

Strange, crystalline veins ran through the stone bark, catching the faint light of the three blue suns and refracting it into soft, ghostly rainbows that danced on the forest floor. The air was cold and still, and felt heavy with the weight of unspoken history.

The ground was carpeted in a delicate, fossilized moss that crunched under their heavy, careless boots, each footstep a desecration.

Jax led them deeper, his movements now surprisingly stealthy, his heavy axe held low. He was a predator in his element. He held up a hand, and the war party froze, melting into the shadows of the stone trees.

Through a gap in the petrified trunks, Ravn could see the shrine.

It was a small, natural grove where a perfect circle of the largest, most ancient petrified trees stood, their branches interlocking overhead to form the dome of a natural cathedral. The silence here was even deeper, a sacred, reverent hush.

In the very center of the circle was a single, massive tree, its fossilized heart exposed and polished smooth like a great, stone altar. Embedded within it was the key: a large, crystalline shard that pulsed with a soft, internal, golden light, casting a warm, gentle glow on the scene.

It looked like the living heart of this dead, petrified forest.

A dozen Husk warriors, their faces painted with white, ash-like symbols, stood in a silent, meditative vigil around the tree. They were not soldiers on guard; they were priests at prayer.

Their heads were bowed, and a low, melodic hum, a sound of pure, peaceful reverence, rose from their circle, a sound that was almost completely absorbed by the ancient stone. They were placing offerings of glowing moss and strange, beautiful, night-blooming flowers at the base of the tree, their movements slow, graceful, and utterly vulnerable.

They were completely unaware of the hundred armed killers hiding in the shadows just beyond their sacred circle.

"Beautiful," Jax whispered from behind Ravn, his voice filled not with awe, but with the gleeful hunger of a wolf watching a lamb. He raised his hand, his fingers slowly curling into a fist. Then he dropped it.

The silence was shattered by a single, deafening blast from a scavenged war horn, its dissonant, braying note a physical blow against the ancient quiet.

The Rust Lords charged into the sacred grove with a storm of fire and noise, their war cries a cacophony of joyous violence. Their heavy boots crushed the delicate, fossilized moss underfoot as they descended on the shrine like a tidal wave of scrap metal and fury.

The Husks, ripped from their meditation, reacted with a desperate, silent fury. They did not scream or shout. They simply moved, their bodies exploding into motion, their bone spears and chitinous blades a blur in the gloom. The melodic hum of their prayer was replaced by the grim, silent work of defending their holy place.

It was a clash of philosophies made manifest. The Rust Lords were a force of overwhelming, chaotic power. A warrior with a flamethrower cackled as he bathed one of the ancient, petrified trees in a torrent of liquid fire. The stone, thousands of years old, began to crack and pop in the intense heat, the delicate, crystalline veins within it exploding in a shower of glittering shards. It was an act of pure, senseless destruction, a joyous desecration.

The Husks, in contrast, were a force of silent, deadly grace. They did not meet the charge head-on. They melted into the shadows of the stone forest, using the terrain their ancestors had worshipped as a weapon.

A heavily armed Rust Lord, roaring as he charged, suddenly pitched forward and vanished, a cunningly disguised pitfall swallowing him whole. Another, aiming his rifle into the gloom, simply slumped to the ground without a sound, a tiny, feathered dart protruding from the soft flesh of his neck, his body convulsing from a silent, fast-acting paralytic poison.

Ravn was in the heart of it, a crude pulse rifle shoved into his hands, a non-combatant in a war between two faiths he could not accept. He scrambled for cover behind a fallen stone log, the air around him a hornet's nest of stray bullets and crackling energy bolts. The Stalker was a low, glowing shadow at his side, its body flattened to the ground, a continuous, terrified hiss rumbling in its chest.

From his vantage point, Ravn was a terrified observer, watching the two alien philosophies tear each other apart.

Jax was a whirlwind of joyous destruction, his double-bitted axe a blur of polished steel. He was not a commander directing from the rear; he was the glorious, brutal heart of the battle. He shattered a Husk's bone shield with a single, mighty blow, his booming laugh echoing off the stone trees as he kicked the warrior to the ground.

He was the embodiment of his creed: the exhilarating, destructive freedom of chaos.

But the Husks had their own champion. The Ascended warrior with the swirling, pearlescent eyes was a terrifying force of nature. He moved with an unnatural speed that the human eye could barely follow.

Ravn saw him take on three Rust Lords at once. He dodged a swing from a spiked club, the weapon shattering against the petrified tree behind him. He disarmed another warrior with a flick of his bone blade, sending a rifle flying. A third charged him, screaming, and the Ascended met him head-on, his chitinous skin deflecting a knife blade that would have killed a normal man. He was not just a warrior; he was an avatar of the Zone's own savage will to survive.

But for all their skill and grace, the Husks were outnumbered and outgunned. The Rust Lords' sheer, brutal force was a tide that could not be turned. They were sacrificing warriors, but they were gaining ground, their heavy boots trampling the sacred offerings of flowers and moss into a muddy paste. The line of Husk defenders around the central tree was thinning, their silent, desperate defense beginning to crumble.

Ravn watched in horror as Jax, flanked by Grit and a handful of his elite warriors, finally broke through. They stood before the great, central tree, the golden light of the crystalline key washing over their jeering, triumphant faces.

Jax raised his massive axe, his laughter echoing through the grove, ready to shatter the stone heart of the shrine and claim his prize.

He saw the key, its golden light pulsing in the heart of the great tree, a beacon in the swirling chaos of smoke and violence. He saw the small, desperate circle of Husk warriors defending it, their numbers dwindling, their silent fury no match for the Rust Lords' overwhelming force. And he saw Jax, laughing as he broke through their final line, raising his massive axe to shatter the stone heart of the shrine and claim his prize.

The world seemed to slow down, the frantic sounds of the battle fading into a dull, distant roar. Time itself seemed to hold its breath, waiting for him.

He was at a nexus, a single point in spacetime where a thousand possible futures branched out before him, and he had to choose one.

A cold, logical part of his mind, the same part that had calculated Caleb's chances of survival, screamed at him. Do nothing. Let Jax take the key. He will see you as loyal. You will be safe. This is the optimal path. Survival is the only variable that matters.

He saw that path laid out before him: a future of loud, empty chaos, of surviving day to day under the thumb of a charismatic tyrant, his own mind a tool to be used for plunder and desecration, the ghosts of his past growing louder and louder in the quiet moments until they finally consumed him.

Then, a flood of other memories—the inefficient, chaotic, human weight—crashed over him, shattering his cold calculations.

He saw Caleb's broken, sobbing form by the iridescent stream, a man left to die because of a percentage point. He felt the searing, stolen memory of Aethelburg, the Cherenkov blue light, the shriek of the alarm, the profound, silent connection of Lena's hand reaching for Aris's in the last moment of their existence. A connection he had failed to honor.

He saw Kaia's ancient, serene eyes, the quiet grace of the Husks who had captured him and offered him sanctuary instead of a cage, a people who, however alien, were dying to protect something they held sacred.

This wasn't a tactical decision. It wasn't about optimizing his own survival.

It was a moral one. It was a choice between the man his fear was turning him into, and a faint, flickering echo of the man he had once been.

He looked at Jax, who was the embodiment of joyful, selfish, destructive impulse. Then he looked at the Husks, who were willing to die for a belief. He had to choose which world he was willing to live in.

He raised the rifle. His hands were shaking, not with fear, but with the terrifying, liberating weight of a final, absolute choice.

He aimed at a leaking fuel tank on a nearby Rust Lord flamer vehicle that was spewing a torrent of fire onto the central tree.

He pulled the trigger.

The explosion was immense, a roaring fireball that engulfed the vehicle and threw the Rust Lord attack into disarray. A shockwave of heat and force ripped through the grove, knocking him and everyone nearby off their feet. Shrapnel whined through the air, and the screams of the warriors caught in the blast were sharp and terrible.

The chaotic assault was momentarily silenced by an even greater, more decisive chaos of his own making.

In the ensuing, ringing silence, Jax, his face blackened with soot, turned and roared in fury, not at the Husks, but directly at him. "TRAITOR!" The word was a definitive, damning sentence.

But before the Rust Lords could turn their rage on him, the Husks seized the opportunity. Led by the Ascended warrior, they fell upon the disorganized, disoriented convoy, not to slaughter, but to drive them back with a sudden, overwhelming ferocity.

The Ascended warrior moved with a speed Ravn could barely track. He ripped the crystalline key from the heart of the now-burning tree, the golden light of the artifact reflecting in his alien eyes.

He met Ravn's gaze across the smoking grove for a single, charged second. There was no warmth in his look, but there was a clear, sharp recognition—a debt acknowledged.

Then he and his soldiers melted back into the petrified woods, vanishing as quickly as they had appeared.

The Rust Lords, their assault broken, their prize stolen, and their leader incandescent with rage, retreated with a chorus of curses and threats, dragging their wounded with them.

Within minutes, Ravn was left alone in the smoking, desecrated grove, a sworn enemy of the only society that had taken him in.

The adrenaline began to fade, leaving him weak and trembling. He had done it. He had drawn a line in the sand. But now he was alone, stranded between the chaos that wanted him dead and the faith that had vanished with his prize.

Just as the cold, absolute reality of his choice began to settle, a figure emerged silently from between the fossilized trees.

It was the Ascended warrior. He stopped a few paces away, the golden, crystalline key held loosely in one hand. He was a silent, imposing figure in the smoky gloom.

He watched Ravn for a long moment with his unreadable eyes.

Then, without a word, he extended his other hand.

Ravn looked at the outstretched hand, then back at the ruin of the shrine, and finally toward the empty wasteland where the Rust Lords had vanished.

He had made his choice. Now, he had to live with it.

14

An Earned Companion

Ravn stood in the smoking, desecrated grove, the silence of the aftermath a ringing in his ears.

The Ascended warrior stood before him, a silent, imposing figure in the smoky gloom, his outstretched hand an undeniable, final term in the equation of the battle.

Ravn looked at the hand, then at the warrior's swirling, pearlescent eyes, which seemed to hold no discernible emotion—neither gratitude nor suspicion, only a deep, alien calm. Taking that hand was a step into a new and unknown world, a world whose most sacred rite was a form of beautiful, ecstatic self-destruction.

But turning away from it meant a return to the wasteland, where the rage of Jax and the cold logic of Rostova were both waiting for him. There was no path backward.

With a slow, weary exhalation of breath, Ravn took the warrior's hand. It was cool to the touch, the skin surprisingly smooth, with the faint, hard texture of thin chitin just beneath the surface.

The warrior's grip was firm, not aggressive, and he held it for a moment before giving a single, sharp nod. The debt was acknowledged. The pact was sealed.

He turned, and Ravn followed, the Stalker a silent, glowing shadow at his heels.

The journey back to the world-tree was a surreal and silent procession. The handful of surviving Husk warriors materialized from the shadows of the petrified forest, their movements fluid and silent. None of them spoke to him. None of them looked at him with any discernible emotion.

The rapturous joy he had seen during the ritual, the silent fury he had seen in the battle—it was all gone, replaced by a placid, unreadable calm. He was not treated like a prisoner. He was not bound or prodded.

He was simply... there, a strange, new piece of their ecosystem that they had not yet categorized.

He walked in their midst, but he was not one of them. He was a creature of metal and sharp edges, of gunpowder and cold, hard logic, and he could feel the immense, silent gulf between his nature and theirs.

The air was thick with the smell of burnt fuel and ozone from his own act of destruction, a scent that felt like a personal accusation in the clean, cold air of the petrified forest.

His mind, a machine that could not stop analyzing, tried to make sense of his new situation. He had made a choice. He had sided with the faith against the chaos. But what had he won? The Ascended warrior was carrying the crystalline key, the first piece of the puzzle that would lead him to the Anchor. He was closer to his goal than ever before, but it was in the hands of a people whose ultimate philosophy seemed to be the dissolution of the self.

How could he ask them for the key? How could he explain his mission to a people who saw his scientific worldview as a disease? His new alliance was a paradox. He had saved them only to, eventually, potentially have to betray them as well.

The weight of this realization settled on him, a cold and heavy thing.

They arrived at the base of the colossal world-tree. He looked up, his neck craning, at the canopy city hidden in the gloom far above. The last time he had been here, he had been a captive, dragged here against his will.

Now, he was returning as... what? A guest? An ally? A dangerous and unstable variable they had reluctantly brought into the heart of their home? He did not know. He only knew that he had drawn a line in the sand, and he had just willingly stepped across it.

The Ascended warrior pointed upward, and the silent, dizzying ascent began once more.

The ascent was different this time. Before, it had been a climb of terror and discovery. Now, it was a slow, solemn procession. As they reached the first of the woven platforms, Ravn saw the cost of the battle he had started.

The city was not celebrating a victory. The air, usually filled with a soft, melodic hum and the gentle sounds of life, was heavy with a mournful, low-frequency chant. He saw Husks tending to their wounded, applying poultices of glowing moss to deep, ugly wounds.

He saw a group of children huddled silently around a warrior who lay still, his skin pale, his bioluminescent patterns faded to a dull, lifeless gray.

He was the cause of this. His desperate, heretical act in his secret grotto had brought this violence, this death, to their peaceful home. The guilt was a physical weight, pressing down on his shoulders, making it hard to breathe.

His silent guides led him through the grieving city, their faces placid and unreadable. He was brought not to a prison, but back to Kaia's chamber, the open-air space woven from the ancient roots at the heart of the tree.

The Ascended warrior who had led him from the grove stood like a silent statue at the entrance, his new, alien eyes watching Ravn with an intensity that was impossible to interpret. Kaia sat in the center of the chamber, her own eyes closed in meditation.

She did not open them for a long time. Ravn stood before her, a prisoner awaiting his sentence, the heavy silence stretching his nerves taut.

Finally, she opened her eyes. They were not filled with anger, but with a deep, ancient sadness.

"The forest is wounded," she said, her voice a soft whisper that carried the weight of a storm. "We have lost kin to the Iron Blight. A pain that was brought into our heart." "I am sorry," Ravn said, the words feeling small and utterly inadequate. "I never intended—"

"Intent is a cage of the logical mind," Kaia interrupted, her voice gentle but firm. "It is a way to separate the cause from the effect, to absolve the self of the consequences of its own nature. Your nature, Physicist, is one of iron and sharp edges. You cannot help but cut the world around you." Ravn flinched as if struck. He had no defense. She was right.

"But," she continued, her gaze softening slightly, "an action can be more than its nature. The Iron Blight came, and you stood against it. You saw a choice between the cold, hard logic of your own survival and the life of another, and you chose another. An illogical, inefficient, and deeply human variable. You chose empathy." She rose with a fluid grace and walked toward him.

"The metal ones value logic. The scrap ones value freedom. Both are cages that separate them from the great song of the world. Empathy... empathy is the beginning of the path home. It is the thread that connects one life to another. You have shown that this thread still exists within you, buried beneath your fear and your logic." She stopped just before him, her shimmering eyes searching his.

"For that reason, you are not our enemy. But you cannot be one of us. Not as you are. You are a dissonant chord in our song. You think in a dead language. You see the world as a thing to be measured, not felt. You cannot walk our path until you can speak our language. And it is not a language of words." This was it, then. The judgment. He was to be an outcast, a tolerated but separate thing, forever an outsider.

"I am offering you a chance to learn," she said, as if reading his thoughts. "A chance to find a new translator. To build a bridge between your world of sharp edges and our world of life." She turned and gestured for him to follow her out of the chamber, her expression now unreadable, a mixture of hope and profound, solemn gravity.

"There is one who may be willing to teach you. But the choice must be his, and his alone. Come." She led him away from the central platforms, down a spiraling pathway he hadn't seen before, toward a more remote and secluded part of the canopy city. The ambient hum of the community faded behind them, replaced by the soft rustling of the colossal leaves and the strange, melodic calls of unseen canopy creatures.

The Husks they passed watched them with a new kind of reverence, their gazes shifting from Ravn to Kaia and back again, as if witnessing the beginning of a sacred ceremony.

They arrived at a place that felt older and wilder than the rest of the city. It was a grotto, a natural hollow in the side of the great tree's trunk, hidden behind a curtain of thick, silvery moss that cascaded down like a waterfall.

Kaia pushed the living curtain aside, and gestured for him to enter.

The air inside was cool and damp, and smelled of rich earth, wet stone, and something else—something musky, wild, and predatory.

The grotto was a place of serene, natural beauty. The only light came from the walls themselves, which were covered in a different kind of glowing moss, this one a soft, ethereal blue that grew in intricate, spiraling patterns reminiscent of a distant galaxy. The light reflected in a small, perfectly still pool of clear water at the center of the grotto, making it seem as if the stars were captured in the water's surface.

Curled beside the water, almost invisible in the deep shadows, was a creature that seemed to be carved from shadow and starlight.

At first, it was just a dark, sleek shape. Then it moved, lifting its head, and Ravn's breath caught in his throat.

It was a predator, powerfully built, with the sleek, fluid grace of a feline. But its skin was not fur; it was a smooth, dark, seamless chitin that seemed to absorb the blue light, giving it a soft, velvety sheen. Its feet ended in silent, obsidian-hard claws that were currently retracted but hinted at their lethal sharpness.

Along its spine and flanks, intricate, glowing patterns, the same color as the moss on the walls, pulsed with a soft, slow, rhythmic light, like a sleeping heartbeat.

It raised its head as they approached, and its eyes, when they opened, were intelligent, almond-shaped pools of liquid night.

It let out a low, guttural growl, a simple statement of deadly potential. The bioluminescent patterns on its body immediately shifted, their slow, gentle pulse replaced by a sharp, agitated flickering. Its muscles coiled, a silent promise of explosive speed.

Ravn instinctively took a step back, his hand moving toward the knife he no longer carried. The scientist in him was in awe, cataloging a magnificent apex predator he had never encountered. The survivor in him was screaming that he was in a cage with a monster.

"He feels your fear," Kaia said softly, her voice calm and steady, not moving from the entrance. "He feels the sharp edges of your logic. He smells the iron of your old world on you. It is a scent he has learned to associate with pain." "What is it?" Ravn whispered, his eyes locked on the creature.

"This is a Stalker," Kaia said, her voice filled with a deep reverence. "It is a child of the Zone, both hunter and guardian, spirit and flesh. We do not command them. We do not tame them. We walk with them, as equals. They are companions, but only to those they deem worthy." She looked at Ravn, her expression unreadable. "This is your test, Physicist. He is the language you must learn to speak. He is the bridge." "He is the bridge," Kaia said, her voice a soft echo in the grotto.

Then, with a final, lingering look at Ravn, she turned and slipped out through the curtain of moss, leaving him alone in the blue-lit chamber with the predator.

The silence that descended was thick and heavy, charged with a predatory tension. Ravn remained perfectly still, his heart a frantic drum against his ribs. The Stalker watched him from across the pool, its body a coiled spring of dark chitin and muscle, its low, guttural growl a constant warning in the quiet.

The bioluminescent patterns on its flanks were flickering rapidly now, a clear, agitated signal of hostility. He was trapped. One wrong move, one sign of aggression, and he knew the creature would cross the small space between them in a silent, lethal blur.

He had to calm it down. He had to calm himself down.

He fell back on his training, on the cold, rational protocols for dealing with a cornered, terrestrial predator. He made his movements slow, deliberate. He lowered himself to one knee, making himself smaller, less of a threat.

He avoided direct eye contact, keeping his gaze respectfully lowered to the mossy ground.

The Stalker was unmoved. Its growl deepened, a resonant vibration that he could feel in the stone floor. This world's animals did not follow the old rules.

He tried analysis. He subtly angled his wrist, trying to get a reading from the Aperture without making a threatening move. The data flickered into his vision, cold and unhelpful.

SPECIES: UNCATALOGUED. DESIGNATION: STALKER. THREAT LEVEL: 7 (LETHAL).

BIOMETRICS: ELEVATED ADRENAL RESPONSE. DOMINANT THREAT DISPLAY.

PROBABILITY OF ATTACK IF PROVOKED: 99.7%. The device's scan, a faint, almost imperceptible pulse of energy, was not as subtle as he had hoped. The Stalker's head snapped up, its almond-shaped eyes fixing on the Aperture.

The light on its skin flared, and it took a single, menacing step forward, its obsidian claws extending with a soft click on the stone.

The data was not helping; it was making things worse. The creature could sense the cold, analytical nature of the device. It could sense him trying to measure it.

He suppressed the urge to check the data again and moved to his next logical step. Appeasement.

He slowly reached into his pack and pulled out one of the pale, chalky tubers he had foraged. He placed it on the ground, pushing it gently across the moss toward the creature. A classic gesture of peace, a sign that he was a source of food, not a threat.

The Stalker didn't even glance at the offering. Its dark, intelligent eyes remained fixed on him, on the source of the fear, the logic, the cold, hard, and alien nature that was a poison in its world.

He had failed. All his logic, all his analysis, all his carefully considered procedures were useless. They were a barrier, a wall of cold science between him and this creature of pure, vibrant, and dangerous life.

He remembered Kaia's words, her gentle accusation that felt like a physical blow: *You see the world as a thing to be measured, not felt.*

He was still doing it. He was treating the Stalker like a problem to be solved, a variable to be controlled, and the creature knew it. He understood. This was not a test of his intellect. It was a test of his soul.

He had to let go. He had to surrender.

With a slow, deliberate movement that felt like the most dangerous thing he had ever done, he reached for the strap on his wrist. The Stalker's growl intensified as he moved, its body tensing. He ignored it. He unstrapped the Aperture.

The familiar weight on his arm vanished. He felt naked, vulnerable, stripped of his only advantage, his only connection to the logical world he understood. He was giving up his armor. He was giving up his mind.

He held the perfect, black dodecahedron in his palm for a moment, then placed it gently on the mossy ground. With an open hand, he pushed it across the floor, past the rejected offering of the tuber, until it came to a rest in the center of the grotto.

It was an offering of a different kind. An act of absolute trust. A gesture of surrender.

He remained on one knee, his head bowed, his hands open and resting on his thighs. He was defenseless. He waited for the end.

The growling stopped. The silence that followed was even more terrifying.

He heard a soft, almost inaudible padding sound on the stone. He didn't look up. He forced himself to remain still, to control the frantic tremor in his muscles.

He felt a presence before him, the warmth radiating from a living body. He felt a warm, strange puff of air as the creature exhaled against his cheek, its musky, alien scent filling his senses.

Then, he felt a gentle, heavy weight on his shoulder.

He slowly lifted his head. The Stalker was standing beside him, its head resting on his shoulder, its dark, liquid eyes looking at him with a calm, appraising intelligence. The agitated, flickering light on its skin had softened into a slow, steady, and welcoming blue-green pulse that seemed to sync with his own now-slowing heartbeat.

He had passed the test. He had spoken the language. He had been chosen.

He slowly raised a hand and, for the first time, placed it on the creature's smooth, chitinous flank.

It was not a scientist touching a specimen. It was a man, a lonely and broken man, finding his first, true anchor in a new and impossible world.

15

The First Hunt

The bond was a tentative, fragile thing, a silent thread of trust woven in a grotto. In the two cycles that followed, Ravn and the Stalker learned the strange, new rhythms of their coexistence. The creature was not a pet. It did not fetch or follow commands. It was a silent, ever-present observer, a shadow of dark chitin and soft, glowing light that trailed him through the canopy city.

It would watch him with its intelligent, almond-shaped eyes as he tried to make sense of this new world, its head tilted in a gesture of profound, animal curiosity. In turn, Ravn learned to read the subtle shifts in its bioluminescent patterns—the quick, agitated flicker that signaled a perceived threat, the slow, gentle pulse of contentment as it slept at the foot of his mossy bed.

They were two anomalies, a man of dead logic and a creature of living magic, learning to orbit each other.

On the third cycle, Kaia summoned him. This time, he was not led to her reverent chamber of roots, but to one of the large, gourd-like homes that housed the Husks' infirmary. The air inside was heavy with the scent of medicinal pollens and a low, mournful hum that was very different from the city's usual vibrant energy.

Several Husks were gathered around a sleeping mat. On it lay an elder, a warrior whose skin was a roadmap of ancient scars, but whose powerful frame was now frail and still.

Ravn saw the sickness immediately. All Husks possessed the faint, glowing patterns on their skin, a sign of their connection to the Zone's life-force. The elder's patterns were barely visible, a dim, stuttering flicker like a dying ember, and his skin was a pale, almost translucent gray.

His breathing was shallow, a faint whisper in the quiet room.

"He suffers from the Fading Light," Kaia said, her voice a low, sorrowful whisper. "It is a sickness of the spirit, a disconnection from the great song of the world. His light goes out. If it is not rekindled, he will be consumed by the silence." Ravn looked at the dying warrior, and for the first time, he felt not as an observer, but as a member of a community with a shared grief. "What can be done?" he asked.

"There is a cure," Kaia said, turning her ancient eyes to him. "A moss that holds the memory of light. The Husks call it Sun-Glow. It grows only in the deepest, darkest places, for it feeds not on the suns, but on the life-energy of the rock itself." She pointed on a small, woven map she carried. "It can only be found in the heart of the Whispering Caves." A ripple of unease passed through the other Husks in the room at the name. Ravn saw one of them unconsciously touch the glowing patterns on their own arm.

"The caves are a place of great power, and great danger," Kaia continued, her gaze fixed on Ravn. "It is a place of profound, unnatural silence." "Silence?" Ravn asked, confused. "This entire forest is silent to me."

"No," Kaia said, shaking her head. "You are deaf to the great song, but you are not deaf to the world. You hear with your ears, you see with your eyes. We... we are different. Our strength, our grace, our very sense of self comes from our connection to the song of the Zone. It is how we know where to walk, where to hunt, what to fear. The Whispering Caves have a strange resonance, a quality in the rock that absorbs the song completely. Inside, we are cut off. We are deaf and blind in a way you can never understand. We are as lost and afraid as your people were in the first days." She looked from Ravn to the Stalker, who had padded silently into the room and now stood at his side.

"But you... you are already deaf to the song. You do not rely on it. You rely on your logic, your senses, and your tools." She nodded toward the

Aperture on his wrist. "And he," she said, gesturing to the Stalker, "is a child of the Zone. Its silence will not blind him as it does us. He feels the world in a way we do not." The weight of her request settled on him. She was asking him to go to a place her own bravest warriors feared to tread. It was a mission only this strange, hybrid team—the man of dead logic and the creature of living magic—could accomplish.

It was his chance to repay their sanctuary. It was his first opportunity to act not for his own survival, but for the survival of another. It was a test.

"We'll go," Ravn said, his voice firm with a sense of purpose he hadn't felt in a very long time. He looked down at the Stalker. The creature seemed to understand, its bioluminescent patterns brightening into a steady, determined glow. They had a mission.

They left the canopy city with the silent, hopeful gazes of the entire Husk community on their backs. It was a heavy burden, the weight of a life entrusted to them.

The journey began with a slow, careful descent down the living trunk of the world-tree. This time, the climb felt different. It was no longer a terrifying ordeal, but a purposeful, methodical process. The Stalker moved ahead, a silent, fluid guide, its claws finding purchase with an easy confidence, its bioluminescent patterns a soft, reassuring beacon in the gloom.

Once on the forest floor, they followed the directions of Kaia's woven map, heading into a part of the Zone Ravn had never seen before. The landscape grew wilder, more aggressive. The fungal trees were larger, their caps casting the forest in a deeper, more permanent twilight. Strange, carnivorous plants, like pitcher plants the size of a man, lay in wait, their sweet, cloying scent a deadly perfume.

They paused for a brief rest near a stream of iridescent water. Ravn checked the Aperture for their bearings. The device hummed, its interface crisp and logical against the chaotic backdrop of the forest.

His eyes drifted to the corner of the display, to the locked file that had taunted him since the beginning: [ROOT].

He tapped the icon. A window flared open, filling his vision with complex, shifting fractals of encryption.

ACCESS DENIED. ENCRYPTION LEVEL: OMEGA.

Ravn frowned, his fingers dancing in the air, manipulating the holographic interface. He tried a brute-force decryption algorithm he had designed during the long nights in Valhalla's archives. The code slammed against the firewall like a moth against a lantern glass.

ACCESS DENIED.

He tried again, inputting a sequence of prime numbers derived from the Fibonacci spiral of the flawed pinecone.

ACCESS DENIED.

He lowered his hand, frustration bubbling in his chest. The file was a fortress, encrypted. It was sealed with a logic he couldn't yet parse.

It required a key, he realized, staring at the unyielding prompt. *A sequence or a unique biometric signature—perhaps Lena's or Aris's. The ultimate program was locked behind the ultimate human key.*

He closed the window. The mystery would have to wait. The mission was here.

It was in this more dangerous territory that their partnership was first truly tested. They came to a wide, deep chasm that was not on Kaia's map, a new wound in the earth.

The Stalker, who had been padding silently ahead, suddenly stopped, its entire body going rigid. A low, guttural growl, a sound of deep, instinctual warning, rumbled in its chest. Its glowing patterns, which had been a calm, steady blue-green, shifted to a sharp, agitated yellow. It stared into the chasm and refused to move.

Ravn approached the edge cautiously. He saw nothing. The chasm was about twenty meters across, its bottom lost in shadow. A thick, fallen log, slick with moss, formed a natural, if precarious, bridge to the other side. To his eyes, it was a simple, physical obstacle.

"What is it?" he whispered, placing a hand on the Stalker's flank. The creature's muscles were coiled as tight as a spring. It did not look at him, its dark, intelligent eyes fixed on the empty space above the chasm.

Trusting his companion's senses over his own, Ravn raised the Aperture.

He ran a standard scan. The device's display remained clear. No biological signatures detected. No anomalous energy readings. According to the data, the chasm was empty. But the Stalker's terror was real.

He remembered Kaia's words: *You see the world as a thing to be measured, not felt.* The Stalker was feeling something his instruments could not measure. He had to try to see the world as it did.

He accessed the Aperture's deeper settings, the raw sensor feed. He began to adjust the parameters, shifting the scanner's focus away from simple heat and energy and toward the strange, low-frequency resonance of the Zone's own life-force, a variable he was only just beginning to understand.

The display flickered, the image dissolving into static. He fine-tuned the frequency, and a new, ghostly image began to resolve.

The chasm was not empty.

It was filled with a colossal, shimmering, and almost perfectly transparent web. The strands, thick as his arm, were woven in an intricate, geometric pattern that stretched from one side of the chasm to the other. They were made of some kind of crystalline silk that did not reflect light in the normal spectrum.

It was a beautiful, deadly trap. And in the shadows at the bottom of the chasm, the Aperture now picked up the faint, cold bio-signatures of the massive, spider-like creatures that had spun it.

He looked from the terrifying image on his display to the Stalker. The creature was still staring at the web, its patterns now pulsing a deep, warning red. It had seen it all along, not with its eyes, but with some deeper, primal sense.

He felt a profound sense of respect. His technology had only confirmed what the Stalker's instinct already knew. They were a team. He was the analyst, and the Stalker was the sensor.

"Okay," he said softly, as if the creature could understand his words. "We find another way." He used the Aperture's topographical map to chart a new course, a long, difficult path around the head of the chasm. The Stalker led the way, its senses on high alert, a silent, living early-warning system. The bond between them, once a fragile, tentative thing, was now a tool, a weapon, a partnership forged in mutual trust and respect.

They were ready for the caves.

After another hour of navigating the treacherous, overgrown terrain, they arrived. The entrance to the Whispering Caves was a dark, jagged mouth in the side of a sheer cliff face, a wound in the rock that seemed to swallow the faint, ambient light of the forest.

A palpable cold emanated from the opening, a deep, unnatural chill that had nothing to do with the temperature. The air was still and dead. Even the ever-present, low-level hum of the Zone's life-force seemed to go silent here.

The Stalker stopped at the threshold, its body low to the ground, its bioluminescent patterns flickering with a nervous uncertainty. It looked from the dark opening back to Ravn, a low whine escaping its throat.

"I know," Ravn whispered, placing a reassuring hand on the creature's back. "Kaia said it would be like this." He took a deep breath, the cold air stinging his lungs, and stepped across the threshold, plunging from the dim twilight of the forest into a realm of absolute, suffocating blackness.

The darkness was a physical presence. It was a thick, velvety, and total absence of light that his eyes, no matter how long he waited, could not adjust to. He was instantly blinded, his sense of direction and distance completely erased. For a terrifying moment, he felt like he was floating in an infinite, empty void.

Then, the Stalker padded in behind him, and its soft, blue-green bioluminescence pushed back the oppressive gloom, carving out a small, lonely island of light in an ocean of black. The light seemed weak here, somehow dampened, its glow barely reaching the walls of the passage.

But the silence was the true horror. Kaia had called it a "psychic dead zone," and now he understood. The constant, low-level connection he had begun to feel to the world through his companion, the shared, instinctual sense of their surroundings, was gone. It had been severed the moment they stepped inside, as if a switch had been thrown.

He felt profoundly, utterly alone, even with the Stalker standing so close he could feel the warmth radiating from its body.

They moved forward, deeper into the cave. The acoustics of the place were a violation of physics. A small pebble he dislodged with his boot fell to the stone floor with no sound at all, as if the rock itself had absorbed the vibration completely. A moment later, a single drop of water from the high, unseen ceiling landed in a puddle, and the sound boomed and echoed as if a boulder had been dropped in a cathedral.

But the echoes were wrong. They came from in front of him, then behind him, then from both sides at once, a disorienting cacophony that made it impossible to get a sense of the chamber's size or shape. His own footsteps were a maddeningly inconsistent rhythm. One step would be completely silent, the next would boom and reverberate through the passage.

Keep this one. It's a strong thematic line. It was a place where the fundamental laws of sound propagation were broken, a place designed to drive a logical mind mad.

He was in a state of high alert, his senses straining, his scientific mind trying to find a rational explanation. Strange geological composition? Phase cancellations caused by the unique geometry of the rock? A localized temporal distortion affecting the speed of sound? The theories were useless. He was in a place where his primary sense for detecting danger— hearing—was being actively and maliciously deceived.

He was blind and deaf in a way that mattered more than sight or sound.

He stopped, holding up a hand. The Stalker froze beside him. They were deep inside now, the entrance long since swallowed by the darkness behind them. And in the profound, disorienting silence, he heard it. A new sound.

A faint, dry, chittering that seemed to come not from one direction, but from all directions at once, a sound like a thousand tiny, chitinous legs skittering across bare rock.

The Aperture's display, which had been mostly dark, flared to life with a swarm of crimson icons. Dozens of small, fast-moving biological signatures were converging on their position, emerging from a network of tunnels in the walls, the floor, and even the ceiling, tunnels he hadn't even been able to see in the gloom. They were surrounded.

The Stalker flattened itself to the ground, its bioluminescent patterns dimming to a bare, ghostly glow, a low, dangerous hiss escaping its throat.

Into their small, lonely island of light, the first of the Chittering Folk emerged.

It was a nightmare of evolution. It was the size of a large dog, its body a pale, almost translucent white, like something that had never seen the light. It moved on six, multi-jointed limbs that bent at impossible angles, allowing it to scuttle across the floor and up the wall with the same, jerky, stop-motion speed.

It had no eyes, its head a smooth, featureless dome of cartilage. But as it scented the air, its head split open vertically, unfurling a grotesque, flower-like maw filled with hundreds of needle-like, black teeth.

The first one was a scout. An instant later, dozens more poured out of the hidden tunnels, a pale, chittering tide of eyeless hunger that flowed across every surface.

"Back!" Ravn yelled, his voice sounding both too loud and too small in the disorienting space. "Back the way we came!" They began a desperate, fighting retreat through the winding, dark tunnels. The battle was a claustrophobic, terrifying chaos. Their greatest asset—the Stalker's light—was also their greatest liability. The soft, blue-green glow was the only thing that allowed them to see, but it also made them a perfect, solitary target in the absolute blackness, a beacon for the sound-hunting creatures.

The Stalker was a blur of dark, fluid motion at the center of the light. Its obsidian claws were a whirlwind of destruction, tearing through the pale, soft bodies of the Chittering Folk. Its powerful tail, tipped with a hard, bony spur, lashed out, crushing the creatures against the rock walls.

But for every one it killed, three more would take its place, swarming over their fallen kin, their needle-like teeth chittering with a mindless, voracious hunger.

Ravn fired his pulse rifle, the weapon's sharp, energetic crack a deafening roar in the strange acoustics of the cave. The blue bolt of energy vaporized the first three creatures in a flash of steam and foul-smelling smoke. But the sound of the blast, instead of scattering the swarm, seemed to excite it, attracting even more of them from the deeper, unexplored tunnels.

He was forced to use it sparingly, firing single, precise shots to clear a path or to blast a creature that had managed to leap onto the Stalker's back.

They were fighting not just the swarm, but the cave itself. The disorienting echoes made it impossible to tell where the next attack was coming from. The narrow, claustrophobic tunnels forced them into single file, preventing them from defending their flanks. The absolute darkness just beyond the Stalker's small circle of light was a constant, oppressive threat, a black curtain from which new horrors could emerge at any second.

The battle was taking its toll. Ravn felt a searing pain in his calf as one of the creatures, scuttling low to the ground, managed to bite him before the Stalker crushed it with a single, powerful stomp. The Stalker itself had several deep gashes in its dark, chitinous hide, its movements growing slightly slower, its bioluminescent patterns flickering with strain.

Ravn's energy pack for the rifle was running low, its indicator light blinking a cautionary amber. They were being overwhelmed. They couldn't outrun them, and they couldn't kill them all. He stumbled backward out of a narrow passage and into a much larger, open space. A vast cavern. It was their only chance.

"Here!" he shouted to the Stalker. "We make our stand here!" They were in a vast, open cavern, their backs to a solid wall of rock. But it was not a sanctuary. It was a kill box.

The chittering horde poured into the cavern from a half-dozen tunnels, their pale, eyeless forms a skittering, nightmarish tide that flowed across the floor and up the walls. The Stalker stood its ground, a low, furious growl rumbling in its chest, its glowing body the lonely, defiant epicenter of a closing circle of death.

There were too many to fight. For every one the Stalker tore apart, five more swarmed forward. Ravn's pulse rifle was nearly depleted, and every shot he fired only seemed to draw more of the creatures from the deeper recesses of the cave.

His mind, sharpened by a flood of pure, survival-driven adrenaline, raced, a high-speed processor searching for a variable he had missed, an exit to an equation that was rapidly resolving to zero.

He scanned the cavern with the Aperture, his eyes darting over the topographical data, ignoring the swarm of red [HOSTILE] icons that threatened to overwhelm his vision. He was looking for a flaw in the system, a weakness in the environment itself.

And then he saw it.

High above them, hanging from the cavern's ceiling like the tooth of a dead god, was a massive stalactite.

It was a colossal spear of stone, dozens of meters long and weighing hundreds of tons, and it was positioned directly above the main tunnel from which the majority of the Chittering Folk were emerging. The Aperture's structural analysis highlighted its base in a flashing, critical red.

[STRUCTURAL INTEGRITY: 4.7%. FRACTURE PROBABILITY (w/ KINETIC IMPACT): 98.2%]. A plan, desperate, loud, and suicidally risky, formed in his mind. It was a terrible gamble, a plan that required a level of communication and trust that he and his wild companion had not yet earned. But it was the only plan he had.

He moved to the Stalker's side, placing a hand on its flank. The creature was a tense, vibrating knot of fury and aggression.

"Listen to me," he said, knowing the words were useless. He had to make it understand. He pointed his small chemical light stick, its beam a thin, white line in the blue-green glow, up at a high, defensible ledge on the far side of the chamber, well away from the stalactite's projected impact zone. Then he pointed at the Stalker.

He was asking it to become a lure. To draw the entire swarm to a single point. To put its life in the hands of his aim.

The creature looked from the ledge, to the swarm, and then to him. Its intelligent, almond-shaped eyes seemed to search his own, looking for a certainty he did not feel. This was the ultimate test of the bond they had forged in the grotto. A test of faith.

For a heart-stopping second, it did nothing. Then, it gave a single, sharp nod of its sleek, dark head. It understood.

While Ravn braced himself, raising his pulse rifle and taking careful aim at the stalactite's base, the Stalker became a blur of motion.

It was a streak of shadow and light, leaping up the cavern wall with an impossible, gravity-defying agility, its obsidian claws finding purchase in the barest of cracks. It reached the high ledge and turned to face the swarm.

And then it let out a piercing, challenging shriek, a sound that was utterly alien to the chittering of the horde. It was a deliberate, defiant cry that echoed through the cavern, a singular, focused sound in a world of disorienting echoes.

The effect was instantaneous. Every single one of the eyeless creatures stopped its advance on Ravn and turned its head toward the source of the new, dominant sound. The entire pale, chittering tide of bodies changed course, scrambling over each other in a frenzy, flowing directly into the kill zone beneath the massive stone spear.

"Now," Ravn breathed.

He held his breath, the world narrowing to the glowing red target on the stalactite's base. He squeezed the trigger.

The pulse rifle bolt struck the rock with a deafening crack that shook the entire cavern. For a heart-stopping second, nothing happened.

Then, with a deep, grinding groan that seemed to come from the mountain itself, the massive stone spear tore free from the ceiling. It fell for a timeless, silent moment before crashing down onto the passage below with a cataclysmic, world-shaking impact.

A cloud of thick, gray dust exploded through the cavern, and the sound of a thousand, shattering bodies was mercifully lost in the roar of the rockslide. The tunnel was gone. The swarm was gone. The rest of the Chittering Folk, cut off from their prey, screeched in frustration before their chittering faded, retreating into the darkness.

Silence, profound and absolute, returned. The Stalker leaped gracefully back down to his side, its body battered and bleeding, but alive. They had survived.

In the now-quiet cavern, he saw it. A soft, gentle, golden light emanates from a small alcove now cleared of the swarm. The Sun-Glow moss. He walked toward it, his legs trembling, and carefully harvested the life-saving plant.

As he did, the Stalker nudged his hand with its head, its bioluminescent patterns shifting from the red of battle to a calm, steady, reassuring blue.

The fragile thread of trust had been forged in darkness and violence. It was now a bond. For the first time since he had lost everything, Ravn Vidar felt the profound, grounding weight of a companion at his side.

16

The Reality Tear

They returned to the canopy city not as a curiosity, but as heroes. Their arrival was met with a quiet, profound reverence from the Husks. The sight of Ravn, the strange man of iron and logic, carrying the sack of gently glowing Sun-Glow moss, and the Stalker, battered but alive at his side, was a powerful, symbolic image. They had journeyed into the silent dark where the Husks could not go and returned with the light of life.

Kaia met them at the entrance to the city, her ancient eyes filled with a deep, serene gratitude. She led them directly to the infirmary, where the elder warrior lay still, his own inner light fading into the final darkness.

The air in the gourd-like chamber was heavy with a mournful, humming chant. The ritual was simple and beautiful. Kaia took the Sun-Glow moss, its golden light a cheerful, living beacon in the gloom, and ground it into a luminescent paste using a smooth, stone mortar.

She mixed it with a single drop of her own blood, and then, with a touch as gentle as a falling leaf, she anointed the elder's forehead, chest, and hands with the glowing balm.

For a long moment, nothing happened. Then, the faint, flickering patterns on the elder's skin seemed to stabilize. A soft, warm, golden light began to spread from the points where Kaia had touched him, flowing through his veins like a revitalizing current. The stuttering rhythm of his bioluminescence grew stronger, steadier, until it pulsed with a calm, healthy beat.

A deep, shuddering breath racked his body, and his eyes fluttered open, no longer clouded with the gray film of the Fading Light. A collective sigh of relief and joy filled the chamber. Ravn had not just completed a task; he had saved a life. He had earned his place.

Later, as the city settled into its quiet, twilight rhythm, Kaia sought him out. She found him sitting with the Stalker at the edge of a platform, looking out over the vast, alien forest.

"You have a strong spirit, Physicist," she said, her voice a soft rustle beside him. "You faced the silence and were not consumed by it. You have proven that your way of seeing, though different, has its own power." Ravn said nothing, simply stroking the Stalker's smooth, dark flank. The creature, for its part, leaned into his touch, its own light a calm, steady pulse of contentment.

"Your bond with him is strong now," Kaia continued, watching them. "It has been forged in darkness and trust. You are ready for the next step. The world has need of you both." She led him back to the derelict observatory, back to the dusty chamber where the holographic map of the Fracture Zone still hung in the air, a silent, blue ghost of a dead science.

The journey was a strange one, a silent pilgrimage from the living heart of her world to the rusted, logical tomb of his. Inside the dome, she pointed a slender finger at the second of the three pulsing, golden lights on the map.

It was located in a region of the wasteland that the map labeled with a single, ominous tag: *Reality Tear.*

"The Unwoven Place," Kaia whispered, her voice losing some of its serenity, replaced by a note of profound, ancient awe. "It is a wound in the world, a place where the laws of your old world and the new have not yet settled their argument. Time does not flow straight there. The ground is not always solid. Your senses, the ones you trust so dearly, will lie to you." Ravn stared at the pulsing light, his own scientific curiosity warring with a deep, instinctual dread. "What is the key?"

"The key you seek there is a thing of perfect Order," she explained, her eyes fixed on the map. "A spinning cage of logic, a gyroscope of impossible, perfect motion. But it is imprisoned in a place of pure Chaos. To claim it, you must force a constant upon a variable that refuses to be solved. It is a dangerous paradox."

"And it's guarded," Ravn stated, recalling the legends he'd heard from Jax.

"It is," Kaia confirmed. "But not by a creature of flesh and blood like the ones in the caves. The Tear has a guardian, an Anomaly. It is a spirit of the chaos itself, a living piece of the Unwoven Place, a creature made of paradox and broken physics. It is a shard of a shattered mirror that reflects a world that should not be." She turned to him, her gaze seeming to pierce through to the new, crystalline lattice in his own eyes.

"Be careful, Ravn. Some things are not meant to be understood, only endured." He looked from the map to the Stalker at his side. The creature seemed to feel his resolve, its glowing patterns brightening. He had a mission, a map, and a companion he now trusted with his life. He was ready.

They journeyed for two days, leaving the vibrant, living territory of the Husks behind and venturing back into the desolate, rust-colored wastelands. The Stalker moved with a quiet, confident grace, its senses attuned to the familiar dangers of the open plains. Ravn followed, the Aperture's compass a steady, guiding line, his mind focused on the impossible, paradoxical mission ahead.

On the third day, the world began to change.

It started subtly. The air, usually clear and thin in the wasteland, began to shimmer with a faint, heat-haze distortion, even though a cold wind was blowing from the north. Sounds became unreliable; the crunch of Ravn's boots on the gravel would sometimes echo strangely, as if from a great distance, while at other times it would be swallowed completely, making no sound at all.

The Stalker sensed it first. The creature's calm, loping stride faltered. It stopped, its head raised, sniffing the air with a low, worried whine. Its bioluminescent patterns, usually a calm, steady blue-green, began to flicker erratically, shifting to a pale, uncertain yellow.

As they pressed forward, the phenomena grew more pronounced. They entered a field of shattered, black rock, and Ravn watched in stunned disbelief as a boulder the size of his head slowly lifted from the ground, bobbed in the air for a moment like a cork in water, and then drifted serenely to the west, following some invisible, private current of gravity.

The Stalker let out a guttural growl and gave the floating rocks a wide berth.

The light from the three blue suns, once a constant, oppressive source of cold twilight, began to bend and fracture as if passing through a flawed, celestial prism. Shifting, vibrant rainbows of impossible colors washed across the ground, making it difficult to judge distances and turning the desolate landscape into a disorienting, beautiful, and deeply nauseating funhouse.

Ravn's scientific mind, the part of him that clung to the immutable laws of physics, was screaming in protest. He used the Aperture to try and measure the phenomena, but the device was as confused as he was. The gravimetric sensors produced a stream of error messages. The light spectrometer returned impossible, contradictory readings. He was in a place where the universe's source code was not just broken, but actively and maliciously corrupted.

The final and most terrifying violation of reality came as they navigated a narrow pass between two jagged cliffs.

A grove of the familiar, sickly-green, pulsating trees stood before them. As they approached, the trees began to flicker. One moment they were solid and real; the next, they were translucent, ghostly afterimages; and then they vanished completely, leaving an empty space where they had been seconds before.

The Stalker let out a terrified yelp and flattened itself to the ground, its patterns now a frantic, warning red.

A moment later, the trees reappeared, not where they had been, but a dozen meters to the left, phasing back into reality with a sound like tearing static.

"It's okay," Ravn said, his voice a dry whisper, trying to soothe the terrified creature, though his own heart was hammering against his ribs. "It's just... a localized decoherence event."

The clinical words felt like a child's prayer against the dark.

He understood Kaia's warning now. This was a place where his logic, his greatest tool, was a liability. He could not analyze his way through this. He had to trust something older, more primal.

He put away the Aperture, knelt beside the Stalker, and placed a hand on its trembling flank. "You lead," he said.

The creature seemed to understand. It rose, and from that moment on, their roles were reversed. Ravn became the follower, his scientific certainty surrendered to the Stalker's pure, animal instinct. The creature guided them, its senses attuned to the wrongness of the world. It would shy away from patches of ground that looked solid but that it somehow knew were unstable. It would navigate by scent and some deeper, unknown sense, finding a safe path through the beautiful, deadly chaos.

Finally, they crested a final ridge and looked down. They had arrived at the heart of the Tear.

It was a shimmering, bowl-shaped canyon, where the air itself seemed to vibrate with a visible, chaotic energy. They had found the Unwoven Place.

They began their descent into the bowl-shaped canyon, the epicenter of the Unwoven Place.

The air grew thick and heavy, vibrating with a visible, chaotic energy that made Ravn's teeth ache and the crystalline lattice in his eyes shimmer with a painful, internal light. The ground beneath his feet felt unstable, shifting subtly as if he were walking on the deck of a ship in a heavy sea. The Stalker moved at his side, its body a tense, low crouch, every muscle coiled, a continuous, low growl rumbling in its chest.

As they reached the canyon floor, the surreal phenomena intensified to a terrifying crescendo. The shifting, prismatic rainbows were so bright they were almost blinding. The sound was a disorienting, atonal hum, the sound of a thousand different realities all vibrating at the wrong frequency.

And in the very center, there was a small island of impossible calm.

On a pedestal of what looked like shifting, slowly rearranging crystal, sat the second key.

It was a gyroscope of interlocking, golden rings, each one spinning silently and smoothly in a complex, counter-rotating pattern that seemed to defy the laws of friction and momentum. The rings wove through each other in a beautiful, non-Euclidean dance, a machine of perfect, perpetual motion.

It was a thing of absolute, unshakable Order, a perfect, logical constant in the heart of a maelstrom of pure Chaos.

As a physicist, Ravn was utterly mesmerized. It was the most beautiful, impossible machine he had ever seen. He took a step toward it, his hand reaching out instinctively, his scientific curiosity momentarily overriding all sense of caution.

The Stalker let out a sharp, warning bark.

The air in front of the pedestal began to shimmer, to coalesce. The atonal hum of the canyon focused into a single, sharp point. The fractured light and shifting rainbows seemed to pour into one spot, weaving together like threads of impossible color.

A figure began to form, coalescing out of the chaotic energy of the Tear itself.

It was the Anomaly.

It was a living mirage, a creature made of fractured light and shimmering, transparent crystal. It had no discernible features, no face, only a smooth, reflective surface that mirrored a distorted, broken version of Ravn, the Stalker, and the warped world around them.

It was a guardian that was a living reflection of the brokenness it guarded. It was a spirit of the chaos itself, a living paradox given form.

Ravn raised the Aperture, but the data stream was a cascade of nonsensical errors.

[ERROR: TARGET IS NON-EUCLIDEAN]

[ERROR: BIOLOGICAL SIGNATURE UNDEFINED]

[ERROR: TEMPORAL STATE UNSTABLE]

[ERROR: PARADOX DETECTED]

His tool of logic was useless against a creature that was a living violation of logic.

The Stalker, however, did not need data. It saw a threat.

It lowered its head, its obsidian claws extending and scraping against the crystalline ground, its bioluminescent patterns flaring a deep, defiant red. It let out a guttural roar, a primal, organic challenge to this thing of pure, abstract chaos.

The Anomaly did not react with a roar of its own. It simply shifted, its form de-rendering for a nanosecond, and then re-rendering a dozen meters closer to them, its every motion a silent, instantaneous glitch in spacetime.

The standoff was over.

The Stalker, a creature of pure, primal instinct, reacted first. It did not wait for a command. It saw a threat, and it lunged. It was a blur of dark chitin and fury, its obsidian claws extended, aimed directly at the shimmering center of the Anomaly's vaguely humanoid form. It was a perfect, lethal strike, delivered with all the explosive power of a coiled spring.

And it did nothing.

The Stalker passed directly through the Anomaly as if it were a projection of light, a harmless hologram. The creature's own momentum, meeting no resistance, sent it tumbling end over end, its claws scraping uselessly against the crystalline ground on the other side.

The Anomaly didn't even seem to notice. It hadn't phased or dodged. It had simply existed in a state where the physical laws that governed the Stalker's body did not apply to its own. Physicality was irrelevant.

Ravn's mind reeled at the impossibility of what he had just seen. If a physical attack was useless, then he had only one other option.

He raised his pulse rifle, his hands slick with sweat, and fired.

A bolt of coherent, super-heated plasma, a weapon capable of vaporizing steel, shot across the small space. It flew true, aimed directly at the creature's core. But as the bolt neared the Anomaly, it began to bend.

The air around the creature warped, the trajectory of the energy bolt curving in a perfect, graceful arc around the shimmering form, as if caught in a localized gravitational field. The bolt continued on its new path and slammed into the canyon wall far behind the creature, exploding in a shower of molten rock and searing blue light.

Technology was also irrelevant. They were facing a being that could casually rewrite the laws of physics in its immediate vicinity. They could not touch it. They could not harm it. The fight was over before it had even begun.

The Anomaly, which had been passive until now, seemed to finally register them as a mild annoyance. It did not lunge. It did not strike. It simply raised one of its shimmering, translucent arms, its fingers—if they could be called that—splayed in a gesture that was almost casual.

And the world twisted.

The ground beneath Ravn's feet ceased to be the ground. The fundamental law of gravity, the most constant and predictable force in his entire universe, was not just negated; it was inverted. He was falling, not down, but up, a horrifying, vertigo-inducing plummet toward the shimmering, rainbow-streaked sky.

The Stalker, caught in the same field, was a flailing, terrified shape of dark chitin beside him, its powerful limbs useless in a world without purchase.

He screamed, but the sound was swallowed by the atonal hum of the Tear.

His vision fractured, the world dissolving into an infinite, spinning kaleidoscope of shattering light and impossible colors. He was not just falling; he was being disassembled, his sensory inputs shredded into a meaningless stream of chaotic data.

He felt a single, surgical impact of impossible force against his chest. It was a pure, conceptual blow, the feeling of a law of physics being applied directly to his body like a weapon.

Then, nothing.

He awoke with a violent gasp, his body arching off the hard, crystalline ground.

The silent, conceptual impact was gone, but a phantom, echoing agony still resonated through his every cell. He sat up, his mind a maelstrom of confusion, and frantically checked himself for wounds. His hands ran over his chest, his arms, his legs, searching for the evidence of the impossible, reality-bending attack that had just annihilated him.

There was nothing. No wounds. His clothes weren't even torn. He was whole. He was alive.

The paradox of it, the stark, impossible contradiction between the perfect, high-fidelity memory of his own death and the undamaged state of his body, was a chasm of madness that threatened to swallow him whole.

He looked around, and the true, soul-crushing nature of his situation became horrifyingly clear.

He was back at the edge of the canyon, the same "safe" spot from which he had started. And the world was gray.

The vibrant, beautiful, and terrifying chaos of the Reality Tear was gone. The shimmering, rainbow-streaked air was now a flat, featureless gray static. The floating, crystalline rocks were dull, lifeless shapes, stripped of their prismatic glow. The atonal, vibrating hum of the Unwoven Place had been replaced by the familiar, grating silence of a dead world, a silence broken only by the sharp, glass-like crackle of his own movements.

He was Desynchronized.

The hollow, aching void in his chest, the physical sensation of a missing piece of his soul, was a familiar, soul-crushing presence. It was the undeniable proof of his own death, a wound that no physical healing could mend. The world was a leached, corrupted photograph of a reality he could no longer touch.

And he was alone.

He frantically scanned the gray, stuttering landscape for the comforting, blue-green glow of his companion.

The Stalker was nowhere in sight. It was not here with him in this purgatory. It was still back there, in the real world, in the vibrant, chaotic heart of the canyon, trapped with the impossible creature that had just executed him with a casual, god-like indifference.

He had failed. He was a ghost, trapped in a gray hell, and his only friend, his only anchor in this mad universe, was in the hands of a monster that could not be fought.

17

The Echo's Prison

He was on his knees at the edge of the canyon, the gray, dead reality pressing in on him. The horror of the Desynchronized State was a familiar poison, but this time, it was laced with a new, more potent despair.

He was a ghost in a gray hell, and he was utterly, completely alone.

The Stalker was gone.

The realization was a cold knife in his gut, a wound deeper and more terrifying than the hollow ache in his chest. His companion was still back there, in the real world, in the vibrant, chaotic heart of the canyon, trapped with the impossible creature that had just executed him with a casual, god-like indifference.

The cold, analytical part of his mind, the part that had survived for five years in exile, the part that had run the brutal calculus on Caleb, began to assert itself. It was a defense mechanism, a retreat into the sterile safety of logic in the face of an overwhelming emotional trauma.

Asset compromised, the voice in his head stated, its tone as flat and impersonal as a Legion report. The Stalker is a biological entity. Its probability of survival against a Class-7 reality-bending Anomaly is functionally zero. The asset is lost.

The logic was sound. It was irrefutable. The mission, as dictated by the Axiom, was to *Survive, Understand, Find the Heart.* The Stalker, for all its worth, was a tool, a variable that had proven useful but was ultimately expendable in service of the primary objective.

The optimal path was clear: cut his losses. Leave the asset behind. Continue the mission alone.

To re-enter the Tear, a place that had killed him with effortless ease, for a creature that was likely already dead, was not just risky. It was a statistical absurdity. It was illogical.

He tried to cling to that logic. He tried to force himself to stand, to turn his back on the canyon and walk away.

But he couldn't move.

Because another, newer part of him, a part he thought had died at Aethelburg and had only just begun to reawaken, was screaming in protest.

It was the part of him that remembered the quiet, profound trust in the grotto. The part that remembered the Stalker's warm, living presence on the long, lonely journey. The part that remembered their perfect, silent synergy as they navigated the invisible webs, his science and its instinct woven together.

The Stalker was not an asset. It was his anchor. It was the only living thing in this entire, broken universe that had chosen to walk with him.

The memory of Caleb's face, his eyes vacant with a despair of Ravn's own making, flashed in his mind. He had left a man to die for a percentage point. He had listened to his screams and called it logic.

He had survived, and the guilt had become a ghost that haunted his every waking moment. To leave the Stalker now would be a betrayal of the same magnitude. It would be a final, definitive surrender to the cold, soulless calculus that was his own worst demon.

He would be ensuring his own survival, but he would be losing what was left of his soul in the process.

He would not be that man again. He refused.

The mission had changed. *Survive.* Yes. *Understand.* Yes. *Find the Heart.* Yes. But now there was a new, overriding directive, one that came not from a cosmic entity, but from the fragile, flickering core of his own rediscovered humanity.

Leave no one behind.

The primary objective was no longer the key. It was a rescue mission. He had to go back in.

The decision settled over him, not with a sense of heroic resolve, but with a cold, quiet, and absolute terror. He was choosing to willingly walk back into the place that had just effortlessly erased him from existence.

He was a ghost, preparing to assault a god, to save the life of a friend.

He took a deep, shuddering breath of the thin, sterile, gray air, and turned to face the shimmering, dead canyon once more.

He began his descent back into the Unwoven Place. The air grew colder as he moved down the slope, and the grating, digital silence of the Desynchronized State deepened, as if the canyon were a psychic dead zone that swallowed even the corrupted sounds of this purgatorial reality.

The journey was a new kind of nightmare. The surreal phenomena of the Reality Tear, which had been disorienting but possessed a strange, chaotic beauty in the real world, were now just another layer of hostile, monochrome horror.

The rocks that had floated with a serene, dream-like grace were now jerky, unpredictable obstacles. They would hang motionless for a long moment, then lurch sideways with a sudden, silent speed, their movements the chaotic jitters of a crashed simulation.

He had to navigate the field of them with extreme care, his eyes constantly scanning for the next erratic movement, the Aperture's proximity alerts a constant, useless scream of data in his vision.

The flora that had phased in and out of existence was now an even greater threat. In the gray, flickering light, the trees and plants were often completely invisible, nothing more than a faint distortion in the air. He would be walking across a seemingly empty patch of ground, only to have a wall of solid, gray, crystalline thorns render into existence directly in his path, forcing him to recoil.

The world was a treacherous, shifting maze where the obstacles themselves were ghosts. And the Glimmers were everywhere.

The unstable, chaotic nature of the Tear seemed to act as a breeding ground for them. They drifted between the floating rocks and phased through the flickering trees, their shimmering, distorted forms a constant, menacing presence.

He moved with a practiced, desperate stealth, timing his movements to the stuttering pulse of the world's light, using the deep, information-less shadows cast by the lurching rocks for cover. He was a ghost, hunted by other ghosts, in the heart of a dying machine.

But this time, there was a difference. He was not just a victim. He was on a rescue mission.

The terror was a cold, constant presence, but beneath it was a bedrock of grim, unshakable resolve. He focused the Aperture's scanner, ignoring the constant stream of environmental error messages, and pushed it to search for a specific energy signature on a different dimensional plane.

He was looking for the faint, familiar, life-giving glow of his companion.

After a moment of scanning, he found it. A tiny, faint, but steady, blue-green pulse, a single point of warm, living color in his gray, dead world. It was the Stalker's bioluminescence. It was still alive. It was at the bottom of the canyon, and it wasn't moving.

The sight gave him a surge of desperate strength. He pushed forward with a new urgency, dodging a swarm of static-like Glimmers that would have sent him reeling, scrambling down the final, treacherous slope of the canyon with a reckless abandon born of pure purpose.

He reached the canyon floor, his body trembling with the strain of the journey. He had made it back to his own grave. He moved forward, his footsteps silent on the gray, crystalline dust, his gaze fixed on the center of the canyon where the faint, blue-green pulse of the Stalker's life-force glowed in his vision like a dying star.

The scene before him was a surreal and horrifying tableau, a piece of impossible, living sculpture carved from paradox and pain.

The Anomaly was there. It was not moving. It stood perfectly still, its form a horrifying anchor of stability in the faded, flickering world. Even in this gray reality, it retained a core of its crystalline structure, a shimmer of distorted light that seemed to bend the very static of the air around it.

It was not a ghost like him, or a Glimmer. It was a god, and this was its domain. And it was standing guard.

Next to it, shimmering like a heat-haze mirage, was his own Echo. The ghost of his spirit, a silent, looping recording of his own final, terrifying moments.

He watched, a cold, sick feeling of violation coiling in his gut, as the phantom of himself fell upwards, dissolved into a silent, screaming burst of light, and then reformed to repeat the sequence. It was a desecration of his memory, a wound in spacetime that refused to heal.

The Anomaly seemed to be watching it, its featureless, reflective surface mirroring the ghostly replay. Was it drawn to the spiritual energy? Was it keeping a trophy of its kill? Or did it even perceive the Echo in the same way he did? He didn't know.

But the most agonizing part of the scene was the one he could barely see.

Through the Aperture's dimensional scanner, the faint, blue-green signature of the Stalker was a crumpled shape on the ground in the "real" world, lying directly at the Anomaly's feet, between the guardian and the ghost.

Still not moving. He didn't know if it was unconscious, or wounded, or dead. The uncertainty was a separate torture all its own.

He was a ghost, facing a god that was guarding his own ghost, which was haunting the body of his only friend. The sheer, layered impossibility of the situation was enough to make his frayed mind snap.

He had to get to the Stalker. But to do that, he had to reclaim his Echo and become whole again. And to do that, he had to get past the Anomaly.

He knew from his last, fatal attempt that a direct approach was suicide. The creature was too fast, its power too absolute. He couldn't fight it. He couldn't outrun it.

He had to out-think it. He crouched behind a low, gray, crystalline outcrop, his mind racing, trying to formulate a new plan, a new variable for an unbeatable equation.

He was a ghost. He could not be harmed by physical force, but he also could not exert it. His only weapon was distraction. The creature had turned last time when he'd thrown the stones. It had reacted to sound. That was his only clue. That was his only hope.

He had a plan. It was a thin, desperate thing, a plan built on a single, unverified data point: the Anomaly reacted to sound.

He moved with a slow, painstaking stealth, a ghost creeping through his own grave, his gaze flicking between the stationary, shimmering form of the Anomaly and the looping, silent agony of his own Echo.

He found what he was looking for near the canyon wall: a loose pile of the same crystalline shards he had noticed on his previous, fatal attempt. They were gray and lifeless, but they would make a sound. It was his only weapon.

He gathered several of the larger, sharper pieces, their edges feeling unnaturally cold and solid in his phantom hands. He took a deep, steadying breath that wasn't really a breath and prepared himself. He had one chance. A window of only a few seconds.

With a desperate, silent prayer to a god of logic that no longer existed, he threw the shards with all his might.

They flew in a high arc, a spray of gray fragments against a gray sky, aimed at the far side of the canyon, as far as possible from his Echo. They struck the rock wall with a sharp, grating, glass-like sound, a violent tearing in the dead silence of the Desynchronized State.

The Anomaly reacted instantly. Its entire being dissolved into a shimmer of static and, in the same nanosecond, reappeared twenty meters away, standing next to the spot where the shards had shattered.

It had taken the bait.

It was the opening he needed. He burst from behind his cover and sprinted. His ghostly legs felt heavy and slow, as if he were running through deep water. The ground seemed to resist him, the distance to his Echo stretching out into an impossible, elastic infinity.

He pushed forward, his entire being focused on the single, horrifying goal ahead: the shimmering, heat-haze silhouette of himself, falling upwards in an endless, silent loop of death. He was running toward the epicenter of his own trauma.

He was meters away, his hand outstretched, his phantom fingers reaching for the shimmering form. He could feel the cold, psychic terror radiating from it, his own fear echoing back at him through time.

He ignored it. He was so close.

He lunged, a desperate, final push of will. His fingers grazed the shimmering form. For a fraction of a second, he felt it. A jolt of cold, a flicker of returning reality, the faintest whisper of color at the edge of his gray vision.

He was about to become whole.

In that exact instant, the Anomaly reappeared. It was back in its original position, standing directly before him with an impossible, silent speed.

He had not been fast enough.

He braced himself for the reality-bending attack, for the fall into the sky. But the Anomaly's attack was different this time. It was more precise.

Its crystalline arm, a blade of fractured light, moved with a surgical, contemptuous speed. It did not aim for him.

It aimed through him.

The arm phased harmlessly through the ghostly, insubstantial form of his Echo to strike the real, spiritual man behind it.

The creature had not been fooled. It had distinguished between the bait and the hunter.

The world twisted again, faster this time, more efficient. The fall into the sky. The kaleidoscope of shattering light. The single, conceptual impact of impossible force. And then, for the second time, nothing.

He awoke with another gasp, a ragged, desperate sound, his back slamming against the cold, crystalline ground.

He was at the edge of the canyon. Again. The same spot. The same gray, stuttering, dead world. The repetition was no longer just a strange phenomenon. It was a rule. It was a prison.

He didn't bother checking his body for wounds this time. He knew he was whole.

He also knew he was more broken than ever before.

The hollowness in his chest was a physical pain now, a gnawing, aching wound where a piece of his soul used to be. He felt thinner, more frayed, more translucent than the last time.

He held up a gray, phantom hand and could almost see the dead, gray landscape through it. He was a rope that had been unraveled and re-woven too many times, and with each violent re-threading, a few more essential fibers of his being had been lost.

How many more times could he be pruned from a timeline before there was nothing left to restore? A profound, soul-crushing despair, heavier and colder than anything he had ever known, settled over him. He had failed.

His desperate, selfless plan to save his friend, the one choice he had made that felt truly, fundamentally right, had failed.

The Anomaly was not just a guardian; it was a warden, a perfect, logical system designed to prevent his success. The Reality Tear was not just a location; it was a cell. And this gray, desynchronized purgatory was the solitary confinement ward.

He was trapped in a perfect, inescapable loop. He dies. He returns. He is a ghost. He tries again. He dies. He returns. It was a closed system with no exit, a recurring, computational error that had been quarantined.

He raised the Aperture, its flickering display a mirror of his own fractured spirit. He looked through the dimensional veil and saw the faint, blue-green signature of the Stalker. It was still there.

Still lying motionless at the feet of the Anomaly. The sight, which before had been a source of desperate hope, was now just a new and exquisite form of torture.

He was trapped here, a ghost forced to watch over the body of his only friend, separated by a barrier he could not break, unable to help, unable to leave, unable to die.

The Glimmers at the edge of the canyon seemed to watch him, their silent, shimmering forms a mocking audience to his private hell.

He sat at the edge of his purgatory, his head in his hands, utterly, completely defeated.

The universe had presented him with an equation he could not solve.

18

Anomalous Essence

Despair was a luxury he couldn't afford, yet it was the only thing he had in abundance.

Ravn sat at the edge of the gray canyon, his back against a cold, crystalline boulder that felt more like a solid block of static than stone.

He wasn't sure how long he had been there. Time in the Desynchronized State was a slippery, unreliable variable. It felt like days. It felt like seconds.

He had stopped counting the attempts after the twelfth death.

The cycle was always the same. He would descend. He would try a new tactic—stealth, speed, distraction, erratic movement. He had tried approaching from the cliff face. He had tried waiting for the Anomaly to turn. He had even tried screaming, a ghost howling at a machine, hoping to provoke a new reaction.

The result was always identical. The Anomaly would shift. The world would twist. He would fall into the sky. The conceptual blow would land. And he would wake up here, gasping, a little less of him returning each time.

He held up his hand. It was translucent now, a gray smudge against the darker gray of the sky. He could see the jagged outline of the canyon wall through his own palm.

He was fading. He was a signal losing its strength, a file that had been copied and compressed too many times, the data degrading with every iteration.

He knew, with a cold, mathematical certainty, that he had perhaps one or two attempts left before his consciousness simply failed to reboot. Before he became just another Glimmer, a mindless patch of static drifting in the wind.

He looked down into the canyon. The scene below was frozen in a horrific tableau. The Stalker lay crumpled in the real world, its blue-green light dim and pulsing with a weak, irregular rhythm. The Anomaly stood over it, motionless, a shimmering idol of broken physics. And next to it, the loop of his own death played out, over and over, a silent, mocking gif of his failure.

It's a closed system, he thought, the words drifting through his mind like smoke. *A perfect, infinite loop. There is no exit variable.*

But he was a scientist. Even here, at the end of his existence, stripped of his body and his hope, the core of who he was remained. He couldn't simply accept the result. He had to analyze the data. If he was going to fade into nothingness, he would do so knowing why he failed.

He forced himself to watch the Anomaly. Not with fear, but with the cold, detached scrutiny of a researcher observing a hostile organism under a microscope.

He watched it kill his Echo. Again. And again.

He looked for the pattern. Every system, no matter how complex, had a pattern. Every program had a syntax. Even chaos had rules.

He watched the Anomaly shift. It edited its position. It de-rendered at point A and re-rendered at point B. It was instantaneous.

No, he corrected himself. *Nothing is instantaneous. Not even light. There is always latency.*

He narrowed his eyes, focusing on the shimmering edge of the creature's form as it executed the kill stroke on his Echo.

He watched it ten times. Twenty. And then, on the twenty-first iteration, he saw it.

It was microscopic. A temporal hiccup that lasted for perhaps a nanosecond.

Just before the Anomaly struck, just before it bent the laws of gravity to send his Echo falling into the sky, its shimmering, chaotic form... solidified.

The fractured light coalesced. The shifting crystal stopped shifting. For that single, infinitesimal moment, the creature ceased to be a probability wave and became a particle.

It became real.

Ravn sat up straighter, the fog of despair clearing slightly. It made sense. To affect the physical world—to strike him, to grab the Stalker, to rewrite the local laws of physics—the Anomaly had to interact with the base code of reality. To write to the hard drive, the read/write head had to touch the platter. To execute the command, the processor had to commit to a state.

It was a vulnerability. A flaw in the god.

During that nanosecond of solidity, the Anomaly was bound by the laws of physics. It had mass. It had location. It was touchable. And if it was touchable, it was killable.

But the window was impossibly small. No human reflex could exploit it. He couldn't pull a trigger or throw a stone in a nanosecond. He was a ghost, anyway; he couldn't interact with it even if he timed it perfectly.

He needed a partner. He needed someone in the real world, someone with reflexes faster than a human, someone who could strike with the speed of pure instinct.

He looked at the crumpled form of the Stalker. It was alive, but barely. It was trapped in the same cage he was, separated by a dimensional veil. But they were bonded.

Kaia had said it: *He is the bridge.*

A desperate, terrifying plan formed in Ravn's mind. It required timing that would make a quantum synchronization look clumsy. It required him to die one last time, or perhaps something worse. But the equation had changed. It was no longer unsolvable.

He stood up. The gray world seemed to sharpen around him. He was fading, yes. But he was not gone yet. He had one last variable to play.

The plan hinged on communication. He had to tell the Stalker when to strike. But how could a ghost speak to the living?

He looked at the Aperture on his translucent wrist. In this gray reality, the device was a flickering, unstable mess, its interface a storm of static.

162

But it was still connected. It was a quantum device, designed to measure and interact with the very fabric of reality that was currently keeping them apart.

He raised his arm, his thumb hovering over the interface. He didn't try to send a voice message or a data transmission. Those complex signals would be scrambled by the dimensional barrier. He needed something simpler. A binary signal. On. Off.

He accessed the device's manual diagnostic tools and found the control for the haptic feedback engine—the small motor that made the device vibrate against the skin. He cranked the intensity to maximum.

He looked down through the dimensional veil at the crumpled form of the Stalker.

Please, he thought, a desperate prayer to a universe that had never listened before. *Feel this.*

He tapped out a rhythm. Three short pulses.

In the real world below, the Stalker's ear twitched.

Ravn's heart leapt. It had felt it. The Aperture, still strapped to his physical body somewhere in the ether, or perhaps resonating with the creature's own sensitivity to the Zone, had bridged the gap.

He tapped it again. Three short pulses.

The Stalker's head lifted slightly. Its bioluminescent patterns, which had been dim and fading, flared with a sudden, confused brightness. It looked around, its dark eyes searching the empty canyon. It couldn't see him, but it knew he was there.

Ravn tapped a new rhythm. One long pulse. Wait. One long pulse. Wait.

He watched as the creature struggled to its feet. It was battered, one of its legs favoring a deep gash, but the lethal grace was still there. It looked at the Anomaly, then seemed to look through it, scanning the air where Ravn stood in the gray world.

It let out a low, questioning whine. It was waiting for a command.

Ravn took a deep, steadying breath of the vacuum-thin air.

He moved into position, standing directly in front of the Anomaly in the gray world. He was the bait. He had to force the creature to solidify, to commit to killing him one last time. And in that single nanosecond of solidity, the Stalker had to strike.

He tapped the signal for "ready." A rapid, fluttery pulse.

The Stalker crouched, its muscles coiling, its obsidian claws extending into the dirt. It understood. It was a hunter, and it knew the rhythm of a trap.

The stage was set for a battle across two dimensions.

Ravn screamed. It was a soundless, psychic howl in the vacuum of the Desynchronized State, a projection of pure, suicidal intent.

He bent down and scooped up a handful of the gray crystalline gravel—the only weapon he had—and hurled it straight at the Anomaly's face.

The stones passed through the shimmering image without making a sound, but the intent landed. The Anomaly reacted.

It shifted, its form dissolving into static and, in the same nanosecond, reappeared directly in front of Ravn.

It raised its arm, the gesture that would rewrite gravity and send him falling into the sky.

Ravn didn't flinch. He didn't try to run. He stared directly into the featureless, reflective surface of the god-machine and waited for the glitch.

He saw the arm rise. He saw the air begin to warp, the gray static twisting into a vortex.

And then, he saw it. The microscopic stutter. The nanosecond where the probability wave collapsed. The Anomaly solidified.

NOW.

He slammed his thumb down on the Aperture's interface, sending a single, continuous, screaming pulse of haptic feedback.

In the real world, the Stalker exploded into motion. It launched itself with a force that cracked the stone beneath its feet. It was a streak of black lightning, aimed not at the shimmering ghost in its world, but at the exact point in empty space where the solid Anomaly stood in Ravn's.

The timing was perfect. Impossible.

The Stalker slammed into the Anomaly in the exact instant it became real. This time, it didn't pass through.

There was a sickening, thunderous sound like a hammer striking a bell underwater, a noise that transcended the barrier between the worlds.

The Anomaly shrieked, a sound not of vocal cords, but of tearing metal and scraping static that spanned both dimensions.

The impact threw the creature back, slamming it against the canyon wall. Its concentration broke. The gravity field around Ravn collapsed before it could fully form, dropping him to his knees.

He watched, mesmerized and terrified, as the battle unfolded.

The Stalker was a whirlwind of fury. It had pinned the Anomaly to the rock face. Its claws, which had found no purchase on light, were now tearing into the semi-solid, crystalline substance of the creature's body. Shards of glowing, unstable reality flew like sparks from a grinder.

The Anomaly thrashed, its form flickering violently between solid and intangible, trying to de-render, trying to escape the physical laws it was suddenly bound to. But the Stalker held on, its jaws clamped onto the creature's shoulder, anchoring it to the earth with the weight of pure, angry biology.

The Anomaly lashed out, a pulse of chaotic, violet energy exploding from its core. The shockwave threw the Stalker back a dozen meters. The companion hit the ground hard, rolling, but it was up in an instant, snarling, its bioluminescence flaring a defiant red.

The Anomaly was damaged. A massive, jagged crack ran down its torso, leaking a blinding, white light that spilled onto the canyon floor like liquid stars. It was unstable. It was vulnerable.

Ravn saw his own Echo, the looping ghost of his death, flicker and fade as the Anomaly's power waned. The loop was broken.

But the Anomaly was not dead. It was gathering itself for a final, cataclysmic discharge.

The air around it began to boil with violet energy, the static in the gray world rising to a deafening scream. It was going to wipe the canyon clean.

"Finish it!" Ravn screamed, though no one could hear him. He didn't need to speak.

The Stalker, sensing the build-up of energy, didn't retreat. It charged.

It leaped straight into the gathering storm of violet light, its claws extended for a final, killing stroke aimed at the glowing crack in the creature's chest.

There was a flash of blinding white light that obliterated the gray world, the real world, and everything in between.

The blinding white light faded, leaving spots dancing in Ravn's phantom vision.

He blinked, his gray, translucent hands trembling as he pushed himself up from the crystalline dust. The canyon was silent.

The atonal hum of the Reality Tear had ceased, replaced by the familiar, dead silence of the Desynchronized State.

He looked down into the canyon floor. The Anomaly was gone. In its place lay a pile of dull, gray shards, like a shattered mirror.

The Stalker lay nearby in the real world, its chest heaving, its biolumines-cence dim but steady. It was alive.

They had won.

But Ravn was dying.

The effort of the psychic scream, the strain of the connection, and the sheer time spent in this purgatory had taken their final toll. He tried to stand, but his legs gave way. He looked at his hands again; they were barely visible now, mere smudges of gray smoke against the landscape.

He could feel his consciousness unspooling, his memories becoming slippery and indistinct. The void in his chest was no longer a vacuum; it was an expanding event horizon, consuming what little was left of him.

He looked toward his Echo, the looping ghost of his own death. It was still there, shimmering faintly near the canyon wall. But it was too far. A hundred meters might as well have been a lightyear. He didn't have the strength to reach it.

He was going to fade here, a ghost in a dead machine, watching his friend survive alone.

Then he saw it.

Where the Anomaly had died, amidst the gray shards of its body, something was glowing.

It was a shard of crystal, but unlike everything else in this dead world, it possessed a light of its own. It pulsed with a soft, internal luminescence— not the blue of the Stalker or the green of the forest, but a shifting, prismatic light that contained every color of the spectrum at once.

It was the creature's core. Its Essence. A concentrated knot of raw, reality-bending energy that had survived the creature's destruction.

The Aperture on his wrist, flickering and dying along with him, flared with a final, desperate diagnostic.

[ANOMALOUS ENERGY SIGNATURE DETECTED]

[COMPATIBILITY: UNKNOWN]

[POTENTIAL STABILIZING AGENT]

It was a choice. A terrible, impossible choice. He could fade away, remaining human until the end. Or he could reach out and touch that alien light.

He could fill the void in his human soul with the essence of a monster.

He could survive, but he would be polluting his own fundamental nature. He would be patching his own code with a virus.

He looked at the Stalker, alone and wounded in the real world. He thought of Aris and Lena, trapped in the Anchor. He wasn't done. He couldn't be done.

He crawled. It was an agonizing, inch-by-inch struggle, his spirit dragging itself across the gray rock.

He reached the glowing shard. Up close, the light was mesmerizing and terrifying, a swirling nebula of impossible physics trapped in a crystal cage. He could feel the power radiating from it, a cold, chaotic fire.

"I am a variable," he whispered to the silence, his voice a fading breath. "And I will adapt."

He reached out and closed his translucent hand around the Essence.

The pain was absolute.

Not the physical agony of nerve endings firing; he had no nerves left in this gray, phantom state. It was a conceptual agony, the feeling of a square peg being forced into a round hole with the force of a collapsing star.

It was the sensation of his human soul, a thing of soft memories and fluid emotions, being soldered to a power source made of hard, broken physics.

The gray world didn't just fade away; it shattered. It exploded outwards in a shockwave of sensory overload that felt like being born and dying in the same instant.

He was back in his body, but his body was a stranger. His senses were screaming, his synapses firing with a voltage they were never designed to handle.

But amidst the chaos of reintegration, his mind was assaulted by something else.

The Essence he had absorbed acted as a prism, fracturing his perception of time and causality. For a single, terrifying second, he wasn't just on the canyon floor. He was everywhere.

He was standing on a balcony of white steel, looking out over a city of impossible, geometric perfection. The air was sterile and cold. Below him, thousands of people walked in perfect, synchronized lockstep, their faces blank, their minds united in a terrifying, peaceful silence. *Order.*

The vision ripped away. Now he was deep in a humid, suffocating jungle. The air was thick with spores. He felt a billion minds humming in a single, hive-mind chorus, a sensation of absolute belonging that erased his identity like a drop of water falling into the ocean. *Nature.*

Rip. He was gripping the wheel of a roaring machine, the smell of gasoline and rust filling his nose. The world was a blur of fire and speed, a chaotic, adrenaline-fueled race across a burning wasteland where only the strong survived. He felt a wild, nihilistic joy. *Chaos.*

Rip. He was floating in a void of streaming data, a digital heaven where bodies were obsolete. He was code. He was pure information, flowing through the veins of a god-machine, eternal and cold. *Information.*

These weren't dreams. They were potential futures, latent realities existing in a superposition of possibility, and he had just touched the raw stuff that they were made of. He had seen the paths he could take, the worlds he could create.

Then, the visions collapsed into a single, searing memory from his own past, triggered by the trauma of the integration.

The flash of futures was replaced by the flash of Aethelburg. The Cherenkov light was blinding. But this time, he wasn't watching Aris. He was feeling Lena.

He felt the heat of the reactor on her skin. He felt the vibration of the console under her fingers. And he felt her final thought as the light consumed her. It wasn't fear. It wasn't love.

It was a profound, icy regret. She was looking at the data, at the beautiful, destructive equation of the Axiom, and her final thought was a correction.

The variable, she thought, her mind dissolving into the cascade. *We forgot to carry the variable.*

The memory slammed shut.

Ravn gasped, arching his back, air rushing into his real, physical lungs with a desperate, rasping sound.

He was lying on the crystalline ground of the canyon floor. The Reality Tear was quiet. The floating rocks had fallen. The rainbows were gone. The world was stable.

He pushed himself up. His body felt heavy, solid, and incredibly powerful. The deep, cellular weariness that had plagued him for weeks was gone, replaced by a humming, electric vitality that buzzed in his veins like a trapped hornet.

He looked at his hands. They were solid. He was alive.

He turned to the Stalker. The creature was standing a few feet away, watching him. But it wasn't approaching. Its body was tense, its ears flattened against its skull. It let out a low, uncertain whine.

It didn't recognize him.

Ravn moved to a polished slab of black crystal that jutted from the canyon wall, moving with a fluid speed that surprised him. He looked at his reflection.

The face that stared back was his, gaunt and bearded, caked in dirt and dried blood. But the eyes... the eyes were a stranger's.

The warm, familiar hazel was gone. His irises were now a striking, unnatural structure—a complex, crystalline lattice that seemed to catch the ambient light and refract it into faint, shifting spectrums of blue and violet.

They glowed with a soft, internal luminescence, independent of the suns, the same light that had pulsed within the Essence.

He touched his face, his fingers trembling. He had filled the void. He had survived. But the price was staring back at him. He had taken a piece of the Zone inside himself, bonded it to his own soul.

He was no longer just a man. He was something new. Something adapted. A hybrid of the old world and the new.

He turned back to the Stalker and held out a hand. "It's me," he rasped, his voice rough and unused. "I'm still here."

The creature hesitated, sniffing the air. It could smell him, the familiar scent of the man it had bonded with. But it could also smell the ozone and static of the Anomaly, the scent of the thing they had just killed.

Slowly, cautiously, it stepped forward. It nudged his hand with its wet nose, then licked his palm. It accepted him. But the bioluminescent patterns on its skin remained a wary, flickering yellow.

Ravn looked down at the gyroscope key, now resting silently on its pedestal, the chaos around it tamed.

He picked it up. It was heavy, cold, and perfect.

He had the second key. He had a map to the third. And he had a new, terrifying power humming in his blood.

He was ready for the final leg of the journey. He was ready for the Drowned City.

19

The Sunken Archive

T he return from the Reality Tear was a silent, somber affair.
Ravn walked with a new, heavy tread, his boots crunching on
the gravel of the wasteland. He felt different. It wasn't just the
exhaustion of the ordeal or the lingering phantom pains of his multiple
deaths, though those were present, dull aches that echoed in his bones. It
was a fundamental shift in his physiology, a low-frequency hum of foreign
energy that vibrated in his marrow like a second heartbeat.

He stopped by a small, stagnant pool of rainwater gathered in the hollow
of a rock. The water was dark, slick with an oily sheen, but it was still
enough to serve as a mirror. He knelt, bracing himself with hands that felt
strange and new, and looked at his reflection.

The face that stared back was his—gaunt, bearded, caked in gray dust and
dried blood—but the eyes were a stranger's.

The warm hazel of his past was gone. His irises were now a striking,
unnatural structure—a complex, crystalline lattice that seemed to catch the
weak, diffuse light of the blue suns and refract it into shifting, microscopic
spectrums of violet and indigo. They glowed with a soft, internal luminescence, independent of the ambient light. They were beautiful. They were
monstrous. They were the eyes of a man who had looked into the source
code of a broken universe and blinked.

The change went deeper than the surface. His vision was sharper, laced with a faint, permanent overlay of geometric patterns that he couldn't blink away. He could see the heat rising from the stones in shimmering waves of infrared. He could see the magnetic field lines of the earth, faint, arcing ribbons of pale blue light stretching across the sky.

The Essence he had absorbed was not just a battery; it was a lens, forcing him to see the world not as a human, but as something more.

He closed his eyes, but the patterns remained, burned into his optic nerve.

He looked over at the Stalker. The creature was pacing a few meters away, its body tense, its ears flattened against its skull. It wouldn't come closer. Since he had absorbed the Essence, the bond between them had strained.

The Stalker, a creature of pure biology, could smell the singed air and static of the Anomaly on him, a scent of wrongness that no amount of wind could scrub away. It watched him with wary, confused eyes, its bioluminescence flickering between a calm blue and an agitated yellow.

He reached out a hand, and the creature flinched, a tiny, involuntary motion that broke his heart more than any physical wound could have.

"It's still me," he whispered, the words feeling heavy and rough in his mouth. "I promise." They returned to the observatory first, a necessary detour to reorient themselves. Kaia met them there, having traveled from the canopy city to await their return.

She stood in the dusty shadows of the dome, her ancient eyes widening slightly as she saw Ravn's face. She stepped forward, her gaze intense and searching, seeing the change not as a deformity, but as a mark of passage.

"The Zone gives, and it takes," she said softly, reaching up to gently touch the air near his face, sensing the energy radiating from him. "You walked into the fire, Physicist. And you did not burn. But you have been forged." "I had to," Ravn said, his voice rough. "It was the only way to survive. It was the only way to save him." He nodded toward the Stalker, who hovered at the edge of the room.

"Survival is a harsh master," Kaia agreed. She looked at the Stalker, sensing the distance between them. "He will learn to accept the new scent of your soul. But it will take time. Trust is a living thing; it can be wounded." She turned her attention to the great, brass orrery, still humming in the center of the room, projecting the map of the Fracture Zone. She pointed a slender, moss-woven finger at the final pulsing light.

It was located far to the south, in a region marked by a vast, dark depression in the topography.

"The final key," she said. "It lies here." "The Drowned City," Ravn said, recognizing the coordinates from his own pre-Fracture knowledge. "Oakhaven."

"It is a place of deep silence," Kaia warned, her voice dropping to a whisper. "The forest does not grow there. The beasts do not hunt there. It is a city asleep beneath a still, gray lake. A tomb for the ghost of pure Information. Be careful not to wake its dreams." Ravn looked at the map. Oakhaven. Before the Convergence, it had been a hub of data storage and server farms, a city built on the flow of digital information. It was fitting that the Key of Information would be buried there. It was a place of ghosts, and he was becoming more like a ghost himself every day.

"We leave now," Ravn said, turning from the map. He looked at the Stalker. "Are you with me?" The creature hesitated, looking at his glowing, alien eyes. Then, slowly, it stepped forward and nudged his hand with its wet nose. It was a tentative gesture, but it was enough. They were still a team, even if the terms of their partnership had changed.

They turned south, toward the silence of the drowned world.

They journeyed south, leaving the jagged peaks and the high, thin air of the observatory behind. The descent was a slow transition from the cold, sterile heights to a humid, oppressive lowlands where the air hung heavy and thick.

The landscape changed with every kilometer, the sharp rocks giving way to a sludgy, oil-slicked marshland where the ground sucked at their feet with a wet, rhythmic squelch.

The Stalker moved with a tense, low-to-the-ground posture, its claws clicking softly on the shattered pavement of what was once a highway. It was a raised causeway, a feat of pre-Fracture engineering that now served as a broken spine for the swamp, its concrete pillars cracked and wrapped in thick, choking vines.

The road surface was buckled and heaved, reclaimed by the aggressive flora, but the faded yellow lines were still visible, cracked and overgrown with slime, stretching out into the murky distance until they disappeared beneath the rising water.

Ravn walked behind the creature, his new eyes picking up heat signatures in the muck—small, burrowing things that scuttled away from their vibrations. He tried to focus on the mission, on the map to Oakhaven, but the sight of the road, stretching out like a memory, triggered something in him.

It wasn't a tactical thought or a scientific observation. It was a ghost.

He stopped, staring at the double yellow line.

Suddenly, the smell of rot and oil vanished, replaced by the scent of stale coffee and pine air freshener. The humidity on his skin evaporated, replaced by the cool, conditioned air of a climate control system. He felt the vibration of a steering wheel under his hands, not the grip of a pulse rifle.

He was driving a road just like this one, perhaps this very road, but the sky above was a brilliant, aching blue, devoid of alien suns or purple bruises. The trees rushing by were green pines, standing straight and tall, not black fungal nightmares.

Aris was in the passenger seat, his feet up on the dashboard, leaving a scuff mark on the plastic that Ravn would later scold him for. His brother had a laptop open on his lap, tapping furiously at the keys, a half-eaten bag of sunflower seeds balanced precariously on the console.

"It's spooky action at a distance, Ravn," Aris was saying, grinning around a mouthful of seeds, his eyes bright with the joy of the argument. "That's what Einstein called it. He hated it. But the math doesn't lie. Two particles, separated by a universe, but they still feel each other. Distance is an illusion. Separation is a lie." "Distance is a physical constant," Ravn heard his own voice reply, calm and pedantic, the voice of the man he used to be. "You can't just wave it away because the math is poetic."

"Poetry is just math with a soul," Aris laughed, tossing a seed shell out the open window.

Music was playing from the dashboard, a simple, weightless melody with a driving beat. The sun was warm through the windshield.

It wasn't a memory of a grand breakthrough or a terrible tragedy. It wasn't the flash of the Aethelburg reactor or the scream of the alarm. It was a memory of nothing important at all. Just a Tuesday afternoon drive to a conference they didn't want to attend.

The memory was so vivid, so painfully mundane, that for a moment, Ravn forgot to breathe.

The loss of Aethelburg was a sharp, stabbing wound, a trauma that defined him. But the loss of this—of the simple, boring, beautiful world where he could drive a car and argue with his brother about physics while the sun shone—was a dull, crushing weight that made his knees weak.

It was the realization that he hadn't just lost his brother; he had lost the entire context in which his brother existed.

He blinked, and the vision dissolved. The blue sky became purple. The green pines became black stumps. The music was replaced by the lonely lap of oily water against the ruined causeway.

He was back in the nightmare. Aris was gone, trapped in a crystal cage at the end of the world. And Ravn was a monster with crystal eyes, standing in a swamp.

He shook his head, physically dislodging the ghost, and forced himself to take a step. Separation was not a lie. In this world, it was the only truth he had left.

"Come on," he whispered to the empty road.

The Stalker looked back at him, its head tilted, sensing the sudden spike in his heart rate, the chemical scent of his grief. It let out a low, questioning whine. Ravn didn't answer. He just kept walking, following the yellow line down into the water.

They arrived at the city proper as the three blue suns began to dip below the jagged horizon, casting long, mournful shadows across the water.

The transition from the swamp to the metropolis was not marked by a sign or a wall, but by the changing shape of the horizon. The gnarled, organic silhouettes of the fungal trees gave way to the hard, vertical lines of shattered architecture.

Oakhaven was a necropolis.

The water level had risen dozens of meters since the Convergence, drowning the streets, the parks, and the smaller buildings completely. It was a world erased. Only the tallest towers remained, their steel and glass skeletons jutting from the murky water like the tombstones of a race of giants.

Some had collapsed against each other, forming rusted, precarious bridges. Others stood in solitary, defiant ruin, their glass facades shattered, their steel bones stripped bare by the wind and rain. Vines as thick as a man's leg strangled the structures, weaving through empty windows and hanging in ragged curtains from the upper floors, a green shroud for the dead city.

The silence was profound. It was not the tense, predatory silence of the jungle or the dead, vacuum-silence of the Reality Tear. This was the heavy, settling silence of a place where time had simply stopped.

There were no bird calls, no insect hum, no wind whistling through the girders. The water was perfectly still, a flat, gray mirror that reflected the bruised purple sky with a clarity that was almost dizzying. It felt less like a flooded city and more like a perfect, three-dimensional photograph of the end of the world.

Ravn stood on the end of the ruined causeway, the water lapping gently at the asphalt a few inches from his boots. He felt a deep, resonant sadness. This city had once been a hub of human achievement, a place of light and noise and commerce. Now, it was just a wet, rotting monument to failure.

The Aperture on his wrist chimed softly, a digital sound that seemed violently loud in the quiet. He brought up the scanner, and the display overlaid the ruins with a wireframe map of the pre-Fracture city. It was a ghost map, showing streets and subways that were now deep underwater. TARGET IDENTIFIED: OAKHAVEN MUNICIPAL DATA ARCHIVE. *LOCATION: SUB-LEVEL 4. STATUS: SUBMERGED.* He followed the guide, his eyes moving from the blue lines on his wrist to the dark shapes in the distance.

The target was a massive, brutalist structure in the city center, a concrete fortress of information designed to withstand bombs and earthquakes. It had not been designed to withstand the ocean.

It was almost completely underwater. Only the very top of its flat, concrete roof was visible, a dark, rectangular island in the middle of the gray lake, draped in a thick carpet of alien moss.

"It's down there," Ravn murmured, his voice flat.

The Stalker approached the edge of the water. It lowered its head, its nostrils flaring as it sniffed the surface. It recoiled instantly, letting out a sharp, disgusted hiss, shaking its head as if to clear the scent.

Ravn knelt beside it and activated the Aperture's chemical analyzer. He dipped the sensor probe into the water. The readout scrolled across his vision in a series of flashing red warnings.

WARNING: TOXICITY LEVELS CRITICAL. ANALYSIS: HEAVY METAL CONTAMINATION (LEAD, MERCURY, CADMIUM). BIOLOGICAL: UNKNOWN MICROBIAL PATHOGENS DETECTED.

LIFEFORM SCAN: MULTIPLE CLASS-4 AQUATIC PREDATORS DETECTED. He stared at the dark, oily water with a new horror. It wasn't just a flood; it was a chemical soup. The city's industrial runoff, its sewage, its chemical stockpiles—all of it had been released and concentrated in this stagnant basin.

To swim in it would be suicide. The toxins would burn his skin and poison his blood within minutes, and whatever "Class-4" horrors were swimming in the gloom below would finish the job.

He stood up, wiping his hand on his trousers. He needed a way to enter the archive without getting wet. He needed to part the Red Sea.

He scanned the surrounding area, pushing his new, crystalline eyes to their limit. He ignored the wireframe map and looked at the world as it was. He saw the thermal gradients rising from the water, the faint magnetic anomalies of the buried power grid. He was looking for infrastructure.

Oakhaven had been a marvel of engineering, built on a floodplain. It had to have flood controls.

He saw it a kilometer away, built into the side of a large hill that rose above the current water line. It was a massive, blocky structure of reinforced concrete, its intake pipes the size of subway tunnels vanishing into the lake. Faint, residual heat signatures, the ghost of a geothermal power source, radiated from its core.

"There," he said, pointing. "The pumping station. If the city's grid had a fail-safe, that's it."

It was a long shot. A desperate, engineering long shot. But if he could restart those pumps, if he could clear the water from the basin, he could walk to the archive's front door. It was the only way.

"We have to go around," he told the Stalker, turning away from the poisonous lake. "We have to wake the machine." Reaching the pumping station was a journey through a vertical labyrinth. With the streets drowned under ten meters of toxic sludge, the rooftops were the only safe ground.

Ravn and the Stalker moved across the skeletal remains of the city, leaping from one crumbling cornice to another. The Stalker moved with a fluid, predatory grace, its claws digging into the concrete to secure its landings.

Ravn followed, his movements heavier, less natural. But the Essence he had absorbed in the Reality Tear was surging in his blood, enhancing his strength and reflexes. He cleared gaps that would have been impossible for the man he was a week ago, his boots slamming onto wet gravel with a force that shook his bones. He was no longer just a man; he was an engine running on alien fuel.

They reached the pumping station, a massive, blocky fortress of rein-forced concrete built into the side of a hill that rose above the water line. It was a relic of the late-stage Anthropocene, a brute-force solution to a changing climate, designed to move millions of gallons of water against the will of gravity. Now, it was silent, a tomb of industry.

They stood before the main service entrance, a pair of heavy steel doors sealed tight by rust and time.

Ravn placed his hand on the locking wheel. He didn't need to hack it; the electronic lock had corroded into useless slag years ago. This was a problem of simple physics. Friction and mass.

He gripped the cold, wet metal of the wheel. He gritted his teeth, the muscles in his back coiling. He pushed. For a moment, the door refused to yield, the rust welding it shut.

Then, with a shriek of tearing metal that echoed across the silent lake like a scream, the seal broke. He spun the wheel, the mechanism grinding in protest, and shoved the heavy door open.

The smell hit him first—a dense, heavy odor of old grease, stale hydraulic fluid, and the damp, earthy scent of a cave.

They stepped inside. The interior was a cavernous space, a cathedral of pipes and turbines. The intake pipes were the size of subway tunnels, vanishing into the darkness of the floor. The turbines themselves were colossal, sleeping giants of steel and copper, silent and cold.

Catwalks crisscrossed the space high above, rusted spiderwebs in the gloom.

The Stalker whined, its bioluminescence dimming. It hated this place. It was a dead space, devoid of the Zone's life-force, yet filled with the heavy, looming presence of dormant power. It stayed close to Ravn's leg, its eyes darting to the shadows.

Ravn ignored the dread and focused on the problem. He climbed the metal stairs to the main control room, a glass-walled office that overlooked the turbine hall. The panels were dead, the analog gauges frozen at zero, covered in a thick layer of gray dust.

He began to trace the power conduits, his new vision allowing him to see the faint, ghostly path of the circuitry behind the metal panels. He followed the lines down through the floor, deeper into the facility's guts.

"The main reactor is dead," he muttered, his voice flat in the acoustic dead zone of the control room. "Fuel cells are spent. Decayed." He moved to a secondary panel, brushing away the dust to reveal the label: *EMERGENCY STARTUP / CAPACITOR BANK.*

He pried the panel open. Inside sat a row of massive, industrial capacitors, cylinders the size of oil drums designed to hold a massive electrical charge for a kick-start. He scanned them with the Aperture. They were intact. The seals were good. But they were empty. Drained by years of standby mode.

He needed a jump start. A massive, sudden jolt of energy to wake the sleeping giants.

He looked at the Aperture on his wrist. He had done this before, channeling energy into the radio slate and the orrery. But those were delicate, low-voltage systems. This was a piece of heavy industrial machinery. The current required to charge these capacitors would be immense. It would be like trying to start a freight train with a watch battery.

He checked the Aperture's energy reserves. *CAPACITY: 84%.*

It might be enough. Or it might drain the device completely, leaving him blind, mapless, and defenseless in the dark. Or worse, the feedback could fry the Aperture's delicate quantum circuitry, destroying the only key he had to the final door.

It was a terrible gamble. But the alternative was to turn back, to leave the key at the bottom of the toxic lake and accept defeat. And Ravn Vidar was done with defeat.

"Stand back," he warned the Stalker. The creature chuffed, backing away toward the door, sensing the build-up of tension in the air.

Ravn set to work. He found a coil of heavy-gauge copper cable in a maintenance locker. He stripped the ends using a sharp shard of scrap metal he found on the floor, his movements precise and frantic. He clamped one end to the main input bus of the capacitor bank.

The other end he fashioned into a crude interface loop.

He unstrapped the Aperture from his wrist. It felt impossibly heavy in his hand, a dense knot of potential. It wasn't just a battery; it was a conduit. It couldn't generate this much power on its own—it needed a source.

Ravn realized with a grim certainty that the source was him.

The Essence he had absorbed in the Reality Tear was a reservoir of raw energy, and the Aperture was the tap.

He grabbed the contacts. "Do it," he whispered. He pressed the port against the copper loop.

The effect was instantaneous. He didn't just feel heat; he felt his own cells withering, his muscle tissue metabolizing in a flash-fire of caloric burn to feed the machine. He screamed as the arc of electricity jumped, draining the vitality from his marrow.

80%... 60%...

He was pouring his own life into the copper. His vision blurred, gray spots dancing in the ozone-filled air.

40%...

The device was drinking him dry. "Come on," he growled, his voice a dry rasp, his skin turning gray and papery. "Wake up." *20%...*

A series of heavy, mechanical clunks echoed from the turbine floor. Relays were engaging. The sleeping giants were stirring.

10%... SYSTEM SHUTDOWN IMMINENT.

"Enough!" Ravn shouted, though it came out as a wheeze.

He yanked the Aperture free, collapsing against the console as the connection broke.

For a second, there was silence. Then, a deep, rising whine filled the station. The lights on the control panel flickered, then blazed to life. The analog needles on the gauges jumped.

[STARTUP SEQUENCE INITIATED]

Down in the hall, the massive turbines began to spin. It started as a groan, then a rumble, and finally a deafening, earth-shaking roar. The floor vibrated violently. Dust that had settled for five years danced into the air.

The pumps were running.

Ravn scrambled for the Aperture. He tapped the screen. Nothing. He tapped it again, his heart hammering. Please.

The screen flickered. The logo spun. Then, the interface returned.

ENERGY RESERVES: 4% (CRITICAL). RECHARGE MODE: ACTIVE.

It was alive. He let out a breath he didn't know he was holding and slumped against the console. He had risked everything, and he had won.

Now, he just had to watch the water fall.

The pumping station roared. It was a deafening, mechanical symphony that seemed to vibrate in the very marrow of Ravn's bones. The ancient pumps, built to last a thousand years and silent for five, had engaged with a series of earth-shaking clangs, and now they were screaming in triumph.

Ravn slumped against the console, cradling his burned hand, his chest heaving. The Aperture was warm against his skin, drinking in the ambient static of the station to slowly rebuild its charge. It had survived. He had survived.

He pulled himself up and limped to the observation window, wiping away a layer of grime with his sleeve.

Outside, the world was changing. The placid, gray mirror of the toxic lake was gone, shattered by a violence of hydrodynamics.

In the center of the submerged city, a massive vortex had formed, a swirling, hungry mouth of sludge and debris that rotated with a terrifying speed. The water was being sucked down, drawn into the city's massive subterranean reservoirs and outflow channels with a force that made the submerged skyscrapers groan.

The water level began to drop. It wasn't fast—this was a volume of water measured in gigatons—but it was visible. It was a reverse deluge, a resurrection of the drowned.

Ravn watched, mesmerized. He saw the upper floors of office buildings emerge from the murky depths, water cascading from their broken windows like a thousand weeping eyes. He saw the rusted skeletons of transmission towers break the surface, draped in heavy curtains of slimy, black algae. He saw cars, trapped for years in the silt, tumble and roll as the currents shifted, tumbling down into the darkening streets.

The Stalker paced nervously behind him, whining at the noise, its claws clicking on the metal grating. It hated this place. It hated the noise, the smell of hot grease, the sheer, overwhelming weight of the machinery. To the creature, this wasn't a triumph of engineering; it was the awakening of a sleeping beast.

Hours passed. The three blue suns dipped below the horizon, and the violet gloom deepened into night. The only light came from the sparks spitting from the station's overworked generators and the faint, bioluminescent glow of the dying aquatic life stranded on the emerging rooftops.

Finally, the roar of the pumps changed pitch, shifting from a strained scream to a steady, rhythmic thrum. The bulk of the work was done.

Ravn looked out. The lake was gone. In its place was a vast, muddy basin, a nightmare landscape of slime-coated ruins and drying mud. The city of

Oakhaven had been reclaimed, but it was not the clean, gleaming city of the past. It was a corpse that had been dredged from the deep, bloated and covered in rot.

But the path was clear.

In the center of the basin, the Municipal Data Archive stood revealed. It was a dark, windowless monolith of concrete, stripped of its water camouflage. The toxic soup had been drained away, leaving a carpet of treacherous mud around its base.

And at the bottom of the structure, a wide, sealed blast door, once hidden deep beneath the surface, was now accessible. It was wet, rusted, and imposing, a gate to the underworld.

"It's open," Ravn whispered, his voice cracking. He turned from the window. "We're done here." Leaving the roaring station felt like stepping out of a hurricane. They descended from the hill, navigating the newly exposed landscape. The going was difficult; the streets were choked with ten feet of mud and debris.

They had to stick to the high ground, leaping from the roofs of lower buildings, traversing makeshift bridges of fallen debris. The smell was atrocious—the stench of a billion decaying organisms exposed to the air for the first time in years.

They reached the plaza in front of the Archive. But they were not the first to arrive. Scattered across the stone slabs in front of the blast door were three bodies. They were Legion tech-specialists, their gray armor scorched and blackened. A heavy-duty plasma drill lay abandoned nearby, its bit fused into a lump of slag against the door's surface.

Ravn knelt by one of the corpses. The soldier's faceplate was shattered, his expression frozen in a rictus of agony. "They tried to force it," Ravn whispered.

He ran his hand over the blast door. The metal was still warm. "They tried to cut through the lock logic with heat." The Archive's automated defense protocols hadn't shot them; the door had simply fed their own energy back into them. A feedback loop. "They didn't have the key," Ravn said to the Stalker. "They thought it was a vault. They didn't know it was a question."

He could feel the hum of the facility's internal power, a faint vibration that told him the archive was not dead. It was waiting.

He looked at the Stalker. The creature was shivering slightly, its blue-green light reflecting off the puddles of toxic slime. It looked at the door, then at Ravn, its eyes filled with a deep, animal mistrust.

"One more," Ravn said, patting its flank. "One more key. Then we find the Anchor. Then we fix this."

He didn't know if he believed it anymore. The "fix" felt further away than ever. But he had the map, he had the will, and he had the door.

He reached for the manual release lever of the blast door. It was stiff, frozen by corrosion. He gritted his teeth, the Essence in his veins flaring, granting him the strength to force the metal to yield.

With a shriek of protesting steel that echoed through the silent, muddy city, the wheel turned.

The blast door groaned and began to slide upward, revealing a mouth of absolute darkness that smelled of dry paper and dust.

Ravn switched on the Aperture's flashlight function, casting a clean, white beam into the gloom.

He stepped across the threshold, the Stalker a reluctant shadow at his heels.

They were leaving the world of mud and rot and entering the tomb of pure information. The final test had begun.

20

The Informational Constant

T
he manual release wheel shrieked, a banshee wail of metal shearing against years of accumulated rust, before finally surrendering. With a deep, shuddering groan that vibrated through the soles of Ravn's boots, the massive blast door began to rise.

It jerked and rattled, fighting the gravity of its own weight, shedding flakes of rust and dried mud like old skin. As the gap widened, a gust of air rushed out from the darkness within.

It smelled of dry paper, and stagnant, recirculated dust. It was the smell of a tomb that had been sealed tight against the apocalypse, a breath of air exhaled from a world that had been dead for five years.

Ravn clicked on the flashlight function of the Aperture. A beam of clean, clinical white light cut through the gloom, dancing with the motes of dust that had been disturbed for the first time in half a decade.

"Stay close," he whispered to the Stalker, his voice sounding unnaturally loud in the stillness.

He stepped across the threshold. His boots, caked in the toxic sludge of the lakebed, left thick, black smears on the pristine white tiles of the atrium floor. It felt like a violation, a muddy footprint on a shroud.

The lobby of the Oakhaven Municipal Data Archive was a frozen tableau of the moment the world ended. The reception desk, a sleek curve of polished polymer, was unmanned, a coffee mug sitting next to a dead terminal, the liquid inside evaporated into a dark stain. Rows of waiting area chairs sat in neat, orderly lines, some overturned as if their occupants had left in a hurry, others still perfectly aligned.

It was a ghost town, but not of people. It was a ghost town of bureaucracy.

The Stalker followed him inside, but it moved with a profound reluctance. Its obsidian claws clicked softly on the tile, a nervous, skittering rhythm. Its bioluminescent patterns, usually a calm blue or a wary yellow, had dimmed to a ghostly, barely-there gray.

It whined low in its throat, a sound of deep, instinctual revulsion.

To the creature, a child of the vibrant, chaotic, and interconnected Zone, this place was an abomination. It was a dead space. There was no biological hum, no mycelial network singing in the walls, no scent of prey or predator.

It was a vacuum of life. Yet, it hummed with a ghostly energy that the Stalker could sense but not understand—the latent potential of petabytes of sleeping data, the silent scream of a billion frozen thoughts. The creature pressed its side against Ravn's leg, seeking a physical anchor in this sea of dead conceptual space.

Ravn ran his hand along the reception desk. His finger came away coated in a thick layer of gray dust. He felt a strange, hollow sadness. The petrified forest had been tragic, a natural beauty frozen in stone. But this... this was tragic in a mundane, human way. This was where people had come to file permits, to look up birth records, to pay fines. It was the banal machinery of civilization, halted mid-cycle.

He checked the Aperture. The signal from the third key was strong here, a steady, rhythmic pulse that seemed to sync with the new, alien thrum in his own blood.

TARGET DETECTED: KEY_GAMMA. PROXIMITY: 400 METERS (VERTICAL OFFSET). STATUS: DORMANT. The signal wasn't coming from this level. It was pulling him down.

"We have to go deeper," Ravn said, his voice flat.

The emergency lights, triggered by the sudden influx of power from the pumping station Ravn had reactivated, flickered to life with a reluctant, buzzing hum. They cast the atrium in a stark, flickering, hospital-white light that was aggressive and harsh after weeks of the Zone's soft, bioluminescent twilight.

The shadows jumped and twitched. The Stalker hissed at the lights, snapping its jaws at a flickering bulb.

"It's okay," Ravn said, though he didn't feel okay. The facility felt like it was waking up, but it wasn't waking up like a living thing. It was waking up like a zombie, a reanimated corpse of steel and silicon shuffling through its old routines.

He looked toward the bank of elevators. They were dead, their doors pried open to reveal empty shafts plunging into the dark. Beside them was a heavy door marked *STAIRWELL ACCESS*.

He pushed it open. The air that drifted up was colder, smelling of concrete and deep earth.

"Down," he said to the Stalker.

They began their descent into the underworld of information, leaving the muddy footprints of the new world on the clean, dead floor of the old. The stairwell was a spiraling helix of steel and reinforced glass, a spinal cord connecting the brain of the city to its body.

The air grew colder with every step, the temperature dropping from the cool, stale air of the lobby to a chill that seeped into Ravn's bones. The emergency lights flickered to life in a staggered, reluctant wave ahead of them, casting the stairwell in a stark, clinical white light.

Ravn's boots clanged on the metal grates, the sound echoing up and down the shaft like a dropped coin in a well. The Stalker moved silently, its claws retracting to pads, but its distress was palpable. It pressed close to the wall, as far from the open drop of the central shaft as possible.

They reached the first landing. A heavy fire door, propped open by a rusted wedge, revealed the expanse of Level 1: Civil Registry & Public Records.

Ravn paused, drawn by a morbid curiosity. He stepped through the doorway into a vast, open-plan office filled with rows of silent, black obelisks—server racks dedicated solely to the bureaucracy of existence.

Placards on the walls, their typography clean and optimistic, labeled the zones: *Birth Certificates. Marriage Licenses. Property Deeds. Census Data.*

It was the administrative DNA of a civilization. Here, in these silent machines, were the digital ghosts of millions of people. Their loves, their homes, their children, their debts—all reduced to binary code, stored in a tomb designed to withstand a nuclear war but not a reality collapse.

Ravn looked at the servers with his new, crystalline eyes. He could see the faint, residual magnetic fields clinging to the drives, a ghostly aura of latent information. It was a graveyard, but there were no bodies, only names. It was a tragedy of profound, mundane silence.

They continued down. Level 2: Cultural Heritage & Media. The atmosphere here was different. The walls were lined with dead holographic projectors that would have once displayed art, history, and music. Now, they were dark, gray mirrors.

This floor held the collective memory of Oakhaven's art, literature, and news. Ravn imagined the petabytes of music, the libraries of novels, the thousands of hours of news footage documenting the slow, creeping rise of the sea levels before the Convergence changed the rules of the game.

He felt a sharp pang of loss. People died. That was a biological constant. But art... art was supposed to outlive the artist. Here, it was trapped in a coffin of silicon, unobserved and unremembered. Without an observer, did the art still exist? Or was it just magnetic patterns in the dark?

The Stalker let out a low, warning growl, snapping Ravn out of his reverie. The creature was staring down the stairwell, its ears swiveled forward. It smelled something deep below. Not a predator—the scanner was clear—but something heavy.

They descended to Level 3: Infrastructure & Municipal Control. This was the guts of the city. The walls were covered in schematics, framed blueprints of the pumping station, the power grid, the subway lines.

It was a testament to human ingenuity, to the arrogance of engineers who thought they could tame the water. Ravn ran his hand over a blueprint of the flood wall, tracing the lines of a defense that had ultimately failed. He felt a strange kinship with the engineers who had built this place. They were men of logic, like him. And the universe had simply changed the variables on them.

Finally, they reached the bottom of the shaft. Sub-Level 4: The Server Nexus.

The air here was frigid, maintained by a dedicated climate control system that had miraculously, or perhaps cursedly, survived the flood. It bit at Ravn's exposed skin.

The door to the level was different from the others. It wasn't a simple fire door; it was a heavy security bulkhead, a slab of reinforced plasteel designed to protect the city's most critical data from anything short of a direct orbital bombardment.

A bold yellow stripe ran diagonally across the gray metal, stenciled with the words: *RESTRICTED ACCESS. AUTHORIZED PERSONNEL ONLY.*

They were not the first to arrive.

Scattered across the stone slabs in front of the blast door were three bodies. They were Legion tech-specialists, their gray armor scorched and blackened. A heavy-duty plasma drill lay abandoned nearby, its bit fused into a lump of slag against the door's surface.

Ravn knelt by one of the corpses. The soldier's faceplate was shattered, his expression frozen in a rictus of agony.

"They tried to force it," Ravn whispered. He ran his hand over the blast door. The metal was still warm. "They tried to cut through the lock logic with heat."

The Archive's automated defense protocols hadn't shot them; the door had simply fed their own energy back into them. A feedback loop.

"They didn't have the key," Ravn said to the Stalker. "They thought it was a vault. They didn't know it was a question."

Ravn approached the control panel. It was dead, the keypad fused by a short circuit years ago. He placed his hand on the door itself. It was locked tight, the magnetic seals engaged and frozen in place by time and corrosion.

He tried to pry his fingers into the seam, gritting his teeth and engaging the enhanced strength the Essence gave him. The metal groaned, but it didn't budge. He was strong, but he wasn't a hydraulic press.

He stepped back, frustration rising. Then, he looked at the Stalker.

The creature was pacing nervously, its claws clicking on the concrete. It was agitated, desperate to leave this dead place, but it was also powerful. It was a creature of the Zone, built of dense muscle and diamond-hard chitin.

"I need a little brute force," Ravn said, his voice echoing in the stairwell. He pointed at the seam of the door.

The Stalker stopped pacing. It looked at the door, then at Ravn. It seemed to understand the problem. It approached the bulkhead, sniffing the seam where the rubber seal had rotted away. It didn't need to be told twice. It wanted to get through this obstacle just as much as he did, if only to find a way out.

The creature reared up, jamming its obsidian claws into the microscopic gap between the doors. It snarled, a sound of pure exertion. Muscles coiled and bunched beneath its dark chitin, rippling with bioluminescent energy. The Stalker planted its feet and pulled.

For a second, the door held. Then, with a screech of tearing metal that set Ravn's teeth on edge, the magnetic seals shattered. Sparks showered from the frame. With a final, thunderous CLANG, the doors were forced apart, sliding into the walls with a grind of protest.

A gust of freezing, sterile air rushed out from the gap, carrying the hum of a thousand sleeping machines.

They stepped through the breached bulkhead and into the dark heart of the archive. If the upper levels were a graveyard, this was the inner sanctum, the holy of holies of a civilization that had worshipped at the altar of information.

The Server Nexus was a cavernous, circular space, vast enough to house a cathedral. The ceiling was lost in shadows high above, hidden behind a complex lattice of cooling ducts and cable runs that hung like dormant vines of copper and steel.

The air here was frigid, bitingly cold against Ravn's skin. It smelled of nothing—no dust, no rot, no ozone. It was the smell of a vacuum, a sterile void where biological life was an intruder.

Ravn raised his flashlight, the beam cutting through the cold air. It revealed row upon row of towering black server racks, arranged in perfect, concentric rings around the center of the room. They stood like silent, obsidian monoliths, thousands of them, their indicator lights dark, their fans silent.

Ravn walked down the central aisle, his boots making a sharp, clicking sound on the raised metal floor. He felt a profound sense of insignificance. To his left and right slept the sum total of a city's knowledge. Every traffic camera feed, every medical scan, every private email, every bank transaction—petabytes of human experience reduced to magnetic patterns on spinning platters, waiting in the dark for a command that never came.

It was a necropolis of binary.

The Stalker hated it. The creature moved with a low, creeping posture, its belly fur brushing the floor. Its bioluminescence, usually a vibrant display of its mood, had dimmed to a faint, sickly gray, as if the oppressive sterility of the room was draining its spirit. It let out a continuous, high-pitched whine, its ears flattened against its skull.

To a creature of the Zone, this room was a horror. It was a place of absolute separation, where data was siloed, categorized, and frozen. It was a cage for the mind.

"Stay close," Ravn whispered, his breath pluming in the cold air. "We're almost there."

They reached the center of the room. Here, the rows of servers stopped, creating a wide, open circle. In the middle of this open space rose a raised platform of polished black glass, accessible by a short flight of stairs.

And on the platform, piercing the gloom, was a single column of shimmering, blue light.

It was a containment field, a cylinder of pure, coherent energy that hummed with a low, dangerous frequency. It cast long, sharp shadows across the floor, illuminating the dust motes that danced in the frigid air.

Suspended within the field, floating in a frictionless void, was the key.

Ravn ascended the stairs, drawn to it like a moth to a flame. He stopped a few meters away, the blue light washing over his face, reflecting in the crystalline lattice of his new eyes.

It was the most alien of the three objects he had found. The first key, the crystalline shard, had been organic, warm, a piece of the living earth. The second key, the brass gyroscope, had been mechanical, a beautiful clockwork engine of the old physics.

This one was... absolute.

It was a complex gyroscope carved from a material that looked like polished obsidian, yet it seemed to absorb the blue light of the containment field rather than reflect it. It had no visible seams, no rivets, no power source.

Its inner rings spun in intricate, counter-rotating patterns, moving with a speed that should have produced a hum, a whine, a displacement of air. But it was silent. It moved without friction. It moved without heat. It moved without sound.

It was not a machine of moving parts; it was a physical algorithm. It was a piece of pure data given form, a Platonic ideal of motion captured in solid matter.

It was the Key of Information, and looking at it made Ravn feel a strange, cold vertigo. It represented a perfection that biology could never achieve, a sterile, eternal, and terrifyingly flawless order.

"The final variable," Ravn murmured.

He looked past the containment field to the object that controlled it. A master control terminal stood at the edge of the platform, a sleek, black slab of glass rising from the floor.

As he approached, it detected his presence. The glass surface woke up. A holographic interface bloomed into existence, projecting a complex, rotating geometric lock into the air. It cast a cold, blue glow over Ravn's face, highlighting the gaunt hollows of his cheeks and the alien geometry of his eyes.

SECURITY PROTOCOL: ENGAGED. AUTHORIZATION REQUIRED.

Ravn looked at the prompt. There was no keyhole. There was no lever to pull. There was no monster to fight. The Guardian of the Reality Tear had been a creature of broken physics; the Guardian of the Archive was a wall of pure logic.

He placed his hands on the cold console. He didn't have an authorization code. He didn't have a keycard. But he had something else. He had a mind honed by years of quantum theory, enhanced by the Essence of the Anomaly, and driven by a desperation that transcended logic.

He looked at the Stalker, who was pacing at the bottom of the stairs, refusing to come up to the platform. The creature snarled at the blue light, sensing the unnatural energy.

"Watch my back," Ravn said.

He turned to the terminal. He cracked his knuckles, the sound loud in the silence. For weeks, he had been a survivor, a hunter, a diplomat. Now, he had to be something else.

He had to be Aris. He had to be a hacker.

He began to type. His fingers danced across the holographic light-keys, querying the system, probing the perimeter of its logic. The security architecture was pre-Fracture, robust, and military-grade. It wasn't a static wall; it was a living, shifting maze.

It used a polymorphic encryption algorithm that scrambled its own cypher keys every 4.7 seconds. Brute force was impossible; the system would detect a forceful intrusion and lock down the facility permanently after three failed attempts.

He had to outthink it.

He leaned in close, ignoring the text on the screen and focusing on the light itself. He pushed his vision, activating the crystalline lattice that now structured his irises. The world shifted.

The blue glow of the hologram sharpened, breaking down into its constituent photons. He could see the refresh rate of the display, the microscopic flicker of the projector.

And he saw the pattern.

Beneath the chaotic shifting of the code, there was a rhythm. The encryption wasn't truly random—nothing in a closed system ever was. It was based on a seed value, a complex variable derived from the system's internal atomic clock and the radioactive decay of a small isotope sample within the server core.

It was a math problem. A problem of entropy and time.

Ravn closed his eyes for a moment, visualizing the equation. He needed to predict the next cypher shift before it happened. He needed to be exactly one second ahead of a machine that could think a million times faster than he could.

He felt the hum of the Essence in his blood, a cold, electric vitality that sharpened his thoughts to a razor's edge. He opened his eyes. The numbers on the screen weren't just data anymore; they were a flow, a current he could navigate.

He began to write code. He wasn't writing a bypass or a virus. He was writing a mirror. He built a synchronization protocol, a digital shadow that would latch onto the system's internal clock and mimic its decay rate. He was trying to teach his intrusion software to dance with the firewall, matching its steps perfectly until the system couldn't tell the difference between the intruder and itself.

His fingers flew, a blur of motion. Sweat beaded on his forehead, freezing instantly in the frigid air. The terminal flashed amber.

ANOMALY DETECTED. VERIFYING CREDENTIALS...

"Come on," Ravn whispered, his heart hammering against his ribs. "Don't look at me. Look at the dance." He adjusted the variable, tweaking the decay rate of his shadow program. The amber light pulsed, faster and faster. The system was suspicious. It was running a Turing test on his code, searching for the hesitation of a human mind.

He couldn't hesitate. He had to flow. He channeled the memory of Aris— his brother's reckless brilliance, his ability to leap across logical chasms without looking down.

Symmetry is a cage, Ravn. True security lies in elegant imperfection.

He introduced a flaw. A deliberate, calculated error in his own code, a stutter that mimicked the natural decay of the system itself. The terminal paused. The amber light held steady.

VERIFICATION...

The seconds stretched out, agonizing and long. The Stalker let out a sharp bark from the bottom of the stairs, sensing a shift in the room's energy.

...COMPLETE.

The screen flashed a brilliant, welcoming green.

ACCESS GRANTED. WELCOME, ADMINISTRATOR. The heavy, dangerous hum of the containment field pitch-shifted down. The column of blue light groaned, a sound of discharging energy, and then collapsed with a soft hiss like a dying breath.

The obsidian gyroscope, no longer held by the field, drifted gently down to rest on the black pedestal. It sat there, an object of pure, terrifying perfection, waiting for him.

Ravn let out a ragged breath, bracing his hands on the console to keep from falling. He had done it. He had beaten the machine on its own ground. He wiped the sweat from his eyes and turned toward the prize.

He reached out. His hand hovered over the object for a second, his crystalline vision picking up a faint, distortion haze around it—not heat, but a bending of light caused by its sheer informational density.

He grasped it.

It wasn't cold or hot. It felt like nothing. It possessed no texture, no friction, no thermal conductivity. It felt like holding a hole in the world, a void cut in the shape of a sphere.

But the moment his skin made contact, a shockwave of sensation traveled up his arm, bypassed his nervous system, and slammed directly into his brain.

No pain. Just noise.

A screeching, high-bandwidth datastream that sounded like a billion voices speaking at once exploded in his mind. It was the raw data of the archive—census records, weather patterns, stock market ticks, personal emails, video logs—all of it discharging into him in a single, chaotic burst.

He gasped, his knees buckling under the psychic weight of an entire city's history forcing its way into his skull. He staggered back, clutching the key to his chest, his breath coming in ragged gasps.

The Stalker snarled, leaping onto the platform, its body interposed between Ravn and the terminal as if the machine were a predator that had just bitten him.

But the assault wasn't over. The terminal he had just hacked let out a sharp, piercing tone. The screen flared white, casting harsh shadows against the server racks.

[EXTERNAL DECRYPTION KEY DETECTED]
[INTERFACE: APERTURE // USER: R. VIDAR]
[INITIATING HANDSHAKE...]

The Aperture on his wrist vibrated violently, its own screen glowing with a matching white light. It wasn't Ravn hacking the system anymore. The system was hacking him.

The obsidian key was a bridge, and it had just opened a connection between the Aperture and the archive's deepest, most protected databanks.

[ATTEMPTING PARTIAL DECRYPTION OF FILE: ROOT]

Ravn froze, his heart hammering against his ribs. The [ROOT] file. The encrypted ghost that had been sitting on his wrist since the beginning, the locked door he could never open.

The key in his hand was vibrating now, humming in resonance with the Aperture.

"No," Ravn whispered, his voice tight with panic. "Stop." He tried to pull the Aperture away, but his arm wouldn't move. His muscles were locked, held by a localized electromagnetic seizing. He was a conduit.

Lines of text began to scroll across his vision, projecting directly from the Aperture into his optic nerve. It wasn't the corrupted code of the Zone or the clean text of the Legion. It was raw, universal machine language. It was a cascade of impossible symbols and mathematical functions that seemed to describe the very fabric of reality.

He saw equations for the curvature of spacetime. He saw the code for the binding energy of an atom. He saw the variables for human consciousness.

And then, the scrolling stopped. The code cleared. A single, terrifyingly simple definition remained, burning in the center of his vision like a brand.

AXIOM = [UNIVERSAL_INFORMATIONAL_CONSTANT]
STATUS: AWAKE.
DIRECTIVE: PRESERVE POTENTIAL.

The connection severed. The light died. Ravn fell to his knees, the obsidian key clattering to the floor of the platform. The silence rushed back in, heavy and suffocating.

He stared at the empty air where the text had been. He understood.

The realization hit him with the force of a physical blow, staggering him more than the data stream had. The Axiom. The voice in his head. The thing Aris had found. It wasn't a god. It wasn't a spirit. It wasn't an AI built by humans.

It was a law of physics that had woken up.

It was a fundamental constant of the universe—like gravity, like electromagnetism—that possessed sentience. It was the Information that underpinned all reality, the code that told an atom to be an atom and a star to be a star.

And they had woken it up. They had poked it with their experiment, and it had looked back at them.

And now, it had a directive. *Preserve Potential.*

What did that mean? Preserve the potential of what? Of the universe? Of humanity? Or was it preserving the potential of the story it was currently writing, treating them all as characters in a cosmic simulation?

"You have opened the library," a voice whispered.

It wasn't in his head. It was real.

Ravn spun around, snatching his pulse rifle from the floor and leveling it at the shadows. The Stalker hissed, its bioluminescence flaring a violent red.

Standing at the entrance to the server room, silhouetted against the light of the stairwell, was a figure.

It was a hologram, but it was corrupted, glitching. It was the avatar of the Archive's AI, a woman in a pre-Fracture librarian's uniform, but her image was tearing and re-forming every few seconds. Her face was a mask of static, but he could see her eyes. They were white, blind, and leaking a faint, black smoke of digital corruption.

She wasn't looking at him. She was looking at the empty pedestal where the key had been.

"The Silence is broken," she whispered, her voice sounding like dry leaves skittering on pavement, layered with the sound of a dial-up modem screaming. "You woke the Constant. Now the variable must be solved."

"Who are you?" Ravn demanded, his finger tightening on the trigger.

The avatar smiled, a terrifying expression that stretched too wide, revealing teeth made of jagged code.

"I am the Memory of this city. And I remember when the sky looked back." She raised a flickering hand, pointing upward, through the millions of tons of rock and water, toward the surface. "He sees you now. The Red Eye is open."

Before Ravn could react, the avatar stepped back into the shadows of the doorway and simply... disassembled. There was no fade-out. She shattered into a cloud of voxels that drifted to the floor like digital snow.

The Stalker growled, the hair on its back standing up. It sensed the wrongness of the entity, the violation of natural law she represented.

Ravn grabbed the obsidian key and shoved it into his pack. He didn't know what the avatar was, or if it was just a malfunctioning subroutine of a dead city. But her words chilled him deeper than the liquid nitrogen air. *The Red Eye is open.*

"Let's go," he said to the Stalker, his voice tight. "We're leaving. Now."

They ran from the archive, climbing back up the spiral stairwell, their footsteps ringing on the metal. They burst out of the lobby and into the muddy, ruined streets of Oakhaven.

The three blue suns were setting, casting long, mournful shadows across the drained basin. But as Ravn looked up, checking his bearings, he froze.

High above, in the darkening zenith of the purple sky, a single, new star had appeared. It was not blue. It was a deep, baleful crimson. It stared.

It was a steady, unblinking point of red light, watching him.

The Axiom was watching.

Ravn looked at the Stalker, then down at the three keys now resting in his pack—Nature, Chaos, and Information.

He had found the keys. He knew the nature of the lock. Now, all that remained was to find the door. To find the Anchor.

And to face the judgment of the red eye in the sky.

21

The Hunt

Ravn stood in the ankle-deep sludge of what had once been a city plaza, his chest heaving, the cold sweat of the Archive turning to ice on his skin. The silence of Oakhaven was back, but it had changed. Before, it had been the heavy, settling silence of a graveyard. Now, it was the held breath of a predator before the strike.

He adjusted the straps of his pack, wincing as the canvas dug into his shoulder. It should have weighed perhaps thirty pounds—a collection of survival gear, a few rations, and three small objects. But it felt like he was carrying a collapsed star. The weight wasn't just mass; it was significance. It was gravity.

He could feel the three keys interacting through the fabric of the bag, a discordant, vibrating hum that traveled up his spine and resonated in the crystalline lattice of his new eyes. They were not inert objects. They were active, potent variables of reality, and they hated being so close to one another.

He could distinguish their individual frequencies against his own skin.

The First Key, the crystalline shard from the Husk shrine, felt like a living heart pressed against his lower back. It was warm, pulsing with a slow, rhythmic beat of organic energy. It whispered of growth, of roots cracking stone, of the relentless, crushing inevitability of life. It wanted to expand.

The Second Key, the golden gyroscope from the Reality Tear, was a knot of erratic, kinetic potential. Even wrapped in oilcloth, he could feel it twitching, its inner rings spinning up and slowing down in a chaotic rhythm that defied conservation of energy. It buzzed like a trapped hornet, radiating a prickly static that made the hair on his arms stand on end. It wanted to break.

And the Third Key, the obsidian sphere he had just torn from the Archive, was a void. It sat between the other two, a cold, silent singularity. It didn't pulse or spin. It absorbed. It drank the warmth of the crystal and the static of the gold, dampening them, categorizing them, digitizing them. It felt like a block of dry ice burning his skin through the layers of fabric. It wanted to know.

Together, they created a magnetic anomaly so strong that Ravn felt physically unbalanced, as if the magnetic north of the planet had shifted to the center of his backpack. He wasn't just a courier anymore. He was the containment vessel for the three fundamental forces of the new world—Nature, Chaos, and Information. He was a walking bomb, and the fuse was lit.

"We need to move," he rasped to the Stalker. "We can't stay in the open." The creature was pacing in tight, anxious circles, its claws squelching in the toxic mud. It kept looking up, not at the horizon, but at the zenith of the sky. Ravn followed its gaze, and the dread he had felt in the Archive solidified into a cold, hard certainty.

The three blue suns were dipping low, painting the sky in familiar shades of permanent, aching dusk. But the sky was no longer empty. High above, locked in a geostationary position directly over the drained city, was the Red Eye.

It wasn't a star. It was too bright, too solid. It was a single, unblinking point of crimson light, harsh and baleful, like the laser sight of a sniper rifle magnified a billion times. It didn't cast shadows; it seemed to erase them, bathing the ruined city in a flat, bloody glow that clashed violently with the twilight.

It was the Axiom. The entity was no longer a passive voice in his head or a line of code on a screen. It had manifested. It was watching him.

Ravn felt the weight of that gaze, a sensation of being observed so intense it made his skin crawl. He was a microbe on a slide, and the Eye was the microscope lens, burning him with its scrutiny.

System Corrupt, the voice had said weeks ago. Now, the System was looking directly at the Corruption. And Ravn realized, with a jolt of terror, that he was the Corruption. He was the variable carrying the keys to the system's reboot.

The Stalker let out a sharp, piercing bark, snapping Ravn's attention back to the ground. The creature's bioluminescence flared a sudden, violent red. It spun around, facing the north, toward the ridge where the pumping station stood.

Ravn strained his hearing, pushing his enhanced senses past the thrum of the keys and the pounding of his own heart. At first, there was only the wet slap of the dying fish in the mud. Then, he heard it. It was a sound he knew well, a sound that haunted his nightmares of the wasteland.

It was a low, rhythmic vibration that grew rapidly into a roar. It was the sound of unrefined ethanol exploding in rusted cylinders. It was the scream of metal grinding on metal. It was the war cry of an internal combustion engine.

A single, black shape crested the ridge of the pumping station, silhouetted against the Red Eye. Then another. Then a dozen.

The Rust Lords had arrived. And they hadn't just found the city. Guided by the energy signature of the keys or the light of the Red Eye, they had found him.

The silence of the Drowned City didn't just break; it was murdered.

It began with the individual roar of the lead bikes cresting the ridge, but within seconds, that sound was swallowed by a much larger, earth-shaking vibration.

The Grinder had arrived. Jax's mobile fortress, the colossal, tracked mining platform that served as the heart of the Rust Lord tribe, breached the horizon line behind the pumping station. It silhouetted itself against the baleful glow of the Red Eye, a jagged mountain of welded steel and smokestacks that blocked out the stars.

As it tipped over the crest and began its descent into the drained basin, its massive engines revved—a sound so deep and loud it wasn't heard so much as felt, a seismic event that rattled the remaining glass in the skyscrapers around Ravn.

Then came the lights. Dozens of high-intensity spotlights, salvaged from stadium rigs and anti-aircraft batteries, snapped on simultaneously. They cut through the purple twilight like physical beams, sweeping back and forth across the muddy ruin of Oakhaven.

They turned the shadows into stark hiding places and the open mud flats into a blinding, exposed stage. The Stalker let out a pained yelp, flattening its ears against its skull. To a creature of the Zone, whose senses were tuned to the subtle bio-rhythms of the forest, this was an assault. The noise was a physical weapon, a wall of decibels that disoriented and terrified.

Ravn grabbed the creature's harness, grounding it. "Stay with me," he shouted, though he could barely hear his own voice over the rising cacophony.

The convoy poured down the slope like a landslide of metal. There were swift, three-wheeled interceptor bikes that bounced over the debris; heavy, armored war-rigs with harpoon guns mounted on their roll cages; and modification-heavy "technical" trucks spewing black exhaust.

They didn't care about the mud or the ruins. They smashed through the skeletal remains of the outlying suburbs, crushing walls and flattening the dead, waterlogged trees. They weren't searching aimlessly. They were tracking him.

Ravn felt a sudden, violent spike of heat from the Second Key in his pack—the golden gyroscope of Chaos. It was vibrating wildly, buzzing like a hive of angry hornets. It was resonating. The chaotic, entropic energy of the Rust Lords—their engines, their violence, their sheer, anarchic will—was feeding the key, and the key, in turn, was acting as a beacon. It was singing to them.

Jax's voice, amplified by a massive, distorted speaker system mounted on the front of the Grinder, boomed across the basin, echoing off the skyscrapers with a terrifying, god-like authority.

"I SEE YOU, BRAINIAC!" The sound wave hit Ravn, rattling his chest.

"YOU THINK YOU CAN HIDE?" Jax roared, his laughter underlining the words with a manic edge. "THE SKY IS WATCHING YOU! THE ENGINE IS SINGING FOR YOU! THERE IS NO HIDING FROM THE CHURNING!"

A spotlight swept over them, missing Ravn by mere meters, illuminating a patch of toxic sludge and turning it into a glistening, white-hot mirror.

"GIVE ME THE PRIZE, AND I'LL MAKE IT QUICK!" Jax bellowed. "RUN, AND I'LL MAKE IT FUN!"

The psychological weight of the moment crashed down on Ravn. He was no longer a scientist on a quest. He was a fox in a box, and the hounds had just been released. The city, which had been a tomb, was now an arena.

He looked at the terrain. The basin was a nightmare of deep, sucking mud and treacherous debris. To the Rust Lords, with their high-torque engines and tracked vehicles, it was difficult ground, but passable. To Ravn, on foot, it was a trap. If he tried to run in the open, they would run him down in minutes.

But he had one advantage. He had the Aperture. And he had eyes that could see the world as a wireframe.

He activated the scanner, overlaying the terrain with a structural analysis. He saw the mud not just as sludge, but as density maps. He saw the hidden basements beneath the street level that would collapse under the weight of a heavy truck. He saw the narrow alleyways between the skyscrapers where a war-rig couldn't fit.

"We don't run away," Ravn yelled to the Stalker, pulling the creature toward the dense cluster of high-rises. "We run through."

The lead bikes reached the basin floor, their engines screaming as they hit the mud, kicking up roosters of toxic slime. They accelerated, fanning out in a wide hunting formation. The hunt was on.

The chase began not with speed, but with a chaotic struggle for traction. Ravn and the Stalker sprinted away from the exposed mud flats and toward the dense cluster of skeletal skyscrapers that formed the city's dead heart.

The ground was a nightmare—a thick, sucking slurry of toxic silt, industrial runoff, and the decaying matter of a million aquatic organisms. Every step was a battle against suction. The mud clung to Ravn's boots like heavy, wet iron, threatening to drag him down with every stride.

Behind them, the roar of the Rust Lord engines rose to a deafening crescendo as the lead bikes hit the basin floor. The lighter, three-wheeled interceptors skidded and fishtailed, their spiked tires carving deep gouges in the slime, kicking up roosters of black sludge that rained down like oil. But they found purchase. They accelerated, their engines screaming, closing the distance with terrifying speed.

The heavier war-rigs were slower, their massive treads churning the mud into a frenzy, but their momentum was unstoppable. They plowed through the debris of the drowned city—crushing cars, shattering fallen masonry—like icebreakers moving through a frozen sea.

"Faster!" Ravn gasped, his lungs burning with the exertion and the chemical stench of the air.

He didn't look back. He looked forward, engaging the crystalline lattice in his eyes. The world shifted into a high-contrast wireframe of structural density. To a normal eye, the basin floor was a uniform expanse of mud. To Ravn, it was a minefield of variable viscosity.

He saw patches of deep, unstable silt that would swallow a man whole, highlighted in warning red. He saw buried causeways of concrete and rebar, hidden beneath inches of slime, glowing with a solid, reassuring green.

"Left!" he shouted, veering sharply toward a collapsed overpass.

The Stalker, trusting him implicitly, scrambled after him. They hit the buried concrete, and their pace instantly doubled. They were running on a hidden road, moving with a sudden, jarring speed while the mud on either side remained a treacherous trap.

A pair of Rust Lord bikes, seeing their prey accelerate, roared in pursuit. They tried to cut the angle, swerving off the hidden causeway to intercept. Ravn saw it happen in slow motion. He saw the red density warning of the mud patch they were driving into. He didn't warn them.

The lead bike hit the soft spot at eighty kilometers an hour. The front wheel didn't skid; it sank. The bike stopped instantly, buried to its axle in the blink of an eye. The rider was launched over the handlebars, a flailing ragdoll that disappeared into a deep pool of toxic water with a splash that was swallowed by the engine noise.

The second bike tried to swerve, lost traction, and spun out, its rider pinned beneath the hot, hissing engine block as it sank slowly into the mire.

Two down. Dozens to go.

They reached the skyscrapers. The alleyways here were narrow, choked with debris and fallen glass. It was a vertical labyrinth that offered cover from the blinding spotlights of the Grinder, which was now trundling down the slope like a mobile mountain, its heavy cannons booming as it fired blind, suppressing shots into the city.

Shells whistled overhead, slamming into the upper floors of the buildings. Showers of concrete dust and shattered glass rained down on them, clattering against Ravn's pack and the Stalker's chitin.

"Keep moving!" Ravn yelled, shielding his head.

They weren't just running; they were being herded. He checked the Aperture's tactical overlay. The Rust Lord convoy was splitting up. The smaller, faster vehicles were racing down the parallel avenues, flanking them, trying to cut off their escape to the north.

The heavier rigs were smashing through the center, driving them forward. They were trying to box him in against the northern cliff face of the basin, where the drained lake ended in a sheer wall of rock.

He needed a chokepoint. A place where their numbers wouldn't matter.

He scanned the map. To the northwest, cutting through the basin wall, was a narrow, winding fissure—an old outflow channel for the dam system. It was a slot canyon, barely wide enough for a single vehicle.

"The channel!" he pointed. "We have to make the channel!"

It was a kilometer away, across open ground. They broke cover from the alleyway and sprinted.

A war-rig, a modified dump truck plated in jagged scrap metal, burst through the wall of a building to their right. It was huge, loud, and terrifyingly close. A gunner on the roof opened fire with a heavy stubber, the bullets chewing up the mud in a line that walked rapidly toward Ravn's heels.

He dove, rolling through the slime behind the cover of a rusted city bus. The bullets punched through the thin metal of the bus, sparking and whining. The Stalker snarled, its bioluminescence flaring red. It looked at the war-rig, then at the tires.

"No!" Ravn grabbed its harness. "Too big! Run!"

They scrambled up and over the bus, dropping down the other side and putting the wreck between them and the gunner. They kept running, weaving through a graveyard of rusted cars, the mud sucking at their energy with every step.

The entrance to the slot canyon loomed ahead, a dark crack in the cliff face. It was their only hope. But between them and the entrance, a pack of four interceptor bikes was racing to cut them off. They were going to lose the footrace.

Ravn's mind raced. He looked at the terrain. The approach to the canyon was a slight incline, covered in loose, wet scree. Above the entrance, precariously balanced on the edge of the cliff, was a massive, rusted billboard frame, its supports eaten away by years of water.

He stopped. He unslung his pulse rifle.

"Go!" he screamed to the Stalker. "Get to the entrance!" The creature hesitated, then obeyed, sprinting for the gap.

Ravn raised the rifle. He didn't aim at the bikes. He aimed high, at the rusted, groaning supports of the billboard. He engaged the weapon's overcharge capacitor, dumping half the clip into a single shot.

The blue energy bolt struck the metal with a blinding flash. The support sheared. With a groan of tortured steel that echoed over the roar of the engines, the massive billboard toppled forward.

It crashed down onto the slope directly in the path of the interceptor bikes, triggering a landslide of wet rock and twisted metal. The lead bikers braked hard, skidding sideways, but they couldn't stop. They slammed into the debris field, their machines tangling in the wreckage.

The path was blocked for them. But there was just enough room for a man and a beast to squeeze through.

Ravn turned and sprinted for the gap, diving into the shadows of the slot canyon just as the heavy war-rigs smashed through the bus behind him.

He was in. But he knew, with a sinking heart, that he had only bought himself minutes. The Rust Lords would clear the debris. And the hunt would continue in the dark.

22

The Hammer and the Anvil

The spotlight didn't just break; it imploded.

Ravn's pulse rifle bolts struck the reinforced glass with the force of a sledgehammer, shattering the filament and vaporizing the reflector dish in a shower of sparks. The blinding white eye of the war-rig winked out instantly, plunging the cul-de-sac back into a profound, suffocating darkness.

For a single heartbeat, there was silence. It was the stunned, ringing silence of a predator that has just been slapped by its prey.

Then, the canyon erupted.

The Rust Lords didn't react with tactics or discipline; they reacted with pure, chaotic rage. A dozen weapons opened up simultaneously. Heavy stubbers, automatic shotguns, and scavenged pulse rifles fired blindly into the gloom.

The sound was a physical assault. In the confined acoustics of the slot canyon, the gunfire didn't just bang; it screamed. The noise bounced off the basalt walls, amplifying and overlapping until it became a solid wall of pressure that vibrated in Ravn's teeth and rattled his bones.

He threw himself to the ground, curling into a ball at the base of the cliff, pulling the Stalker down with him. The air above their heads became a kill zone of flying lead and superheated plasma.

Bullets struck the canyon wall inches above him, sending showers of razor-sharp rock splinters raining down on his back. Ricochets whined through the dark like angry hornets, sparking against the stone.

It was a sensory nightmare. The darkness was punctuated by the frantic, strobe-light flashing of muzzle flares. In those brief, stuttering bursts of light, Ravn saw snapshots of hell: the jagged silhouette of the war-rig, the masked face of a gunner screaming in silent fury, the twisting smoke of the exhaust.

The air filled with the acrid stench of cordite, unburnt fuel, and pulverized rock.

The Stalker was a vibrating knot of muscle against his side. It wasn't cowering; it was coiling. Every time a bullet struck near them, the creature let out a sharp, aggressive bark, its bioluminescence flaring a violent red that illuminated the dust choking the air.

It wanted to fight. It wanted to launch itself into the darkness and tear at the metal beasts that had cornered them.

"Stay down!" Ravn yelled, his voice lost in the roar. He gripped the creature's harness with white-knuckled force. There was no fighting this. This wasn't a battle; it was an execution by volume of fire.

He checked the Aperture, shielding the screen with his body. The tactical display was a useless wash of red static. The acoustic sensors were overloaded, the thermal imaging blinded by the heat of the muzzle flashes. He was blind, deaf, and pinned.

The barrage slackened for a moment as the Rust Lords reloaded. In the brief lull, the voice of Jax boomed from the rig's speakers, distorted by static and rage.

"YOU WANT THE DARK, BRAINIAC? WE CAN DO DARK!" The engine of the lead war-rig revved, a deep, guttural roar that shook the ground. The driver slammed the gears. The massive machine lurched forward, its spiked tires grinding on the stone floor. They weren't going to shoot him anymore. They were going to crush him. They were going to ram the rig into the canyon wall and smear him into a paste.

Ravn squeezed his eyes shut. He clutched the empty fabric of his pack, his knuckles white against the worn canvas. He had failed. He had found the keys, solved the puzzle, and survived the nightmare, only to die as roadkill in a dead-end crack in the earth.

He thought of Aris. He hoped, with a desperate, sudden clarity, that the "Pruning" he had experienced before was real. He hoped that when the metal hit him, he would simply de-render, that his consciousness would be stripped away before the pain could register.

The roar of the engine grew louder. He could feel the heat of the radiator washing over him. He braced himself for the impact. He counted the seconds in the darkness. One. Two.

The impact never came.

Instead, a new sound cut through the guttural roar of the diesel engine. It was a high-pitched, descending whine, piercing and clean, like the scream of a falling turbine. It had no place in the wasteland. It belonged in a laboratory, or the nose cone of a fighter jet.

Ravn opened his eyes just as the darkness of the canyon was banished—not by the warm, yellow beams of the Rust Lord spotlights, but by a sudden, blinding wash of clinically pure, azure light.

The sky above the canyon rim, a thin ribbon of violent violet, erupted.

A volley of energy bolts, thick as tree trunks and humming with lethal coherence, rained down from the cliffs. They didn't fall like artillery shells; they struck with the speed of light.

The lead war-rig, the one mere meters from crushing Ravn, was the first casualty.

A beam of blue fire struck its engine block. There was no explosion, no expanding fireball of gasoline. The physics of the impact were far more terrifying. The heavy steel armor of the rig's hood simply vaporized, sublimating instantly from solid to gas.

The engine block beneath it turned molten, glowing cherry-red and then white-hot in the span of a heartbeat. The massive vehicle's momentum carried it forward another few feet, its tires melting into the stone floor, before it collapsed in on itself with a groan of tortured metal.

The driver, silenced mid-scream, was gone, consumed by the heat flash. The rig slumped into a heap of slag, radiating a heat so intense it singed the hair on Ravn's arms.

Silence, absolute and stunned, filled the canyon for a single second. The Rust Lords, deafened by the sudden energy discharge, froze.

Then, the rain began in earnest.

Ravn looked up, shielding his eyes against the glare. Lining the rim of the canyon, silhouetted against the alien stars like gargoyles of the old world, were figures. Dozens of them. They stood in perfect, spaced intervals, their armor sleek and uniform, their silhouettes distinct from the jagged, scrap-metal shapes of the Rust Lords.

They were Legionnaires.

They didn't cheer. They didn't scream war cries. They simply fired. It was a display of disciplined, synchronized violence. Pulse rifles chattered with a rhythmic, electric thrum-thrum-thrum, sending a curtain of smaller blue bolts cascading down into the cul-de-sac.

Heavy weapon specialists, braced on the edge of the cliff, fired shoulder-mounted cannons that spat balls of superheated plasma. The canyon floor became a kill box.

The Rust Lords, packed tight in the narrow fissure, had nowhere to go. The rear vehicles tried to reverse, grinding their gears, crashing into the rigs behind them in a chaotic tangle of metal. The warriors on foot scrambled for cover, but the high angle of the Legion attack left them exposed.

A technical truck, its bed loaded with fuel drums, took a direct hit. It exploded, this time with a conventional, chemical fury, sending a mushroom cloud of oily fire rolling up the canyon walls. The shockwave knocked Ravn flat against the rock.

The Stalker was going mad. The creature snarled, snapping its jaws at the air, its head whipping back and forth between the burning Rust Lord machines and the cold, blue death raining from the sky. It hated the Rust Lords for their cruelty, but it hated this—this sterile, vacuum-scented destruction—even more. It sensed the unnaturalness of it, the violation of the Zone's chaotic order.

Ravn grabbed the creature's head, forcing it to look at him. "Down! Stay down!"

He looked up at the rim again. Amidst the firing line, he saw a figure standing taller than the rest, wearing the officer's crest of a high-ranking commander. Even at this distance, he recognized the rigid posture.

It was General Rostova. She wasn't firing. She was observing, her hands clasped behind her back, watching the slaughter with the detached interest of an exterminator clearing a nest.

A cold realization washed over Ravn, chilling him more than the fear of death. They hadn't tracked the Rust Lords. They had tracked him. They had followed the energy signature of the Aperture, or perhaps the unique radiation of the keys.

This wasn't a rescue mission. It was an acquisition.

"They're not here to save us," Ravn whispered, the words lost in the cacophony of exploding metal. "They're here to clean up the mess." The canyon floor transformed from a trap into a cauldron. The initial shock of the Legion's ambush lasted only seconds. The Rust Lords were not disciplined soldiers, but they were survivors of the harshest environments in the Zone. They lived in a state of perpetual war against the elements, the beasts, and each other. They did not panic; they raged.

Recovering from the blinding flash of the lead rig's destruction, the remaining Rust Lord vehicles roared their defiance. Heavy stubbers mounted on roll cages spun up, spitting streams of high-caliber tracers that streaked upward like angry red comets against the falling blue rain. Rockets spiraled from shoulder-mounted launchers, leaving corkscrew trails of gray smoke before impacting against the cliff face.

The Legionnaires on the rim held the high ground, but the sheer volume of fire coming from below forced them to seek cover. The pristine, rhythmic thrum-thrum-thrum of their pulse rifles was broken by the jagged, tearing sound of heavy slugs chipping away at the basalt lip of the canyon.

Ravn was no longer a participant; he was debris. He pressed himself into a shallow depression at the base of the cliff, curling his body around the Stalker.

The air above them was a crossfire hurricane of conflicting physics. The superheated ozone of the Legion's plasma clashed with the acrid, sulfurous smoke of the Rust Lords' gunpowder.

To his left, a Legion heavy trooper fired a plasma cannon. The orb of white-hot energy descended slowly, almost gracefully, before striking a cluster of Rust Lord bikes. The explosion was silent for a microsecond as the air was sucked into the thermal vacuum, followed by a thunderclap that ruptured eardrums. The bikes didn't explode; they melted, fusing together into a singular, grotesque sculpture of burning metal.

To his right, a Rust Lord technical truck, its driver screaming a war cry that was audible even over the din, rammed the burning wreckage of the lead rig, using it as a ramp. The truck launched into the air, its turret gunner firing wildly as they arced toward the cliff face.

It was a suicidal, impossible maneuver born of pure adrenaline. The truck smashed into the canyon wall twenty meters up, exploding on impact, but not before the gunner managed to rake the Legion line with a burst of armor-piercing rounds, sending two gray-clad figures tumbling from the heights to smash onto the canyon floor below.

It was a clash of philosophies made manifest in violence. The Rust Lords fought with a chaotic, organic fury, expending ammunition and lives with reckless abandon. They were a fire that wanted to burn everything, including themselves. The Legion fought like a machine, their fire disciplined, their target prioritization logical and ruthless. They were an ice sheet, crushing and extinguishing everything in their path.

And Ravn was the stone caught between the hammer and the anvil.

A stray bullet sparked off the rock inches from his face, sending a shard of stone slicing across his cheek. He didn't flinch. He watched the battle with a terrifying, hyper-focused clarity, his crystalline eyes recording the trajectories, the thermal blooms, the shifting tactical map.

He saw Jax. The warlord had bailed from his command rig before it took a direct hit. He was on foot now, wading through the smoke like a demon of the old world. He wielded a massive, scavenged rotary cannon ripped from a downed aircraft, holding it by the barrel shroud with heat-resistant gloves.

He was laughing, a sound that cut through the explosions, as he sprayed a continuous wall of lead at the cliff top. He wasn't trying to survive. He was trying to drag the sky down with him.

"We can't stay here," Ravn yelled into the Stalker's ear. The creature was trembling violently, its sensory organs overwhelmed by the overload of noise and energy. Its bioluminescence was flashing a chaotic, strobe-like pattern of fear and aggression.

The canyon walls were beginning to destabilize. The heavy weapons fire was chewing away the rock face. Boulders the size of cars were breaking loose from the rim, crashing down into the narrow space, crushing Rust Lords and blocking the retreat. The cul-de-sac was becoming a tomb.

Ravn checked the Aperture. The tactical display was a mess of red and blue icons merging into a single blob of conflict. But underneath the chaos, the topographical map showed him something he had missed in his panic. Fifty meters back, near where the burning technical truck had crashed, the explosion had fractured the canyon wall.

A deep, jagged fissure had opened up behind a veil of falling scree. It was narrow, dark, and possibly unstable. But it was a way out. It was a path that led away from the kill box.

But to get there, he would have to run a gauntlet of fire. He would have to sprint across fifty meters of open ground, through the heart of the crossfire, while two armies tried to annihilate each other around him.

He looked at the Stalker. "One more run," he whispered. "One more run and we're gone."

He tightened his grip on his empty pulse rifle, not as a weapon, but as a shield. He waited for a lull in the barrage, for the split second when the Rust Lords paused to reload and the Legion's heat sinks cycled.

The rhythm of the battle shifted. A heavy mortar shell from the Rust Lords struck the rim, sending a cloud of dust over the Legion's position. The blue rain faltered for a heartbeat.

"Now!"

He sprang from cover, the Stalker matching his pace instantly. They dove into the smoke, running not away from the battle, but directly across its bloodied, burning center.

They broke cover, leaving the relative safety of the rock wall for the open, suicidal insanity of the canyon floor. To a normal observer, the fifty meters between their position and the fissure would have been a blur of smoke and noise. But to Ravn, with the adrenaline of the Essence flooding his system and the crystalline lattice of his eyes fully engaged, the world slowed down.

It became a terrifyingly high-resolution study in ballistics and thermodynamics.

He didn't just see the battle; he felt the math of it. He saw the trajectory of the Legion's plasma bolts as lines of searing white light, calculating their impact points milliseconds before they struck. He saw the chaotic, spiraling arcs of the Rust Lord rockets, tracing their erratic flight paths through the smoky air.

He was a pedestrian running across a highway where the cars were made of death.

"Low!" he screamed, shoving the Stalker's head down. A heavy stubber round, a slug the size of his thumb, cracked the air where the creature's head had been a fraction of a second before. It struck a boulder behind them, spraying them with stone shrapnel.

They scrambled over the wreckage of a burning technical truck. The heat was intense, searing Ravn's eyebrows. Inside the cab, the driver was a charred, screaming husk, thrashing against the melted steering column. Ravn didn't look away; he couldn't afford to. He vaulted over the hood, his boots slipping on the slick, boiling oil leaking from the engine.

The Stalker was a shadow at his heels, moving with a frantic, terrified agility. It was no longer fighting; it was purely surviving. It juked and weaved, its body low, dodging debris and fire with an instinct that was older than any technology.

They reached the middle of the kill zone. Here, the crossfire was densest. The air was a solid wall of noise.

A Legionnaire on the rim, tracking their movement, fired a suppression burst. The blue bolts stitched a line of craters across the ground in front of Ravn, forcing him to skid to a halt. He looked up, locking eyes with the soldier for a split second—a faceless, gray helmet against the purple sky.

The soldier adjusted his aim. Before he could fire again, a Rust Lord on a bike, trailing smoke and fire, launched off a ramp of debris. The biker wasn't aiming for the Legionnaire; he was just a projectile of pure, nihilistic rage. The bike slammed into the canyon wall just below the rim, exploding in a massive fireball that engulfed the ledge.

The Legionnaire vanished in the blast.

Ravn didn't pause to celebrate. He used the distraction, sprinting through the smoke of the explosion. He was analyzing the battlefield with a cold, detached part of his mind.

The Rust Lords were losing, but they were dying hard. Their erratic movements, their refusal to take cover, their sheer volume of fire—it was creating a chaotic entropy that was disrupting the Legion's targeting algorithms. The Legion wanted a clean fight; the Rust Lords were giving them a bar brawl.

And in that chaos, there was a path.

Ravn saw it as a thread of green light in his vision—a probability vector winding through the carnage. Left at the burning tire. Under the collapsed axle of the war-rig. Jump the crater.

He followed the line. He grabbed the Stalker's harness and hauled the creature over a pile of jagged scrap metal. His hand was sliced open on a rusty fender, but he didn't feel it. They were close.

The fissure in the rock wall was ten meters away, a dark, jagged wound beckoning them to safety.

But the path was blocked.

A Legion heavy trooper, his armor bulky and pristine, had rappelled down from the rim to secure the flank. He landed with a heavy thud directly in front of the fissure. He raised a heavy rotary cannon, the barrels spinning up with a high-pitched whine.

He wasn't looking at the Rust Lords. He was looking at Ravn.

TARGET ACQUIRED. CLASS-1 ANOMALY.

The voice boomed from the trooper's external speakers, synthesized and devoid of humanity.

Ravn skidded to a halt, his boots digging into the gravel. He was in the open. He had no cover. The pulse rifle in his hands was empty, a useless club. He looked at the spinning barrels. He calculated the firing arc. There was no escape. The probability of survival dropped to zero.

Then, the Stalker moved.

Attacking the environment. The creature slammed its tail into the ground, not at the trooper, but at a precarious pile of loose rock and debris that the heavy trooper was standing next to—the remnants of the landslide caused by the earlier explosion.

The impact dislodged a key keystone. The pile shifted. A massive slab of basalt, weighing tons, slid forward. The trooper sensed the movement and tried to turn, his rotary cannon firing a wild burst that chewed up the sky. But he was too slow. The slab crashed down, pinning the trooper's legs and the lower half of his armor to the canyon floor.

The cannon fell silent. The trooper struggled, his servos whining, but he was anchored.

"Go!" Ravn roared.

He didn't wait. He sprinted past the trapped, thrashing Legionnaire, diving headfirst into the darkness of the fissure. The Stalker scrambled in after him, its claws scrabbling on the stone.

They squeezed through the jagged crack, the rock scraping the skin from Ravn's shoulders. The roar of the battle behind them was instantly muffled, replaced by the damp, cool silence of the earth. They were through. They were alive.

Ravn collapsed against the rough wall of the tunnel, gasping for air, his heart hammering a frantic rhythm against his ribs. He checked the Stalker. The creature was trembling, patches of its chitin scorched by near-misses, but it was whole.

He looked back toward the entrance of the fissure. Through the narrow crack, he could see a sliver of the canyon. It was a furnace of blue and orange light, a cauldron of destruction.

Then, the world turned white.

A massive, concussive blast shook the ground, knocking Ravn flat. Dust rained from the ceiling. The Rust Lords, in a final act of spite, had detonated the fuel reserves of the Grinder.

The explosion consumed the cul-de-sac, vaporizing the trapped vehicles, the bodies, and the very air. The shockwave slammed into the fissure, a physical hammer of compressed air that lifted Ravn off his feet and threw him deeper into the dark.

He hit the stone floor hard, the breath driven from his lungs, as the world behind him ended.

A deafening, grinding roar echoed down the tunnel—the sound of millions of tons of rock giving way. The entrance to the fissure, the narrow slice of purple sky and burning orange light, vanished.

A cloud of choking dust billowed over them, instantly coating Ravn's mouth and nose with the taste of pulverized granite. He lay in the absolute darkness, coughing, his ears ringing with a high-pitched whine that drowned out his own heartbeat. He waited for the ceiling to collapse, for the crushing weight of the mountain to finish what the Rust Lords had started.

But the rumble faded. The dust began to settle. The tunnel held.

Ravn fumbled for the Stalker in the dark. His hand brushed against warm, trembling chitin. The creature was curled into a tight ball, its head tucked beneath its tail. It let out a low, terrified whimper.

"It's okay," Ravn rasped, his voice sounding small and flat in the confined space. "We're alive."

He activated the flashlight on the Aperture. The beam cut through the swirling dust, revealing a jagged, claustrophobic tunnel that wound upward into the rock. Behind them, where the entrance had been, was a solid wall of fallen boulders. They were sealed in. The only way was forward.

"Come on," he urged, pulling gently on the Stalker's harness.

They began the climb. It was a grueling, silent ascent through the veins of the earth. The fissure was narrow, forcing them to squeeze through gaps that scraped the skin from Ravn's shoulders and snagged on his pack.

The air grew colder and thinner with every meter they climbed. The sounds of the battle—the roar of engines, the scream of plasma—were gone, replaced by the wet, rhythmic scuffing of their boots and the Stalker's claws.

After what felt like hours of climbing, the air current changed. A draft of cold, dry wind touched Ravn's face, carrying a strange, sharp scent. The smell of ozone or burning fuel faded away. It began to smell of clean minerals and static electricity.

Ahead, the tunnel widened. A faint, prismatic light spilled from an opening above. They scrambled up the final slope and emerged from the earth, gasping for the clean air.

Ravn stood up and looked around, his breath catching in his throat.

They had not emerged back into the muddy basin of Oakhaven, nor onto the rust-colored plains. They had surfaced in a new world entirely.

They were in a forest, but it was a forest of glass.

The trees here were petrified, their organic matter replaced over centuries by a translucent, quartz-like mineral. They soared into the sky, sharp and angular, their branches shattering the light of the three blue suns into a million fractured rainbows.

The ground was not soil, but a carpet of diamond-dust and shattered crystal shards that crunched loudly underfoot. It was breathtakingly beautiful. And it was terrifyingly silent.

There was no wind to rustle the glass leaves. There were no insects humming. The silence was sharp, brittle, and absolute. It was a landscape of perfect, frozen clarity.

Ravn looked back the way they had come. The fissure they had emerged from was hidden beneath the roots of a massive, crystalline oak. To the south, miles away, he could see a column of black smoke rising into the sky—the funeral pyre of the Rust Lord convoy and the Legion vanguard.

He checked the Aperture. The signal from the keys was quiet here, dampened by the unique resonance of the crystal forest. But the tactical display was clear.

REGION IDENTIFIED: THE CRYSTAL LABYRINTH. ACOUSTIC PROPERTIES: HIGHLY AMPLIFIED. STATUS: EXPOSED. The Stalker didn't like it. It moved with exaggerated caution, wincing every time its claws clicked against the glass floor. It sensed the danger. In the canyon, noise had been a weapon. Here, noise was a death sentence. Every footstep was a gunshot in the silence.

Ravn realized their situation. They had escaped the hammer and the anvil, but they had walked into a house of mirrors. They were no longer running from a noisy, chaotic army. They were about to be hunted by something far more dangerous: silence.

He looked at the endless, glittering maze of trees ahead.

"We have to move," he whispered, and even his whisper seemed to echo. "And we have to be ghosts." They stepped into the Crystal Forest, leaving the war for the world behind them, and entering the silent, deadly hunt for the final door.

23

The Hunted

They emerged from the fissure into a world that had been held in a breath of silence for a thousand years.

The transition was absolute. One moment, Ravn was breathing the stale, dusty air of the underground escape tunnel, his ears still ringing with the phantom echoes of the Rust Lord explosion. The next, he was standing in a cathedral of frozen light.

The Crystal Forest stretched out before them, a vast, glittering expanse that defied the organic logic of the Zone. These were not trees in any biological sense. Ages ago, they might have been wood and bark, but the strange, mineral-rich alchemy of the Fracture Zone had transmuted them. They were now towering sculptures of translucent quartz and silicate, their trunks soaring fifty meters into the air like pillars of jagged ice.

Their branches were not soft or swaying; they were sharp, geometric fractures that split the light into razor-edged beams. Their leaves were sheets of diamond-thin mica that chimed softly, like wind chimes, in the thin, cold breeze.

It was breathtakingly beautiful. And it was a death trap.

Ravn took a step, and the sound was like a gunshot.

CRUNCH.

The ground was carpeted not in moss or soil, but in a thick layer of crystal dust and shattered shards, the detritus of a million years of silent erosion.

His boot grinding into the surface sent a sharp, brittle echo ricocheting through the trees. The sound didn't die; it amplified, bouncing off the hard, faceted surfaces of the forest, multiplying until it sounded like a dozen men marching.

The Stalker flinched violently, its claws scrabbling for purchase on the slick, glass-like ground. It let out a low, involuntary whine of distress, and even that sound was amplified, twisting into a ghostly, moaning echo that seemed to come from everywhere at once.

"Quiet," Ravn hissed, freezing in place.

He looked around, his heart hammering against his ribs. The forest was a house of mirrors. The light from the three blue suns and the baleful Red Eye of the Axiom above was caught in the billions of facets of the trees. It was refracted, bent, and scattered until the air itself seemed to be made of solid light.

He saw his own reflection a thousand times over—distorted, stretched, fragmented in the trunks of the trees. He saw the Stalker multiplied into a pack of glowing ghosts.

And above it all, the Red Eye was fractured into a million tiny, crimson points of light, staring at him from every surface. The Axiom wasn't just in the sky; it was in the trees, in the ground, in the air. It was a panopticon of crystal.

Ravn raised the Aperture, squinting against the glare. The tactical display was a mess of ghost signals. The laser rangefinder was useless, the beam bouncing off a dozen surfaces before returning confused data. The thermal scanner was blinded by the reflections of his own body heat mirroring back at him.

ENVIRONMENTAL WARNING: HIGH ACOUSTIC REFLECTIVITY.
VISUAL DISTORTION: EXTREME. STEALTH INDEX: 0%.

"We're exposed," he whispered to the Stalker.

The creature was crouching low, its belly fur brushing the sharp dust. It hated this place. Its primary senses—smell and hearing—were being assaulted. The air smelled only of cold minerals and static charge, devoid of biological scent trails. The acoustics were a maddening funhouse of false echoes. The Stalker was blind and deaf in a world made of hard, cold light.

Ravn looked back toward the fissure. It was hidden beneath the roots of a massive, crystalline oak, invisible from ten meters away. They had escaped the anvil of the Legion and the hammer of the Rust Lords, but they had walked into something far more insidious.

They were no longer being pursued by roaring engines, but by something far more dangerous: ghosts. They were in a place where the environment itself was a sentry.

He looked ahead, into the glittering maze. He needed to cross this biome to reach the Aethelburg Basin. It was miles of open, treacherous ground. If the Legion had scouts in here—and Rostova was too smart not to have a perimeter—they wouldn't need scanners to find him. They would just need to listen.

"We have to move," Ravn whispered, forcing himself to unclench his jaw. "But we have to be ghosts. No running. No sudden movements. Watch where you step." He took another step, placing his foot with agonizing slowness, rolling his weight from heel to toe to minimize the crunch. It was quieter, but still terrifyingly loud in the absolute stillness.

He **shifted his refractive focus**. The world shifted. The glare of the reflections dulled, and he saw the forest as a network of stress lines and angles. He saw the patches of ground where the crystal dust was thinner, packed down into a semblance of silence. He saw the angles of refraction that would hide him from a watcher on the ridge.

He was a creature of the Zone now, adapted and changed. He signaled the Stalker with a hand motion. Follow. Low. They moved into the Crystal Forest, two shadows trying to pass through a world of glass without breaking it. The Hunt was no longer a chase; it was a game of breath and heartbeat, played out on a board where every mistake rang like a bell.

They moved deeper into the labyrinth, two silent anomalies in a world of static perfection. The Crystal Forest was not a place that welcomed life; it tolerated it with a cold, brittle indifference. Every breath Ravn took felt like inhaling powdered glass, the air dry and sharp in his lungs.

He checked the Aperture. The display was a chaotic mess of false positives.

The refractive index of the trees was playing havoc with the sensors, creating "ghost" signals—phantom heat signatures that drifted through the crystal trunks like spirits.

But amidst the noise, a pattern emerged.

A series of cold, precise blips appeared on the edge of the scanner's range. They weren't drifting. They were moving in a grid search pattern.

"Contact," Ravn whispered, the word barely forming on his lips.

He pulled the Stalker down behind the faceted trunk of a massive, petrified oak. They waited.

The hunters emerged from the glare like specters. They were Legion scouts, an elite reconnaissance unit outfitted in advanced, light-bending camouflage cloaks. In any other environment, they would have been invisible. But here, in the Crystal Forest, their tech betrayed them.

The cloaks tried to mimic the surroundings, but they couldn't process the millions of complex refractions fast enough. As they moved, they shimmered with a digital lag, creating glitchy, pixelated silhouettes against the pristine glass.

There were four of them, moving in a silent, spread-out line. They held suppressed carbines, weapons designed for wet-work, for quiet kills. They weren't here to capture him. They were here to erase him.

Ravn watched them through the trunk of the tree, the crystal acting as a thick, distorted lens. He saw the lead scout pause, raising a hand. The soldier tapped his helmet, adjusting his optical sensors. He was confused.

Ravn realized the irony with a grim satisfaction. The Legion's greatest strength—their reliance on superior technology—was their fatal flaw in this biome. Their HUDs were likely screaming with target locks that weren't there. They were seeing reflections of reflections, thermal echoes of their own body heat bouncing back at them from the mirrors all around.

One scout raised his rifle and fired three quick, silent bursts into a dense cluster of saplings to his left. The blue bolts shattered the crystal branches, sending a shower of glittering dust into the air. There was nothing there. Just a reflection.

"They're blind," Ravn murmured. "Or seeing too much."

He looked at the Stalker. The creature was tense, its muscles vibrating. It wanted to attack, to close the distance and tear the intruders apart. But Ravn put a hand on its neck, shaking his head. A fight here would draw the rest of the squad. This wasn't a battle; it was a puzzle of angles and light.

He engaged the crystalline lattice in his eyes. The world shifted again. The glare subsided, replaced by vectors and lines of sight. He traced the scouts' path. They were sweeping north, pushing toward the Aethelburg Basin. They were blocking the only route forward.

He needed to create a gap in their line.

He scanned the environment. Ten meters to his right, a large, smooth slab of quartz jutted from the ground at a forty-five-degree angle. It was a natural mirror.

He picked up a small, heavy chunk of rock from the ground. He weighed it in his hand, calculating the trajectory. He didn't throw it at the soldiers. He threw it at the quartz slab.

The rock struck the crystal with a sharp, resonant clink. The acoustics of the forest amplified the sound, throwing it sideways.

To the scouts, the noise didn't come from Ravn's position; the reflection of the sound wave made it seem like it originated from a ridge fifty meters to their left.

The entire squad spun, weapons raised. The lead scout signaled, and they broke formation, advancing aggressively toward the source of the noise, their boots crunching loudly in their haste.

They had taken the bait. The grid was broken.

"Move," Ravn signaled.

He and the Stalker slipped through the gap in the line, moving low and fast while the scouts were distracted. They ghosted past the soldiers, so close Ravn could hear the hum of their armor servos and the low, frustrated chatter on their comms.

"Target phantom... re-calibrating sensors... too much noise..."

They left the scouts behind, hunting shadows in the glass. But Ravn knew this was only the first wave. The Legion wouldn't give up. They would adapt. They would realize their tech was failing and switch to older, more reliable methods. And when they did, the game would change from hide-and-seek to a footrace against a bullet.

They pushed on, the forest growing denser, the trees taller and sharper. The silence returned, heavier now, pregnant with the threat of what lay ahead. They were ghosts in the glass, but they were leaving footprints.

They moved deeper into the labyrinth, the silence of the Crystal Forest pressing against Ravn's eardrums like a physical weight. They had evaded the scout team, slipping through the gaps in their search grid like smoke, but the feeling of being watched didn't fade. It intensified.

It wasn't the chaotic, panicked sensation of the canyon chase. It was a cold, prickling focus centered between his shoulder blades.

Ravn stopped, holding up a hand. The Stalker froze instantly, one paw raised, its body a statue of dark chitin against the glittering background.

Crack.

A section of the crystal tree directly next to Ravn's head exploded. A shard of razor-sharp quartz, the size of a knife, sheared off and spun past his cheek, drawing a thin line of blood.

The sound of the shot didn't come until a second later. And when it arrived, it was a lie.

The crack-thump of a high-velocity kinetic slug echoed from the left, then the right, then from behind them. The acoustics of the forest took the sound wave and shattered it, bouncing it off a thousand hard surfaces until it was impossible to locate the source.

"Down!" Ravn hissed, throwing himself behind a ridge of jagged, translucent rock.

The Stalker dove beside him, its bioluminescence flashing a startled, angry red before dimming to nothing. They were pinned.

"Sniper," Ravn whispered, pressing his back against the cold stone. He touched his cheek, his fingers coming away wet with blood. "Kinetic rounds. No energy signature to track. He's good." He risked a glance around the edge of their cover. A second shot rang out instantly, chipping the rock inches from his face. He pulled back, his heart hammering.

This wasn't a scout. This was a hunter. A Legion specialist who understood the environment better than the others. This sniper wasn't relying on high-tech sensors that got confused by reflections. He was using the forest's geometry as a weapon. He was firing from a concealed position, likely masked by a refractive angle, and using the echoes to hide his location.

Ravn checked the Aperture. *THREAT DETECTED: TRAJECTORY UNKNOWN.* The device was useless. It couldn't calculate a vector from a sound that came from everywhere.

He closed his eyes and took a breath, forcing the adrenaline to settle. He couldn't out-shoot this enemy. He had to out-think him. He had to use the house of mirrors against its master.

He engaged the crystalline lattice in his eyes. The world shifted into high-contrast geometry. He didn't look for the sniper; he looked for the shot. He focused on the shattered scar on the tree trunk where the first bullet had hit. He traced the angle of impact, drawing a mental line back through the air.

The line pointed to a cluster of diamond-shaped boulders eighty meters away, perched on a high rise. But that was too obvious. A sniper wouldn't expose himself on a crest.

Ravn looked closer. He traced the reflection of that cluster in the smooth, polished trunk of a nearby tree. The reflection showed a gap between the boulders, a perfect, protected firing lane that was invisible to the naked eye from Ravn's position.

The sniper wasn't shooting directly at him. He was shooting through a gap in the refraction, using a specific alignment of the crystals to magnify his scope's view while remaining completely hidden behind solid rock.

"I see you," Ravn breathed.

He looked at the Stalker. The creature was coiled tight, waiting for a target. It couldn't smell the sniper over the ozone of the forest. It couldn't hear him over the echoes. It needed eyes.

Ravn grabbed a loose, flat shard of crystal from the ground. It was polished on one side, a natural mirror. He looked at the Stalker and pointed a finger to the left, indicating a wide, flanking route through a dense thicket of glass saplings.

"Go," he mouthed. "Wait for the flash." The creature understood. It melted away, moving with a silence that defied the brittle ground, its body low, weaving through the shadows of the refraction.

Ravn waited. He counted the seconds, estimating the Stalker's speed. Ten seconds. Twenty.

He shifted his position, propping the crystal shard on the edge of the rock. He angled it carefully, using his enhanced vision to calculate the reflection. He wasn't trying to see the sniper. He was trying to blind him.

He waited for the suns to shift a fraction of a degree. The light hit the shard. A beam of concentrated, reflected sunlight shot out, bouncing off a tree trunk, angling through the gap in the boulders, and striking the sniper's scope directly.

It was a momentary flare, a blinding flash of white light in the sniper's eye. The sniper flinched. A reflex shot rang out, wild and high, shattering a branch far above Ravn's head.

The position was revealed. The muzzle flash bloomed from the gap in the boulders, a momentary star in the shadows.

"Now!" Ravn yelled, though the Stalker couldn't hear him. It didn't need to. It had seen the flash.

From the shadows behind the boulders, a dark shape erupted. The Stalker cleared the distance in a single bound. There was no roar, no challenge. Just the wet, heavy sound of an impact, a brief scuffle of boots on stone, and a single, choked cry that was abruptly cut short.

Then, silence returned to the forest.

Ravn waited a beat, then two. He stood up slowly, his eyes fixed on the high rise. The Stalker appeared on top of the boulder. It shook its head, a spray of red droplets staining the pristine crystal ground. It looked down at Ravn and let out a soft, chuffing breath. The path was clear.

Ravn exhaled, the tension draining from his muscles. They had survived the hunter. But as he looked at the endless miles of glittering forest still ahead of them, he knew the game of attrition was far from over. They were winning the battles, but they were slowly losing the war against exhaustion.

They walked.

The tactical adrenaline of the sniper encounter faded, leaving behind a hollow, rattling exhaustion that settled into Ravn's bones like lead. Time lost its meaning in the Crystal Forest. The suns moved across the sky in a slow, mocking arc, their light fracturing through the canopy into a kaleidoscope that never dimmed, never changed, never offered the mercy of true darkness.

It was a death march through a diamond.

They had been moving for what felt like days, though the Aperture's internal chronometer insisted it had been only twelve hours since they escaped the canyon. But biological time is measured in calories and hydration, and by that metric, Ravn was ancient.

He had eaten the last of his nutrient paste two days ago. His canteen was dry, the water reclamation filter clogged with crystal dust. He was running entirely on the Essence.

The alien energy he had absorbed in the Reality Tear was a cold, electric fire in his veins. It kept his heart beating. It kept his muscles firing. But it was a dirty fuel. It burned hot and fast, and he could feel it consuming him from the inside out, metabolizing his own muscle tissue to keep the engine running.

He felt light, hollow, as if a strong wind could blow him away like a dry leaf. The silence of the forest, once a tactical threat, became a psychological torture. The only sound was the crunch-crunch-crunch of his boots on the glass floor, a rhythm that synchronized with the pounding of his headache.

And then, the forest began to speak.

It started as a whisper in the wind chimes of the mica leaves.

Ravn...

Ravn stumbled, his head snapping up. He scanned the faceted trunks of the trees. There was no one there. Just his own reflection, multiplied a thousand times, staring back at him with glowing, crystalline eyes.

But the reflections were wrong.

In the polished surface of a massive, quartz oak, his reflection didn't move when he did. It stood still. And it wasn't wearing his ragged survival gear. It was wearing a white lab coat.

It was Aris.

His brother stood inside the tree, trapped in the crystal like a fly in amber. He was holding a marker, tapping it rhythmically against the glass. *Tap. Tap. Tap.*

"The math doesn't work, Ravn," the reflection mouthed, the voice sounding like it was coming from inside Ravn's own skull. "You forgot to carry the variable. You always forget." Ravn squeezed his eyes shut, shaking his head violently. "You're not real," he rasped, his voice a dry croak. "You're dead. You're in the Anchor."

When he opened his eyes, Aris was gone. But ten meters further on, in the facet of a fallen branch, he saw Lena. She wasn't screaming in terror as she had in his memories. She was smiling, that wry, brilliant smile she used to give him when he missed the punchline of a joke.

"It's beautiful here," she whispered, her voice refracted through the glass. "Why are you running away from the beauty?" He kept walking, but the ghosts were everywhere now. The forest was a hall of mirrors reflecting his own guilt. He saw Caleb, his face twisted in accusation. He saw the Husk warrior Kael, his eyes swirling with madness. He saw himself, dead and gray, falling into the sky of the Reality Tear.

The line between the world and his mind was dissolving. The Essence, which heightened his perception, was now amplifying his delusions. He was hallucinating in high-definition.

He stumbled over a root of solid glass. His knees hit the sharp ground hard, shredding his trousers and slicing his skin. He didn't feel the pain. He just felt the overwhelming gravity of the earth pulling him down.

It would be so easy to stay here. To lie down on the bed of crystal dust and let the lights take him. To stop running. To stop thinking.

He slumped forward, his forehead resting against the cool ground. The Red Eye of the Axiom stared down at him through the canopy, a judgmental star.

System failure imminent, a distant part of his mind noted. *Biological shutdown in 3... 2...*

Something nudged his shoulder. Hard.

He groaned, trying to push it away. "Leave me."

The nudge came again, forceful and insistent. A wet, rough tongue licked the side of his face, rasping against his beard.

Ravn opened his eyes. The Stalker was standing over him. The creature was in no better shape. Its sleek, dark chitin was dull and scratched, covered in gray dust. Its ribs showed through its flank. Its bioluminescence was a faint, flickering ember. It was starving, thirsty, and exhausted. But it wasn't stopping.

It looked down at him with those dark, intelligent almond eyes. There was no pity in them. There was a challenge. It let out a low, chuffing sound, then lowered its body, presenting its shoulder to him. It was offering support.

Ravn looked at the creature. It didn't care about Aris or Lena. It didn't care about the Axiom or the keys. It cared about him. It was the only thing in this entire hallucination of a world that was undeniably, physically real.

He gritted his teeth. He reached out, grabbing the Stalker's thick mane. With a groan of exertion that tore at his throat, he hauled himself up. He leaned heavily against the creature's flank. The Stalker braced its legs, taking his weight without complaint.

"Okay," Ravn whispered, tears cutting tracks through the dust on his face. "Okay." They began to move again. A three-legged, stumbling organism made of man and beast. The Stalker took the brunt of the effort, guiding Ravn's steps, steering him away from the sharpest rocks.

The hallucinations didn't stop. Aris still watched him from the trees. Lena still whispered in the leaves. But Ravn didn't look at them. He looked at the ground. He looked at the Stalker's paws. *Step. Step. Step.*

They were dying. He knew it. The attrition was winning. But they were dying forward. And as long as they were moving, the equation wasn't solved yet.

They stumbled out of the Crystal Forest not with a triumphant burst of speed, but with the desperate, lurching momentum of a machine running on its last drop of fuel.

The transition was as abrupt as the entrance had been. The canopy of razor-sharp quartz and wind-chiming mica simply ended, giving way to a steep, crumbling slope of gray scree. The blinding, refracted light of the forest vanished, replaced by the dull, flat illumination of the bruised purple sky.

Ravn fell to his knees, his breath tearing at his throat like a rasp. The Stalker collapsed beside him, its chest heaving, its bioluminescence faded to a dull, rhythmic pulse that barely registered against the gray rock.

They were alive. They had crossed the house of mirrors.

Ravn wiped a mixture of sweat and crystal dust from his eyes. He looked up, his vision swimming, and saw the destination.

Below them lay the Aethelburg Basin.

It was a wound in the world. A circular depression ten kilometers wide, where the very fabric of reality had been scooped out and put back wrong. The ground was a sterile, lifeless gray dust, devoid of the Zone's vibrant flora. There were no trees, no moss, no movement. It was a dead zone, a scar of absolute silence in the center of a screaming world.

In the center of the basin, a dark fissure cut through the earth—the entrance to the subterranean research facility. The tomb of his brother. The womb of the Axiom. It sat there, a black singularity, pulling his gaze toward it with a gravitational force that felt sickeningly physical.

"We made it," Ravn whispered, the words feeling dry and brittle.

But as his eyes adjusted, focusing through the crystalline lattice of his new vision, he realized they were not the only ones arriving at the finish line.

To the west, a cloud of dust rose against the horizon. He zoomed in, his vision clicking into telescopic focus. It was the Legion. A column of armored personnel carriers and heavy walkers was navigating the treacherous slope of the basin, moving with a grim, inexorable discipline. They had circled around the Crystal Forest, choosing the long way over the dangerous way. Rostova was coming.

To the east, a more chaotic dust cloud choked the air. It was smaller than the Legion's force, a ragged collection of surviving buggies and bikes, led by a single, smoking war-rig that looked like it had driven through hell.

The Rust Lords. Jax had survived the canyon ambush, and his rage had only fueled his engine. He was burning a direct path toward the center, ignoring the terrain, driven by pure, spiteful momentum.

And from the south, emerging from the tree line like ghosts, he saw the shimmer of movement. The Husks. A war party of Ascended warriors, moving with a terrifying, fluid speed across the gray dust. They carried no banners, made no sound, but their intent was clear. They were coming to reclaim the heart of their world.

Ravn stared at the converging lines. Three armies. Three philosophies. One point of impact. It wasn't just a destination anymore. It was the center of a target.

He looked at the Stalker. The creature had pulled itself up, its head low, growling at the distant shapes of the war machines. It was ready to fight, even on its last legs.

Ravn reached into his pack and touched the cold, vibrating surface of the obsidian key. He had Nature, Chaos, and Information. He had the map. He had the will.

But he had run out of time. The race was no longer about distance. It was about seconds.

He stood up, swaying slightly. The Essence in his veins flared one last time, a reserve of cold fire pushing back the exhaustion. He looked down at the dark entrance in the center of the basin.

"One last run," he said to the Stalker. "For everything."

He began to slide down the scree slope, descending into the scar. The hunt was over. The war for the Anchor had begun.

24

The Descent into Aethelburg

The descent was not a climb; it was a controlled fall.

Ravn slid down the steep embankment of the basin, his boots surfing on a landslide of loose, gray scree. Dust billowed around him, a choking, dry cloud that tasted of pulverized concrete and ancient ash.

The Stalker scrambled beside him, its claws digging deep furrows in the loose rock to slow its momentum, a low, terrified whine vibrating in its throat. They hit the basin floor with a jarring impact that rattled Ravn's teeth. He rolled, absorbing the shock, and came up into a crouch, his pulse rifle raised, his eyes scanning for threats.

But there was nothing.

The Aethelburg Basin was a void. After weeks of navigating the aggressive, verdant chaos of the fungal forests, the rust-colored fury of the wastelands, and the sharp, glittering malice of the Crystal Labyrinth, this place was shocking in its sterility. It was a ten-kilometer-wide circle of absolute nothingness.

The ground was a flat, featureless expanse of compacted gray dust, baked hard by the initial energy release of the Anomaly five years ago. There were no trees here. No glowing moss. No insects. No wind. It was a dead zone, a place where the life-force of the planet had been cauterized.

The air shimmered with a latent, oppressive energy. It wasn't the clean, electric hum of the Crystal Forest; it was a heavy, static pressure that made the fine hairs on Ravn's arms stand up and his teeth ache. It felt like standing under a high-voltage power line during a thunderstorm. It was the feeling of potential energy waiting to be kinetic.

Ravn stood up, brushing the gray dust from his shredded clothes. He looked back up the slope. High above, on the rim of the basin, the silhouette of the Crystal Forest glittered like a crown of jagged ice. But down here, the light was flat and shadowless, the three blue suns filtered through a haze of suspended particulate matter.

He checked the Aperture. The display was glitching, the readout scrolling with random characters before settling on a single, flashing warning.

WARNING: HIGH ENERGY SATURATION. LOCAL REALITY INDEX: UNSTABLE. PROXIMITY TO ANCHOR: 5KM.

"We're close," he rasped.

He looked at the Stalker. The creature was pressing itself low to the ground, its ears flattened, its tail tucked between its legs. Its bioluminescence, usually a vibrant indicator of its mood, was dark, completely extinguished.

To a creature of the Zone, an organism connected to the great, throbbing web of life, this place must have felt like a vacuum. It was a psychic dead zone.

"I know," Ravn whispered, reaching out to touch the creature's cold, trembling flank. "I feel it too." He felt it in the hollow ache of his chest, in the resonance of the three keys in his pack. This wasn't just a location. It was a wound. It was the exact spot where he and Aris had torn the world open, and the scar tissue had never healed.

He turned his gaze to the center of the basin. Five kilometers away, a dark, jagged shape broke the flatness of the gray plain. It looked like a piece of broken obsidian jutting from the earth.

It was the entrance to the subterranean research facility. The main blast doors, blown outward by the force of the event, stood like twisted, metal sentinels guarding the descent into the underworld.

It was the finish line. But they were not the only ones running the race.

Ravn overlaid the wireframe view, zooming in on the horizon. To the west, a cloud of dust rose against the horizon. He could see the individual shapes of the Legion's heavy walkers, their hydraulic legs churning up the gray dust. They were moving in a phalanx, a wall of steel and plasma cannons. Rostova pushed her machines hard; they were already deploying at the rim, setting up a firing line to lock down the basin.

To the east, the chaotic swarm of the Rust Lords was tearing across the flats. Arriving late but moving fast, Jax's war-rig, trailing black smoke, was in the lead, its engine roaring a challenge to the silence. They were reckless, heedless of the terrain, driving with the manic energy of berserkers, aiming to smash the Legion line before it could solidify.

And from the south, the shimmering mirage of the Husks was resolving into a terrifying reality. The Ascended warriors were sprinting, their movements a blur of supernatural speed. They carried no supplies, no armor, only their bone weapons and their fanatical devotion. They were closing the distance faster than the machines.

The three armies were converging. They were three points of a triangle, collapsing inward toward the center. Toward Ravn.

He checked the position of the Red Eye in the sky. It was directly overhead now, a baleful, unblinking pupil staring down into the iris of the basin. The Axiom was watching the end of its experiment.

"We have to move," Ravn said, his voice tight. "They'll be here in less than an hour."

He started to run. It wasn't a sprint; he didn't have the energy for that. It was a loping, rhythmic jog, a pace born of desperation. The Stalker fell in beside him, moving silently on the hardpan.

They were two specks of life moving across a dead ocean, racing against the tide of war that was rising on all sides.

They ran until the gray dust of the basin floor turned into a field of shattered concrete and twisted rebar. The looming shape of the facility entrance grew from a dark smudge on the horizon into a towering monument to catastrophe.

Up close, the scale of the destruction was breathtaking. The main entrance to the Aethelburg Research Facility had not been designed to be imposing; it had been a standard, secure access point for government contractors and scientists. But the Anomaly had transformed it. The massive, blast-proof doors, slabs of reinforced steel three meters thick, had not been opened. They had been blown out.

They lay twisted and crumpled on the ground a hundred meters from the entrance, like discarded pieces of tin foil tossed aside by a petulant giant. The force required to do that was beyond calculation. It wasn't an explosion; it was a directional release of pressure from a universe trying to fit into a space too small to contain it.

Ravn slowed to a walk, his breath ragged. He approached the gaping maw of the tunnel. The concrete archway was cracked and scorched, the rebar protruding like the blackened ribs of a skeleton. Above the breach, a metal sign hung by a single bolt, swinging slightly in the static-charged air.

It was scorched and illegible, but Ravn didn't need to read it. He knew what it said.

Aethelburg Quantum Research Division. Authorized Personnel Only.

He stopped at the threshold, the line where the gray dust of the Zone met the cracked linoleum of the old world.

The Stalker stopped with him. But while Ravn was frozen by memory, the Stalker was frozen by a primal, biological wrongness. The creature whined, a high-pitched, fearful sound that Ravn had never heard it make, not even when facing the Reaper.

It crouched low, its belly fur brushing the dust, its ears flattened against its skull. Its bioluminescence was flickering rapidly, a chaotic strobe of yellow and gray. It looked at the dark tunnel, then back at the open basin, and let out a sharp, warning bark.

To the Stalker, a child of the Zone, the wilderness was dangerous, but it was right. It was a system of predator and prey, growth and decay. This place—this geometric tomb of dead angles, processed air, and synthetic materials—was an abomination. It smelled of things that had never lived. It felt like a void in the ecosystem.

"I know," Ravn whispered, kneeling beside the creature. He ran his hand over its trembling flank, feeling the muscles bunched tight with the urge to flee. "It's dead. It's just a dead place." He was lying. It wasn't dead. He could feel the facility humming in his own bones, resonating with the keys in his pack. It was sleeping.

He stood up and stepped across the line.

The transition was instantaneous and jarring. The moment he passed under the concrete arch, the oppressive, static-charged atmosphere of the basin vanished, replaced by a chill, stagnant air that smelled of dry rot, old plastic, and the copper tang of ancient, fried wiring.

The light changed. The flat, gray illumination of the three suns was cut off, replaced by a deep, heavy gloom. But it wasn't total darkness. Deep within the tunnel, emergency lights, triggered by some phantom sensor or residual power loop, flickered with a sickly, intermittent orange glow.

Ravn clicked on the Aperture's flashlight. The beam cut through the dusty air, illuminating a scene that hit him harder than any monster in the Zone.

It was the security checkpoint. He saw the metal detectors, now toppled and rusted. He saw the glass booth where the guard, a man named Miller who used to talk about his grandkids, would sit and check badges.

The glass was shattered, the booth empty save for a layer of gray dust. He saw the turnstiles, frozen in place.

A ghost of a memory overlaid the ruin. He saw himself walking through here on a Tuesday morning, holding a travel mug of coffee, swiping his badge with a practiced, thoughtless motion. He heard the beep of the scanner, the clack of the turnstile, Miller's cheerful "Morning, Dr. Vidar." It was a memory of a world so safe, so boring, and so orderly that it felt like a hallucination. The contrast between that Tuesday morning and this gray, ruined reality was a physical pain in his chest. He had walked through these doors a thousand times to go to work. Now, he was walking through them to end the world.

He looked back at the Stalker. The creature was still outside, pacing the line of the threshold, refusing to enter.

"I can't do this alone," Ravn said, his voice echoing in the dead tunnel. He held out a hand. "Please." The Stalker looked at him, then at the dark, unnatural tunnel. It let out a low growl, a sound of supreme unhappiness. But the bond they had forged in the Whispering Caves, the trust earned in the Reality Tear, was stronger than its fear.

It stepped across the line.

Its claws clicked on the linoleum, a sharp, unnatural sound that made the creature wince. It moved close to Ravn, pressing its side against his leg, seeking a physical anchor in this alien world of straight lines and dead stone.

"Good," Ravn whispered.

He unslung his pulse rifle, checking the charge. It was low, but functional. He checked the Aperture. The map of the facility was already loaded, a schematic burned into his own memory.

TARGET: PRIMARY REACTOR CHAMBER. DEPTH: SUB-LEVEL 5.

"We go down," he said.

They moved past the ruined security checkpoint and into the main atrium, leaving the gray light of the Zone behind and descending into the haunted dark of the human past.

The transition was like stepping into a strobe light. The facility was not dead. It was seizing.

The emergency lighting system, triggered by the Anomaly five years ago, had never shut down. But the power grid was corrupted, bleeding energy into the surrounding rock. The result was a frantic, erratic flickering of deep orange sodium lights.

They buzzed like angry wasps, snapping on and off in a chaotic rhythm that made movement look disjointed. One second, the atrium was plunged into total darkness; the next, it was bathed in a harsh, amber glare that threw long, jumping shadows against the walls.

The air pressure was wrong. It fluctuated wildly, popping Ravn's ears every few steps. A low, throbbing hum permeated the walls, a sound that wasn't quite mechanical and wasn't quite organic. It sounded like a massive lung struggling to draw breath through a crushed windpipe.

The Stalker hated it. The creature moved in a low crouch, its claws clicking nervously on the cracked terrazzo floor. It snapped its head back and forth, growling at the empty air, its bioluminescence flashing a confused pattern of threat and submission.

It couldn't lock onto a target because the threats weren't physical. They were temporal.

Ravn saw the first one near the elevators.

In a flash of orange light, a figure appeared. It was a woman in a lab coat, clutching a sheaf of papers to her chest. She was running, her face contorted in a silent scream of absolute terror. She wasn't solid; she was translucent, a smudge of light and motion like a double-exposure on a film photograph.

The light flickered off. Darkness. The light snapped back on. The woman was gone.

Ravn stopped, his heart hammering. He knew what this was. He and Aris had theorized about it—"Temporal Echoic Resonance." When a high-energy event shattered the local spacetime manifold, it could imprint moments of extreme emotional or kinetic intensity onto the environment.

These weren't ghosts. They were recordings. The facility was playing back the moment of its own murder on an infinite loop.

"It's not real," Ravn whispered, his voice trembling. He reached down to touch the Stalker, whose hackles were raised. "It's just a movie. A recording." They pushed forward, moving deeper into the administration wing. The corridor was a tunnel of flickering horror. The echoes became more frequent. He saw a security guard firing his sidearm at an invisible enemy, the muzzle flash a silent bloom of light. He saw two technicians supporting a wounded colleague, their mouths moving in frantic, soundless shouts. He saw a man he recognized—Dr. Vance, a senior analyst—curled in a fetal ball under a desk, his hands over his ears.

The silence of the vacuum outside began to bleed away. A sound started to rise from the walls, faint at first, then growing steadily louder.

It was the sound from his nightmare. The containment alarm.

It wasn't the full, ear-splitting shriek of the memory. It was a ghostly, distorted version of it, sounding tinny and distant, like a radio tuned between stations.

Whoop... whoop... static... whoop...

240

It grated on Ravn's nerves, scraping away the callus of five years of survival. He felt the urge to run, to join the panicked, silent figures rushing past him in the gloom. He felt the phantom heat of the reactor on his skin.

The Stalker lunged. The creature roared, swiping its claws at a flickering figure that had suddenly appeared directly in their path—a man stumbling, reaching out as if to grab them.

The Stalker's claws passed through the figure harmlessly, meeting only air. The echo dissolved into a cloud of static particles. The Stalker stumbled, confused, sniffing the air where the man had been. There was no scent. No blood. Just the smell of ozone and fear. The creature looked back at Ravn, its eyes wide with a primal panic.

It couldn't fight things it couldn't touch.

"I know," Ravn said, his own grip on his pulse rifle tightening until his knuckles turned white. "Ignore them. Look at me. Just look at me."

He forced the creature to focus on him, on the solid, physical reality of his presence.

They had to keep moving. They reached a junction. The corridor to the left led to the cafeteria and the dorms. The corridor to the right led to the elevators for the lower levels.

Ravn looked left. In a long flash of the emergency lights, he saw the cafeteria doors burst open. A crowd of echoes poured out, a stampede of terrified light. He recognized faces. Friends. Rivals. People he had shared coffee with. People whose names he had forgotten but whose terror was now etched into his mind forever.

He turned away, nausea rolling in his gut. He turned right, toward the elevators.

The elevator doors were fused shut, melted by a surge of heat. The call button was a lump of slag.

"Stairs," Ravn muttered. "Always the stairs." He found the access door to the emergency stairwell. He grabbed the handle. It was hot—not burning, but feverishly warm, vibrating with the facility's dying pulse. He pulled it open.

The darkness of the shaft swallowed the orange flicker of the hallway.

From deep below, from the throat of the facility, came a sound that was not an echo.

It was a mechanical screech, the sound of metal grinding on metal, followed by the heavy, rhythmic thud of a servo-motor stepping on concrete.

The facility wasn't just haunting him. It was waking up to stop him.

Ravn turned on the Aperture's flashlight, the beam cutting a white cone into the dark.

"We're not alone down there," he said to the Stalker.

The creature growled, a low, solid sound of aggression. Finally, a threat it could bite.

They stepped into the stairwell, the heavy door slamming shut behind them, cutting off the silent screams of the ghosts and locking them in with the monsters.

25

The Reactor's Gut

The heavy steel doors of the service elevator slid shut with a finality that echoed like a prison sentence. The seal engaged with a pneumatic hiss, cutting off the view of the shattered Observation Deck and sealing Ravn and the Stalker inside a box of cold, brushed steel.

For a moment, there was only silence and the hum of the magnetic levitation coils engaging beneath the floor. Then, the sensation of weightlessness hit.

The elevator dropped.

It wasn't a smooth, modern descent. It was a lurching, mechanical fall. The ancient guides screamed in protest, a high-pitched shriek of metal on metal that vibrated through the walls of the cage. The air inside the small space instantly grew heavy and stale, smelling of hydraulic fluid and the copper tang of old electricity.

The Stalker panicked. To a creature born of the open, limitless Zone, this was a special kind of hell. It was trapped in a blind, moving box that defied its understanding of movement. It scrambled for purchase on the metal floor, its claws screeching against the steel.

It threw its weight against the walls, snapping its jaws at the invisible force that was pulling its stomach into its throat. Its bioluminescence flared a chaotic, strobe-like white, illuminating the cage in harsh, terrified flashes.

"Easy," Ravn said, though his own voice was tight. He reached out, grabbing the creature's harness to anchor it. "It's just a machine. It's taking us down." He leaned back against the wall, sliding down until he was sitting on the floor next to the beast. He needed to conserve his strength. The encounter with Aris's ghost in the atrium had drained him, leaving him feeling hollowed out and raw.

He looked up at the floor indicator above the door. In the old world, it would have been a simple LED display counting down from Observation to Level 5. But here, close to the Anchor, simple causality was breaking down.

The digital numbers were glitching. They didn't count down; they scrambled.

05... 04... 03...

Then *88*. Then a series of nonsensical alien symbols. Then a negative number that spiraled downward into infinity.

-12... -135... -4000...

Time in the elevator became elastic. Ravn felt like they had been descending for minutes, then hours. He checked the Aperture on his wrist. The chronometer was spinning wildly, the seconds ticking by too fast to read.

Temporal dilation, his mind noted, a cold, scientific observation surfacing through the fear. *The gravity of the Anchor is bending time around the core. We are descending into a gravity well.* The air pressure fluctuated violently. His ears popped, then popped again. The air grew hot, then freezing cold, cycling through extremes in seconds. Frost formed on the metal walls, tracing intricate, fractal patterns that bloomed and melted in the span of a breath.

He closed his eyes, trying to center himself. He could feel the three keys in his pack vibrating against his spine. They were singing. A low, discordant harmony of energy—the organic thrum of the Crystal, the chaotic buzz of the Gold, and the cold silence of the Obsidian—all reacting to the proximity of their mother-source.

They were magnets being dragged toward a lodestone.

The Stalker whined, pressing its head into Ravn's lap. It was trembling.

"I know," Ravn whispered, stroking the creature's chitin. "We're almost there." Suddenly, the descent changed. The feeling of weightlessness vanished, replaced by a crushing G-force as the elevator began to decelerate. The shriek of the guides deepened to a groan. The floor shuddered violently, knocking Ravn's head against the wall.

The digital display froze on a single word, burning in bright, ominous red:

CORE.

The elevator slammed to a halt with a bone-jarring thud. The lights flickered and died, plunging them into total darkness for a heartbeat before the emergency red lighting kicked in, bathing the cage in the color of blood.

The pneumatic seal hissed again, a long, dying breath that echoed into the vastness beyond. The heavy steel panels shuddered and slid apart, revealing not a room, but a void.

Ravn stepped out of the red-lit cage and onto a metal grating that hung over an abyss. He clicked his pulse rifle's flashlight to maximum intensity, but the beam was swallowed by the darkness. The air here was different— super-cooled, motionless, and carrying the distinct, metallic taste of cold iron and ionized dust.

It tasted like the inside of a lightning bolt.

He raised the Aperture, adjusting the gain on its sensors, and swept the beam across the chamber. As the light cut through the gloom, the scale of the Aethelburg Reactor Floor revealed itself, and Ravn felt his knees weaken.

It was a cathedral of the machine age.

The chamber was a colossal cylinder, half a kilometer wide and plunging down into the bedrock. The walls were lined with millions of shock-absorbing acoustic tiles, giving the space a textured, geometric complexity. Catwalks and gantries crisscrossed the empty air like spiderwebs of steel, connecting massive, towering machines that rose from the floor like the pillars of a ruined temple.

But it wasn't the size that stole his breath. It was the shape.

In his memory, this place was a masterpiece of Euclidean geometry— straight lines, perfect circles, right angles. It was a monument to precision.

Now, it was a surrealist nightmare. The Anomaly hadn't just destroyed the machinery; it had rewritten the rules of matter that held it together.

The massive cooling towers, three stories tall and built of reinforced concrete, were not cracked or crumbled. They were twisted. They spiraled upward like wringed-out towels, the concrete stretching and flowing like taffy before freezing instantly in place.

The particle accelerator ring, a perfect loop of superconducting magnets that had once encircled the room, was shattered. Sections of it floated in the air, suspended by locked pockets of gravity, while others had dripped down the walls like molten wax, pooling on the floor in puddles of hardened, silvery alloy.

It was a frozen explosion. A snapshot of a moment where steel became liquid and gravity became a suggestion.

"My god," Ravn whispered, the sound vanishing into the acoustic baffling of the walls.

He walked to the edge of the gantry, looking down. The floor of the chamber was a landscape of wreckage. The primary emitter arrays—multi-ton devices of gold and ceramic—had been pulled from their mountings and dragged toward the center of the room, fusing together into a jagged, metallic mountain range.

The Stalker crept out of the elevator, its body low. It looked out at the twisted landscape and whined, a sound of pure sensory confusion. To the creature, matter was binary: hard or soft, solid or liquid. This place was a violation of that basic truth. It sniffed the air, but there was no scent of decay, only the sterile, terrifying smell of physics gone wrong.

It refused to step onto the grating, its claws digging into the threshold of the elevator.

"It's solid," Ravn promised, though he wasn't entirely sure. "It's just… wrong." He engaged the crystalline lattice in his eyes. The darkness receded, replaced by a wireframe view of the chamber. He saw the stress lines in the twisted metal, glowing with residual energy. He saw the pockets of high radiation, blooming like invisible flowers of death.

And he saw the path.

The central gantry, the main bridge that led to the inner core, was gone—twisted into a corkscrew and severed. To reach the Anchor, they would have to descend to the reactor floor and navigate the wreckage of the emitter arrays.

"We have to go down," Ravn said, pointing to a service ladder that seemed relatively intact, though it twisted dangerously to the left halfway down.

He began the descent. The metal rungs were cold enough to burn his hands through his gloves. Every step sent a vibration through the structure, a groan of metal that hadn't moved in five years.

They reached the floor. Up close, the destruction was even more disturbing.

Ravn walked past a bank of supercomputers that had melted into a single, solid block of silicon and plastic, the keys of the interface still visible in the smooth surface like fossils in amber. He passed a support pillar made of I-beams that had been tied into a knot.

This was the power of the Axiom. It wasn't malice. It was simply a level of energy that the material world couldn't withstand. It was what happened when you tried to download the ocean into a cup. The cup didn't just break; it changed state.

They navigated through the maze of the melted cathedral, moving toward the center. The silence was absolute, heavy and pressing.

Then, the Stalker stopped.

The creature's head snapped up, its nostrils flaring. It let out a sharp, percussive *chuff*—a warning sound Ravn had learned meant immediate, mortal danger. It backed away, its claws clicking frantically on the metal floor, its bioluminescence flaring a violent, panicked red.

Ravn froze. He raised his pulse rifle, scanning the shadows for movement. "What is it? Drones? Glimmers?"

But the Stalker wasn't looking at the shadows. It was looking at the floor ahead.

Ravn followed its gaze. Ten meters in front of them, the path through the wreckage simply ended. A massive rupture in the primary cooling line, a pipe thick enough to drive a car through, lay across their route.

It had been sheared in half by the torsional forces of the Anomaly. But it wasn't leaking water or coolant. It was leaking light.

A pool of glowing, brilliant blue fluid lay across the floor, blocking the way to the inner core. It shimmered with a deadly, hypnotic beauty, casting a wash of azure light that danced on the twisted metal walls. It rippled, though there was no wind, moving with a slow, viscous sluggishness.

Ravn stepped closer, engaging the crystalline lattice in his eyes to analyze the substance. The data that scrolled across his vision was a stream of terrified mathematics.

WARNING: EXOTIC MATTER DETECTED. STATE: SUPERFLUID. RADIATION LEVEL: LETHAL. TEMPORAL STABILITY: 0%.

"Cherenkov radiation," Ravn breathed, the color triggering a visceral memory of the control room, of Lena's hand dissolving. "But... condensed. Liquid exotic matter." He watched as a loose bolt, dislodged from a gantry above, fell into the pool.

The moment the metal touched the blue liquid before it could even make a splash, it simply ceased to be. It unspooled into raw code. The steel bolt dissolved into a mist of gray static pixels that drifted upward for a moment before vanishing entirely.

It was a moat of pure unmaking. A substance that didn't burn matter, but deleted it from the universe's hard drive.

The pool stretched wall to wall, filling the depression in the floor created by the facility's collapse. There was no way around it. The liquid light was slowly eating into the floor plates, widening the gap.

"We can't cross that," Ravn said, his voice hollow.

He looked up. Above the pool, suspended from the ceiling by groaning, rusted chains, was a network of maintenance gantries. They were twisted, some hanging at forty-five-degree angles, their metal gratings corroded by five years of exposure to the reactor's leakage. But they bridged the gap.

"We have to go up," he said to the Stalker.

The creature looked at the gantries, then down at the pool of unmaking, and whined. It understood the physics of falling. It understood that a slip here meant something worse than death.

"I know," Ravn whispered. "I'm scared too."

He found a service ladder bolted to a support pillar. The metal was cold enough to burn his hands through his gloves. He began to climb, the structure vibrating with every step. The Stalker followed, its claws hooking into the rungs, moving with a nervous, jerky rhythm.

They reached the gantry level, twenty meters above the floor. The heat coming off the blue pool below was intense, a wave of dry, static pressure that made Ravn's skin crawl. The air tasted of ozone and copper.

The walkway ahead was a nightmare. The metal grating was rusted through in places, revealing the lethal blue glow below. The handrails were twisted into abstract shapes.

"Slow," Ravn cautioned. "Test your weight."

He stepped out onto the catwalk. The metal groaned, a high-pitched screech of stress. He gripped the warped handrail, his knuckles white. He moved one foot at a time, keeping his center of gravity low.

The Stalker followed, placing its paws exactly where Ravn's boots had been. It was flattened to the grating, its belly fur brushing the rust.

They reached the midpoint of the crossing, directly over the widest part of the pool. The blue light was blinding here, washing out Ravn's vision. The hum of the liquid was a physical vibration in his teeth.

Suddenly, the gantry lurched.

A support cable, eaten away by the rising fumes of the exotic matter, snapped with a sound like a gunshot. The walkway dropped three feet, tilting violently to the right.

Ravn was thrown against the handrail. The rusted metal creaked, bending outward under his weight. For a heart-stopping second, he hung over the abyss, staring directly down into the swirling, de-rendering blue.

The Stalker let out a yelp as it scrabbled for purchase, sliding toward the edge.

"Hold on!" Ravn screamed. He hooked his arm around a vertical stanchion, pulling himself back from the brink.

He reached out with his other hand and grabbed the Stalker's harness just as the creature's hind legs slipped off the edge. He held the beast's weight, his muscles screaming, the Essence in his veins flaring hot.

He hauled the creature back onto the grating. The Stalker scrambled up, shaking, its claws digging deep gouges into the metal.

They lay there for a moment, pressing themselves into the rust, breathing the ozone-heavy air. The gantry swayed gently, a pendulum over death.

"Go," Ravn gasped. "Move. Now." They scrambled the rest of the way, abandoning caution for speed. They leaped across a gap where a section of grating had fallen away, landing hard on the far platform. They didn't stop until they were back on the solid concrete of the mezzanine level, well away from the edge.

Ravn leaned against the wall, his legs shaking uncontrollably. He looked back. A section of the gantry they had just crossed finally gave way, falling silently into the pool below. It hit the blue liquid and vanished in a puff of gray static.

They were across. But the path to the Anchor wasn't just blocked by physics anymore. It was guarded by the very instability they had created.

He turned away from the light. Ahead, the corridor led to the secondary control cluster. And past that... the final door.

26

The Final Gate

They stood before the Tri-Key Door, two specks of dust at the foot of a monolith.

The journey through the Aethelburg facility had been a descent into noise—the shriek of the elevator, the groan of twisted metal, the hiss of the Cherenkov pool, the chatter of the drones. But here, at the very bottom of the world, the silence was absolute.

It was a pressurized silence, heavy and physical, like the air at the bottom of a deep ocean trench. It pressed against Ravn's eardrums and settled in his lungs, a stillness so profound it felt like the pause between heartbeats of a dying god.

Ravn stepped closer to the door. The black alloy was flawless. Unlike the rest of the facility, which had been twisted and melted by the Anomaly, this barrier was pristine. It was cold enough to radiate a chill that cut through his clothes, yet it hummed with a faint, sub-audible vibration that made the teeth in his jaw ache.

It wasn't just a door; it was a containment lid for a pot that had been boiling for five years.

He looked down at his hands. They were shaking. Not with fear, but with the sheer, overwhelming magnitude of the moment. He was holding the fate of reality in a canvas backpack.

The three keys—Nature, Chaos, and Information—were vibrating against his spine, a dissonant, agitated chord of energy that demanded resolution.

He turned to the Stalker.

The creature had not moved. It sat on its haunches a few meters back, its tail wrapped neatly around its paws, its body posture alert but utterly still. Its bioluminescence had faded to a deep, solemn gray, merging with the shadows of the antechamber.

It looked at the door, then at Ravn, with eyes that held a terrifying, ancient intelligence. It knew.

It knew that the journey—the physical trek across the wasteland, the hunts, the battles—was over. This next step was not a distance to be crossed with paws and claws. It was a threshold of will.

The creature let out a soft, low chuff, a sound of finality. It wasn't going to cross the line. It was the guardian of the gate, not the opener.

"You're staying here?" Ravn whispered, the sound loud in the vacuum.

The Stalker dipped its head once, a slow, regal nod. It shifted its gaze to the dark corridor behind them, the path back through the ruined facility. It bared its fangs slightly, not at Ravn, but at the darkness. It would hold the line.

It would ensure that no ghost, no drone, no converging army interrupted what had to happen next.

Ravn felt a lump form in his throat. He reached out and rested his hand on the creature's head for a long moment. The chitin was cool and smooth. He felt the steady, powerful rhythm of its life, a simple biological truth in a place of complex quantum horrors.

"Thank you," he said. "For everything."

He pulled his hand away. The separation felt physical, like tearing a stitch. He turned his back on his only friend and faced the door. He was alone again. Just him, the math, and the mistake.

He shrugged the pack off his shoulders. It hit the floor with a heavy, metallic thud that echoed like a gavel strike. He knelt and undid the buckles. The interior of the bag glowed with a swirling, chaotic light where the energies of the three keys bled into one another.

He took a breath of the stale, dust-heavy air. He checked the Aperture one last time.

PROXIMITY: 0 METERS. ANCHOR STATUS: CRITICAL. READY.

He reached into the bag. The ritual had begun.

The First Key, the Crystalline Shard, pulsed with a warm, golden-green bio-luminescence. It smelled of deep earth and metallic rain. It hummed with a low, cello-like resonance that Ravn felt in his chest cavity.

The Second Key, the Golden Gyroscope, was a blur of kinetic energy. Its brass rings spun so fast they were a haze of motion, throwing off sparks of static electricity that snapped and hissed against the canvas. It buzzed with the angry, high-pitched frequency of a trapped hornet.

The Third Key, the Obsidian Sphere, was a void in the light. It sat between the other two, absorbing their radiation, drinking their noise. It was silent, cold, and terrifyingly still, a black hole in the center of the storm.

Together, they created a dissonant, agitated chord of energy—a "singing" that wasn't sound, but a distortion of the air pressure in the room. They were the three fundamental variables of the new world—Nature, Chaos, and Information—and they were screaming to be resolved.

Ravn looked up at the Tri-Key Door. From a distance, it had looked like a simple slab of black metal. Up close, under the harsh beam of his flashlight and the chaotic glow of the keys, the surface revealed its true complexity.

The door wasn't smooth. It was etched with microscopic fractal patterns, millions of tiny grooves that seemed to shift and flow like oil on water. It wasn't just a barrier; it was a circuit board, a roadmap of the physics that Aris and Lena had tried to rewrite.

In the exact center of the door, arranged in a perfect equilateral triangle at eye level, were the three sockets. They were deep recesses, bored directly into the neutron-dense alloy.

The top socket was a jagged, organic cavity, lined with what looked like fossilized veins. It was a geode waiting for a crystal, a wound waiting to be healed.

The bottom-right socket was a complex, mechanical housing. Inside, Ravn could see rows of dormant, interlocking gear teeth and tumblers, a clockwork mechanism paralyzed by time.

The bottom-left socket was a smooth, perfect hemispherical port. It was darker than the surrounding metal, a matte-black sensor array designed to interface with pure data.

This was the lock. It wasn't designed to keep intruders out. It was designed to keep the universe stable. It required a consensus. It required the simultaneous input of biology, entropy, and logic to open.

Ravn reached into the bag. The energy field around the keys prickled his skin, making the fine hairs on his arm stand up. He felt the heat of the Crystal, the vibration of the Gyroscope, the chill of the Sphere.

He looked at the sockets. He looked at the keys. The geometry was absolute.

He took the First Key in his hand.

The Crystalline Shard felt heavy, dense with potential life. As he lifted it from the pack, the golden light flared brighter, casting long, dancing shadows against the door. The hum intensified, shifting from a low resonance to an eager thrum.

Ravn stood up. The door seemed to loom over him, a silent judge waiting for his testimony.

"Step one," he whispered to the silence.

He approached the door, the shard held out like an offering. The black metal surface seemed to ripple in response to the key's proximity, the fractal etchings aligning themselves toward the organic socket. The lock was waking up.

As he brought the shard closer to the black metal, the air between them began to distort. The sub-audible hum of the door pitched up, becoming a faint, high-frequency whine. The metal surface around the socket seemed to soften, losing its rigid, light-absorbing matte finish and taking on the sheen of liquid mercury.

It was waiting. It was hungry.

"For the world that grew," Ravn whispered, his voice cracking in the silence.

He pushed the key into the lock.

There was no mechanical click. There was a sound like a deep, drawn-in breath. The shard didn't just fit; it fused. The metal of the door seemed to flow around the crystal, embracing it.

Then, the reaction began.

A pulse of blinding gold light erupted from the key, shooting outward across the surface of the door like a shockwave. But it didn't dissipate. It etched itself into the metal.

Ravn stumbled back, shielding his eyes with his arm. Through the glare, he watched the impossible alchemy taking place. The golden light was tracing a path, branching and splitting with frantic speed. It wasn't a random crack; it was a pattern.

It was a root system.

Thick veins of glowing gold spread from the central socket, diving deep into the black metal. From these main arteries, smaller capillaries of emerald green light shot out, spiraling into fractal fern-shapes and leaf patterns.

The door was being overwritten. The cold, neutron-dense alloy was being forced to accommodate the geometry of life.

The heavy, dead silence of the reactor chamber was shattered. Not by an alarm, but by the sound of a phantom forest. Ravn heard the groaning creak of wood growing at high speed, the rustle of a million leaves in a wind that didn't exist, the snap of roots breaking through stone.

It was the sound of the Husk's world-tree, amplified and trapped within the steel.

The vibration in the floor intensified. The door wasn't opening yet, but it was changing. The top third of the massive circle, once a featureless void, was now a glowing, intricate tapestry of golden roots and green leaves, burned into the metal like a circuit board made of biology.

The light stabilized, pulsing with a steady, rhythmic beat—*thump-thump, thump-thump*. It was a heartbeat. The door was alive.

Ravn lowered his arm, staring in wonder. He looked back at the Stalker. The creature was standing now, its bioluminescence flaring in sympathy with the door, a bright, joyous blue. It threw its head back and let out a howl, a sound of pure, primal recognition. The machine had accepted the flesh.

One lock was open. The variable of Nature had been integrated.

The energy in the room shifted. The golden light cast harsh shadows on the remaining two sockets—the mechanical gear-housing and the dark sensor port. They looked darker now, colder, in contrast to the vibrant warmth above them. They were voids waiting to be filled.

Ravn turned back to his pack. He could feel the second key buzzing against the canvas, agitated by the surge of energy. It was spinning faster, its chaotic potential demanding release.

"One down," Ravn breathed, his heart hammering in rhythm with the door.

He reached into the bag and wrapped his hand around the Second Key. The Golden Gyroscope. The engine of Chaos. It stung his palm with static electricity, biting him even before he lifted it.

It was ready to break the world again.

The Golden Gyroscope was vibrating so hard it blurred in his vision, a restless, kinetic knot of potential energy that refused to sit still. It wasn't humming like the crystal; it was buzzing, a high-pitched, angry frequency like a turbine spinning slightly off-center.

Ravn took a breath, bracing himself. He grabbed it. A jolt of static fired up his arm, making his muscles spasm. The key fought him. It twisted in his grip, the inner rings spinning with a gyroscopic force that tried to wrench his wrist sideways. It was heavy, hot, and aggressive. It felt less like holding a machine and more like holding a live grenade with the pin pulled.

He stood up, fighting the torque of the object, and approached the door.

He looked at the bottom-right socket. Unlike the organic cavity of the first lock, this recess was a complex, machined housing. Inside the black metal, Ravn could see rows of dormant, interlocking gear teeth and tumblers, a clockwork mechanism paralyzed by time and entropy.

It was a lock waiting for a force violent enough to turn it.

The Stalker, watching from the shadows, let out a sharp, agitated bark. It flattened its ears, backing away further. It liked the first key; that was the scent of home. But this... this smelled of the Rust Lords. It smelled of burning fuel, grinding metal, and the terrifying, nonsensical physics of the

Reality Tear.

It smelled of things that broke.

"It's okay," Ravn muttered, though he wasn't sure who he was reassuring—the creature, or himself. "Chaos isn't evil. It's just... movement."

He raised the gyroscope. The spinning brass rings caught the golden light from the crystal above, fracturing it into a spray of dizzying sparks.

He lined up the key with the socket. The internal gears of the door seemed to sense the proximity of the chaotic engine. They didn't soften or flow like the organic lock; they shuddered. A grinding sound, like stone on steel, echoed from deep within the door.

Ravn shoved the key home.

It gave resistance at first then slammed into place with a metallic CLANG that rang like a hammer strike.

For a microsecond, there was a pause. Then, the reaction began. It wasn't a growth; it was an explosion of industry.

The gyroscope spun up, its whine rising to a scream. Sparks—blue, orange, and violet—erupted from the socket, showering Ravn in a cascade of hot light.

He flinched, shielding his face, but he didn't step back.

The black alloy of the door around the socket began to fracture. But it wasn't breaking; it was reconfiguring. The solid metal split into distinct, geometric plates that shifted and slid over one another. Brass gears, some as small as a watch spring and others as large as dinner plates, erupted from the surface of the door, meshing with a violent, perfect precision.

The sound was deafening. It was the roar of the Grinder, the scream of a jet engine, the crash of a rockslide, all compressed into a mechanical symphony.

Heat radiated from the lock, a wave of dry, blistering air that smelled of hot oil and friction. The golden light of the gyroscope bled outward, not in veins, but in jagged, lightning-bolt arcs of electricity that jumped between the newly formed gears.

The transformation spread across the bottom right sector of the door. The static, immovable slab became a wall of frantic motion. Pistons pumped, flywheels spun, and clockwork mechanisms ticked with a manic, accelerating rhythm.

It was the physics of the Reality Tear, tamed and harnessed. It was the energy of the Rust Lords, purified into function.

Then, with a final, heavy THUNK, the mechanism locked into a stable cycle. The sparks died down. The screaming whine settled into a deep, powerful, rhythmic thrum that harmonized strangely with the organic beat of the first key.

Two locks were open.

Ravn lowered his arm, his hand numb and tingling from the residual vibration. He looked at the door. It was two-thirds alive now—a fusion of growing forest and roaring machine, of biology and industry.

But there was still one void left.

The bottom-left sector of the door remained a cold, matte-black expanse of dead metal. The final socket, the smooth, spherical port, sat there like a blind eye, dark and silent. It absorbed the golden glow of the roots and the sparks of the gears, giving nothing back.

It was the void of Information. The silence of the Archive.

Ravn turned back to his pack for the final time. The third key was waiting. It wasn't vibrating. It wasn't hot. It was just there, a heavy, black singularity that anchored the other two.

"Two down," Ravn whispered, wiping sweat and grease from his forehead. "One to go."

He reached for the Third Key. The Obsidian Sphere. The cold logic that would bind the chaos and the life together.

It didn't hum like the crystal. It didn't vibrate like the gyroscope. It simply sat there, a heavy, black singularity that seemed to anchor the canvas bag to the floor. It absorbed the golden light of the roots and the blue sparks of the gears, drinking them in and giving nothing back.

It was the coldest thing in the room.

Ravn reached for it. As his fingers brushed the smooth, black surface, the noise in the room seemed to drop away, dampened by a sudden, heavy pressure in his ears. He lifted the sphere. It felt density-infinite, yet weightless, like holding a hole in the universe.

He approached the final socket: the smooth, spherical port. It looked like a blind eye, staring back at him from the dark metal.

The Stalker, which had howled for the forest and snarled at the machine, went utterly silent. It lowered its belly to the floor, covering its nose with its paws. It didn't fear this key; it was negated by it. This was the variable of anti-life, of pure, sterile abstraction.

Ravn took a breath, steadying his hand against the chill radiating from the sphere. "Three," he whispered. "The constant."

He pushed the Obsidian Sphere into the port.

There was no resistance. No friction. The sphere slid into the socket with a terrifying, silent perfection, as if the metal of the door wasn't there at all.

For a heartbeat, the universe seemed to pause. The grinding gears stopped. The growing roots froze. The noise of the antechamber was severed, replaced by a vacuum of absolute, ringing silence.

Then, the Third Key woke up. It didn't glow. It etched.

From the center of the sphere, a single line of laser-thin, ice-blue light shot out. It moved with the speed of a thought, tracing a geometric path across the black metal. It turned at perfect ninety-degree angles, splitting and branching into a complex, circuitry-like labyrinth.

It wasn't random. It was code.

Lines of glowing blue mathematics, ancient algorithms, and pre-Fracture computer syntax burned themselves into the door's surface. They spread like frost across a window pane, cold and fast.

The code intersected with the golden roots, digitizing them, turning their organic curves into vector graphics. It crashed into the brass gears, analyzing them, optimizing them, turning their chaotic motion into a synchronized, silent rotation.

The Third Key was bringing order to the other two. It was binding the biology and the entropy together with the cold, hard logic of the Axiom.

The vibration in the floor changed. It was no longer a mechanical rumble or a biological pulse. It was a hum. A pure, resonant sine wave that rose in pitch until it was at the very edge of human hearing.

The three sectors of the door—Root, Gear, and Code—flared in unison. Gold, Bronze, and Blue merged into a single, blinding white light that washed out the shadows of the antechamber.

Then, the sound came.

It wasn't a click. It was a deep, mournful thrum, like the plucking of a cosmic cello string. It was the sound of a locking bolt the size of a building disengaging.

THRUM.

A crack appeared in the center of the door, a vertical line of absolute white light.

THRUM.

The crack widened. Dust that had settled for five years danced in the air. The air pressure in the room plummeted, sucking the breath from Ravn's lungs.

THRUM.

With a low, grinding groan that vibrated through the floor and up into his bones, the massive circular gate began to slide sideways. It moved with a slow, unstoppable momentum, retreating into the bedrock walls.

Ravn shielded his eyes against the glare. The light spilling from the opening chamber was not the orange flicker of the emergency systems, nor the gray gloom of the Zone. It was a brilliant, spectral white, a light so intense and pure it seemed to possess mass.

He squinted, his crystalline eyes adjusting, filtering the glare. The door fully retracted. The path was open.

Beyond the threshold lay a space of pure impossibility. The air shimmered, thick with a visible energy that distorted light and warped perspective.

And in the center of that distortion, suspended in the heart of the machine that had broken the world, waited the answer to every question he had asked for five years.

Ravn lowered his arm. He reached back, blindly, until his fingers brushed the Stalker's fur.

"Stay," he commanded softly.

He stepped forward, into the light. The ritual was complete. The tomb was open.

27

The Room with Two Chairs

T
he massive circular gate retracted fully into the bedrock walls with
a final, resonant thud that felt less like a mechanical stop and more
like the closing of a heavy book. The grinding vibration in the
floor ceased, leaving a silence that was absolute and terrifyingly pressurized.

Ravn stood at the threshold, shielding his eyes against the glare.

The light spilling from the open chamber was not merely bright; it was
heavy. It was a brilliant, pearlescent white radiance that didn't behave like
photons. It rolled out of the doorway like a slow-moving fog, clinging to
the floor of the antechamber, swirling around his boots in lazy, hypnotic
eddies. It possessed a physical density, a viscosity that made the air look
thick and liquid.

He lowered his arm, blinking his crystalline eyes. The lattice structure in
his irises spun and adjusted, filtering the intensity and breaking white light
into a complex, shimmering spectrum of data. He saw not just light, but
a tapestry of high-energy particles, a soup of raw quantum potential that
was leaking from the room beyond.

He took a step forward, eager to see the source, to finally understand the
geometry of the disaster.

A sharp, pained yelp stopped him.

He turned. The Stalker had not moved. It sat on its haunches well back
from the threshold, just outside the pool of spilling light. Its ears were

flattened against its skull, its lips pulled back in a grimace of instinctual revulsion.

Its bioluminescence, usually a reflection of its mood, had gone completely dark, as if the creature were trying to make itself invisible to the entity inside the room.

Ravn reached out a hand. "Come on," he whispered. "We're here."

The creature whined, a high, keen sound of distress. It took a single, tentative step forward, placing one paw into the pearlescent fog. It recoiled instantly, shaking the limb as if it had been burned.

It wasn't heat; Ravn could feel the cold radiating from the room. It was wrongness.

To a creature of the Zone, an organism woven from the chaotic, vibrant biology of the new world, the energy inside that room was anathema. It was the anti-life. It was the raw, uncompiled code of existence, and flesh could not survive contact with it.

Ravn understood. The Stalker belonged to the world of roots and blood, the world he had traversed. But the world inside that room belonged to physics and math. It was a place for variables, not animals.

He walked back to the creature. He knelt in the dark antechamber, ignoring the humming, open door behind him. He took the Stalker's head in his hands, pressing his forehead against its cool, smooth chitin. He could feel the rapid, terrified hammer of its heart.

"You can't go in there," he said softly. "I know."

The Stalker nudged him, licking the grime from his cheek with a rough tongue. It was a goodbye. It was letting him go.

"Guard the door," Ravn commanded, his voice thick with emotion. "Don't let them follow me. Hold the line." The creature chuffed, a low, warm sound of affirmation. It pulled away from him and turned to face the dark corridor of the reactor facility, its muscles coiling, its bioluminescence flaring back to life—a deep, defensive red. It was a sentinel. It would hold back the Legion, the Rust Lords, and the ghosts for as long as it drew breath.

Ravn stood up. He felt a sudden, crushing sense of isolation. For weeks, this creature had been his eyes, his ears, and his anchor. Now, he was cutting the rope. He was drifting back into the void alone.

He turned to the light.

He stepped up to the threshold. The air in the doorway shimmered, thick with visible energy that distorted the view beyond like a heat haze over asphalt. It was an event horizon. He took a breath, tasting sulfur and static, and stepped through.

The sensation was immediate and disorienting. It felt like walking underwater. The air resisted him, pressing against his chest and limbs with a gelatinous weight. The sound of his own breathing was muffled, swallowed by the dense atmosphere.

The gravity seemed to shift, pulling him not just down, but forward, toward the center of the room. He pushed through the shimmering veil, his boots heavy, his mind racing. He emerged from the fog of light and into the chamber proper.

The glare subsided, or perhaps his crystalline eyes finally adapted, filtering the intensity down to a manageable spectrum. The white fog thinned, revealing the space beyond.

Ravn stopped. His breath caught in his throat, freezing there.

He had expected a cave, a rough-hewn chamber carved by the sheer force of the energy. He had expected a machine room filled with alien technology, or perhaps a void of pure, empty space.

He did not expect to be home.

The chamber was the Aethelburg Control Room.

But it was not the room as he remembered it. It was a reflection seen in a shattered, melting mirror. The geometry of the space had been seized by a violent, impossible force and twisted like wet clay.

The floor, once a flat expanse of linoleum and steel grating, was rippled like the surface of a pond disturbed by a stone. The waves were frozen in place, solid steel crests and troughs that he had to step over.

To his left, a bank of monitoring consoles—heavy, industrial-grade terminals that had cost millions—had melted. They hadn't burned; they had simply lost their structural integrity, drooping like wax candles in a hot room.

The keyboards were elongated, the keys stretched into long, thin drips of plastic that hung almost to the floor. The monitors were warped into impossible curves, yet they were still active. They flickered with distorted, static-filled telemetry, displaying data from an experiment that had ended five years ago.

The walls were worse. The reinforced concrete was not cracked; it was shattered, caught in the mid-frame of an explosion. Chunks of masonry, rebar, and conduit floated in the air, suspended in a gravity-less void near the ceiling. They rotated slowly, lazily, drifting in currents of air that didn't exist.

It was a museum of the moment of impact. A snapshot of the catastrophe, seized by the Anchor and held in an eternal, unbreaking stasis.

Ravn walked forward, his footsteps silent on the rippled floor. He reached out to touch a floating pen that hung at eye level. It spun away from his finger, leaving a faint trail of ink in the air that didn't dissipate.

The silence was heavy, pressing against his eardrums. But underneath it, he could hear the room groaning. It was the sound of metal under immense torsion, of atoms screaming as they were forced to hold impossible shapes. It was the sound of a reality in pain.

He moved deeper into the room, navigating the maze of floating debris. He recognized personal items amidst the wreckage—a coffee mug with a chip in the rim, floating upside down; a lab coat, frozen in a billow of movement as if worn by an invisible runner.

This was his life. This was his work. All of it, captured and distorted by the very force he had tried to harness. He wasn't just walking into a trap; he was walking into his own memory, made solid and monstrous.

The gravity began to shift. As he neared the center of the room, the floor seemed to tilt upward, though his eyes told him it was flat. He felt lighter, his steps becoming bounding and dreamlike. The air grew thicker, shimmering with heatless radiation.

He looked ahead. In the center of the room, where the main reactor viewing window should have been, the space opened up into a sphere of pure, blinding whiteness.

The Anchor.

But before the light swallowed everything, he saw the final, most terrifying detail of the twisted reflection.

Arranged in a semi-circle around the core, facing the light, were the main control stations. They were not melted. They were not broken. They were pristine, untouched by the chaos that had consumed the rest of the room.

And in the center, two chairs sat empty, waiting.

One was his. The other was Aris's.

Ravn stared at them, a cold dread settling in his stomach that had nothing to do with the alien physics. The room wasn't just a snapshot of the past. It was a stage. And the actors were missing.

He tore his gaze away from the empty chairs. To look at them was to drown in the past, and the present was demanding every ounce of his attention.

He turned toward the center of the room, toward the source of the light.

The Anchor was suspended in the exact geometric center of the chamber, hovering two meters above the warped deck plates. It was a perfect sphere of contained energy, perhaps ten meters in diameter.

It burned, a cold, white incandescence that was absolute. It cast no shadows because it allowed no darkness to exist within its radius.

He took a step toward it, and the universe pushed back.

It wasn't a wall. It was a tide. The air around the Anchor was dense with gravimetric distortion. Every step forward required a physical effort, as if he were walking into a gale-force wind that blew not with air, but with gravity itself.

The keys in his pack were screaming now, a frantic, vibrating weight against his spine that threatened to pull him off balance. The Essence in his veins flared hot, his own internal energy resonating with the colossal power before him.

He gritted his teeth and leaned into the pressure. He was walking into the heart of a singularity.

As he drew closer, the silence of the room shattered. It wasn't replaced by noise, but by a song. It was a resonant frequency that bypassed his ears and vibrated directly in the marrow of his bones.

It was a low, thrumming chord, complex and multi-layered. He heard the deep, geological groan of the earth; the high, crystalline chime of the forest; the chaotic, static hiss of the Reality Tear.

It was the sound of the Fracture Zone, all of it, condensed into a single point. It was the hum of the operating system of reality.

The closer he got, the more the laws of physics began to fray. He watched a piece of floating debris—a shattered monitor screen—drift too close to the sphere. It slowed down. It drifted into the aura of the Anchor and simply... stopped.

Time, in the immediate vicinity of the sphere, was dilated to a near-standstill. The monitor hung there, frozen in a micro-second that would last a thousand years.

Ravn looked at his own hand as he reached out to steady himself against a twisted stanchion. His movement left a trail, a visual echo of his fingers fanning out in the air like a deck of cards. He was moving through a fluid of thick time.

He forced himself forward, fighting the nausea of the temporal distortion. He stopped at the edge of the raised platform that circled the reactor pit. He was only five meters from the sphere now.

The light was blinding, but his crystalline eyes adapted, shifting their refractive index to filter out the glare. He looked into the face of the thing he and Aris had created.

It was terrifyingly beautiful. The surface of the sphere wasn't smooth. It was roiling. Storms of exotic matter swirled across its equator. Arcs of pure information, visible as cascading lines of white code, leaped from pole to pole.

It was a star made of data. It was a knot in the string of the universe.

And it was heavy. Not just physically, but conceptually. Ravn felt the sheer significance of the object pressing down on his mind. This wasn't just a power source. It was the pivot point. The fulcrum upon which the entire leverage of the new world rested.

It was the reason the trees grew black, the reason the suns were blue, the reason the dead walked. Every anomaly, every glitch, every miracle in the Zone radiated from this single, impossible point in space.

He was standing before a naked law of nature. He was a microbe staring up at the boot of a god.

The song in his bones reached a crescendo, a vibration so intense it felt like he was being shaken apart on a molecular level. He fell to his knees, overwhelmed by the proximity to the divine. He was close enough to touch it. Close enough to be unmade by it.

But he had to look. The Axiom had told him to *Find the Heart*. He was here. Now, he had to see what was inside.

He engaged the full power of his crystalline vision, pushing the lattice to its limit, staring past the blinding photosphere of the Anchor and into the core.

The white fire peeled back. The layers of data parted. And the truth revealed itself.

It was not a simple act of focusing. It was a physical exertion, a flexing of a muscle he had only recently acquired. The lattice structure in his irises spun and locked, filtering out the blinding photosphere of the Anchor. The world around him darkened, the twisted wreckage of the control room fading into a dull gray background.

All that remained was the sphere.

He peeled back the layers of light like the skin of an onion. He filtered out the gamma radiation, the hard X-rays, the blinding visible spectrum. He tuned his sight to the specific, impossible frequency of the quantum foam itself.

The white fire parted. The data stream thinned. And the core was revealed.

It was a bubble of perfect, timeless vacuum, a pocket universe no larger than a bedroom, suspended in the center of the storm.

And floating in that void, anchored by nothing but the terrifying gravity of the moment, were two control chairs.

They were standard-issue, ergonomic mesh chairs, the kind found in a thousand labs across the old world. But here, they were artifacts of immense significance. They floated facing each other, tilted slightly back as if blown by a wind that had frozen instantly.

And they were occupied.

Ravn's heart stopped. The air in his lungs turned to stone.

In the left chair sat a man. He was young, his hair a messy halo of dark curls that were frozen in a chaotic, wind-blown tangle. He wore a white lab coat, the tails of which billowed out behind him like the wings of an angel, frozen in mid-flap.

His hands were raised, his fingers splayed, not in defense, but in a gesture of reaching, of grasping for something just out of range. His face was unlined, untouched by the five years of hell that had aged Ravn. His eyes were wide, reflecting the blinding light of his own creation.

His mouth was open in a shout that would never be heard. It was a look of pure, unadulterated, scientific awe.

It was Aris.

In the right chair sat a woman. She was gripping the armrests of her chair with white-knuckled force, her body tense, braced against an impact that was always coming but never arriving. Her lab coat was buttoned wrong, a detail Ravn remembered with a sudden, agonizing clarity—she had been rushing that morning.

Her head was turned, her gaze not on the data, but on the man in the chair opposite her. Her face was a mask of terrified love. Her hand was outstretched, reaching across the void between them, her fingers millimeters from touching his.

It was Lena.

They were perfect. They were pristine. They were like insects trapped in amber, preserved in the exact millisecond of the Anomaly's formation.

They weren't ghosts. They weren't memories. They were flesh and blood, captured and held in a state of quantum suspension.

Ravn fell forward, catching himself on his hands. He crawled toward the sphere, his breath coming in ragged, tearing sobs.

"No," he whispered. "No, no, no." He was close enough now to see the details. He saw the ink stain on Aris's pocket protector. He saw the small, silver earring in Lena's left ear. He saw the individual droplets of sweat frozen on their foreheads, diamonds of human effort caught in stasis.

He saw the tragedy of their final moment. Lena had known. She had seen the collapse coming, and her final act hadn't been to save the experiment, but to reach for Aris.

And Aris... Aris hadn't seen her. He had been looking at the light. He had been looking at the Axiom.

They were trapped in an eternal, unresolved chord. The reach that never connected. The shout that never ended. The love that was never acknowledged.

Ravn reached out a trembling hand, his fingers brushing the edge of the energy field. The hum of the Anchor intensified, a warning vibration that rattled his bones and set his teeth on edge. It wasn't a mechanical hum. It was a scream held at a constant pitch, a harmonious agony of infinite duration.

He understood now. The data flooded his mind, interpreted by the Aperture and his own crystalline eyes, but the conclusion was human, not mathematical.

The "Heart" of the Zone wasn't a machine. It wasn't an alien artifact buried in the earth.

It was them.

Their consciousness, their quantum signatures, their very souls had been caught in the feedback loop of the experiment. They hadn't been destroyed. They had been expanded. They had been uploaded into the fabric of spacetime itself.

Aris, with his wild, chaotic brilliance, was the engine. His mind was the generator, churning out the raw, creative energy that fueled the Fracture Zone's impossible biology and twisted physics. He was the reason the trees grew black and the suns burned blue.

Lena, with her cold, precise logic, was the containment field. Her will was the gravity that kept the chaos from tearing the planet apart. She was the lattice, the structure, the laws of physics holding her brother's wild imagination in check.

They were the binary stars at the center of the universe. The entire Fracture Zone—the fungal forests, the crystal deserts, the gray purgatory—was just the fallout of their eternal, frozen struggle. The universe hadn't just broken. It had snagged on his brother's soul.

Ravn recoiled, stumbling back from the sphere as if it had burned him. He fell to his knees on the warped metal floor, the horror of the realization crushing him.

He had come here to save them. He had come to unlock the door and set them free. But now he saw the terrible truth of his mission.

They weren't prisoners. They were the dam.

If he freed them—if he shut down the Anchor and released their souls into the afterlife—the dam would break. The stabilizing force of the Zone would vanish. The chaotic energy Aris was generating would be unleashed without Lena's constraint.

It wouldn't just be a "correction." It would be a total, catastrophic de-rendering of reality.

He wasn't a rescuer. He was a tomb robber. He was a saboteur standing in the heart of a nuclear reactor, holding a wrench to the control rods.

"I can't save you," he whispered, the words tasting of ash and tears. "If I save you… I kill everything else." He looked at Aris's frozen shout. He looked at Lena's terrified reach. For five years, they had been trapped in this millisecond of trauma, holding up the sky. And he had spent five years trying to tear it down.

A deep, resonant boom echoed through the facility, shaking dust from the high ceiling of the chamber.

Ravn's head snapped up. The sound hadn't come from the Anchor. It had come from the tunnel behind him. From the elevator shaft.

Another boom followed, closer this time. Then the distinct, high-pitched whine of a plasma cutter drilling through metal.

The silence of the tomb was broken.

He scrambled to his feet, turning away from the blinding light of his brother's soul. He looked back toward the open blast door, toward the dark antechamber where he had left the Stalker.

He heard a roar—not the mechanical sound of the facility, but the organic, furious roar of his companion. Then the sharp crack-thump of a heavy slug-thrower. Then the thrum of a pulse rifle.

They were here.

The Legion. The Rust Lords. The Husks. They had converged. They had breached the facility, fought their way down the elevator shaft, and crossed the melted cathedral. They were at the door.

Rostova, coming to impose her order on her sister's ghost. Jax, coming to smash the machine and unleash the chaos. Kaia, coming to assimilate the god into her hive mind.

They were coming to claim the Anchor. They were coming to desecrate the tomb.

Ravn wiped the tears from his face. His hand dropped to his belt, finding the grip of his empty pulse rifle. The drained weapon was useless, a pathetic weight against armies, against ideologies. But it was all he had.

He looked back at the sphere one last time. At the two people he loved most in the universe, suspended in their eternal, terrified embrace.

"I won't let them touch you," he promised.

He turned his back on the light and walked toward the door to meet the war.

28

A Convergence of Wills

Ravn stepped backward out of the Anchor chamber, his eyes still burning with the afterimage of his brother's frozen scream.

He crossed the threshold of the Tri-Key Door, moving from the timeless, suspended silence of the core back into the cold, recycled air of the antechamber.

The transition was physical, a change in pressure that popped his ears. But it was the noise that hit him first.

The silence of the tomb was gone. The Aethelburg facility, which had been a place of ghosts and glitching whispers, was now screaming.

It wasn't the mechanical shriek of the drones or the distorted wail of the alarm. It was the sound of invasion. A cacophony of violence echoed down the elevator shaft and reverberated through the ventilation ducts, a discordant symphony of three armies tearing the world apart to get to him.

He heard the high-pitched, rhythmic *thrum-thrum-thrum* of Legion pulse rifles, a sound like a relentless, digital drumbeat. He heard the guttural, grinding roar of Rust Lord chainsaws and the wet, tearing sound of their harpoon guns punching through metal. And beneath it all, a low, resonant humming, the sound of the Husks chanting as they shattered the concrete with their bone weapons.

The sanctuary had been breached. The seal was broken.

Ravn turned to the Stalker. The creature was standing guard at the far end of the antechamber, positioned directly in front of the crumpled remains of the elevator doors.

It was no longer the calm, mystical guardian he had left moments ago. It was a blur of lethal motion.

The elevator shaft had become a choke point, a funnel for the chaos above. The doors had been blasted open, twisting outward like peeled metal skin. Through the smoke and debris pouring from the shaft, the vanguard of the assault was trying to push through.

A Rust Lord, clad in spiked scrap-armor and wielding a buzz-saw on a pole, leaped from the shaft, screaming a war cry. The Stalker met him in the air. There was a flash of dark claws, a spray of red blood, and the warrior was thrown violently against the wall, his armor shredded.

Before the body hit the floor, a Legion drone, a sleek, spherical kill-bot, buzzed through the smoke, its laser targeting array sweeping the room. The Stalker didn't pause. It rebounded off the wall, its tail lashing out like a whip. The bony spur at the tip struck the drone's drive core, shattering it in a shower of sparks and glass.

The creature landed, snarling, its bioluminescence flaring a violent, warning red that pulsed in time with the muzzle flashes from the shaft.

It was holding the line. It was a singular, biological dam against a flood of steel and fire.

"I'm here," Ravn said, his voice rough. He moved to the Stalker's side, raising his pulse rifle, though he knew the weapon was empty.

He reversed his grip on the rifle barrel, the weight of it pathetic against the scale of the threat.

The Stalker looked at him for a split second, its eyes wild with the battle-lust of the Zone. It chuffed, a sound of acknowledgement, then turned back to the breach.

The noise grew louder. The floor plates vibrated. The air in the antechamber grew hot and choked with the smell of cordite, unwashed bodies, and ionized dust.

"They're coming," Ravn whispered.

He looked back at the open blast door behind him. Through the aperture, he could see the blinding white light of the Anchor, and within it, the faint, tragic silhouettes of Aris and Lena.

They looked so fragile now. Not gods. Just people. People who were about to be trampled by the march of ideologies.

He stepped between the door and the elevator, placing his body in the path of the war. He wasn't a soldier. He wasn't a hero. He was a physicist who had made a mistake, and he was standing guard over the only thing that mattered.

Then, the elevator shaft exploded.

It wasn't a grenade. It was a simultaneous, three-pronged breach. The ceiling of the antechamber buckled as heavy cutting lasers sliced through the reinforced concrete. The wall to the left imploded under the impact of a shaped charge. And the elevator shaft itself vomited forth a fresh wave of smoke and debris.

The vanguard was dead. The leaders had arrived.

The smoke from the breached elevator shaft billowed into the antechamber, a choking gray curtain. For a heartbeat, there was a lull in the noise, a heavy intake of breath before the scream.

Then, the Legion arrived.

They didn't charge. They advanced. Through the smoke, a wall of translucent blue energy materialized—a interlocking phalanx of riot shields held by heavy troopers in pristine, vacuum-sealed armor. They moved with a terrifying, synchronized lockstep, their magnetic boots clanging against the floor plates in a rhythm that sounded like a slow, mechanical heartbeat.

Clang. Clang. Clang.

Behind the wall of shields, pulse rifles fired in controlled, suppressive bursts, filling the air with the whine of capacitors and the smell of static.

In the center of the formation, unshielded and walking with a calm, terrifying arrogance, was General Eva Rostova. She held a heavy officer's pistol in one hand, but she wasn't firing. She was directing the slaughter with sharp, precise hand signals.

Her eyes, cold as glacial ice, swept the room, ignoring the carnage, locking instantly onto the open blast door behind Ravn. She didn't see her sister's tomb; she saw a rogue variable that required immediate stabilization.

But before the Legion could secure the room, the wall to Ravn's left exploded.

It wasn't a tactical breach. It was a demolition. A massive, rusted drill bit, the size of a tree trunk, punched through the reinforced concrete, spraying dust and shrapnel across the Legion's flank.

The wall crumbled, and a monstrosity roared into the antechamber. It was a personal war-rig, a mech-suit built from the chassis of a forklift and the armor of a tank. It belched black diesel smoke that instantly fouled the Legion's clean air.

The cockpit cage threw open, and Jax leaped out. He was a vision of industrial madness, his skin smeared with oil and war paint, his double-bitted axe revving with a modified chain-drive.

Behind him, a horde of Rust Lords poured through the breach, screaming, firing wildly, and throwing homemade explosives. They crashed into the Legion's flank like a tidal wave of scrap metal.

"KNOCK KNOCK!" Jax bellowed, his laughter a jagged, manic sound that cut through the discipline of the Legion. He swung his chain-axe, catching a heavy trooper's shield and shattering the energy field in a shower of sparks. "OPEN THE DAMN DOOR!"

The room descended into a deafening, close-quarters brawl. The clean lines of the Legion's formation broke under the sheer, kinetic weight of the Rust Lords' assault.

Ravn backed up, pressing himself against the frame of the Tri-Key Door, the Stalker growling at his feet. He watched the chaos, his mind trying to track the vectors of violence.

Then, the shadows moved.

While the Legion and the Rust Lords tore at each other on the floor, the ventilation grates high on the walls blew out silently. There was no explosion, no smoke. Just a sudden, fluid motion as a dozen shapes dropped from the ceiling.

The Husks landed in the center of the melee, crouching low, their bone weapons drawn. They moved with a speed that made the soldiers and scrappers look sluggish.

An Ascended warrior, his eyes swirling with light, landed on the back of Jax's mech-suit, driving a chitinous blade into the hydraulic lines.

And walking through the smoke of the elevator shaft, untouched by the crossfire, came Kaia.

She didn't carry a weapon. She walked barefoot on the glass-strewn floor, her robes drifting around her like smoke. The chaos seemed to part around her. A Rust Lord raised a shotgun to fire at her, but a vine, seemingly erupting from the cracked concrete floor, whipped around his ankle and slammed him into the wall.

Kaia stopped in the center of the room, the three-way battle raging around her. She looked at Rostova, then at Jax, her expression one of profound, weary pity.

The three heads of the dragon were here. Rostova, the avatar of Order, firing with cold precision into the mob. Jax, the avatar of Chaos, laughing as he bludgeoned a trooper with the stock of a shotgun. Kaia, the avatar of Nature, standing serene in the eye of the storm, her warriors flowing like water around the rocks of the conflict.

They had all come for the same thing. And they were all willing to burn the world down to get it.

Ravn stood at the threshold of the Anchor, the only thing standing between the war and the peace of the tomb. He raised his empty rifle, a futile gesture. They didn't even look at him. To them, he wasn't the protagonist.

He was just the doorman. And the door was open.

The battle raged in the antechamber, a chaotic swirl of blue plasma, roaring engines, and flashing bone-blades. But in the center of the storm, there was a moment of terrifying stillness.

The three leaders—Rostova, Jax, and Kaia—stood in a loose triangle, ignoring the violence of their followers. Their gazes were drawn past Ravn, through the open frame of the Tri-Key Door, and into the blinding, heart of the Anchor chamber.

The light washed over them, casting long, sharp shadows against the back wall. And as it touched them, Ravn saw the truth of the war. The Anchor was a mirror.

Not showing the reality around them; instead showing them their own desires.

General Eva Rostova stepped forward, her boots crunching on the shattered glass of the floor. She holstered her pistol, her demeanor shifting from combat commander to lead scientist. She pulled a datapad from her belt, her eyes darting between the screen and the sphere of white fire.

Ravn watched her face. He expected to see recognition. He expected to see grief.

Inside that sphere, frozen in time, was her identical twin sister. The silhouette of Lena was visible, her hand outstretched, her face a mask of terror.

But Rostova didn't blink. She didn't weep. Her expression was one of cold, calculating satisfaction.

"Energy output exceeds theoretical maximums," she murmured, her voice clipped and professional, audible only because Ravn was standing so close. "The field is unstable, but the core geometry is perfect. It's a perpetual motion engine. An infinite well."

She looked right at Lena's frozen form and didn't see a sister. She saw a component.

"Deploy the stabilizers!" she shouted over her shoulder to her heavy troopers. "I want containment fields on the perimeter! We are going to shackle this star and power the new world!"

To her, the Anchor was a rogue variable that needed to be disciplined. It was a resource to be strip-mined for the sake of order. The humanity inside it was just a glitch in the readout.

Jax didn't look at datapads. He gunned the engine of his damaged mech-suit, the hydraulic claws snapping the air. He laughed, a sound of pure, manic glee that vibrated in his chest. He stomped forward, ignoring the Husk warrior clinging to his back until he slammed the attacker against the doorframe, crushing him.

"Look at it shine!" Jax roared, shielding his eyes with a grease-stained arm. "It's the biggest engine in the universe, boys! And it's stuck in neutral!"

He looked at Aris's silhouette, at the look of sublime awe on the physicist's face. Jax didn't see a tragedy. He saw a challenge.

"It wants to scream!" Jax yelled, revving his chain-axe. "It wants to burn! We're gonna crack that shell wide open and let the fire out! We're gonna ride the shockwave until the wheels fall off!"

To him, the Anchor was a cage. The order it represented, the stillness of the frozen moment, was an insult to his philosophy of chaos. He wanted to shatter it not to understand it, but simply to see what color the explosion would be.

Kaia moved past them both. She didn't walk; she seemed to drift, her eyes wide and swimming with glistening tears. She fell to her knees at the threshold, ignoring the battle raging inches from her robes. She reached out with trembling hands, as if to embrace the deadly radiation.

"The Seed," she whispered, her voice trembling with religious ecstasy. "The Great Heart."

She looked at the trapped souls and saw deities. She saw the fusion of man and energy not as a horrific accident, but as the ultimate evolution.

"We will plant it," she cried out, her voice rising to a chant. "We will let its roots drink from the earth! We will dissolve into its light and become the forest eternal!"

To her, the Anchor was a god to be consumed by. She wanted to feed her people to it, to merge their consciousness with the singularity in a horrific, beautiful mass suicide that she called harmony.

Ravn stood between them and the door, his heart breaking. They were all insane.

The trauma of the new world had twisted them so deeply that they could no longer see the human cost of their ideologies. They looked at a tomb containing his brother and his best friend—two terrified people who had made a mistake—and they saw a battery, a bomb, and an idol.

He realized then that there was no reasoning with them. You could not debate with a fundamentalist, a nihilist, or a machine. They were not here to rescue anyone. They were here to validate their own broken worldviews.

"Stop!" Ravn screamed, his voice cracking. "It's not a prize! It's a grave!"

But his voice was a whisper in a hurricane. They didn't hear him. Or if they did, they didn't care. They were already moving, stepping toward the threshold to claim their version of the truth.

"Stop!" Ravn screamed again, his voice cracking under the strain of the shouting and the sheer, crushing weight of the moment. "It's not a prize! It's a grave!"

The sheer desperation in his voice cut through the din of the antechamber. For a second, the three leaders paused. They looked at him, not with respect, but with the annoyance of gods being interrupted by a mortal.

Ravn stepped away from the doorframe, placing himself physically between the converging armies and the light of the Anchor. He held his empty pulse rifle across his chest like a barrier, though he knew it offered no protection against mech-suits or heavy troopers.

He turned first to General Rostova. She was the most dangerous, because she was the most convinced of her own sanity.

"Look at her, Eva," Ravn pleaded, using her first name, a breach of protocol that made the heavy troopers tense. He pointed into the blinding light, at the silhouette of the woman reaching out in terror. "That isn't a battery. That isn't a 'perpetual motion engine.' That is Lena. That is your sister."

Rostova's face twitched, a microscopic crack in the ice.

"I saw the photo," Ravn pressed, his voice shaking. "In your office. I know why you built the walls. I know why you hate the chaos. You're trying to build a world where she wouldn't have died. But she is dead, Eva. She's trapped in a millisecond of agony, holding the universe together with her fear. If you tap into that... if you try to regulate that... you aren't honoring her. You're torturing her."

Rostova stared at him. For a heartbeat, Ravn saw the grief-stricken woman from the office, the sister who missed her twin. But then, the General blinked, and the mask slammed back into place.

"Sentiment," she said, her voice flat and metallic, "is a variable we cannot afford. My sister sacrificed herself for science. I will not let that sacrifice be wasted on chaos. She will be the foundation of the new order. It is what she would have wanted."

She had rationalized the horror. She had turned her grief into a machine.

Ravn turned to Kaia. The shaman was watching him with tears in her eyes, but they were tears of pity, not understanding.

"And you," Ravn said, his voice trembling with anger. "You talk about harmony. You talk about the 'song.' I saw your ritual. I saw what you did to Kael."

Kaia smiled, a serene, terrifying expression. "He is happy, Ravn. He is whole."

"He is gone!" Ravn shouted. "You don't want to join the song. You want to drown in it. Look at them!" He gestured to Aris and Lena. "They are individuals. They are terrified. They are screaming for help, not for union. If you feed your people to that... if you merge with that much pain... you won't become a god. You'll become a tumor. You will lose everything that makes you human."

Kaia shook her head slowly. "To be human is to be lonely. To be separate is to be in pain. We offer the end of pain. We offer the silence of the seed."

She was lost in the mysticism. She had stared into the abyss of the Zone for so long that she no longer recognized the value of the self.

Finally, Ravn turned to Jax. The warlord was revving his chain-axe, bouncing on the balls of his feet, practically vibrating with the need to destroy something.

"Jax," Ravn said, his voice low. "You want to break the cage? You want absolute freedom? Look at that light. That is the energy that broke the world the first time. If you smash that containment field... there won't be a wasteland left to rule. There won't be a Grinder. There won't be any scraps left to fight over. It will be the silence of the vacuum. That's not freedom. That's just death."

Jax laughed. It was a wet, ugly sound. He leaned down, his face inches from Ravn's, smelling of oil and rot. "You think I'm crazy?" Jax sneered, the manic light in his eyes dimming for a split second to reveal something sharper, colder. "You think I broke the world? No. *You* did. Your people." He gestured with his revving chain-axe toward the frozen, pristine forms of Aris and Lena in the light. "Look at them. Perfect. Frozen. *Dead.* That's what your 'Order' gets you, brainiac. Statues in a glass case." Jax leaned in closer, his voice dropping to a gravelly rasp that cut through the noise. "I remember the Before. Everyone sitting in their boxes, waiting to die, pretending the concrete would last forever. It was a lie. The rust is the only truth. Things break. They *have* to break to be real." He looked past Ravn at the Anchor, his eyes wide not with hate, but with a desperate, philosophical hunger. "I don't want to rule the ash. I want to wake you all up. If it burns, at least we know it was there."

"I don't want to rule the ash. I want to be the fire."

Ravn stepped back, his back hitting the cold metal of the blast door frame. He looked at the three of them. The General, the Shaman, the Warlord. Order, Nature, Chaos.

They were stone deaf.

The trauma of the Convergence hadn't just broken the world; it had broken the people. It had shattered the collective human psyche into jagged, extremist shards. Rostova couldn't accept a world she couldn't control. Kaia couldn't accept a world where she was alone. Jax couldn't accept a world that had consequences.

They were no longer people. They were avatars of their own damage. They were the same forces he had carried in his backpack, writ large in flesh and blood, and they were about to collide.

"You're wrong," Ravn whispered, the fight draining out of his voice, replaced by a cold, hard certainty. "You're all wrong. There is no right answer here. There is only the choice."

He looked up at the ceiling, through the layers of rock, imagining the Red Eye of the Axiom staring down at this tragic stage play. "And I'm the one who has to make it."

The tension in the room snapped. The words were done. The time for philosophy was over. Now, there was only the physics of violence.

Jax roared, raising his axe. "Talk time is over! Out of my way, doorman!"

Rostova raised her pistol. "Secure the asset!"

Kaia raised her hand. "Claim the seed!"

The three armies surged forward.

Jax didn't wait for a signal. He didn't wait for a tactical advantage. He simply let the entropy inside him boil over. With a roar that sounded more like a grinding transmission than a human voice, he squeezed the trigger of his massive, scavenged rotary cannon.

"PLAYTIME!"

The weapon spun up with a terrifying shriek. A stream of high-velocity depleted uranium slugs, each the size of a finger, erupted from the barrels. He swept the weapon across the room in a chaotic, jagged arc, spraying death indiscriminately.

The first rounds struck the Legion's energy shields, blooming into blinding flowers of blue sparks. The heavy troopers staggered under the kinetic impact, their formation buckling.

Rostova didn't flinch. She shouted a single, sharp command. "Suppression! Clear the zone!"

The Legionnaires dropped to one knee in perfect unison and opened fire. The antechamber was instantly illuminated by a strobing storm of blue plasma. The air turned to superheated static. The sound was a deafening, continuous thunderclap.

Kaia moved. She didn't run; she flowed. As a line of plasma bolts tore through the space where she had been standing, she dropped to the floor, weaving through the legs of the combatants. Her Ascended warriors leaped into the fray, not with guns, but with the terrifying, silent speed of the Zone. One warrior vaulted off the wall, tackling a Rust Lord, driving a bone blade through the man's scrap armor.

Ravn was caught in the center of the meat grinder. A heavy slug sparked off the doorframe inches from his head, sending a spray of hot metal into his face. He flinched, stumbling back. He raised his empty pulse rifle, swinging it like a club to deflect a Rust Lord who lunged at him with a jagged knife.

The blow connected with a jarring vibration, knocking the scavenger back, but Ravn lost his footing on the slick, glass-strewn floor. He fell hard. The breath was driven from his lungs.

Above him, the battle raged. It was a claustrophobic nightmare of flashing lights and screaming metal. A Legionnaire fell next to him, his chest plate melted by a Rust Lord explosive. A Husk warrior, his arm severed by a plasma bolt, continued to fight with his remaining limb, his eyes glowing with a manic, pearlescent fervor.

The Stalker was over Ravn in an instant, a growling umbrella of protection. It snapped its jaws at a heavy trooper who tried to advance, forcing the soldier back. The creature was bleeding from a dozen small wounds, its chitin scored by shrapnel, but it refused to abandon him.

But they were losing ground. The sheer volume of violence was pushing them back. The three armies were pressing inward, their hatred for each other momentarily eclipsed by their desire to breach the door. They were a tidal wave of ideology, and Ravn was a grain of sand.

He looked up from the floor. He saw Rostova advancing behind her shield wall, her eyes fixed on the Anchor. He saw Jax wading through the melee, laughing as he swung his axe. He saw Kaia chanting, her hands glowing with biological energy.

They weren't going to stop. They were going to tear through him, through the Stalker, and through each other to get to the prize.

Ravn realized then, with a cold, clarifying shock, that he could not fight them. Not like this. He couldn't out-shoot the Legion. He couldn't out-brawl the Rust Lords. He couldn't out-maneuver the Husks.

If he stood his ground here, he would die, and the door would be left unguarded. The sanctity of the tomb would be violated by the victor.

He had to change the battlefield. He had to move the conflict to a place where his weapon—his mind, his understanding of the Axiom—was the only one that mattered.

He looked back, through the open blast door, into the blinding white heart of the Anchor chamber. Into the room with the two chairs.

"Back!" he screamed to the Stalker, grabbing its harness. "We have to go back!"

He scrambled backward, crawling like a crab, dragging the reluctant beast with him. He crossed the threshold.

The moment he passed through the doorway, the air changed. The pressure returned. The gravity shifted. He was back in the bubble of the Anomaly.

The battle spilled in after him. A Rust Lord burst through the door, screaming in triumph, only to be incinerated by a stray plasma bolt from the antechamber. His body de-rendered into gray static before it hit the floor.

The reality of the Anchor chamber was too hostile for normal combat. The twisted gravity threw aim off. The time dilation made movements sluggish and dreamlike. But they were still coming.

Ravn scrambled to his feet on the rippled steel floor of the control room. He retreated toward the center, toward the blinding sphere of his brother's soul. He was no longer the guardian at the gate. He was the last line of defense, cornered in the heart of the machine.

He scanned the ruined lab, his eyes frantic, searching for something, anything, that could stop this madness.

His gaze fell on a shadowed alcove beneath the melted remains of the main console, protected by a fallen I-beam. There, blinking with a faint, steady blue light amidst the devastation, was a terminal. It wasn't dead. It wasn't looped. It was waiting.

Ravn looked at the approaching armies, then at the terminal. He realized there was only one move left. A move that wasn't about fighting, but about rewriting the rules of the game.

He grabbed the Stalker's mane. "Run," he whispered.

He turned and sprinted toward the terminal, leaving the war behind him to face the machine one last time.

29

The Legion's Gambit

Ravn slid into the alcove beneath the melted ruins of the main console, his chest heaving.

The space was cramped, a pocket of shadow protected by a twisted I-beam that had once supported the ceiling. In the center of the darkness, the terminal blinked with a steady, inviting blue light—a single, functional eye in a blind face.

He didn't look at the screen yet. He looked back.

The battle didn't stop at the threshold. It poured through the Tri-Key Door like a virulent infection breaching a cell wall.

The first to enter were the Rust Lords, driven by the momentum of their own rage. A pack of three warriors, screaming war cries that were instantly swallowed by the heavy atmosphere, charged into the room.

They expected a fight. They expected solid ground. They found neither.

The moment they crossed the event horizon into the Anchor chamber, the rules of engagement changed. The gravity well of the singularity caught them. They didn't run; they bounded, their heavy boots driving them into long, slow-motion arcs through the air.

One warrior fired his shotgun at a shadow. The pellets didn't fly straight. Caught in the intense, localized gravimetric distortion, they curved wildly to the left, sparking harmlessly against the warped wall. The recoil, amplified by the lack of friction, sent the warrior spinning backward, tumbling end-over-end in a slow, graceful drift until he slammed into a floating piece of masonry.

It was a dream-battle, a conflict fought underwater.

The Legion came next, pushing through the Rust Lord rabble with their shield wall. But their discipline crumbled against the geometry of the room. Their energy shields flickered and shorted out, the coherent fields disrupted by the high-energy radiation of the Anchor. Their formation broke as the floor rippled beneath them, the steel plates shifting like ice floes on a restless sea.

A heavy trooper fired a plasma cannon. The bolt of superheated gas moved sluggishly, trailing a wake of distortion. It didn't explode on impact; it simply dissipated, its energy drunk by the hungry void of the room.

And then the Husks flowed in. They were the only ones who seemed to understand the terrain. They moved low, using their hands and feet, clinging to the warped debris like spiders. They didn't fight the gravity; they rode it.

An Ascended warrior leaped from the doorway, catching a gravity current that slung him across the room in a blur of motion. He landed on the shoulders of a Legionnaire, driving a bone blade through the man's helmet before pushing off again, weightless and lethal.

The melted cathedral had become a warzone, but it was a warzone painted by a madman. The air was filled with the screams of men and the roar of weapons, but the sounds were wrong—stretched and distorted by the time dilation. A gunshot was a low, booming bass note. A scream was a long, drawn-out siren.

Ravn watched, mesmerized and terrified. He engaged his enhanced vision, trying to parse the chaos. He saw the vectors of force, the lines of gravity twisting like snakes.

He saw the Rust Lords firing blindly, their bullets hanging in the air for impossible seconds before accelerating to lethal speeds. He saw the Legionnaires panicking, their tactical computers screaming errors as they tried to target enemies that were effectively in a different time zone.

A Rust Lord, spinning out of control, spotted Ravn in his alcove. The warrior grinned, a slow-motion rictus of hate, and leveled a harpoon gun.

Ravn tried to raise his own weapon, but his limbs felt like lead. He was moving in syrup. The harpoon fired. The heavy steel spear floated toward him, lazy and inevitable.

Then, a shadow eclipsed the light. The Stalker leaped from the roof of the alcove. It moved with a violence that defied the room's lethargy.

It slammed into the Rust Lord in mid-air, the impact driving them both down to the rippled floor. The creature didn't bite; it simply held the man down, pinning him against a patch of floor that was glowing with Cherenkov heat.

The warrior screamed as his armor began to dissolve into gray static beneath him.

The Stalker looked up at Ravn, its muzzle wet with the static-mist. It barked once—a sharp, distorted sound that cut through the sluggish air.

"Work."

Ravn nodded, shaking off the hypnotic horror of the battle. He turned to the terminal.

The blue screen was waiting, a window into the mind of the machine. He placed his hands on the interface, his fingers trembling not with fear, but with the sheer, vibrating power of the room.

The war was raging behind him, a slow-motion apocalypse of physics and flesh. But the real battle was here, in the code.

In the center of the swirling, gravity-warped melee, a sudden, unnatural order began to form.

General Rostova stepped through the Tri-Key Door, moving with a stride that seemed to ignore the rippling floor plates. She didn't look at the chaos around her. She looked only at the Anchor.

She raised her hand, fingers splayed, and then closed it into a tight fist.

"Phalanx," she commanded, her voice amplified by her helmet speakers, cutting through the roar of the battle like a knife. "Secure the perimeter. Deploy the asset."

The Legion heavy troopers responded instantly. Twenty men and women, clad in bulky, vacuum-sealed power armor, moved to the front line. They slammed their tower shields down onto the unstable metal floor, engaging magnetic locking clamps that anchored them to the deck with a synchronized *thud-thud-thud*.

A wall of coherent blue energy shimmered into existence between the shields, linking them into a single, impenetrable barrier.

The Rust Lords, caught in the momentum of their own charge, slammed into it. It was like watching water crash against a cliff. Chain-axes sparked uselessly against the energy field. Improvised explosives detonated against the shields, the force absorbed and dissipated in harmless ripples of blue light.

The Legionnaires didn't flinch. They stood like statues, their pulse rifles firing in controlled, rhythmic bursts through the firing ports of their shields, mowing down the scrappers with mechanical efficiency.

Behind the safety of the shield wall, a second team entered the chamber. These were not soldiers. They were combat engineers, clad in lighter, utility-focused armor. They carried heavy, reinforced cases and spools of thick, insulated cabling.

They moved with a frantic, practiced speed, ignoring the stray bullets that pinged off the floor around them. They set up in the center of the secured zone, directly facing the Anchor.

Ravn watched from his alcove, his eyes wide. He recognized the components they were assembling. A high-capacity capacitor bank. A focusing lens cut from a synthetic diamond. A massive, tripod-mounted emitter array that looked like a cross between a telescope and a railgun.

"The Calibrator," he whispered, recognizing the device from the schematics he had recovered in the archives.

It wasn't a weapon of war. It was a tool for terraforming, designed to stabilize localized atmospheric anomalies. But Rostova had modified it. She had turned it into a cage.

The engineers worked with terrifying precision. They bolted the tripod to the floor. They connected the power cables to portable fusion batteries that hummed with a dangerous, rising pitch. They aligned the emitter, using laser designators to target the exact geometric center of the Anchor.

Rostova stood beside the machine, her face illuminated by the diagnostic screens. She wasn't looking at the battle raging meters away. She was looking at the data streams scrolling across the monitors. She was adjusting the frequency, tuning the weapon to the specific resonance of her sister's soul.

"Field harmonics locked," an engineer shouted over the din. "Capacitors at full charge. Target is acquired."

"Stabilize it," Rostova ordered, her voice devoid of emotion. "Burn the chaos out of it."

The Rust Lords, seeing the massive machine take shape, redoubled their efforts. Jax roared, throwing himself against the shield wall, his mech-suit straining against the blue energy. The Husks dropped from the ceiling, trying to bypass the phalanx from above, only to be met by a disciplined volley of shotgun fire from the Legion's rear guard.

The wall held. The machine was ready.

The lead engineer unlocked the safety firing mechanism. A low, thrumming vibration built in the throat of the emitter, a sound that rose in pitch until it was a scream.

The air around the machine began to distort, sucked in by the gathering energy. Ravn felt the hair on his arms stand up. The Stalker whined, burying its head under its paws.

"Fire," Rostova said.

The lead engineer, his face a mask of terrified concentration behind his polarized visor, pulled the heavy engagement lever.

The Calibrator screamed.

A sound of tearing reality, like a sheet of steel being ripped in half by a giant, erupted from the emitter array. The air inside the Anchor chamber, already thick with gravimetric distortion, instantly ionized. Every hair on Ravn's body stood up.

The Stalker let out a high-pitched keening of pain, burying its nose in the dust of the alcove to escape the frequency.

Then, the beam struck.

It was a solid column of azure light, three meters thick, connecting the emitter to the Anchor in an instant. But as Ravn squinted against the glare, shifting his visual spectrum, he realized it wasn't light at all.

It was data.

The beam was composed of billions of tightly packed, scrolling geometric equations. It was a stream of weaponized mathematics, a high-velocity injection of syntax designed to overwrite the chaotic code of the anomaly. It was a command-line override sent by a god of order to a universe of chaos.

The beam hit the Anchor dead center.

The reaction was immediate and violent. The Anchor, a sphere of roiling, prismatic chaos, didn't explode. It convulsed.

The impact point flared with a blinding, geometric grid—a net of blue laser lines that spread rapidly across the surface of the sphere. It looked like a wireframe mesh, a digital cage clamping down on a living thing.

"Output at 110%!" the engineer shouted, his voice cracking. "The field is holding! We have capture!"

Ravn watched in horror as the Legion's philosophy was applied to the cosmos. The sphere was being forced into a hyper-dense containment lattice. The blue mesh wasn't just a shape; it was a mathematical cage designed to halt quantum spin.

The roiling sphere was forced into the path of least resistance—a perfect, rigid cube—as the Calibrator attempted to freeze the entropy of the core to absolute zero.

It was an attempt to put a straitjacket on a star.

The effect on the room was catastrophic. As the Calibrator forced the local laws of physics to align, the gravity waves in the chamber straightened out with a violent snap. The rippled floor plates slammed flat with a deafening clang. The floating debris—chunks of concrete, rebar, the frozen lab coats— dropped out of the air as if their strings had been cut, crashing to the ground in a rain of heavy matter.

A Rust Lord, who had been using a low-gravity pocket to leap across the room, suddenly found himself subject to standard Earth gravity. He fell mid-arc, plummeting twenty feet and shattering his legs on the steel deck.

The war for the room stopped. The Rust Lords and the Husks cowered, overwhelmed by the sheer, god-like display of the Legion's power. They were watching their deities—Chaos and Nature—being strangled by the cold hands of Order.

Rostova stepped closer to the machine, her face illuminated by the blue glare. She looked triumphant. She looked terrified. She was winning. She was imposing rules on a universe that had dared to break them.

"Stabilize," she whispered, the word a prayer. "Conform."

But Ravn saw what she didn't. Through his enhanced eyes, he looked past the blue cage and into the heart of the Anchor.

He saw the resistance.

The Anchor wasn't just energy. It was consciousness. It was Aris and Lena. And they were screaming.

The cage wasn't calming them. It was crushing them. The blue mesh was compressing their quantum signatures, forcing their infinite, expanding minds into a finite, binary box.

The silhouettes inside the light twisted and warped, their frozen postures of awe and terror stretching into shapes of agony.

The hum of the Anchor changed pitch. It rose from a deep, resonant thrum to a dissonant, shrieking tear. It was the sound of a soul being compressed into a file format it couldn't survive.

"You're killing them!" Ravn screamed, though the sound was lost in the roar of the machine.

He saw a fracture appear on the surface of the Anchor—not a crack in the energy, but a crack in the space around it. A black, jagged line of nothingness that hissed with vacuum. The Calibrator was pushing too hard. It was trying to solder a circuit board with a lightning bolt.

"General!" the engineer yelled, pointing at his monitor, where red warning lights were strobing. "Feedback loop! The target is rejecting the syntax! We're seeing massive destabilization in the core!"

"Hold it!" Rostova ordered, her voice rising to a shout. "Increase the gain! Force it to accept the pattern!"

She wouldn't stop. She couldn't stop. She was trapped in her own logic loop: if the chaos was the disease, then order must be the cure. She would burn the patient to ash to kill the fever.

The Calibrator whined, its capacitors glowing cherry-red. The blue beam intensified, becoming a solid wall of pressure. The Anchor shrank, compressed by the cage, its light turning a bruised, angry violet.

Ravn felt the Essence in his veins recoil. The Stalker was clawing at the floor, trying to dig a hole to escape the noise.

If that machine kept running, it wouldn't just stabilize the Anchor. It would crush it into a singularity. It would delete Aris and Lena, wiping their consciousness from the universe to leave behind a cold, dead battery.

Ravn couldn't let that happen. He looked at his empty pulse rifle. Useless against the phalanx. He looked at the distance to the machine. Fifty meters of open ground, guarded by heavy troopers. Impossible.

Then he looked at the ceiling.

The Calibrator was fed by thick, insulated power cables that ran from the portable fusion batteries on the floor. But to handle the massive load, the engineers had tapped into the facility's surviving grid, running a bypass cable up to a heavy junction box on a hanging gantry directly above the machine.

It was a thin, black line against the white light. A jugular vein.

Ravn grabbed the Stalker's harness. The creature looked at him, its eyes wide with pain and fear.

"Up," Ravn shouted, pointing to the twisted wreckage of the cooling tower that spiraled up toward the ceiling, its catwalks hanging over the Legion's position. "We have to cut the cord!"

The Stalker understood. It didn't need courage; it needed a target. It bared its fangs at the blue beam and nodded.

They broke cover. They didn't run toward the Legion; they ran up.

They scrambled up the twisted spine of the cooling tower, hand over hand, boot over claw. The concrete was warm and slick, vibrating with the immense energy discharging below. Ravn didn't look down. He kept his eyes fixed on the target: the heavy, black junction box bolted to a surviving section of the ceiling gantry, where the thick bypass cable fed the Legion's weapon.

Below them, the scream of the Anchor reached a fever pitch. The blue mesh of the Logic Cage had tightened further, compressing the sphere into a near-perfect, terrifying cube. The silhouettes of Aris and Lena were no longer recognizable as people; they were smears of light, stretched and distorted by the compression algorithm. The air in the chamber felt brittle, ready to shatter.

"Almost there," Ravn gasped, his lungs burning.

They reached the gantry. It hung precariously over the center of the room, swaying in the thermal updrafts of the Calibrator.

Ravn pulled himself onto the grating, the Stalker right behind him. They were directly above the machine now. He could see Rostova, a tiny figure in gray, shouting orders at her engineers. He could see the blue beam firing straight down, a pillar of tyranny.

He crawled to the junction box. The cable was as thick as his arm, wrapped in heavy-duty insulation and armored braiding.

He hacked at it with a sharp piece of scrap metal he'd grabbed from the debris, but the improvised blade skidded uselessly off the protective mesh. It was designed to withstand shrapnel and heat. It laughed at his steel.

"I can't cut it!" Ravn yelled, panic rising in his throat.

The hum of the Anchor pitch-shifted again, rising beyond the range of human hearing into a dog-whistle frequency that made his vision blur. The cube was shrinking. The event horizon was collapsing. If he didn't stop it now, they would be deleted.

The Stalker shoved him aside.

The creature didn't use a tool. It used what the Zone had given it. It opened its jaws, revealing rows of serrated, obsidian teeth capable of crushing bone and tearing through the armor of the Chittering Folk.

It bit down on the live cable.

There was a crunch of tearing insulation, followed instantly by a blinding explosion of sparks. The Stalker's jaws locked onto the copper core. Thousands of volts of raw current surged through the creature's body.

The Stalker convulsed, its muscles seizing, its bioluminescence flaring a blinding, incandescent white. It let out a sound that was half-roar, half-scream, muffled by the cable in its mouth.

The smell of burning chitin filled the air.

"Let go!" Ravn screamed, grabbing the creature's harness.

The Stalker didn't let go. It thrashed, using its own body weight and the spasm of its muscles to tear the cable free.

With a sound like a cracking whip, the cable snapped.

The severed end, spitting blue lightning, whipped down toward the floor. The connection to the Calibrator was severed.

Below, the effect was instantaneous. The blue beam sputtered and died. The geometric mesh surrounding the Anchor vanished.

The reaction of the released energy was violent. The Anchor, compressed for minutes under immense pressure, rebounded. It snapped back from a cube to a sphere in a fraction of a second.

A shockwave of pure, white displacement energy exploded outward from the core.

The engineers were thrown back as if hit by a truck. The Calibrator was knocked off its tripod, crashing to the floor in a tangle of smoking metal. General Rostova was lifted off her feet and slammed against the far wall, her energy shield flaring and dying.

The scream of the Anchor ceased, replaced by the familiar, resonant thrum of the sphere. Aris and Lena returned to their frozen, terrified stasis. They were safe. For now.

On the gantry, the Stalker slumped, releasing the severed cable from its jaws. Smoke curled from its mouth. It was breathing in shallow, ragged gasps, its light dim and flickering.

Ravn fell to his knees beside it, his hands hovering over the burns. "You crazy, beautiful bastard," he whispered.

He looked down at the reactor floor. The Legion was in disarray. Their weapon was broken, their commander down, their lines broken by the shockwave. The room was plunged into relative silence, the blue glare replaced by the pearlescent glow of the Anchor.

But the silence didn't last.

From the breached blast door, a new sound emerged. It wasn't the high-tech whine of the Legion. It was a low, guttural roar that vibrated the floor plates.

Jax had not been idle. While the Legion played with their laser pointer, the Rust Lords had been bringing up the heavy gear.

A massive, armored shape smashed through the doorway, widening the breach. It was a siege engine, a vehicle built of welded scrap and pure hate. A hydraulic ram mounted on the front revved with the sound of a chainsaw tearing through metal.

Jax stood on top of the rig, his face blackened with soot, his eyes wide with the joy of a man who has just seen the biggest toy in the universe.

"MY TURN!" he bellowed.

The threat had shifted. The scalpel was broken. Now came the hammer.

30

The Scrapper's Fury

T he silence that followed the destruction of the Calibrator was brief, but it was heavy. It was the kind of silence that follows a thunderclap, a vacuum in the air where the pressure drops so suddenly it makes the ears pop.

The blue beam was gone. The geometric cage that had been strangling the Anchor had evaporated, leaving behind only the smell of ionized dust and the cooling *tink-tink* of the ruined emitter.

The Anchor itself seemed to heave a sigh of relief, its shape snapping back from the forced, rigid cube to its natural, roiling sphere. The light shifted from a bruised, compressed violet back to a brilliant, blinding white. Aris and Lena, trapped inside, returned to their static, frozen poses of awe and terror, released from the active torture of the compression algorithm.

On the floor of the reactor chamber, the Legion was in disarray. The shockwave of the Calibrator's failure had scattered their engineers like toys. General Rostova was pulling herself up from the wall, her pristine uniform scorched, her energy shield flickering and dying. Her phalanx of heavy troopers, once an immovable wall, was broken, their formation shattered by the sudden shift in gravity when the machine died.

For a few seconds, Ravn, clinging to the high gantry with the panting Stalker, thought he had bought them a reprieve. He had broken the scalpel. He had stopped the surgery.

Then, the vacuum was filled.

It started with a smell. The clean, sterile scent of the Legion's antiseptic air was suddenly choked out by a thick, greasy wave of diesel fumes, unburnt hydrocarbons, and the copper tang of old, rusted blood.

Then came the vibration. The floor plates of the reactor chamber, which had stopped rippling when the Calibrator fired, began to shake again. But this wasn't the smooth, gravimetric distortion of the Anomaly. This was a crude, mechanical earthquake.

From the shadowed maw of the breached Tri-Key Door, a new noise emerged. It wasn't the high-pitched whine of technology. It was a low, guttural roar, a deep, throbbing bass note that grew louder and louder until it drowned out the hum of the Anchor.

It was the sound of a thousand horsepower tearing itself apart.

"Clear the lane!" a voice bellowed from the darkness, amplified by cracked, distorted speakers.

The Legionnaires, still reeling from the shockwave, looked up. They saw two blinding, yellow headlights cut through the smoke in the antechamber.

They didn't have time to regroup. They barely had time to scream.

The wall around the doorframe exploded. The Rust Lords didn't just enter the room; they widened the entrance. A colossal, armored shape smashed through the concrete and steel, tearing the blast door from its tracks and sending it skidding across the floor.

It was a siege engine. A nightmare of welded scrap and industrial fury. It was built on the chassis of a pre-Fracture mining hauler, but it had been stripped down and armored with plates of rusted iron and jagged rebar. Massive, spiked treads chewed up the metal floor, throwing sparks and debris into the air. Exhaust pipes, welded to the sides like the ribs of a skeleton, belched thick, black smoke that instantly fouled the air, creating a dark, artificial storm cloud inside the chamber.

Jax stood atop the rig, riding it like a chariot of the apocalypse. He was strapped to a roll cage welded above the driver's compartment, exposed to the air and the danger. His face was blackened with soot, his eyes wide and white in the grime, burning with the joy of a man who has just found the biggest toy in the universe.

"TEAR IT DOWN!" he bellowed, his voice echoing off the high ceiling.

Behind him, the rest of the Rust Lord horde poured through the breach. They flowed around the massive treads of the siege engine like scavenger fish trailing a shark. They were whooping and cheering, firing their slug-throwers into the ceiling, into the Legion survivors, into the Anchor itself.

The discipline of the room was gone. The cold, mathematical order the Legion had tried to impose was shattered by a sledgehammer of pure entropy.

Ravn watched from the gantry, horror dawning in his gut. He had stopped Rostova from compressing the Anchor, from squeezing the life out of it.

But Jax didn't want to squeeze.

The siege engine didn't stop. It rumbled over the debris of the Calibrator, crushing the delicate optical lens under its treads with a sickening crunch. It was heading straight for the center of the room. Straight for the Anchor. And mounted on the front of the machine, gleaming with oil and menace, was a massive, diamond-tipped hydraulic ram. It was a drill designed to crack mountains.

"He's not going to contain it," Ravn whispered, gripping the railing until his knuckles turned white. "He's going to break it."

The siege engine rumbled forward, its steel treads chewing the reactor floor into a spray of sparks and metal shavings. As it emerged fully from the smoke of the breach, Ravn got his first clear look at the instrument of the world's end.

It was a monstrosity of engineering, a Frankenstein's monster built from the corpses of a dozen different heavy industrial vehicles. The chassis belonged to a pre-Fracture bucket-wheel excavator, massive and squat, but the bucket arm had been torched off and replaced with a nightmare of offensive weaponry. Plates of rusted, jagged scrap metal had been welded over every inch of the hull, forming a chaotic, impenetrable skin that looked like dragon scales made of iron. Trophies hung from the roll cage—helmets of Legionnaires, skulls of Zone beasts, and braided chains of copper wire that swung wildly with the machine's vibration.

It wasn't designed; it was accumulated. It was a rolling accretion of violence.

But the heart of the beast, the weapon that gave it its purpose, was mounted dead center. Projecting from the front of the chassis, supported by hydraulic pistons the size of tree trunks, was a colossal, cylindrical ram. It was twenty feet long, tipped with a rotating, diamond-encrusted drill bit that looked like it had been stolen from a deep-core geothermal rig.

The drill spun with a blurring speed, screaming a high-pitched, mechanical wail that cut through the guttural roar of the engine.

"The Breaker," Ravn whispered, recognizing the machine from the terrified whispers of scavengers he had met in the wasteland. It was a legend. A city-killer.

Jax rode atop it, strapped into a gunner's cage welded to the roof of the cab. He was no longer just a warlord; he was a conductor of entropy. He held the control yoke of the ram in one hand and his chain-axe in the other, revving both in a syncopated rhythm of destruction.

He looked down at the disarray of the Legion forces, at the shattered remains of their delicate, high-tech Calibrator, and he laughed. It wasn't a sound of amusement. It was the sound of a man who had looked at the complex, fragile equation of civilization and decided that the only variable that mattered was force.

"LOOK AT YOU!" Jax bellowed, his voice amplified by the cracked speakers bolted to the rig's flanks. "PLAYING WITH LIGHTS! TRYING TO TALK TO THE GOD!"

He slammed the throttle forward.

The Breaker surged, black smoke pouring from its twin vertical exhaust stacks in a dense, choking cloud.

A squad of Legion heavy troopers, recovering from the shockwave, tried to form a line. They raised their tower shields, engaging the magnetic locks, trying to rebuild their wall of order.

It was a futile gesture. The Breaker didn't even slow down. The massive machine hit the shield line with the force of a tectonic shift. The energy fields flared and shattered instantly. The troopers were tossed aside like plastic toys, their armor crumpling under the weight of the treads. One soldier was caught under the tracks, his scream cut short by the wet crunch of flattened plasteel and bone.

Jax didn't look back. He didn't care about the soldiers. He didn't care about the territory. His eyes were locked on the Anchor.

The sphere of white light hung in the center of the room, pulsing with its silent, terrifying rhythm. To Rostova, it had been a battery. To Kaia, a seed. But to Jax, Ravn realized with a sickening jolt, it was just the biggest, most beautiful thing in the world to break.

"OPEN UP!" Jax screamed at the trapped souls of Aris and Lena. "LET'S SEE WHAT'S INSIDE!"

He engaged the hydraulics. The massive diamond drill bit extended, reaching out like a spear.

The Breaker rumbled over the last of the debris, crushing the remains of the control consoles, and lined up its shot.

It wasn't going to interface with the energy field. It wasn't going to hack it. It was going to physically, violently penetrate the event horizon.

Ravn, watching from the high gantry, felt a wave of nausea. The Calibrator had been torture, a vice squeezing the soul. But this... this was murder.

The drill would disrupt the quantum coherence of the Anchor instantly. It wouldn't just release the energy; it would cause a catastrophic, uncontrolled decoherence. It would be like dropping a grenade into a supernova.

"He's going to kill us all," Ravn said, his voice trembling. "He doesn't care."

The Stalker snarled, its claws digging into the metal grating of the walkway. It felt the threat. It felt the wrongness of the machine.

Below them, the Breaker stopped ten meters from the Anchor. Jax revved the drill to maximum RPM. The sound rose to a shriek that shattered the remaining glass in the observation deck above. Sparks flew from the tip of the drill as it spun against the empty air, hungry for contact.

Jax raised his axe high, a signal to his followers, a signal to the universe. "TEAR IT DOWN!"

Jax slammed the engagement lever forward. The Breaker surged. The massive diamond-tipped drill, spinning at three thousand revolutions per minute, blurred into a cone of silver death. The air around it shrieked, the friction heating the atmosphere until it shimmered.

"BREAK!" Jax screamed.

The drill struck the Anchor.

It wasn't a collision of solid against solid. It was a collision of matter against math. The Anchor's event horizon was a field of infinite density, a wall of pure, condensed spacetime. When the diamond tip made contact, the sound that erupted was not a clang or a thud. It was a scream that spanned the entire audible spectrum, a high-pitched, grinding tear that felt like a dental drill boring directly into the listener's skull.

Ravn clapped his hands over his ears, crouching on the gantry, his teeth rattling in his gums. The Stalker howled, a sound lost in the mechanical cacophony, and pressed its head against the metal grating.

Sparks didn't fly. Instead, arcs of exotic energy sprayed from the contact point—volleys of violet lightning that lashed out like whips. Where they struck the floor, the metal bubbled and hissed. Where they struck the hull of the Breaker, the rusted armor glowed cherry-red.

The siege engine shuddered violently, its massive tracks grinding against the floor plates, smoking as they fought for traction against the pushback of a singularity. The hydraulic pistons supporting the ram groaned, leaking pressurized fluid that vaporized instantly on the hot metal.

But Jax didn't back off. He pushed the throttle past the red line. The engine roared, belching a cloud of black smoke so dense it obscured the ceiling.

"BREAK!" he roared, his voice a distorted crackle over the speakers. "BREAK!"

And the Anchor... yielded.

It wasn't designed to withstand kinetic assault. It was designed to hold energy, not mass.

The drill bit, hardened by the pressures of the deep earth, began to bite. It displaced the light. It bored a physical hole into the energy field, a tunnel of friction and violence forcing its way toward the core.

The sphere of light began to deform. It didn't compress into a cube like it had under the Legion's laser. It rippled. It warped. It stretched like a soap bubble being poked by a needle.

The effect on the room was catastrophic. The gravity field, which had snapped flat when the Legion failed, now went haywire. It started to fluctuate and spasm. Gravity waves radiated outward from the drill site in violent, concussive pulses.

Ravn felt his weight double, slamming him against the walkway. A second later, he was weightless, floating inches off the grate. The debris on the floor—chunks of concrete, twisted metal, the corpses of the fallen—began to dance. They hopped and skittered, thrown into the air by the seismic waves, then slammed back down with crushing force.

The air pressure hammered at his eardrums. *Thump. Thump. Thump.* It was the heartbeat of the machine, magnified by the dying universe.

But the true horror was inside the sphere.

Ravn shifted his visual spectrum, engaging the crystalline lattice in his eyes, staring past the grinding drill and into the core.

Aris and Lena were no longer frozen. The kinetic energy of the drill was transferring into the quantum state of the core. It was shaking them apart.

Their silhouettes flickered. They dissolved into a cloud of binary noise, then snapped back into focus, then de-rendered again. It was a violent, strobe-light disintegration.

Ravn saw Aris's face contort. The look of awe was gone, shaken into a blur of digital noise. His mouth opened wider, the silent shout becoming a scream of frequency that bled through the energy field.

...help...

The word wasn't heard; it was felt. A psychic splinter in Ravn's mind.

Lena's outstretched hand, the one reaching for her love, began to fracture. The fingers drifted away from the palm, floating in the chaos, before snapping back into place. She was being unmade, pixel by pixel.

Jax wasn't opening a door. He was putting a blender into a soul.

"He's tearing them apart," Ravn whispered, tears of pain and rage leaking from his eyes. The sight was unbearable. The physical violence being visited upon the memory of his loved ones was a desecration worse than the Legion's torture. Rostova had tried to freeze them. Jax was trying to mulch them.

A hairline fracture appeared on the surface of the Anchor, spiraling out from the drill tip. It wasn't a crack in the energy. It was a crack in reality. Black, chaotic nothingness bled from the wound. It hissed like escaping steam. Where the black mist touched the drill, the diamond tip turned gray and brittle, aging a million years in a second.

The Breaker screamed, its metal fatigue reaching a critical point. A hydraulic line burst, spraying hot oil across the Anchor's surface, where it ignited into a wreath of chemical fire.

Jax laughed, dancing in the flames. "ALMOST THERE! I CAN SEE THE DARK!"

Nearby, a Rust Lord driver peered through the smoke, his greed turning to ice. He had come for weapons. He had come for fuel. But looking at the black cracks spreading across reality, at the void eating the light, he realized there was no prize. He realized they weren't robbing a vault; they were digging a grave.

He screamed a warning to his pack, scrambling to reverse his rig, but his voice was swallowed by the roar of the drill.

Jax was going to breach the core. And when he did, the release of energy wouldn't be a wave. It would be a detonation.

Ravn looked at the Stalker. The creature was huddled against the railing, terrified by the noise and the shaking gravity.

"We have to stop it," Ravn yelled, pulling himself up against the fluctuating gravity. "He's going to kill everyone!"

He looked for a weakness. The Breaker was a tank. His empty rifle was useless against the heavy plating. The power cables were internal. There was no "off" switch on a machine built of hate.

Except one. The drill.

It was the point of contact. The fulcrum of the violence. It was spinning at thousands of RPM, driven by a massive, exposed chain drive located just behind the ram's housing. The chain was a blur of heavy steel links, slick with grease, roaring as it transferred the engine's power to the bit.

If the chain broke, the drill stopped. But it was guarded by a heavy steel cowling, and Jax was perched right above it with his chain-axe.

There was no way to get close. No way to shoot it.

Unless...

Ravn looked at the heavy, industrial winch hook hanging from the gantry above him—a relic of the facility's construction crane. It was a block of solid steel the size of an anvil, suspended on a thick cable.

If he could drop it. If he could drop it into the gears. It was a one-in-a-million shot. A problem of trajectory, gravity, and timing in a room where all three were broken.

He didn't care. He calculated the angle. He grabbed the release lever of the winch.

"Hey! Scrapper!" Ravn screamed, his voice tiny against the roar.

Jax didn't hear him. But he felt the intent. The warlord looked up, his eyes locking onto Ravn on the gantry.

Ravn pulled the release lever.

The heavy steel winch hook dropped from the gantry. It was a block of iron the size of an anvil, plummeting straight down toward the exposed, roaring chain drive of the Breaker. It was a perfect shot. A kinetic kill-switch.

But the Anchor wasn't done fighting. Just as the hook reached the top of the siege engine, a violent pulse of gravity wave erupted from the drill site. The air distorted. The hook, caught in the sudden shift of physics, didn't fall straight. It curved. It swung wildly to the left, defying momentum, and slammed harmlessly against the armored cowling of the engine block with a deafening CLANG.

It bounced off, swinging uselessly in the air.

Jax looked up, his eyes wide with manic delight. He saw the hook. He saw Ravn clinging to the railing above.

"MISSED ME!" Jax howled, his laughter tearing through the mechanical scream of the drill.

He raised his chain-axe, pointing it at Ravn. "MISSED ME! NOW WATCH IT BURN!"

He slammed his fist down on the throttle. The Breaker surged again.

The diamond drill bit pushed deeper into the Anchor. The sphere of light didn't just ripple this time; it darkened. The brilliant white luminescence was stained by a spreading cancer of void-black ink.

The cracks in reality widened, hissing with the sound of a vacuum breach. The silhouettes of Aris and Lena stretched into impossible, horrifying shapes, their silent screams vibrating the very atoms of the air.

"No!" Ravn screamed, his voice raw. He looked around frantically for another weapon, another loose bolt, anything.

But there was nothing. He was empty. The physics of the room had defeated his math.

He was going to watch them die. He was going to watch his brother be mulched by a madman's machine, and then he was going to be unmade by the explosion.

He slumped against the railing, the strength draining from his legs.

"I'm sorry," he sobbed, the words lost in the roar.

Beside him, the Stalker stood up.

The creature wasn't looking at Jax. It wasn't looking at the Anchor. It was looking at the machine. Specifically, at the blurring, roaring loop of the exposed chain drive that was powering the drill.

It looked at the gears with a cold, alien intensity. It didn't understand mechanics. It didn't know what a combustion engine was. But it understood the Zone.

It understood that to stop a heart from beating, you had to strike it. And it understood that its companion—the man with the strange eyes who had shared his water and his silence—was in pain.

The Stalker turned its head. It looked at Ravn for one timeless second.

Its bioluminescence, which had been a chaotic red, shifted. It softened into a calm, steady, deep blue. The color of the grotto. The color of peace. It let out a low, chuffing breath. A goodbye.

Then, it moved.

It launched itself over the railing, diving straight down into the heart of the beast.

"NO!" Ravn lunged, his hand swiping at empty air, his fingers brushing the tip of the creature's tail.

The Stalker fell. It tucked its body, aiming itself like a missile. It slammed directly into the exposed tensioner arm of the chain drive.

There was no roar of defiance. There was only the sickening, wet crunch of biology meeting industrial steel.

The impact shattered the creature's ribs, but the force knocked the guide wheel out of alignment. The massive steel chain, moving at thousands of revolutions per minute, jumped the sprocket.

It whipped loose with the sound of a cracking whip, slashing through the hydraulic lines. The engine revved freely, disconnected from the drill, screaming as it redlined.

The recoil was catastrophic. The snapped chain whipped around, slashing through the hydraulic lines of the ram. The engine, unable to turn the gears, blew its head gasket, exploding in a geyser of oil and fire.

The drill stopped instantly.

The sudden loss of momentum threw the entire siege engine forward. The rear treads lifted off the ground.

Jax, perched on the gunner's cage and laughing at the sky, was launched like a ragdoll. He flew through the air, his axe spinning away, and smashed into a distant pile of debris.

The Breaker slammed back down, dead. Smoke poured from its engine block.

The drill sat motionless, buried deep in the Anchor's energy field, but no longer turning.

Silence rushed back into the room, heavy and suffocating. The Anchor pulsed, the black stains slowly receding, the white light returning.

The immediate threat of detonation was gone.

But there was no victory in the silence.

Ravn stared down from the gantry, his hand still outstretched, his heart frozen in his chest. He looked at the smoking, ruined mechanism of the chain drive.

Wedged between the gears, broken and still, was a mass of dark chitin and indigo blood.

31

The Husk's Prayer

Ravn knelt in the pool of oil and indigo blood, his hand resting on the cooling flank of the Stalker. The grief was a physical weight, a stone in his throat that made it impossible to swallow.

He looked up at the dead siege engine. The Breaker was now just a smoking monument to kinetic failure. Beyond it, the scattered bodies of the Rust Lords and the Legionnaires lay in heaps of meat and metal strewn across the reactor floor.

The hammer had failed. The scalpel was broken. The violence of men and machines had thrown itself against the Anchor and broken its teeth.

But the war wasn't over. It was just changing states.

The smell hit him first. It cut through the acrid stench of burning diesel, cooked flesh, and copper with a violence that made him gag.

It was sweet. Cloying. It smelled of blooming jasmine, rotting honey, and the musk of a deep, damp cave. It was the scent of a funeral home left to fester in the sun.

Then came the air. A draft blew from the antechamber, but it wasn't the cold, recycled air of the facility. It was warm, humid, and thick. It rolled across the floor, displacing the black smoke of the explosion with a heavy, golden mist.

It wasn't fog. Ravn shifted his visual spectrum, zooming in on the particulate matter drifting around him. It was pollen.

Billions of microscopic, bioluminescent spores, drifting on an artificial wind generated by the collective will of the approaching army.

The mist swirled around the wreckage of the Breaker, coating the rusted iron in a layer of glittering gold dust. Where the pollen touched the oil slicks, it sizzled, drinking the hydrocarbons and blooming into tiny, rapid-growth mold colonies.

The invasion had already begun on a microscopic level.

Ravn coughed, the taste of sugar and dirt coating his tongue.

He grabbed his empty pulse rifle, using it as a crutch to push himself up. His legs shook. He backed away from the Stalker's body, retreating toward the center of the room, toward the Anchor.

"Show yourselves," he rasped, his voice wrecked.

They didn't charge. They didn't roar. They filtered in.

The golden fog thickened at the breach of the blast door. Through the haze, shapes began to materialize. They moved with a fluid, unnerving grace, their feet making no sound on the metal floor.

The Husks.

There were hundreds of them. They flowed into the reactor chamber like water filling a basin. They moved in perfect unison, a single organism with a thousand limbs. They wore no armor, only robes woven from living vines and moss. Their skin was painted with ash and pollen, glowing with the soft, rhythmic pulse of their bioluminescence.

They didn't look like soldiers. They looked like pilgrims.

They stepped over the bodies of the Legionnaires without looking down. They walked around the wreckage of the war-rigs as if they were mere stones in a river. Their eyes, pearlescent and swirling with alien light, were fixed on one thing: the Anchor.

To them, the devastation of the room—the twisted metal, the dead machines—was irrelevant. It was just dead matter to be composted.

Ravn backed up until his heels hit the raised lip of the reactor pit. He was surrounded.

The Husks formed a perfect circle around the core, three deep, enclosing him and the Anchor in a wall of living flesh.

They stopped.

The silence returned, but it was different now. It was vibrating. A low, sub-audible hum emanated from the circle, a collective resonance of a thousand throats vibrating at the same frequency. It sounded like the buzzing of a hive, or the purring of a colossal cat.

Ravn gripped his rifle by the barrel, ready to swing it, ready to die fighting. But they didn't attack.

The circle parted.

From the golden mist near the door, a single figure emerged. She walked slowly, her bare feet leaving glowing footprints in the dust. Her robes were elaborate, woven from iridescent beetle wings and fibers that shifted color from green to gold.

It was Kaia.

She didn't look like a general. She looked like a mother walking into a nursery. Her face was serene, unlined by the stress of the war. Her eyes were pools of infinite, terrifying compassion.

She stopped ten meters from Ravn, standing over the body of the Stalker.

She looked down at the broken creature, and a genuine tear slid down her cheek.

"Poor, lost child," she whispered, her voice carrying effortlessly through the humid air. "He fought so hard to remain separate."

She looked up at Ravn. She didn't see the rifle. She didn't see the threat. She saw a wound that needed to be closed.

"Put down the iron, Ravn," she said softly. "There is no more need for breaking."

Her voice was not a command; it was an invitation. It drifted through the golden haze, carrying a weight of maternal warmth that felt alien in the cold, dead air of the reactor.

She stepped closer, her bare feet silent on the oil-slicked metal. The Ascended warriors behind her held their positions, a wall of silent, glowing sentinels, their weapons lowered but not sheathed.

Ravn tightened his grip on the useless rifle, his knuckles white.

"Stay back," he warned, though his voice lacked the steel he intended. He was exhausted, hollowed out by grief and adrenaline. He was a man holding a stick against a rising tide.

Kaia ignored the threat. She knelt beside the body of the Stalker, heedless of the grime that stained her iridescent robes. She reached out a hand, her fingers trailing over the creature's shattered flank. Where she touched, the dark chitin seemed to soften, the indigo blood stopping its flow as if commanded by the earth itself.

"So much pain," she whispered, looking into the creature's dim, dead eyes. "So much lonely, desperate strength. He fought the world every day of his life. He lived in fear of the silence."

She looked up at Ravn, her eyes shimmering with silvery tears.

"But he does not have to end in silence, Ravn. Nothing ever truly ends. Not here."

She opened her hand. In her palm rested a single, glowing seed, pulsating with a soft, golden light. It looked like a drop of the sun solidified into matter.

"The root remembers," she said. "The earth keeps what is given to it. We can plant him. We can fold his song into ours. He will not be a hunter anymore. He will be the hunt. He will be the forest. He will be safe."

Ravn stared at the seed. He felt a chill that had nothing to do with the temperature of the room. He understood what she was offering. She wasn't talking about burial. She was talking about assimilation. She wanted to feed his friend to the hive mind, to dissolve the Stalker's fierce, individual spirit into the soup of the collective consciousness.

"That's not life," Ravn spat, his voice trembling. "That's digestion. He would be gone."

"He would be whole," Kaia corrected gently. "Is it better to be a broken thing, rotting in the dark? Or to be part of something eternal?"

She stood up, leaving the seed resting on the Stalker's chest. She stepped toward Ravn, moving into his personal space. The smell of the pollen was overwhelming now, a narcotic perfume that made his head swim. He felt a sudden, dizzying urge to drop the rifle, to lie down, to sleep.

"And you," she murmured, reaching out to touch his face. Her fingers were cool and dry. "You carry such a heavy burden, Physicist. I see the ghosts you drag behind you. I see the hole in your heart."

She looked past him, toward the blinding light of the Anchor. Toward the silhouette of Aris.

"You want to save him," she said. "But you know you cannot open the door without breaking the world. You are trapped."

She smiled, a terrifying expression of infinite love.

"We can save him, Ravn. We can embrace the Seed. We can wrap it in roots and love and make it part of the Great Song. He will not be trapped in a moment of terror anymore. He will be everywhere. He will be the rain. He will be the moss. He will be us. And you... you can be with him."

The temptation hit Ravn like a physical blow. To be with Aris. To end the guilt. To stop the endless, grinding struggle of survival and simply... let go. To dissolve into a warm, golden ocean of connection where there was no pain, no loss, no loneliness.

It was the promise of heaven, offered by a monster wearing a mother's face.

For a second, his grip on the rifle loosened. The Essence in his veins hummed, resonating with the biological frequency of the pollen. His crystalline eyes saw the golden light not as a threat, but as a beautiful, complex pattern of integration.

Then, he looked down at the Stalker. He saw the seed resting on its chest.

He remembered the creature's fierce independence, its wary intelligence, the way it had chosen him not out of instinct, but out of trust. It had died fighting for him, not for a collective. It had died as an individual.

To assimilate it would be the ultimate betrayal.

Ravn stepped back, slapping Kaia's hand away from his face. The spell broke. The smell of pollen was no longer sweet; it was cloying, the stench of rot.

"No," he said, his voice hard. "We don't want your peace. We don't want your song."

Kaia's expression didn't change. She didn't look angry. She looked disappointed. "Then you choose pain," she said softly. "You choose the silence of the seed."

She stepped back, raising her arms. The humming of the Husks rose in pitch, becoming a deafening, vibrating drone. The golden fog swirled, thickening into tendrils.

"If you will not give it willingly," Kaia whispered, her voice hardening into the tone of a tectonic plate shifting, "then the earth must take it."

She raised her arms, the iridescent sleeves of her robe falling back to reveal skin covered in swirling, pulsing bioluminescence.

The ritual began.

The low, rhythmic humming of the circle rose in pitch. It ceased to be a sound made by human throats and became a physical vibration, a resonant frequency that rattled the teeth in Ravn's skull.

The golden fog swirling around the room thickened, coalescing into solid, rope-like tendrils of mist that drifted toward the center of the room.

The reactor floor, a foundation of reinforced steel and concrete designed to withstand a nuclear meltdown, began to groan. It was a screeching, tortured sound of metal being stressed beyond its yield point. Then, it buckled.

With a deafening CRACK that echoed like a gunshot, a steel floor plate near the edge of the reactor pit burst upward. A massive, gnarled root, thick as a barrel and glowing with veins of emerald light, erupted from the sub-floor. It tore through the metal grating like wet paper, curling into the air with the muscular, seeking motion of a tentacle.

Then another plate burst. And another.

The room became a garden of violence. Roots and vines surged from the wreckage of the facility, shattering the concrete, wrapping around the twisted remains of the cooling towers, and crushing the dead machinery of the Legion and the Rust Lords. They moved with a terrifying, rapid-growth speed, expanding in real-time, adding feet of biomass every second.

Ravn scrambled back, tripping over the debris of the Calibrator, as a vine the size of a python slammed into the floor where he had been standing. The vine didn't attack him. It ignored him completely. It wasn't interested in flesh. It was interested in the light.

All the growth was directional. The roots, the vines, the tendrils of moss— they were all converging on the Anchor.

The circle of Husks swayed in unison, their eyes rolled back, their hands making pulling motions in the air, as if they were physically dragging the flora from the deep earth. They were the conductors of this biological symphony.

Ravn watched in horror as the vines reached the edge of the energy field. They didn't burn. They didn't de-render. They adapted.

The tips of the vines split open, revealing wet, pink interiors lined with sensory cilia. They touched the blinding white light of the Anchor, testing it, tasting it. The energy field flared, arching with electricity, but the vines held fast. They began to secrete a thick, translucent resin that hardened instantly upon contact with the radiation, forming a protective shell.

Then, they began to wrap.

It was a strangulation. The vines coiled around the sphere of light, crisscrossing, weaving a cage of living wood and glowing sap. They were creating a womb. A chrysalis.

The brilliant light of the Anchor began to dim, choked off by the encroaching biomass. The clean, white radiance was filtered through layers of green and brown, casting the room in a sickly, underwater gloom.

Ravn looked up. The ceiling of the chamber was cracking. Roots from the surface, kilometers above, were responding to the call, drilling down through the bedrock to join the feast.

"Stop!" Ravn yelled, aiming his empty rifle at Kaia. "You're suffocating them!"

Kaia didn't hear him. She was in a trance, her eyes glowing with the same emerald light as the vines. She was no longer an individual; she was a node in the network.

The vines tightened. The hum of the Anchor changed. It wasn't the mechanical scream of the Legion's compression, or the tearing shriek of the Rust Lords' drill. It was a wet, gurgling sound. A drowning sound. The Anchor was being digested.

Ravn saw the silhouette of Aris inside the sphere. A thick vine slithered across the energy field, blocking his brother's face. Then another wrapped around Lena's outstretched hand. They were being buried alive.

The "soft" power of nature, Ravn realized with a jolt of nausea, was just as brutal, just as relentless, and just as destructive as the "hard" power of the machine. It was a slow, crushing inevitability. It was a kudzu vine swallowing a house.

And he was the only thing left in the room that wasn't part of the root system.

Kaia stood before the chrysalis, her arms raised, her face rapturous in the green light. She was no longer an individual. She was the mouth of the forest.

"Become," she commanded, her voice a multi-tonal harmonic that vibrated in Ravn's teeth. "Become us."

32

The Point of Collapse

he Anchor screamed.

It was not a sound that traveled through the air to vibrate eardrums. It was a psychic concussion grenade, a resonant frequency of pure rejection that bypassed the senses and hammered directly into the wetware of the brain. It was the sound of a universe gagging, a violent, spasmodic expulsion of something it could not digest.

The Husks were the first to fall. Because they had opened their minds to the Anchor, because they had woven their consciousness into the attempt to assimilate it, they took the full force of the blow.

Kaia was thrown backward as if she had been hit by an invisible truck. Her back slammed against the metal floor plates with a sickening crunch. Her eyes, usually glowing with wisdom, rolled back in her head, showing only the whites of a mind overwhelmed by static. Thick, indigo blood erupted from her nose and ears, splattering across her iridescent robes.

The Ascended warriors surrounding the core didn't just stumble; they seized. Their synchronized chanting shattered into individual, animalistic shrieks of agony as their neural pathways were overloaded by the feedback loop.

The organic assault had been reversed. The Anchor was vomiting up the meal.

The massive, emerald-veined vines that had wrapped the sphere withered in the span of a heartbeat. They turned from vibrant, pulsing biology into gray, desiccated ash, snapping away from the light and crumbling into dust that coated the floor like snow.

The sweet, cloying scent of the pollen was instantly incinerated, replaced by the sharp, metallic taste of ionized dust and the smell of burning synapses.

But the rejection of Nature was only the beginning. The system was destabilizing across all vectors.

The rejection triggered a catastrophic rebound. The three conflicting energies that had been forcibly injected into the Anchor—the strict, geometric Order of the Legion's compression field; the violent, kinetic Chaos of Jax's drill; and the all-consuming Nature of the Husks' assimilation—did not simply vanish.

They collided in the center of the sphere.

The Anchor's white light went critical.

It flashed a furious, impossible spectrum of colors, cycling through millions of shades per nanosecond. A geometric blue laser grid (the ghost of the Calibrator) fought for dominance against a fractal green vine pattern (the ghost of the Husks) across the surface of the sphere. And where the colors met, a corrosive void-black ink (the void of the drill's rupture) erupted, spitting raw, chaotic matter into the room.

The chamber shook, not with a mechanical vibration, but with a dimensional convulsion. The fabric of spacetime inside the room began to tear. The temperature cycled through impossible extremes in the blink of an eye.

A wave of blistering heat, hot enough to crack the remaining blast glass of the observation deck, washed over the combatants, instantly singeing hair and blistering skin. Before they could scream, it was followed by a wave of cryogenic cold so absolute that the moisture in the air froze instantly, coating the heated metal in a thin, crackling layer of hoarfrost.

The very air tasted of static, friction, and thermal shock.

The physics of the room began to break down. The floor plates, already warped by the earlier gravitational fluctuations, groaned and buckled. Steel treated to withstand nuclear impacts tore like wet paper. A massive chunk of ceiling concrete, heavy and sharp, sheared loose from its rebar moorings and slammed down onto the spot where a Rust Lord was struggling to rise, crushing him instantly into a paste of bone and armor.

The raw energy pulses were hitting the surviving combatants indiscriminately. A Legion heavy trooper, desperately trying to rebuild the shield wall, was engulfed in a wave of the chaotic violet energy. He didn't burn. He didn't explode. He fractured. His armor, his weapon, and his body shattered into millions of perfect, tiny cubes, hanging suspended in the air for a terrifying second before dissolving into gray mist.

The survivors—the Legionnaires clutching their jamming weapons, the Rust Lords cowering behind their wrecked machines, and the shocked, recovering Husks—stopped fighting each other. The war for the prize was over. They were no longer soldiers fighting for an ideology; they were rats trapped in a sinking cage. They were fighting the room itself.

The scream of the Anchor reached a final, deafening crescendo, a sound that defied the very concept of frequency and became a wall of pure pressure. The Anchor was no longer a prize to be won. It was a bomb, and the fuse had burned down to the detonator.

The air in the reactor chamber was thick with the scent of sulfur and the heavy, metallic tang of burnt circuits, but it was the smell of fear that now dominated the space—a raw, biological panic that the Legion's discipline and the Rust Lords' madness could no longer suppress.

The psychological fallout of the Anchor's rejection was immediate and absolute: the Dogma had failed.

General Eva Rostova was the first to convert the metaphysical shock into physical action. She pulled herself away from the wall where the shockwave had slammed her, ignoring the searing pain in her dislocated shoulder.

Her face, usually a study in glacial composure, was contorted with a mixture of terror and absolute, cold fury. She didn't look at the Anchor with reverence or greed anymore. She looked at it as a bomb.

She scrambled past the shattered body of a combat engineer, her boots crunching on the remains of the optical lens, and reached the primary power control console for the ruined Calibrator. The screen was a chaotic mess of red and black warning lights, scrolling data too fast for a human eye to read.

But she didn't need the screen; the sheer violence of the room—the temperature spikes cycling from absolute zero to inferno, the gravity spasms tearing the floor apart, the visual noise of reality de-rendering—screamed the data at her.

The convergence of the conflicting syntax had created a terminal error. Her attempt to impose order had created the ultimate chaos.

Rostova stared at the monitor. The telemetry showed the quantum signature of the Anchor twisting, stretching into a shape of pure agony. For a split second, her hand hovered over the controls, her finger trembling as she recognized the scream pattern. It matched Lena's voice print.

She squeezed her eyes shut, forcing the memory down.

"Increase the gain!" she ordered, her voice shaking. "Force it to accept the pattern!"

"Forget the asset!" Rostova shrieked, her voice amplified by her damaged helmet speakers, cracking with a desperation her troops had never heard. This was a direct, immediate abandonment of her central mission.

"All units! Drop plasma rifles! We need containment gel! Anchor the fusion batteries! I need a temporary field! NOW!"

The Legionnaires, trained for discipline, obeyed instantly. They dropped their heavy plasma rifles—the tools of their order—and began scrambling to recover temporary shield emitters and fusion batteries from the wreckage.

Their dogma of Order collapsed the moment the physics became impossible. They were prepared to fight chaos with rules, but not to fight reality with nothing. They were no longer conquerors; they were engineers trying to shore up a dam that had already burst.

Jax, fueled by the pure spite of defeat, had his own, more primal reaction.

He abandoned the Breaker, his massive siege engine, realizing that the machine itself was now just a massive anchor for the coming explosion. His philosophy of Chaos—the belief that destruction was the ultimate freedom—had reached its ultimate, self-destructive expression.

He stumbled across the heaving floor, his eyes wide and burning with a terrifying realization. He saw the void-black cracks spreading across the Anchor, leaking a darkness that ate the light.

His mind, which prized noise and fire, realized this was an end state. It was a level of entropy that resolved all potential, leaving nothing behind—no scrap, no fuel, no pain, no joy.

It was the true silence he had feared all along.

"No! Not silence!" Jax bellowed, his voice raw with despair and rage. He wasn't yelling at Ravn; he was yelling at the universe. "You don't take the whole damn thing!"

He scrambled toward a functional control terminal on a Rust Lord support rig. He began frantically trying to overload the core in a final, spiteful act. He didn't want to survive. He wanted to maximize the glory of his own annihilation.

He found a functioning thermite charge launcher, a desperate, final weapon. If the world was going to end, he was going to be the one to pull the trigger. He would turn the catastrophic deletion into a huge, glorious explosion that would at least be a spectacle worthy of a warlord's death.

Jax leveled the launcher, his eyes wide not with hate, but with a desperate, manic need to break the silence.

"It's too quiet, Ravn!" he screamed, his voice cracking. "It's always too quiet! Let's make it scream!"

Kaia and the surviving Husks were already retreating. The psychic backlash had shattered their collective mind. The Ascended warriors were wandering aimlessly, weeping, clutching their heads.

Kaia was being dragged away by two of her followers, her eyes vacant, her mouth moving in a silent, broken prayer. Their shared faith in Nature had been utterly broken by the unnatural pain of the rejection. They had sought to join the song, and the song had choked them.

The entire ideological structure of the room had dissolved in seconds. The leaders were reduced to their desperate, individual instincts: Rostova wanted to contain the failure; Jax wanted to ignite the failure; and Kaia simply wanted to escape the failure.

Ravn, pushing himself to his feet amidst the debris, saw the three factions—his whole journey—reduced to a desperate, panicked retreat.

The war was over. The game had gone critical. And he was the only one left standing between their collective failure and the annihilation of everything.

He pulled himself away from the immediate chaos, scrambling backward into the alcove where the functional terminal blinked with its steady, inviting blue light. He pressed his back against the cold steel of the bulkhead, his chest heaving, his lungs burning with the acrid taste of ash and pulverized stone.

The world around him was dissolving into raw entropy. He could hear Rostova screaming for containment protocols that no longer existed. He could hear Jax's manic laughter as the warlord scrambled for explosives to accelerate the end. He could feel the psychic agony of the Husks vibrating in the floorboards. Their failures were absolute.

He looked at the Anchor. The sphere of light was now a maelstrom of destruction, the colliding syntax—blue, green, and black—tearing at its surface like wolves at a carcass.

The core wasn't just destabilizing; it was rejecting the input.

Ravn forced his mind to disengage from the fear. He shifted his visual spectrum, pushing his perception into the raw data stream. He needed to see the math beneath the fire.

He analyzed the three failed solutions, watching the energy pulses clash on the core.

First, he looked at the ghost of the Legion's beam. It was a stream of absolute, geometric truth. It commanded the universe to be $A = A$. It was a binary system where everything was defined, categorized, and locked.

If the Anchor accepted this, the result would be stasis. All motion would cease. All change would be suppressed. The universe would become a crystal: perfect, beautiful, and dead. Potential $= 0$.

Next, he looked at the black void of Jax's drill. It was a violent attempt to enforce infinite entropy. It commanded the universe to be $A \neq A$. It was a system of pure kinetic energy with no structure to hold it.

If the Anchor accepted this, the result would be immediate, total decay. All complex structures—atoms, stars, people—would be ripped apart. Potential $= 0$.

Finally, he looked at the withered vines of Kaia's ritual. It was an attempt to create perfect, all-consuming unity. It commanded the universe to be $A = All$. If the Anchor accepted this, the result would be the end of the individual. There would be no "I," only "We." Without the friction of separation, there is no spark of creation. Potential $= 0$.

Ravn realized the horrifying flaw in all three elegant answers.

The Axiom's core directive, revealed to him in the archive, was to Preserve Potential.

Any system that resolves itself to an absolute state—perfect order, perfect chaos, or perfect unity—is a closed system. It has no unknowns. It has no capacity for surprise. It has no future.

The collapse wasn't a malfunction; it was a defense mechanism. The Axiom was executing a final [DELETE] command to wipe the slate clean and reboot the entire universe back to a state of pure, unpredictable potential, because the alternative was a dead end.

His mind flashed back to the moment he absorbed the Anomaly's Essence, to the one clear memory that wasn't his: Lena's final, desperate thought, echoing through the data streams of a dead world.

The variable. We forgot to carry the variable.

For five years, he had thought she meant a variable in the K-field equation. A missing decimal. A wrong integer. But looking at the collapsing sphere, at the three failed absolutes, he finally understood.

Lena wasn't talking about math. She wasn't talking about a piece of code they forgot to include in the experiment.

She was talking about the human element. She was talking about the flaw.

The unquantifiable factors that defined their lives: grief, curiosity, self-sacrifice, and the capacity for paradox. The ability to hold two contradictory thoughts in one mind. The ability to choose love even when it was illogical. The ability to hope when the probability was zero.

They had tried to create an information substrate—the Axiom—without including the illogical truth that gives information value. They had built a god of logic and forgot to give it a heart.

The core was collapsing because it lacked a piece of Humanity.

Ravn looked at his hands. They were shaking, stained with oil and blood. He wasn't a soldier. He wasn't a general. He was just a man who had made a mistake. And that mistake was the key.

He wasn't supposed to find a solution for the Axiom. He was supposed to find a flaw.

He had to become the variable.

He looked at the terminal. He couldn't type a new physical law. He couldn't create a new element. The syntax of the Axiom was too complex, too infinite for a human keyboard. He needed a direct line.

He had to introduce the paradoxical input that would save the universe by providing the Axiom with the one thing it couldn't compute: a self-sacrificial, illogical flaw that resolves into a higher truth.

The solution wasn't code. It was contact.

"I understand," he whispered to the roaring silence.

He pushed himself away from the alcove, his muscles coiling. He didn't look back at the retreating armies.

He launched his body into a final, desperate sprint toward the functional terminal.

His run was a brutal exercise in applied physics, his fractured gaze automatically calculating the gravity shifts. He timed a massive pulse of downward gravity to flatten a cluster of struggling Rust Lords, creating a brief path over their paralyzed bodies.

He reached the final obstacle: a heavy gantry had collapsed over the console. He scrambled onto the hot, twisted wreckage, tearing the skin from his hands.

The heat coming off the Anchor was immense now, a suffocating, searing pressure that made the crystalline lattice of his eyes glow white-hot.

Behind him, Jax let out a triumphant howl. The warlord had armed the thermite charge. He swung the massive launcher onto his shoulder, aiming directly at the core.

"SAY GOODBYE, RAVN!" Jax roared. "LET'S MAKE IT SCREAM!"

Ravn pulled himself through the final gap in the wreckage, falling onto the functional console. His hip slammed against the hard casing. He ignored the keyboard entirely.

He ripped the Aperture from his wrist, the strap snapping. The device was burning hot, vibrating with the resonance of the end times.

He slammed the Aperture onto the console's universal interface port.

There was no click of keys. There was a screech of digital feedback that tore through the room. The screen flared white, overriding the facility's OS with the Axiom's own language.

Ravn didn't type. He grabbed the device with both hands, forcing the connection, letting the Essence in his veins bridge the gap between the machine and his mind.

He accessed the file marked [ROOT].

It wasn't a program. It was a memory. It was the recording of the Aethelburg disaster—the moment of his own hesitation, the terror of his brother, the illogical hope of a man who refused to accept the end.

He uploaded the concept of 'The Flaw.'

//INPUT RECEIVED: HUMANITY

//ANALYZING VARIABLE: CHOICE...

He looked up, his gaze locking onto Jax's burning, triumphant eyes. He met the pure, destructive nihilism of the warlord with the terrifying certainty of a man who had just bet his soul.

//CONSTANT UNDEFINED.

//RECALCULATING...

"Accept it," Ravn screamed at the machine, pouring the last of his strength into the upload. "Accept the Potential!"

The screen flashed a blinding, pure white.

//NEW PARADIGM ACCEPTED.

The Anchor's collapse did not accelerate. It froze. The scream of the world ceased. The furious, impossible spectrum of colors on the sphere's surface went blinding white, holding still. The black cracks spreading across the core halted, suspended in a state of eternal, agonizing possibility.

The entire universe held its breath.
The final act had begun.

33

The Variable

The sound of the key-press, a small, synthesized *click*, was the last ordinary sound Ravn would ever hear.

It was a trigger pull that didn't fire a bullet, but a law.

The effect was instantaneous. The Anchor's collapse did not accelerate. It froze.

The cessation of action hit the room with the force of a conceptual singularity. The high-pitched, agonizing harmonic of the core—the scream of reality tearing itself apart—was cut off mid-note, replaced by a silence so profound it felt like a physical vacuum sucking the air from the room. The chaotic, searing heat that had been blistering Ravn's skin instantly bled away, leaving the air frigid and perfectly, unnaturally still.

Ravn slumped over the console, his chest heaving, waiting for the shockwave that never came. He opened his eyes, which he hadn't realized he'd closed.

The world had stopped.

It wasn't just quiet. It was static. The dust motes that had been swirling in the turbulent air were locked in place, a glittering, suspended fog. The smoke rising from the ruined gantry above him had ceased to billow; it hung in solid, gray sculptures of turbulence, the eddies and currents trapped in high-definition stillness.

He pushed himself up from the console. His muscles screamed with exhaustion, but they moved. He looked at his hands. He flexed his fingers. He was the only variable in the equation that was still processing.

He stepped out of the alcove, his boots making no sound on the metal floor. The acoustic properties of the air seemed to have been dampened to zero. He was walking through a recording.

He looked up. Directly in front of him, less than ten meters away, hung the death of the world.

The thermite charge Jax had fired was suspended in the air. It was a jagged, ugly cylinder of machined steel, caught in the middle of its flight path. But it was the fire that held Ravn captive. The exhaust plume trailing from the rocket was a solid, three-dimensional sculpture of violence—tongues of yellow and orange flame, perfectly preserved in their chaotic bloom. He could see the individual sparks drifting at the edge of the fire, glowing red-hot but radiating no warmth.

He walked toward it, drawn by a terrified curiosity. He reached out a trembling hand, his finger hovering inches from the frozen flame. No flicker. No burn. It was light without heat, energy without motion. It was a photograph made of matter.

He looked past the bomb to the man who had fired it.

Jax was a statue of annihilating rage. The warlord was caught mid-recoil, his muscles bunched under his soot-stained skin, his body leaning into the kick of the massive launcher. His face was a mask of transcendent fury, his mouth open in a roar that would never be heard. Ravn could see the individual droplets of sweat flying from his brow, suspended like diamonds in the air around his head. He could see the madness in his wide, unblinking eyes, a hunger for destruction that had been denied its meal.

Ravn stepped back, a wave of vertigo washing over him. The pressure in the room was immense, a psychic weight. The Anchor, hovering in the center of the chamber, was no longer a swirling storm of color. It was a blinding white sphere of absolute solidity. The cracks in its surface were black scars, frozen in the act of spreading.

He turned back to the terminal. The screen, which had flashed white with acceptance, was now blinking with a new, urgent prompt. The blue light pulsed in the stillness, a heartbeat of logic.

[NEW PARADIGM ACCEPTED]

[CALCULATING TRAJECTORY...]

[ERROR: HARDWARE LATENCY DETECTED]

Ravn frowned. He leaned closer, his fractured gaze scanning the scrolling code.

[ERROR: INTERFACE INCOMPATIBLE. QUANTUM SIGNATURE MISMATCH.]

[PHYSICAL BRIDGE REQUIRED FOR UPLOAD.]

The acceptance was theoretical. The Axiom had accepted the *logic* of the new paradigm, but the physical machinery of the Aethelburg facility—the old-world wiring, the silicon chips, the copper cables—could not handle the transmission of the new laws of physics. The signal was too dense. It was trying to push a galaxy through a straw.

If he didn't bridge the gap, the freeze would break. The pause would end, and the explosion would resume exactly where it left off.

Ravn looked at his hands. The Essence in his veins was humming, but it wasn't enough. He was a hybrid, yes, but he was still mostly human. He was still carbon and water. He wasn't conductive enough to ground the Axiom's power.

He needed a superconductor. He needed something that was born of the Zone, something that naturally bridged the gap between biology and energy.

He looked down at the floor.

The pool of oil and fluid leaking from the dead siege engine had stopped spreading, frozen in a slick, black puddle. But near the base of the console, there was another pool. It was dark, viscous, and shimmered with a faint, indigo iridescence even in the dim light.

It was the Stalker's blood.

It had pooled on the floor where the creature had died, seeping into the seams of the terminal and dripping down onto the universal interface port where Ravn had slammed the Aperture.

Ravn stared at it. The blood of the Zone. A substance evolved to survive in a world of broken physics. A biological conductor.

He understood. His friend hadn't just died to save him from the machine. The Stalker's sacrifice was the final, necessary component of the machine itself.

Ravn fell to his knees. He reached out, his hands shaking, and dipped his fingers into the pool of indigo blood. It was cold and thick.

He smeared the blood across the interface port, bridging the gap between the Aperture's quantum drive and the facility's hardline connection. He coated the copper contacts, the fiber optics, the steel casing.

He was painting a circuit with the life of his friend.

The terminal screen flared.

[BIOLOGICAL CONDUCTOR DETECTED.]

[BRIDGING SIGNATURE...]

[HANDSHAKE COMPLETE. ADMINISTRATIVE OVERRIDE GRANTED.]

The hum in the room returned, but it wasn't the scream of the collapse. It was a rising, harmonious tone, like a choir taking a breath.

The frozen fire of the thermite charge began to dissolve, fading into mist. The tension in the air released.

Ravn stood up. His hands were stained with indigo. He placed them on the holographic keyboard. He didn't have to write code anymore. The bridge was built. The path was open.

He looked at the frozen forms of Aris and Lena in the Anchor. They were waiting.

"This is the variable," Ravn whispered. "This is the choice."

He typed the final sequence. It wasn't a command to control. It wasn't a command to destroy. It was a command to let go.

> //EXECUTE: CONSTANT = [POTENTIAL]

He hit enter.

The keening shriek from the Anchor stopped. For a single, silent moment, all energy in the room seemed to be drawn inward, the white sphere collapsing in on itself until it was a single, infinitely dense point of light.

Then, with a soundless, atmospheric concussion, it released.

A wave of pure, pearlescent energy erupted from the Anchor. It wasn't a blast of heat or force. It was a wave of rewriting.

It passed through the thermite charge, and the bomb vanished, resolved into its component atoms.

It passed through Jax, and the warlord was thrown backward, his rage disconnected from his muscles.

It passed through Rostova and Kaia, knocking them to the floor.

It passed through Ravn.

He didn't feel pain. He felt a sudden, profound sense of *expansion*. The Essence in his veins flared in resonance with the wave, and for a split second, he wasn't just standing in the reactor chamber. He was standing at the crossroads of four infinite timelines. He saw the Bastion rising from the ashes. He saw the World-Mind waking in the forest. He saw the Rust Lords riding the eternal highway. He saw the silent, digital peace of the Archive.

They were all there, superimposed over one another, existing in a state of perfect, suspended superposition.

The light washed over the crumpled form of the Stalker. Because the creature's blood was the bridge, the wave moved through it first, prioritizing the conduit. The impossible physics of the wave reversed the trauma. The crushed chitin knit back together in a flash of white fire; the severed spine fused. The energy rewrote the creature's ending, pulling it back from the void and holding it in a state of suspended, perfect potential.

Then, the wave expanded outward, swallowing the room, the facility, and the world in blinding white.

34

The Constant

T he light faded not into darkness, but into clarity.

The aftermath was not silence. It was the absence of noise. The roar of engines, the high-pitched whine of capacitors, the guttural chanting—all of it had been sheared away, replaced by a vacuum so absolute it felt like a physical pressure against the eardrums.

Ravn pushed himself up from the console. His body was a wreck, a map of pain drawn in bruises, burns, and lacerations. His hands, stained with the indigo blood of the Stalker and the grime of the machine, trembled uncontrollably.

The adrenaline of the desperate sprint was fading, receding like a tide to reveal the jagged rocks of a cold, hollow exhaustion. He sucked in a breath of air. It was freezing. The chaotic thermal fluctuations of the battle had stabilized into a crisp, sterile chill. It tasted of ionized dust and petrified stone, the scent of a lightning strike frozen in amber.

He turned slowly, his boots making no sound on the metal floor plates. The acoustic properties of the room had been altered by the Wave of Potential; sound waves no longer propagated. They simply died the moment they were born.

He looked out over the reactor chamber.

It was a museum of violence. A tableau of failure frozen in high definition.

The surviving members of the three factions—the Legionnaires, the Rust

Lords, the Husks—were scattered across the floor. They were not dead, but they were not moving. They were statues, caught in the amber of the new physics.

Ravn walked among them, a ghost drifting through a graveyard of ideologies.

He passed a Legion heavy trooper, caught mid-stride. The soldier was leaning forward, bracing against a recoil that would never come. His face, visible through his cracked visor, was a mask of disciplined terror. He was staring at his own weapon, a plasma rifle that had melted into a useless lump of slag in his hands. The blue light of the weapon's discharge was frozen in the air, a solid, jagged bolt of energy that hung suspended like a neon sculpture. Ravn reached out and brushed his finger against the frozen plasma. It was solid. It felt like warm glass.

He stepped over a knot of Rust Lords. One of them, a woman with a mohawk of green feathers, was mid-scream, her mouth a black void, her hands clawed as she reached for a Husk warrior. The Husk was frozen in a defensive crouch, his bone-blade raised to parry a blow that would never land. They were locked together in an eternal struggle, hate and survival fused into a single, sculptural form.

He walked toward the center of the room, toward the leaders.

Jax was a monument to kinetic failure. The warlord had been thrown backward by the wave, his body caught in a sprawling, airborne pose. He hung suspended a few feet off the ground, held there by the localized gravity distortion. His face was a masterpiece of madness, a hunger for the big bang that had been denied its meal. The fire of his rage had been chemically locked in his neurons, preserved forever in a single moment of unsatisfied adrenaline.

Ravn walked under him, feeling the heat still radiating from the warlord's skin.

Near the wall, General Eva Rostova was slumped against a bulkhead. She wasn't suspended; she was crushed by the weight of her own failure. She was frozen in the act of reaching for her sidearm, but her eyes were on the Anchor. The Order she had worshipped, the grid she had tried to impose on the universe, had snapped. She looked small.

And Kaia. The shaman lay on the floor, surrounded by her Ascended warriors. Her hands were clutched to her temples, her back arched in a rictus of psychic agony. The perfect bead of blood from her nose hung in the air, a ruby jewel that caught the light of the room. Her failure was the most tragic of all. She had tried to love the monster, and it had broken her.

They were trapped in the event horizon of his choice. He had stopped the collapse by refusing to let the story end. He had created a world where the outcome was not determined by the strongest army or the loudest ideology, but by the mere potential for something else to happen.

Ravn turned away from them. He looked down at the floor, near the ruined console.

The Stalker was there.

The creature was suspended in the pearlescent field of the wave, caught in the edge of the Anchor's stabilization zone. Its crushed body was no longer a ruin of blood and bone. The white light had wrapped around it, cocooning it.

It wasn't moving. It wasn't breathing. But the gray, deathly pallor was gone, replaced by the faint, steady blue luminescence of deep sleep. It was held in a state of perfect stasis. It was a statue of life, preserved in the moment before its heart beat again.

Ravn knelt beside it. He touched the creature's head. It was warm.

"Sleep," he whispered, his voice raspy in the quiet air. "The world isn't ready for us yet."

He knew, with a certainty that came from the Essence in his blood, that the Stalker wasn't dead. It was paused. It was waiting for the signal, for the timeline to unspool, for the new world to wake up.

He stood up. He adjusted the straps of his pack. It felt lighter now. The keys were silent, their energy spent, their purpose fulfilled.

He looked at his hands. The indigo blood was gone, absorbed into the machine or vaporized by the wave. His skin was gray with dust, scarred and burned, but his hands were steady.

He turned his gaze to the center of the room. To the Anchor.

It was no longer a shimmering, unstable sphere. It was stable. A constant. It hovered in the center of the reactor pit, motionless, silent, and terrifyingly pure.

And within that light, the silhouettes returned.

Ravn saw Aris. He was no longer twisted by terror. His mouth was closed. His hands were no longer raised in a desperate defense; they were lowered, relaxed at his sides. He looked peaceful. He looked like he was sleeping, drifting in a warm, white ocean.

And Lena. She was no longer reaching in panic. She was turned toward Aris, her expression soft, the lines of fear erased from her face. She looked calm. She looked whole.

They were no longer prisoners trapped in a millisecond of trauma. They were willing sacrifices.

As Ravn watched, their forms began to lose their cohesion. They didn't shatter or de-render. They dissolved. Like ink dropped into clear water, their silhouettes began to spread, thinning out, becoming part of the pearlescent mist of the sphere.

Their consciousness was breaking apart, unspooling from the tight knots of their individual identities and weaving itself into the foundational code of the universe. Aris's creativity became the engine of the new physics. Lena's logic became the lattice that held it together.

They were fading into the infrastructure of existence.

Ravn felt a sob build in his chest. He stumbled forward until he was standing right at the edge of the energy field. He reached out a trembling hand and placed his palm on the cool, smooth surface of the interface barrier.

"Goodbye," he whispered. The word didn't echo. It was absorbed by the sphere.

There was no voice. There was no memory. Just a sensation.

It started in his fingertips and traveled up his arm, settling in the hollow void where his soul used to be. It was a faint, lingering echo of his brother's presence. It was the feeling of a Sunday afternoon. It was the warmth of a shared joke.

It was peace. It was gratitude. It was forgiveness.

Then, it was gone.

Ravn opened his eyes. He was standing in the silent heart of a world reborn.

He turned away from the light and looked toward the open blast door, toward the dark tunnel that led back to the surface. The facility was frozen. The basin was frozen. The entire Fracture Zone was held in the breath of the Axiom.

But Ravn could move.

He checked the charge on his empty rifle, then tossed it aside. He wouldn't need it where he was going.

There were four paths ahead of him. Four ways the world could unspool from this single, frozen knot. He could walk toward the order of the Legion, the chaos of the Rust Lords, the unity of the Husks, or the silence of the Archive.

He didn't know which path was right. He only knew that the choice was finally, truly his.

He took the first step toward the door, the sound of his boot on the metal the only noise in the universe.

His journey through the Fracture Zone was over. The journey into the world he created had just begun.

Did you enjoy Fracture Zone?

Thank you for traveling through the Anomaly with Ravn. As an independent author, I rely on readers like you to help others find my work.

If you enjoyed the book, please consider leaving a brief review on Amazon or Goodreads. Even a sentence or two makes a massive difference.

Contact the Author: contact@caincyberlabs.com

About the Author

Christian Cain is a cybersecurity expert and U.S. Marine Corps veteran with over a decade of experience in Information Technology and Security. Holding a Master of Science in Cybersecurity and Information Assurance, along with advanced industry certifications including the CASP+, PenTest+, and CySA+, Christian brings a terrifying level of technical authenticity to his fiction.

He applies his real-world knowledge of system architecture, encryption, and vulnerability assessment to construct the complex, logic-driven magic systems found in Fracture Zone. He writes science fiction for readers who want to know not just that the machine works, but how. When he isn't writing about broken realities and god-machines, he explores the intersection of automation and security through his work at CainCyberLabs, LLC.

www.ingramcontent.com/pod-product-compliance
Lightning Source LLC
Chambersburg PA
CBHW030638260626
47157CB00007B/2393